Jack Carr is a former Navy SEAL who led special operations teams as a team leader, platoon commander, troop commander, and task unit commander. Jack retired from active duty in 2016 and lives with his wife and three children in Park City, Utah. His debut novel, *The Terminal List*, was adapted into the #1 Prime Video series starring Chris Pratt. He is also the host of the top-rated Danger Close podcast. Visit him at OfficialJackCarr.com and follow Jack on Instagram, X, Facebook, and YouTube @JackCarrUSA.

M.P. Woodward is the *New York Times* bestselling author of the Jack Ryan, Jr. series and The Handler CIA espionage series (*The Handler* and *Dead Drop*). He served as a US naval intelligence officer before going on to an international career in tech and streaming media. He lives in Redmond, Washington.

THE FOURTH OPTION

JACK CARR
AND M.P. WOODWARD

SIMON &
SCHUSTER

London · New York · Amsterdam/Antwerp · Sydney/Melbourne · Toronto · New Delhi

First published in the United States by Emily Bestler Books / Atria Books,
an imprint of Simon & Schuster LLC, 2026

First published in Great Britain by Simon & Schuster UK Ltd, 2026

Copyright © Tomahawk Creative, Inc., 2026

1 3 5 7 9 10 8 6 4 2

Simon & Schuster UK Ltd, 1st Floor
222 Gray's Inn Road, London WC1X 8HB

Simon & Schuster Australia, Sydney
Simon & Schuster India, New Delhi

www.simonandschuster.co.uk
www.simonandschuster.com.au
www.simonandschuster.co.in

The authorised representative in the EEA is Simon & Schuster Netherlands
BV, Herculesplein 96, 3584 AA Utrecht, Netherlands. info@simonandschuster.nl

Simon & Schuster strongly believes in freedom of expression and stands against
censorship in all its forms. For more information, visit BooksBelong.com

A CIP catalogue record for this book is available from the British Library

Paperback ISBN: 978-1-3985-6683-5
eBook ISBN: 978-1-3985-6684-2
Audio ISBN: 978-1-3985-6685-9

Interior design by Kyoko Watanabe

Printed and Bound in the UK using 100% Renewable Electricity
at CPI Group (UK) Ltd

Now Roman is to Roman
More hateful than a foe,
And the Tribunes beard the high,
And the Fathers grind the low.
As we wax hot in faction,
In battle we wax cold:
Wherefore men fight not as they fought
In the brave days of old.

—**Thomas Babington Macaulay, "Horatius"**

PREFACE

I HAVE LONG wanted to set a novel in New Orleans. The history, music, architecture, cuisine, festivals, cemeteries, superstitions, and fusion of French, Spanish, African, and Caribbean cultures make it an appealing backdrop for the action and suspense of a thriller.

I first visited New Orleans while in SEAL Qualification Training. I remember doing our last static line jump of the week in Southern California and then zipping to the airport to meet friends for Jazz Fest in the Big Easy. I went back with my first SEAL platoon while we were training a few hours away at the Joint Readiness Training Center at Fort Polk. New Orleans is a city that stays with you.

The Fourth Option is a blend of the crime, political, and military thriller genres, with an underlying foundation that comes from experiences in places like Iraq and Afghanistan. The idea for this novel has been simmering for years. It was one of the concepts I wanted to explore when I first spread all my executive summaries out on a table in 2014, studying them to decide which would become my first novel as I was getting ready to leave the SEAL Teams. I decided on *The Terminal List*, but *The Fourth Option* would not leave me. Then, in the summer of 2021, in our final days of filming *The Terminal List* for Prime Video in Los Angeles, I took some time to write out a few ideas for possible books, television shows, and movies outside the James Reece Terminal List universe, and I revisited *The Fourth Option*, now more thoroughly fleshed out on the page. That fall, I turned that robust executive summary into a forty-page Power-Point presentation with actors attached to characters, location photos, and stills from films and television shows to capture the mood of the project. I started the treatment with these words: "When law enforcement, the courts, and the prison system fail . . . there is a fourth and final option."

I thought of *The Fourth Option* as a modern tribute to the 1950s–1960s television show *Have Gun—Will Travel* and the classic "stranger comes to town" narrative that so resonated with me as a kid watching westerns with my dad. I bought the full *Have Gun—Will Travel* DVD box set at the PX in Baghdad in 2004. They remain in my collection today. Richard Boone stars as Paladin, a Civil War veteran and gun for hire. The white knight chess piece was his symbol and featured heavily in the opening credits. It was on his holster, business card, and one of his rifles. It made such an impression that I had the knight chess piece incorporated into business cards I made up for my platoon in the wake of September 11, 2001. They were emblazoned with Steve McQueen's line in *The Magnificent Seven*—We deal in lead, friend—SEAL Team Five Delta Platoon Scout-Snipers—an idea inspired by Stephen Hunter's masterpiece, *Point of Impact*. I thought we might use them the way Bob Lee Swagger does in that book. We never did. I still have one of the cards.

Though *The Fourth Option* is firmly seated in the mythology of Paladin and the Old West, it is also an homage to some of the other books, television shows, and movies that were so impactful on me during the formative years of my youth, even helping set the course my life would follow, a testament to the influence of popular culture. The astute reader will note elements of *Shane, The Magnificent Seven, High Plains Drifter*, and *Pale Rider* along with themes explored in books by Louis L'Amour and Zane Grey. Fellow Gen Xers will recognize whispers of *Magnum, P.I.; The Equalizer;* and *Airwolf* with a dash of *The A-Team* for good measure. Comic book fans will identify a nod to *Batman*. Some may see contemporary links to *The Shield, Dexter,* and *True Detective*. In the pages ahead, you will find a couple of direct references to *Lethal Weapon*—yes, of course it's a Christmas movie, but it's also a film that threw gasoline on the fire of the 1980s cop buddy movie subgenre while exploring justice through the eyes of two Vietnam veterans turned Los Angeles police officers.

As I pushed forward with the *Terminal List* series—with the growing demands of books and television shows in that universe—I began to realize that I might never get to *The Fourth Option*. That prospect weighed heavily on me as it remained important that I tell this story. As a reader of Tom Clancy and admirer of his contributions to the worlds of literature and entertainment, I was acutely aware that after his seventh novel he branched out into nonfiction and after his eighth he created the Op-Center series outside the Jack Ryan universe. With that example in mind, in April 2023, I decided to pitch *The Fourth Option* to my publisher and editor Emily Bestler as a cowritten thriller. I got the green light immediately. That left finding a coauthor who shared my vision and wanted to collaborate. As soon as I read *The Handler* by former Naval Intelligence officer M.P. Woodward, I knew I had found the right person. I reached out to him in late 2024, and he didn't hesitate—he was in.

I sent him the forty-page PowerPoint treatment for *The Fourth Option,* and we got to work on the outline via texts, emails, and Zooms. Once the outline was complete, M.P. dove into the rough draft of the manuscript and delivered it in August 2025. I then worked on it from August through December and sent it to Simon & Schuster at the end of 2025. Edits continued into early 2026, at which point I switched gears to the new James Reece Terminal List series novel—yes, James Reece will be back!

This story explores disillusionment, abandonment, idealism, corruption, vigilantism, purpose, and despair. It examines the role of violence in the pursuit of peace and justice. As I wrote in my initial summary of *The Fourth Option* all those years ago, "Disillusioned by the government and institutions he dedicated his life to serving, former Navy SEAL and CIA Ground Branch operative Chris Walker is about to end his life, when he receives a call that saves it." The book asks the question, Do you burn the system down that has enabled unthinkable evils, or do you work to expose corruption and ultimately fix it? Is fixing it even possible? This narrative incorporates those questions plaguing discourse in the American social and political zeitgeists through the medium of popular fiction.

The foundation of this story was laid when I was in the single digits enthralled with *Have Gun—Will Travel.* It was further envisioned during my final years of service and then more solidly developed in the summer of 2021 as I watched the disastrous withdrawal from Afghanistan, an event that plays heavily into *The Fourth Option.* The novel in your hands finally came to fruition over the past year, but it has been a lifetime in the making.

Turn the page and strap into a vintage VW camper van with Chris Walker and his Belgian Malinois, Paladin, as they make their way to New Orleans to repay an old favor. Walker is a modern-day gunslinger and philosopher, a man whose soul belongs to a previous generation, a generation that believed sometimes the only way to uphold justice was by breaking the law.

Get ready. That justice is coming.

Jack Carr
Park City, Utah
January 2026

PROLOGUE

Quinault Indian Nation, Washington State, Pacific Coast
Present Day

THE PISTOL IN Chris Walker's hand felt heavier than he remembered.

The 1911 was as familiar to him as the tendons that moved his fingers, an extension of training and instinct. But this evening, the steel felt colder. The grip, rougher.

Combat altered the senses. Elevated them. It sharpened sight, amplified sound, magnified scent; ancient survival mechanisms etched into the human genome. But that was the kinetic kind. In that type of fight, muscles moved before the mind caught up.

This was a different battle, one that required thought. And with that thought came the weight.

Sitting on the rear built-in sofa of his customized '84 Volkswagen Westfalia Vanagon, parked on a bluff in the rain overlooking the rough waters of the Pacific, Walker pressed the cold steel of the 1911's barrel to his temple.

This was the edge of the abyss, and Walker's senses were in hyperdrive.

The round Navy Chelsea clock bolted above the bookshelf ticked with surgical precision. He had salvaged it during a wreck dive off Algeria with a few buddies from his first SEAL platoon and had it restored by a Swiss watchmaker who had once repaired timepieces for submariners. Now it clacked like a metronome. A steady drip from the cedar bough over the van's roof snapped like a snare drum. Rain lashed the side windows in gusts, the hiss of cymbals in a storm-born symphony. Beneath it all, the ocean's bass drum rolled, deep, patient, eternal.

If he weren't about to end his life, Walker might have tapped his foot to it.

He had always felt alive when listening to the crashing waves, howling wind, and torrential rain of the Pacific Northwest, preferring it to the deserts and mountains of Iraq and Afghanistan. He shifted the pistol from the side of his head and repositioned it under his chin. If he was going to take his life, it was going to be with a 1911 and not the Austrian-made Glock he had carried across continents, through wars, and into the shadows as a paramilitary officer in the CIA's Ground Branch.

Afghanistan was where he had failed, and now it was time to join the friend he was responsible for putting in the grave. He imagined the bullet going through the roof of his mouth and tearing through his brain, perhaps embedding itself in the thin mattress of the pop-top. Walker wanted the shot to blend into the natural symphony, one more beat in time. He could hear it all now, the waves, the rain, the staccato drip from the cedar bough.

Thunder.

It didn't roll in. It crashed, abrupt and graceless, like a mortar round landing too close. It shattered the rhythm, tore through the fragile harmony of the forest like shrapnel.

Then it passed.

Walker exhaled. He lowered the pistol to his lap, waiting for the rhythm to return.

It was important that he die in the proper rhythm.

A flip phone sat open on the table in front of him. He reached for it with his left hand, his thumb hovering over the power button, waiting for the right moment.

The wind rocked his home on wheels, the rain pounded harder. Walker looked up at the headliner of the old Vanagon, marveling at how the pop-top camper wasn't leaking. Having served in tropical hellholes and frozen wastelands, crossed squalling seas and spiny mountain ridges, he had never heard precipitation like this.

Enough.

His thumb stabbed the phone's power button. He closed his eyes and pressed the phone to his ear, waiting for it to find a signal.

Then came the bark, sharp, guttural, urgent. *Paladin.*

Walker opened his eyes. Thunder cracked again. Paladin, his Belgian Malinois, a veteran of countless explosive door breaches and firefights, was going berserk. The dog howled, snarled, and clawed at the door, defying all his training. He had never done that before.

Damn it.

Not only was the rhythm off now, but Walker couldn't stop thinking of Paladin. It was bad enough to leave the dog outside, even if he was protected by the awning.

Fuck.

He swiveled the Vanagon's compact table aside and got to his feet, leaving the open phone on the cushion, powered up, and placed the pistol on the cutting board that covered the sink in the port-side galley kitchen. He would calm Paladin, say one more goodbye, then make the call and finish what he started.

His beard hid an angular jaw. It was highlighted with hints of gold that differentiated it from his greasy blond hair. An ex-girlfriend and undergraduate creative writing major at NYU had once told him that his hair was the color of wheat and that his eyes reminded her of a cloudless summer afternoon. She had gone on to write poetry.

Walker wasn't a tall man. People called him rangy because of his wiry build and the distant look in his eyes, the gaze that most said was a function of his former vocation, Navy SEAL turned CIA operator.

Yet those who knew him well, and there weren't many, understood the look wasn't about the fighting or the bad memories. It was about the way he thought, the perception of his surroundings and his place within it, even more than that, mankind's place within it. Half of Chris Walker's soul was that of a philosopher, a soul that seemed in constant conflict with its other half, that of a warrior. That battle had run its course. Both sides were exhausted. Walker would finish the clash with a single bullet to his head.

He bent his knees and twisted the handle on the sliding side door of the Syncro four-wheel drive Vanagon. He ducked and stepped outside.

Under the crack of thunder and the strobe of lightning, Paladin lunged from the shadows, forcing Walker into a seated position on the step outside. The dog's breath was frantic, his tongue desperate, licking at Walker's face like he was trying to pull a man from a coma.

Walker didn't resist. He let the dog's panic wash over him, grounding him. Barely sheltered by a fabric awning, he stroked Paladin's head with a trembling hand, fingers brushing the scars behind the ears.

Beyond the edge of the canopy, the rain didn't fall so much as collapse; vertical surf pounding the earth, retreating, then crashing again.

The forest swayed under it, cedar limbs writhing like the arms of monsters. No wonder Paladin was losing it. Out here, the world looked like it was coming undone.

And maybe it was.

Walker dropped to a knee on the patch of AstroTurf under the awning, the soaked green square squelching beneath his weight, and tucked a strand of shoulder-length dirty blond hair behind his ear. He leaned in close, forehead to fur, and thought of the commands taught to Paladin in his training, a combination of Dutch and German, a canine language of obedience, of control, of war.

"Nothing really covers this, Pal, does it?"

Despite all his canine combat training, Paladin wasn't buying it. The dog's light brown eyes flickered. His breath came in ragged spurts. Paladin had taken shrapnel to the neck during a raid in Kandahar, leaving a scarred hole in his windpipe. When he panted, it sounded like a hacksaw cutting through a pipe.

"It's all right now," Walker soothed, pulling the dog close.

He shifted to the camp stool near the cooler and stroked Paladin's head. To the right of the door, firmly secured by black rigger's tape, was an envelope in a Ziploc bag that read: "ATTN TOMMY HAWKEYE. INSTRUCTIONS AND MONEY FOR PALADIN'S CARE." Tommy was a Vietnam vet who lived with his wife not far away on the reservation. They would give Paladin a good home.

Walker had used his vintage Navy-surplus Royal Quiet De Luxe to hammer out the instructions. The typewriter, stowed in its olive-drab case, rested between freeze-dried food packets, Tupperware containers, and barbecue tools in the camper. Everything had its place in the van.

Those instructions included the commands the dog would understand, guidance for his exercise and food, and most importantly, the phone number of a fellow former SEAL in Southern California who ran a combat dog rehabilitation and rescue camp in case Hawkeye and his wife needed it.

More thunder. Paladin whined.

"Just take it easy, boy," Walker said, staying with English as the dog licked his hands. Paladin would be okay. He wouldn't be alone for long. Walker stood up to head back inside.

"*Blijf*," he said halfway through the door, telling the dog to stay. "*Baywaken*," he added, a command to guard the site. "Attaboy."

He slammed the door shut and tried to block out Paladin's growls.

Back in the van, he snagged the pistol off the cutting board and resumed his seat on the cushion. It was time. *Just do it*, he told himself. Like yanking a Band-Aid.

A headshot would take care of the memories. Of Afghanistan. Of John Staub.

Walker checked the ship's clock and retrieved the phone, which blinked with a flashing light that he ignored. His right hand held the .45-caliber pistol, his left the phone. He stabbed the preprogrammed number for the tribal cops with his thumb.

One shot at this, he said to himself, pausing for a second to appreciate the double meaning.

As he waited on the tribal police dispatcher to pick up, he surveyed the interior of his van, eyes passing over his books, tomes from NYU and a few others he had picked up since abandoning his postgraduate education, a collection of philosophers: Plato, Voltaire, Bacon, Spinoza, Kant, Schopenhauer. Next to these great teachers of the West, he had arranged texts on the Eastern faiths and philosophies: Hinduism, Taoism, Shintoism, Buddhism.

I guess I'm finally going to see which of you guys was right.

Above the books were other letters for the authorities, more envelopes taped to the cabinet doors, one for the wife of a long-gone friend.

His eyes lingered on his guitar, the instrument he played only for himself. He would miss it.

"*Quinault Nation Tribal Police*," a female voice answered.

"Hello," Walker said. "I'm calling from the Lower Quinault River, close to the estuary. I need to report a dead body."

"*A dead body? We'll get someone right out. Do you have any idea as to the identity of the individual, sir?*"

"Yes."

"*Who is it?*"

"It's me."

———

Walker snapped the phone shut, set it down, and lifted his pistol. He pressed it to the underside of his chin, pushed down on the thumb safety, and set his finger on the trigger. The doctors had said his head was broken. They were right.

Outside, amid the swishing branches and crashing skies, Paladin howled as had his ancestors, wolves that had once hunted these very lands.

Walker closed his eyes, telling himself it was a fitting send-off. Paladin had seen a lot of death. He would understand. Time to . . .

Bleep-bleep.

Walker removed his finger from the trigger. What the hell was that? An irritating little sound that did not blend with the natural rhythms of the storm.

My death has to be in rhythm.

He glanced at the phone and saw a flashing light.

Fuck it. Doesn't matter. Do it, Chris.

Bleep-bleep.

He closed his eyes tighter than before, willing the unnatural sound away, sliding his finger back into place on the trigger.

Ignore it and press.

Do it!

Bleep-bleep.

His heart was racing.

It wasn't supposed to be like this.

Arrhythmic.

Bleep-bleep.

Fuck!

Walker engaged the thumb safety and lowered the gun to his lap, sucking in deep breaths, the religion and philosophy texts on his shelf coming back into focus. The sound was a text indicator and a message was on the phone's outer LCD screen.

Hey Chris, it's Leigh Ann Staub. Hope you're well. I've been calling you but not getting an answer. Trying this—hope it works. Please call me back as soon as you can. It's important.

Walker stared at it in disbelief.

A message from Leigh Ann just as he was about to join her husband in Valhalla?

What kind of timing was that?

He looked back to the books.

John Staub, his master chief in the SEAL Teams whom he had followed into Ground Branch, was dead because of Walker. Now his wife just spared Walker's life?

He fought to control his breathing as Paladin's howls took on a pain he had not noticed before.

You trying to talk me out of this, buddy?

Thunder rumbled, more distant than it had been moments earlier.

Was the storm passing?

Walker tilted his head to look out the side window and up into the dark clouds, his inner philosopher kicking into gear, questioning the workings of the universe, the unity of nature, thought, and consciousness. His mind flashed over Spinoza, who wrote that there was no good or evil, just substance and elements; even thoughts were elements.

He looked down at the pistol resting in his hand on his right leg, then up to an envelope taped just below his books. Earlier in the day he had written on it in Sharpie: "LEIGH ANN STAUB, NEW ORLEANS."

Substance and elements. What the hell was going on?

Tired of you, inner philosopher.

The destruction, the loss, the injustice—those were his substance and elements, and they demanded atonement. Dignity. Finality.

He could not quell the question.

Leigh Ann Staub? Now?

He saw John's lifeless body in the Afghan dirt, then alive and laughing in the CIA bar of Kabul's Arania Hotel, a Kipling quote written on the wall behind him:

> *When you're wounded and left on Afghanistan's plains,*
> *And the women come out to cut up what remains,*
> *Jest roll to your rifle and blow out your brains*
> *An' go to your Gawd like a soldier.*

The sound that tore from Walker wasn't a scream, it was a rupture. A raw, guttural cry, the pain of a soul ripped from its body.

Walker raised the 1911, pushed down on the thumb safety, and pressed the trigger.

PART ONE

"*The soul is dyed the color of its thoughts.*"

—Marcus Aurelius, *Meditations*

CHAPTER ONE

"HOW MUCH DOES one of these Defenders go for back in the U.S.?" John Staub asked from the front passenger seat.

Walker scanned the vehicle's interior. The Rover was a four-door 110 version with the longer wheelbase. The back seats were of the dual, inward-facing bench style. The windows were blacked out, but it was otherwise a standard model from the mid-nineties.

Walker scratched his beard. Like Staub, he had grown out his facial hair. The more robust, the more respect it garnered from the Afghans. While Walker's retained the golden shade of his hair, resulting in his call sign "Viking," Staub's beard was starting to transition from jet black to the gray that had appeared at his temples. "I don't think you could afford one in the States," he replied. "Plus, you barely fit in here."

"Yeah, why don't these seats go back farther?" asked the barrel-chested frogman.

"I think the engineer was a little guy," Walker responded.

Staub took a closer look at the utilitarian metal dash and manual transmission. He twisted to inspect the rear seats. "Maybe we can smuggle this thing back in a shipping container? Agency will never know. We can call it a combat loss. Leigh Ann has always wanted a Range Rover."

"This isn't a Range Rover. It's a *Land* Rover."

"Same thing."

"Not really."

"Huh?"

"Believe me, Leigh Ann will know the difference."

"Well, whatever. I like this one. I'm going to see if I can get it home when we pull stakes and leave this shithole."

"The U.S. is never leaving this shithole," Walker replied. He shifted to neutral, coasted, and touched the brakes. "You have your ID? They don't know us on this side of the runway."

Walker stopped and cranked down the manual window. He presented his blue badge ID card to a pair of soldiers stuck with gate duty. Staub handed his green CIA identification card across the center console. The difference in colors signaled their differing roles. Blue badgers were management. Green badgers were muscle.

One of the soldiers disappeared inside the guard shack. The other inspected the undercarriage of the Rover with a lighted mirror on a pole. While they waited, Staub remarked, "I can totally see Leigh Ann driving this thing."

"I can't."

"Be like riding in a tank for her and Connor."

"How old is Connor now?"

"Sixteen. Growing up too fast."

"Sounds like you need a Volvo. Nice and safe."

"I don't think Leigh Ann is a Volvo person. Plus, this is one hell of a capable four-by-four."

"It's not like you have mountains in New Orleans. The one time I passed through Louisiana, I thought the whole state was a bridge."

"Exactly. See the snorkel?" Staub nodded at the hood corner where a thick black tube crawled up the front door post. "Katrina wasn't the last hurricane to blow through that town. Something like this would be an evacuation machine, you know? I should take it for that reason alone."

"It's right-hand drive."

"Good point. Maybe I just need to buy one. I read they're coming out with a new design later this year. First time they're selling Defenders in the U.S. since '97."

Walker watched the soldiers at the guard shack. "You'd blow all that extra combat pay you've banked over here."

"Exactly what that money's for. Tax-free, Mr. Philosopher," Staub said, using the nickname Walker had acquired very early on in the SEAL Teams.

Chris stared doubtfully at his older teammate. Although Staub was brilliant when it came to tactics, he was capable of the worst possible financial decisions.

"We're different," Staub said, correctly sensing the judgment.

"Thank God for that."

"No, I mean, Leigh Ann and I don't like restoring old crap. You fixed up your mom's house and car. You rebuild engines. You haul around that surplus typewriter of yours and clack away at your homework—"

"Dissertation."

"Whatever. My point is, I bet you'd take this beat-up old right-hand drive over a brand-new made-for-America Defender, wouldn't you?"

"In a heartbeat."

"Then why do you still wear that issued G-SHOCK?"

"Because it's practical."

"And this isn't?" Staub said, pointing to the Tudor timepiece on his left wrist.

"It's shiny."

"You of all people should appreciate the history."

"Oh, I do. That doesn't make it any less shiny."

"Some supply guy was taking a hammer to all the old Tudors at my first SEAL Team," Staub said. "Have I ever told you this story?"

"About a hundred times."

"Said he was ordered to do it to get them out of the system. Said it was illegal to take them. I reminded him of the age-old naval tradition of 'gun-decking,' and in exchange for the last four Tudor Subs, I rewarded him with a case of beer. I saved a bit of history that day. You know, the Team guys who jumped in after the Apollo astronauts when they splashed down were wearing these."

"Yes, I'm aware."

"Gave one to my chief, one to my LPO, and one to my BUD/S swim buddy. One day this one will go to Connor when he graduates college."

"What's he interested in?"

"Journalism. Works on the school paper. Big reader. He's not like me. He's smart enough to make a living with a pen, not the sword."

"Well, let's hope so," Walker said as a soldier arrived with a clipboard.

The sergeant handed the badges through the window.

"We're picking up a new arrival," Walker said. "He would have checked in last night. Name's Lawrence."

"Lawrence the first name or last?" the soldier asked.

"Both. He should be staying in visiting officer quarters."

The other soldier approached with the clipboard. After a half-minute search, he tapped the clipboard. "Got him. He's in the CHUs. A-16, third alley to your left."

"Thanks." Walker shifted into gear and let out the clutch.

The CHUs—container housing units—were the high-rent district on the Bagram base, boasting metal walls and Mitsubishi mini-splits for heating and cooling. Staub was working on requisitioning one of them to set up out in the swamps as a hunting cabin back in Louisiana.

"You worked much with Fisk?" Staub asked as they coasted to a stop by a container.

"We were in the same class at the Farm. But after that, he went the case officer route."

"Not a gunslinger?"

"Too smart." Walker smiled, killed the engine, and yanked the parking brake.

"Come on, no one's smarter than you, genius."

Walker rolled his eyes.

"I'll hop out and give him the front seat," Staub said. "And I can check out the cargo volume of my future ride."

Walker found container A-16 at the center of a rat maze of narrow passages. In addition to the stenciled A-16 address, a laminated card had been inserted in a slot that read: "L.L. LAWRENCE, OGA." Other Government Agency was the catch-all term for the various government groups that cycled through Bagram: CIA, FBI, DEA, DSS. But for all intents and purposes, the term had become synonymous with the CIA. The nondescript alias was another dead giveaway.

"Hey, Chris," Leonard Fisk said in greeting. "Long time."

Walker shook hands with the taller, skinnier man. "Welcome to Kabul, Lenny."

"Thanks. Come on in."

Walker climbed the steps and entered the corrugated metal wall container. "How's the jet lag? How are things at Langley?"

"Langley's Langley and jet lag is my standard operating condition," Fisk answered, pushing his reading glasses up the bridge of his nose. "Give me a second to close out this email, then we'll get going." Fisk sat on a desk chair and typed while Walker remained standing by the door.

After half a minute, bespectacled face to the screen, Fisk asked, "What's your contact's name again? Just putting together a quick synopsis for the station before we head out."

"Naji Mansour," Walker replied.

"And how did you make contact?"

"Believe it or not, Staub bought a rug from him. Mansour hinted at having information that might be of interest to us, so I went in and bought a rug too. The hints became more than that."

Fisk stopped typing and studied Walker through his glasses. "Really? It was that random?"

"Life's like that sometimes."

Fisk resumed typing. After a few more strokes on the keys, he shut the laptop and threw his glasses in a case. "Ready," he said, standing. "Oh— and from now on, we're to refer to this asset as Mongoose."

"Mongoose," Walker repeated. "Who came up with that?"

"The Agency's cryptonym generator."

"It was a good choice. They eat snakes."

CHAPTER TWO

Quinault Rain Forest, Washington State, Pacific Coast
Present Day

THE RINGING IN Walker's ears was so loud and shrill that it was almost physically painful.

That was fucking stupid, he thought, looking at the books on his shelves as if they would speak to him.

He laid the pistol to his side on the sofa bench seat and leaned forward, setting his elbows on his knees and pressing his palms to the side of his head.

Just some ringing.

The noise shifted in tone and Walker lifted his head, running his fingers through his hair.

His eyes went to the bullet hole in the headliner, thinking that the rain would soon seep into the mattress above and would eventually start to drip into the interior.

Is there anything you don't fucking ruin?

That bullet is going to come down somewhere, you selfish son of a bitch.

The buzzing in his brain gave way to the sounds of Paladin scratching at the door.

Paladin, from the knights of Charlemagne's court; a champion for a cause.

Was Walker that cause?

He leaned to the side and opened the sliding door. The dog leaped in, tail wagging, and bound into Walker's lap, licking his face while whining as if the two had been separated for months instead of minutes.

"Okay, Pal, it's okay. I'm all right."

Paladin, not convinced, slid to Walker's side and curled into a ball, setting his chin on his guardian's lap, looking up with soulful brown eyes.

Walker stroked Paladin's head. "Thanks, boy. I'm okay for now." Then he looked to the phone.

Leigh Ann.

He took a deep breath and dialed her number.

"Chris?" Leigh Ann Staub said after two rings.

"Yeah, it's me."

"Thank God."

There was a brief silence as if neither party knew what to say.

Walker cleared his throat. What did you say to the widow of the man you were responsible for killing?

"Where are you, Chris?"

Leigh Ann had always been inquisitive.

"I'm uh . . ."

"Out of the country or something? You're not back with the Agency, are you?"

"I'm still medically retired. Just a little remote. Pacific Northwest."

"Sounds like there's static on the line."

"Rain on the roof. Ocean beyond windows. Storm's rolling in off the Pacific." His voice was gravelly and hollow.

"Are you alone?" The concern in her voice evident.

"I'm on an Indian reservation."

"A reservation?"

"Yeah."

Paladin gave a slight growl.

"Well, not quite by myself."

"How are you, Chris?"

Walker's eyes went to the pistol on the bench seat next to him and replied after two seconds of introspection. "I'm doing great."

Chris knew the pause did not go unnoticed. Leigh Ann had always been in tune with other people's mental states, far more so than her late husband. She had been the ballast in the Staub marriage.

"Yeah?" she asked gently. *"How are you feeling?"*

"You mean, how's my head?"

"Well, yes. I'm a nurse, remember?"

The traumatic brain injury had been the final nail in his CIA career. "I didn't forget. Head's good."

He glanced back at the gun on the seat beside him, his eyes traveling to the bullet hole in the ceiling. It had started to leak, the hole staring back at him like an accusation.

Leigh Ann's tone shifted into nurse mode. *"Blurred vision? Dizziness? What meds are you on?"*

Walker had forgotten that Leigh Ann was a talker.

"Was just about to try a new one, actually," he replied, his eyes going back to the 1911.

"Which one?"

"Nothing you'd recommend."

"It's good to hear your voice."

"You too. Been a minute, hasn't it?"

"Too long."

"Leigh Ann, I'm so sorry, I . . ."

"No, we've been through this and that's not why I'm calling."

"Oh?"

"I reached out because something's going on down here. God, it's . . ."

"What?"

She coughed as if stalling for time.

"Connor . . . is . . ." A sharp breath.

"Leigh Ann?"

"I've got to get used to saying this." She paused. *"Connor's dead."*

Walker's spine stiffened. Paladin raised his head, sensing the shift.

Connor Staub. John and Leigh Ann's son. Dead? Last Walker heard, the kid was headed to a master's program at Columbia University Journalism School after finishing his undergrad at LSU.

As an NYU grad, Walker respected the move to the Big Apple, the ambitious swing. He had even taped an envelope to the cabinet with Leigh Ann's name on it, meant to help with Connor's tuition.

"He's . . . how? When?"

Leigh Ann's voice was muffled, as if speaking through gauze. *"A month ago. He was chasing a story, his first real one. Wanted it to be big. An exposé. It got attention from the wrong people. He got too close."*

"He was murdered?"

Leigh Ann's voice came through weaker now. *"Yes."*

"Who did it?"

"I don't know, I mean I do know."

Walker could hear her sobbing.

He waited a few seconds before speaking.

"Leigh Ann, I am so sorry."

Her sobs turned to deep breaths as she regained her composure.

"If there is anything I can do?" The words felt hollow.

A memory intruded, one of knocking on doors in his service dress blues. He pushed it away. That was a different life.

"*There is, Chris.*" Her voice was stronger now.

"Anything." He saw John Staub looking up at him, knowing he would never make it home.

"*I need you to find out who did it.*"

"What? Leigh Ann, I'm not the police."

"*I know. That's why I need you.*" She paused, selecting her words. "*John told me that if I ever needed help, you were the man to call.*"

John's blood pooled in the dust.

"*Chris?*"

"I'm here."

"*He said I could trust you.*"

"You can."

"*Then help me.*"

Walker looked back at the pistol. He could barely help himself.

"Do the police have any leads?"

"*Yes.*"

"Then why do you need me?"

"*Because they were in on it.*"

Walker closed his eyes. His jaw clenched. The ringing that had subsided surged in conjunction with a migraine, sharp and blinding. He pinched his temples.

"*I need help, Chris. Connor was an only child. He was all I had after John died.*"

And that was my fault, Walker thought.

He felt dizzy, but inside, the gyros began to turn.

"Tell me."

"*Connor worked on his investigation for more than a year,*" Leigh Ann said.

"What kind of investigation?"

"*An exposé on overdoses, the drug trade.*"

"Fentanyl?"

"Maybe, but maybe worse. I don't know. Connor thought it was something new. I've seen some of those kids rushed into the ER. Maybe a synthetic."

Walker stared at the envelope, the one marked for Leigh Ann Staub, the one he had meant to be opened only after he was gone. The timing of her call spoke to him. Impossible? Absurd? Divine? Cruel?

Walker's mind, always a battlefield for long dead philosophers, lit up with arguments.

Spinoza whispered about substance and attributes.

Schopenhauer reminded him that desire was immutable.

The Tao offered no comfort, only inevitability.

The pistol beckoned him. He could almost feel the cold metal that had nearly ended it all. And now her voice, alive, urgent, familiar.

Connor was dead. Just like his dad.

Connor Staub. The kid with ambition. Gone.

Walker couldn't help but recall the main points of the NYU dissertation he had abandoned after Afghanistan, the debates on determinism versus free will. His thesis supported the ideas of Arthur Schopenhauer, the German nineteenth-century philosopher who believed that while man's actions are free, his predetermined, unchangeable desires are not. A man could physically alter his actions, but not the core drivers of his soul.

As he listened, Leigh Ann's voice cracked, steadied, and then cracked again as she painted a picture of Connor's final months, his obsession with the story, the trail of overdoses, the coded journals, the bricks of heroin planted in his car. The cops said Connor was a dealer. The headlines agreed.

Walker closed his eyes.

Somewhere in the heavens, another thunderclap. Paladin barked and hopped off his seat. He stood in the narrow passage between the van's sliding starboard door and port-side galley. Walker suddenly remembered the call.

The tribal cops. Shit.

"Leigh Ann, let me call you back. Give me one minute."

He pressed END and then dialed another number.

"Quinault Nation Tribal Police."

Time to put some of his CIA training from the Farm into use.

"I am so sorry," he began, explaining that a drunk friend had taken his phone and called them earlier in a poor attempt at a practical joke. He assured them that his friend was now sleeping it off and that all was well. Annoyed, the dispatcher hung up. Walker called Leigh Ann back.

"Sorry about that. You were about to tell me how you know the cops had something to do with Connor's death," Walker said, bringing the conversation back on track.

"I have some of his notes, from the story he was working on."

"Notes?"

"He kept journals."

"And the journals point to police?"

Leigh Ann paused. *"Not exactly. He wrote key items like places and people in a kind of code that I haven't yet figured out. But there is something to do with bribes to people in high places. I can see that much. I think he was framed."*

"But it's just notes? Did he ever discuss his project with you?"

"No. He kept me at arm's length, telling me I'd get the big reveal when he was done."

"I see."

"Chris, I would not ask if I thought I had anywhere else to turn."

And maybe because you know I can't possibly say no, not after what I did to your husband. He pushed the thought from his mind.

You owe her, Chris. And you owe Connor.

Is that why you didn't put a bullet in your brain?

"Journals," Walker whispered.

"What? I think the connection is breaking up."

"Nothing," Walker said, thinking of the intercepted phone calls that had led to the deaths of terrorists on the Agency's target list over the years. "Leigh Ann, give me your address. I'll be there in a few days."

After Walker had written down the address and said his goodbyes to a tearful and grateful Leigh Ann Staub, he stroked Paladin's head, the rain still coming down in torrents.

I owe them.

"Dein platz," he ordered, pointing to the front passenger seat.

Paladin sprang to the front of the van but positioned himself so as to keep a watchful eye on his master. The passenger seat worked on a swivel, facing aft when the vehicle was parked as it was now.

Walker removed an aluminum rod from under the table that allowed him to fold it out of the way, then he pushed himself off the bench seat that separated the cabin from the rear cargo area where a SCUBA tank was strapped against a thin vertical closet. Fins, mask, snorkel, weight belt, and wet suit were in a nylon duffel under a deflated free-diving buoy and a Riffe Marauder speargun with a breakaway system and Kinetic Grip he had customized with his friend Brendan O'Malley for a trip down to Mexico was strapped to the ceiling. He flipped the thin backrest into the cargo space and pulled the rectangular seating cushion off the bench seat to reveal a storage compartment with a push-button cipher lock. Walker had constructed it himself. He punched in a four-digit code and swung open the hatch.

A traditional Osage orangewood bow, backed with western diamondback skins, he had crafted by hand with his SEAL teammate Trevor Thompson was seated in a cutout section of foam, along with arrows made from dogwood fletched with wild turkey feathers and wrapped in elk sinew, their points chipped from Texas chert and Oregon obsidian. Stacks of cash separated by denomination sat in their own rectangular silos. He lifted the foam insert out and set it in the rear cargo area.

The second layer held a 12-gauge Winchester Model 1897 trench gun with bayonet, a pre-64 Winchester Model 94 .30-30, a Colt Single Action Army "Peacemaker" in .45 Colt, and an empty right-angle cutout for the 1911 that had been pressed to his head twenty minutes earlier.

Walker picked up the pistol he had almost used to end his life, felt its weight in his hand.

He heard Paladin growl behind him.

"Not today," he whispered as he pressed it into the foam. He let his fingers linger on its cold steel a moment. The final layer was one he had not visited since he had hidden the items there years earlier when he returned home after he had lost John Staub. He hesitated. He had used the bow and the .30-30 many times over the years, hunting as he explored the country. The 1911 had been his carry pistol, yet he had never gone into the last layer of his vault. Much like what was hidden in his soul, he knew what was there, but he dared not expose it. The tools of his previous life opened the door to darkness.

Then why had he kept them?

Maybe because it was fate that he would need them again?

He took a breath and pulled the heavier second layer out, sliding it on top of the first one in the rear cargo area. Then he looked down at the final tier.

Embedded in the foam were the weapons of his former trade.

He set his hand on the Bravo Company Recce-16 rifle in .300 Blackout with Huxwrx suppressor topped with a Vortex Razor 1-6x24 scope and throw lever. Affixed to the top rail was an L3Harris ATPIAL infrared aiming device, and on the left side was a SureFire Mini Scout light. A Viking Tactics sling was attached. Just below and to the left of the rifle was his Ops-Core ballistic helmet with PVS-14 monocular night optical device, a NOD. He found himself wishing he had snagged a PVS-15 or 31 or, even better, a GPNVG18 panoramic four-tuber before he left the Agency, but someone may have missed that one. He had sometimes used the monocular as a staff officer at GB because as the ground force commander he found it easier to manipulate the radios in the vehicles to communicate with the Agency's experimental manned and unmanned aircraft when on target. No helping that now. Next to the helmet and NOD was a Glock 19 with Trijicon HD Night Sights and an Al Salvitti–designed Regiment Blade with wood grips in a low rider sheath. He removed the pistol and knife and set them to the side.

Then, with the bench seat lifted, Walker grabbed the envelopes from the galley cabinets, the envelopes that contained his death letters, and raised the last layer of foam, stuffing them underneath.

"For another day."

CHAPTER THREE

THE TRUCK RATTLED over the corrugated dirt roads between Bagram and the market bazaar district. After parking among other dusty vehicles, the three CIA men exited.

This area was technically inside the perimeter of a zone where Americans and other coalition security personnel were supposed to be safe. As proof of the increased security, a hulking Army MRAP—Mine Resistant Ambush Protected—moved through traffic with a sergeant in the turret.

Afghan men in *payraan* overshirts with *kulla* caps and women in *parahaan* dresses shuffled to the walls lining the alley, avoiding the steel monster. Americans in Kevlar body armor, helmets, ballistic sunglasses, and black weapons stood out as foreign invaders and always reminded Walker of *Star Wars* stormtroopers manning checkpoints on Tatooine, which was why he, Staub, and Fisk were dressed in earth-tone civilian clothes.

They shouldered between vendors on the market street, with Staub at the six position, checking security, stopping at irregular intervals to mingle with the vendors, to better fit in with the flow of the pedestrians going about their days. They also used the stops as opportunities to observe.

It was mid-September, and the sun was still bright, but the signs of winter were emerging as occasional winds swept over the glacier peaks into mile-high Kabul. The shadows cast by the mud structures stretched longer than they had at this same time just a month prior.

"Posting up here," Staub said at a crossroads, dropping back. "Comms check."

"Lima Charlie," Walker responded into the mic hidden in his collar. Lima Charlie meant loud and clear in milspeak.

"Good copy," Staub replied. "I'll check in with ISR."

Walker fought off the urge to look skyward. ISR was intelligence, surveillance, and reconnaissance, an Agency drone somewhere high overhead. An operator in Nevada was behind the controls, but it was monitored back at Kabul Station. It was Staub's job to keep an eye on any emerging threats and extract them from the meet if things went south.

"That's it, there," Walker said after twenty additional paces. He head-gestured toward a sign that read *Pan Arabian Fine Rugs,* a shop twenty yards ahead on the left. The sign was coated in dust, but the pride taken in the careful lettering shined through. "Let's give John a minute to take a spin around the block."

Walker and Fisk looked over a vendor's cart stuffed with cheap wallets—counterfeits labeled Gucci, Chanel, and Coach with misspelled brand names—as Staub worked his way through the crowds looking for anything out of place.

"Stay put for a second," Staub announced into Walker's earpiece. "I got some burkas coming down the street with a mullah leaning on a doorjamb. One of the burkas is a big ol' gal."

"Roger."

"And, CW, if you see a Gucci lady's wallet that looks somewhat real, pick it up for me. Leigh Ann loves that shit."

"I'm running low on cash."

"The hell you are. And you owe me a favor for finding this guy in the first place. Use some of Fisk's contingency account. Have to spend it on something."

"Problem?" Fisk asked as he checked out a leather passport cover with a blotchy Coach stamp.

"Group of women in burkas around the corner," Walker said quietly. "That's how they hide bombs or disguise Taliban fighters."

"Got it. Should we have that MRAP circle back?"

"No. That would disrupt the natural rhythm and possibly raise suspicions."

Fisk nodded.

A minute later Staub came back over comms. "Okay, we're good. All clear. You see a good wallet?"

"Negative on Gucci. We're going in."

"Good copy. Monitoring the alleys."

A bell jingled when Walker opened the door. He stepped inside and waited for his eyes to adjust. Oriental rugs blocked the light from the windows. The cozy shop smelled of incense, camphor, and musty wool. Boshret Kheir played through decades-old speakers on either side of the cash register.

Fisk tapped his ear. "That shit drives me crazy."

Walker listened to the music while they waited for Naji to come out from the residential part of the shop. "Good tempo," he said. "Think of it as cover."

Lifting a maroon rug with dark blue geometric shapes from a pile, Fisk examined the label. "Tabriz," he said. "Iranian carpet."

"Mongoose gets around. That's one of the reasons you're going to like him."

A man emerged from the back, his smile genuine, his eyes tired but kind.

"Ah! Mr. Chris, you brought a friend!" Naji Mansour looked to be in his late thirties, his dark hair streaked with premature gray. He wore a pressed tunic and moved with quiet dignity.

"Hello, Naji. Great to see you again." Walker turned to Fisk. "This is the man I wanted you to meet. His name is Lawrence."

Fisk placed his hand over his heart, leaned forward in a slight bow, and shook Naji's hand.

"Mr. Mansour, a pleasure to make your acquaintance. I have heard many wonderful things about you and your business."

Walker retreated to a corner and keyed his transmitter while Fisk made small talk about rugs.

"How we looking?" he asked Staub.

"*NSTR, brother,*" Staub responded, using the acronym for nothing significant to report.

"ISR?"

"*Clear. No electronic emanations from the target area.*"

Staub and a Ground Branch technical specialist had swept Naji's shop three weeks ago as part of their surveillance package. All indications since then showed that Naji was clean, a genuine asset who wanted to turn things around for his country.

Over tea and a labored negotiation, Naji had dropped certain hints—namely that he got around, which allowed him to learn things about certain Taliban leaders. He was willing to trade information for U.S. citizenship and relocation to Fremont, California, home to such a large Afghan community that it was known as Little Kabul.

After sending his report on Mansour through Agency channels, Walker was cleared to proceed with an approach. However, as a blue-badge officer in the CIA's Special Activities Center's Ground Branch, Walker's primary role was tactical operations. Fisk, meanwhile, was a case officer responsible for managing confidential informants, whom the Agency referred to as assets. Consequently, this meeting was Fisk's show.

Walker leaned into Fisk and whispered while the music bounced along. "We're clear."

Fisk nodded and turned to Naji. "You mind if we turn that down a little?"

"Of course," Naji replied. He ducked behind the counter to fiddle with his stereo.

With the asset out of sight, Walker instinctively reached for the Glock beneath his light cotton jacket. The music lowered and Naji's head popped up half a second later.

Fisk withdrew his phone from his jacket and swiped the screen. "Can you read English?" he asked Naji.

"I completed my business degree at King's College, London, before returning to Afghanistan," Naji replied.

Fisk shot a glance at Walker, a half smile on his face. No doubt about it, Naji could be a true unicorn: access to senior Taliban ranks, Western-educated, and with the perfect cover to travel.

Walker said to Naji, "Lawrence works closely with our headquarters people. He's here to help you."

"I see."

"There are just some things I'm going to need," Fisk added. "I have a form for you to digitally initial for—" He cut himself off at the sound of an interior door creaking.

A woman in a fawn-colored head scarf looked inquisitively at Walker. He could only see her eyes because the scarf wrapped the lower half of her face. He had met her during the second meeting with Naji.

Walker touched Fisk's elbow. "Naji's wife, Rina. They have two daughters. This is their home as well as their shop."

Fisk instinctively buried his phone in his pocket.

"Mr. Lawrence, I would like you to meet my wife and daughters."

Fisk shifted uncomfortably on his feet.

"It's okay," Walker said to both Naji and Fisk, his voice calm and confident.

With the price of Mansour's intel being U.S. citizenship, Fisk needed to meet the family.

Rina stepped forward, her daughters following, their maroon dresses clean and carefully pressed. They stood beside their mother, eyes wide with curiosity. "Good afternoon, sir," they said in practiced English, their voices barely above a whisper.

"This is Fatima and Zahra," Walker said.

Fatima was around eight with sharp, inquisitive brown eyes, while Zahra was not yet five, her wide eyes full of wonder.

Fisk shook all three of their hands politely as Walker reached into his pocket and offered Tootsie Rolls he had picked up on base.

When they went back to the residence area, Fisk pulled his phone from his pocket.

"Now you have a sense of the future exfil package," Walker said.

Fisk turned to Naji. "I need something before we go much further." He reversed his phone so the screen faced Naji. "This is the form. Just click here. That'll be your signature."

The rug seller did as asked, and handed the phone back to the CIA case officer.

"Thank you." Fisk swiped and turned it around again. "Do you recognize this man?"

Naji studied the device. "Yes. He's Mullah Farj."

"Do you know where he lives?"

Naji glanced at Walker, who nodded. "This is how we get you out of here. That's the deal."

———

Walker covered the first quarter mile through the dust and blaring horns of Kabul traffic, weaving past cars, trucks, buses, scooters, and the occasional donkey with no sign of a tail.

Fisk was in the passenger seat, his head buried in his phone while Staub scanned for threats from the rear bench seat.

"How'd it go? We have a new asset?" Staub asked.

"Looks that way," Walker replied from behind the wheel. "What'd you think, Lenny?"

"A lot of potential here," the case officer responded.

"So, you made the deal?" Staub asked.

"Yes," Fisk answered. "As long as Mongoose delivers, he'll get a special visa to come to the U.S. After a year of what amounts to probation he'll become an American citizen, but . . ."

"But what?" Walker asked.

"He has to deliver."

CHAPTER FOUR

Quinault Rain Forest, Washington State
Present Day

AS THE RAIN hammered down and the ocean thundered, Walker rolled up the awning, folded his chair, and packed up camp. Paladin had been fed and Walker had roasted three rockfish he had killed spearfishing that morning in the Queets River estuary.

Next, he collected Paladin's fetch toys, which he had arranged around the campsite so the dog would have something to do while waiting for the authorities to arrive. His last packing task was to lower the pop-up tent atop the VW and secure his tan Bison cooler to the cargo shelf extending from the rear bumper. When he was finished, the van rumbled to life with that familiar whistle that afflicts old Volkswagens. Walker put it in gear, twisting the parking brake handle to the right and pushed it forward. He engaged the windshield wipers and slowly pulled from his campsite onto a dirt logging road.

Why am I still alive?

A shaft of light filtered through a break in the clouds as Walker pulled into Tommy Hawkeye's driveway five miles away. A U.S. Marine Corps flag marked Tommy's single-story rambler on the outskirts of town. Walker had met Hawkeye, a Vietnam veteran, on a hunting trip in eastern Washington State. The old man had noticed Walker's trad bow. Hawkeye appreciated the nod to heritage and tradition. Walker had asked him about the faded USMC tattoo on his right forearm. Through a federation of Indian tribes, Hawkeye had led Walker onto the hunting lands of the Yakama Nation. Together, they had taken a bull elk using traditional bows.

"You leaving?" Tommy asked through the screen door, as a reality show about finding love blared from an older-model television. Walker could see Tommy's wife in an easy chair, her hands busily crocheting. The couple was well into their seventies.

"It's time," Walker said. He was in jeans, a flannel, his Iron Ranger boots, and wearing a black hat now faded to gray with a barely visible symbol on the front, that of an eagle over a tommy gun and what appeared to be an anchor.

Hawkeye looked at him through the screen. He reminded Walker of a priest peering through a confessional.

Tommy pushed the screen door open. It creaked on its hinges.

"Did you get what you came for?" the Vietnam veteran asked, nodding past Walker at the forest.

"No luck on a blacktail, if that's what you mean. I did some spearfishing, ate a lot of rockfish, went for a beach dive, and collected clams."

"That's not what I mean."

Walker remained quiet.

"Where you off to now? Home?" Hawkeye asked, his face lined and creased with the vestiges of time.

"For a bit."

"And then?"

Walker paused.

"Then I'll be heading south."

The van was not designed with speed or aerodynamics in mind.

His first two hundred miles brought him into the majestic Cascade Mountains. On the eastern side, he decided that the van's overworked engine needed a break, so he stopped in the town of Cle Elum for fresh groceries.

After his resupply, he drove along Highway 97 toward the Teanaway River Valley, where, under a fading sky, he set up camp in a grove of mixed cottonwoods, maples, firs, and pines. The river, still swollen from melting snow, hissed and gurgled.

Natural rhythms.

The gloomy storms that battered the west side of the state were kept at bay by the mountains. Here on the eastern slope, the sky was clear, and the stars flickered in the night just as they had during bivouacs in

Afghanistan's Hindu Kush. Walker had operated with his SEAL troop and then the CIA under these same stars. He thought of moving through the Spīn Ghar Mountains in Nangarhar Province with Staub, navigating via GPS and NODs.

Walker pushed the memory aside, throwing a fresh cedar bough onto the fire. Its sap was a highly flammable accelerant and hit the flames like gasoline, sending embers skyward.

With Paladin settled near the warming rocks, Walker grilled two steaks he had bought in Cle Elum, at Owens Meats. After two weeks on the Quinault Reservation eating fish, he went for two pounds of prime rib eye, one for himself, the other for Paladin.

While the steaks sizzled, Walker found the bottle of Four Branches bourbon in the van's galley. He didn't drink often, but after surviving a near-death experience earlier in the day and being thoroughly tired of listening to the philosopher in his head, it felt like the right remedy as he accepted his decision to remain among the living, at least in the short term, until he got this one last thing done for his old friend. Then he would revisit the .45.

Sitting on a thick flannel sleeping bag, bundled in his blanket-lined Carhartt, Walker reclined on an elbow and stroked his dog as the fire crackled. Though a philosopher at heart, his studies led him to history and human motivations. He thought about ancient wolves, and the finely tuned weapon curled up by his side. There was a wolf pack that lived in the Teanaway. He wondered if Paladin could sense them beyond the glow of the fire.

Walker kept the .30-30 nearby. It stayed there that night as he slept, his dog nuzzled against him, briefly at peace.

———

Seventeen hours later, he turned the van into the driveway of the house that used to belong to his foster mother, Teri. According to the typed letter in an envelope under the gun tray, proceeds from the sale of the house were to go to the Rescue 22 Foundation, an organization providing fully trained service and support dogs to veterans dealing with the physical and emotional trauma of the battlefield.

"Sorry, guys," Walker said, looking up at the modest home. "You're going to have to wait a little longer."

He exited the vehicle and punched a code into a box on the side of the garage that opened the door. After he pulled in and shut down, the van's engine clicked, and Walker could smell a faint trace of burning oil. Worse, he could hear dripping onto the garage floor. While Paladin leaped out, Walker lowered himself to the concrete for an inspection. Sure enough, there was a growing puddle, which meant he would need to replace the van's water pump again, or at least its seals, a recurring problem.

The house remained exactly as his mother had left it, her clothes hung in the closet, while the other two bedrooms were dedicated to her hobbies, sewing and music. It was fully paid off when she had passed away when Walker was still in his teens and she had left him just enough money to make sure he could keep it. Walker slept on the sofa. There were too many memories in his old room.

In the morning, he practiced dog-whistle drills with Paladin and then went on a long run through the high desert sage with the Belgian Malinois at his side. Later, he did his laundry and sifted through an old milk crate of cassettes to stock his vehicle with different tapes. Around three that afternoon, he drove the van onto two steel ramps and worked on the water pump.

His tools and spare parts hung on a pegboard as neatly as a NAPA auto store. It took him all of three seconds to locate the spare gaskets for the pump, even less to find the right sockets and wrenches.

Then he used a sealant to fix the .45-caliber bullet hole in the roof and checked the vehicle's power system. Walker had mounted a six-hundred-watt solar array on the roof of the van, which was enough to keep the batteries topped off after a full day in the sun. The charge controller fed a steady twelve volts into the lithium bank that powered the fridge and interior lights.

After dinner, he prepared the van for departure. He swapped out the LP gas tank, filled the potable water jerry can, and ensured he had the correct tools to adjust the engine on his journey, stowing them in the van's kit with the intricacy and care of a Zurich watchmaker. He ensured the fan that circulated air throughout the cabin for Paladin was in working order, as he had not checked it in a while with the cooler weather and the fact that Walker rarely, if ever, left his dog alone in the van.

Before he set off, Walker knew he had to flip a switch. He had designed the three levels of the storage vault under the back bench seat that separated the living area from the cargo area to be interchangeable. Since he left the Agency, he had prioritized his more primitive weapons on the top. That was about to change. He pulled up the seat and removed the layer that held his trad bow in place. Then he pulled up the middle one that contained his trench gun, .30-30, Colt Peacemaker, and 1911. Lastly, he detached the level with his Bravo Company AR, helmet, and NOD. While the 1911 felt at home in a Milt Sparks Summer Special 2 leather holster, the Glock 19 was secured in a Kydex Tenicor like he had used overseas on the enemy's turf. He then replaced the layers starting with his bow, next the guns with wood furniture, and finally, on top went the instruments of his former profession.

When the van was stocked and organized, Walker pulled a bag from a shelf in the garage and removed his Velocity Systems plate carrier and low-profile chest rig. The bloodstains from the last time he had worn it were visible. He had never cleaned it off. The blood wasn't his. It remained infused with dried dust and memories of Afghanistan.

CHAPTER FIVE

Afghanistan
2020

NESTLED AMONG THE stark hills three miles north of Hamid Karzai International Airport, the former brick factory was now a compound consisting of climate-controlled trailers, a faux training village, shooting ranges, a burn pit, and a holding facility known as the Salt Pit. Those who had been held there had another name for it: the Dark Prison.

Covered with antennas, watchtowers, and sandbags, the base spanned over two square miles. If Afghanistan was the main event of the Global War on Terror, Eagle Base was the ticket office, and it was the compound where Walker and Staub lived, worked, and trained. It was home to the Zero Units, the Afghan paramilitary teams, vetted and trained by the Americans, and it was from Eagle Base that the CIA ran the secret war.

In the narrow chute before the main gate, Walker zigzagged the Rover through a complex maze of barricades. At the final barrier, bearded contractors in ball caps and body armor, holding M4s, inspected the car with mirrors and sensors. They popped the hood and trunk and asked Staub and Walker to stand outside while they looked through the passenger compartments. It wasn't so much that they didn't know or trust the two CIA operators; it was that they needed to know their car hadn't been sabotaged with an IED that could be triggered by a cell phone. A decade earlier seven CIA officers and contractors along with a Jordanian intelligence officer and Afghan driver had been killed when a triple agent detonated a suicide vest at FOB Chapman after a lapse in security protocols. The contractors at Eagle Base were not about to let that happen here. There were always eyes in the hills waiting on the Americans to let their guard down.

"Hey, Clorox," Staub said to the supervising contractor. "Who's on overwatch right now?"

CIA contractors usually used call signs while in country. "Clorox" had earned his nickname by claiming that his blond hair and beard were natural.

"That's Toad in the south tower, Garbo to the east," Clorox said.

Staub waved at the two men in helmets and black balaclavas. Toad, the man farthest from him, returned the wave with a middle-finger salute.

"What's his problem?" Walker asked.

"I kicked his ass in yesterday's bench press competition," Staub explained.

"He said you cheated," Clorox said.

"I didn't. Chris will back me up on that."

Clorox leaned in to look at Walker, who nodded.

"Here's a little friendly advice, fellas," Clorox suggested. "Always be nice to the guy who has you sighted in through his high-powered scope."

"Good tip," Staub replied.

Walker drove the Rover past the compound's vast motor pool of indigenous vehicles before parking at the low two-story operations building where the case officers met. It was originally built by the Soviets in the eighties, but the Agency had expanded it with several wings.

"Welcome back," Leonard Fisk said, greeting them at the entrance. Though Fisk spent most of his time at Bagram or Langley, direct action operations were planned at Eagle Base. "Come on, I have us set up in a SCIF upstairs." He pronounced the acronym as *skiff*, a sensitive compartmented information facility.

Fisk led them inside. After swiping their IDs at a locked door, they passed through an inner room they called Cortex, where raw ISR feeds were displayed on monitors bolted to the wall. A half dozen officers, technicians, and specialists sat glued to screens much like air traffic controllers in towers guiding and directing aircraft on the ground and in the skies. After clearing Cortex, they entered a stairwell and hustled to the second-floor SCIF.

The entire operations building was hardened against incoming and outgoing radio transmissions, but the mission planning center was so sensitive that it was, effectively, a SCIF within a SCIF. Walker and Staub secured their cell phones in a honeycomb of lockboxes before following Fisk through the windowless maze, eventually arriving in a six-seat conference room filled with the detritus of CIA case officers on the hunt: binders, bulletin boards, Post-it notes, and photos of high-value targets. A sixty-inch Samsung flat-screen was affixed to the front wall.

Fisk plugged an HDMI cable into his laptop and began typing while Walker and Staub settled in.

"Movie?" Staub asked.

Fisk didn't reply. After a few more keystrokes, the Samsung lit up with a PowerPoint presentation title screen, a blue background with the Agency seal in one corner and a single word across the center in fifty-point font: "BACKDRAFT."

"Already seen it, Lenny," Staub said. "Quite the cast."

"Okay," Fisk said. "I'm reading you both in on BACKDRAFT, a capture-kill op targeting leadership elements of HQN. Chris, you'll have lead."

HQN, the Haqqani Network, was a semiautonomous offshoot of the Taliban closely related to al-Qaeda.

"Which elements?" Walker asked.

Fisk punched a key on his laptop. The TV screen shifted to a series of surveillance photos of a man in his fifties. "This guy, Abdul Nasr, is on a little field trip to Lashkar Gah. He's been HQN's weapons supplier for the past year."

"He'd be a big get for us," Walker said.

"Indeed. We've been looking for him in Cairo, but we obtained new source reporting that he's here, in Afghanistan. Further reporting indicates this house in Lashkar Gah, five hundred clicks southwest of us, is one of his safe houses."

Fisk flipped the chart forward to reveal photos of a dull mud house that could be anywhere in Afghanistan. The pictures were oddly angled because they were taken covertly by an asset in Lashkar Gah, the distant, dusty capital of Afghanistan's Helmand Province.

"How do we know this is the house?" Walker asked.

"We'll discuss that in a minute. But it was confirmed by a second source, here."

"And by here, do you happen to mean something coming out of the Pit?" Staub asked, referring to Eagle Base's interrogation and detention facility.

"Need to know," Fisk said, using the intelligence colloquial for "I can't answer that."

Some case officers regarded the men from the CIA's Special Activities Center as equal colleagues. Others, like Fisk, maintained a class distinction between the paramilitary knuckle-draggers and what some considered the more cerebral work of the case officers. Walker had detected the first signs of Fisk's attitude when they had been training together at Camp Peary, the Virginia CIA training base better known as the Farm.

"And who's source?" Walker asked

"Mongoose."

Walker and Staub traded a glance.

Staub smiled. "Let me guess, Abdul Nasr wanted to deck out his vacation house in lovely Lashkar Gah and for that, he needed some new rugs."

"Correct."

"And the confirmation may or may not have come from some poor bastard in the Salt Pit."

Fisk remained noncommittal.

"Quite a risk for him to take these pictures," Walker noted.

Fisk didn't reply. He flipped to the next chart, a high-resolution satellite image. "Given the long distance to Lashkar and the crowded urban environment, the chief wants this to be a light footprint."

"Meaning," Walker said, "no involvement from JSOC."

The CIA's Special Activities Center was akin to a specialized military force unto itself, comprising three branches: Ground, Air, and Maritime. Walker and Staub were both with Ground Branch. Depending on the mission scope, direct action ops were either conducted by the CIA and their Afghan partner forces or farmed out to forces falling under Special Operations Command, SOCOM, or JSOC, the Joint Special Operations Command, comprised of tier one units that included the Army's Delta Force and the Navy's SEAL Team Six.

"Conventional military assets for the quick reaction force, but the main effort is Agency and Agency assets."

Walker gazed at the images. "This everything?"

"We're working up a threat assessment package on Taliban strength in Lashkar Gah. Right now, it's looking like there are two or three active cells, platoon-strength, though that varies."

"Why does it vary?" Walker asked.

Fisk paused, as though weighing whether he should share more sensitive intelligence. "We think Nasr is training them. Cells are rotating through, learning how to make bombs, using his house as a base of operations. Clearly, we'll time the op based on a gap between intervals. I need you two to concentrate on the house and Nasr."

"Uh-huh," Staub said with a dose of cynicism, because he'd been in a hundred meetings like this over his career in the SEAL Teams and Ground Branch. "We're going to need a lot more than a few pictures from the outside of the house. We need to know if the doors open right or left, who exactly is inside, back doors, window placement, disposition of the neighbors."

"Understood," Fisk said. "Which is why I'm sending Mongoose back out there."

"Under what pretext?" Walker asked.

"Let us worry about that. I told him what we need. He'll get back in the house, but this time wired for video. You'll get the take."

"When?"

"He's leaving for a sales trip to that region tonight."

"I thought he was just there. These pictures you have are new."

"Like you guys said, they're not enough. I'm sending him back."

———

Free of the operations building, Walker and Staub made their way along a dirt sidewalk that led to their vehicle, eyes adjusting to the bright sunlight. Now that an op was taking shape, Walker wanted to head back to Bagram to coordinate a QRF—Quick Reaction Force—with the conventional Army battlespace owner.

"I heard Fisk has orders back to Langley," Staub said.

"Not surprised," Walker replied. "He's punched his ticket here in the hot zone. Now he can do an administrative tour stateside and move on to Europe as deputy chief. He speaks French."

"He speaks douchebag. Hope that French lands him in some shithole like Cameroon."

They were nearing the parking lot when a pair of Air Force A-10 Thunderbolts rocketed overhead, ascending out of Bagram Air Base, fifteen miles north of Eagle Station. After the roaring echoes died away, Staub caught the distant look in Walker's eyes. "Overthinking something again?"

"Maybe," Walker replied.

There was no reason to lock the Land Rover on the fortified base, so Walker simply opened the door, turned the key in the ignition, and started the engine. He performed a three-point turn to leave the parking lot and waved as he passed through the security gate.

"I don't like the idea of Fisk sending Naji back out there so soon after his last visit. If Taliban fighters are using this bombmaker's house, then they're going to figure out who Naji is and what he's up to. A lot of Westerners visit his shop. While he's in Lashkar, I could imagine a Tali contingent scooping up his family for leverage."

"Isn't he supposed to be getting out of here soon?"

"Yes. He's over his year commitment already. The last time I saw him, he told me Fisk is dragging his feet on the special immigrant visas for his family. Now we're sending him halfway across the country while his family is exposed. I'm starting to wish I'd never sent in that contact report."

Staub kept his eyes focused on the distant hills as the truck neared the exit gate. "Who's up on favors right now?"

"I am," Walker said. "For backing you up on that bench press."

"Time was, you would back me up on that and not count it as a favor."

"Time was, you wouldn't have had to cheat."

Staub laughed. "So, let's just say I owe you one."

"You do."

Staub surveyed the Afghan countryside, took a deep breath, and turned back to his partner.

"I'm not feeling good about this either. Let's get a Zero Unit surveillance team to keep an eye on Naji's family."

"I was thinking the same thing."

"Great minds," Staub replied.

"Fisk might not go for it. If they get burned, it might compromise the mission."

"He'll never know."

CHAPTER SIX

American West
Present Day

GLAD I GAVE *myself a week,* Walker thought as he pushed the van across the fat bottom of Idaho, Paladin curled up on the front passenger seat.

Worried that he might pop a fan belt or burst a hose, he felt obligated to avoid interstate traffic and instead nursed the vehicle along U.S. Highway 20, also known as the Medal of Honor Highway. Walker hadn't planned for this to be a tribute ride, but seeing the signs every ten miles, he couldn't help but think of the men he knew who had received the nation's highest award for valor. His mind shifted through the variables that resulted in some missions ending in glory and others in shame.

Snap out of it.

He reached over to pet Paladin and distract himself from the signs.

At fifty-seven miles an hour, Walker managed about four hundred miles a day.

When he hit Boise, he navigated to Scheels, where he stocked up on ammo.

What are you doing? You are not going to war, are you?

That night found him under the stars of the Morley Nelson Snake River Birds of Prey National Conservation Area. The next, in the desolate expanse of Craters of the Moon National Monument, northwest of Pocatello, the juniper wood burning in the campfire hissing and popping, filling the air with the sweet, resinous scent of the West. The high desert sage and distant red hills reminded Walker of Afghanistan, and he was relieved when the sky finally surrendered its colors and turned to black.

With clear skies, he slept outside on the ground rather than in the rooftop tent, Paladin next to him on two wool blankets by the fire.

His morning started with cowboy coffee for him and whistle drills for

Paladin. Whistle commands were not something they used in the Teams, but Paladin had gone from the military to a former SEAL's dog rehab center in Southern California that provided Hollywood with dogs trained to act on set responding to whistle command and hand signals from a distance. Before packing up, he went for a run to clear his head, Paladin at his side.

The following night, near Jackson, Wyoming, they camped in the shadow of the Tetons. Crickets chirped, owls called, and bats darted beneath a sky so thick with stars it looked like glowing smoke. The air was colder at elevation, but Walker couldn't resist the view. After a dinner of trout fried over the fire, he leaned back and let his mind drift to time, space, and eternity. As always, the old philosophers came whispering, asking the fundamental questions that have plagued mankind since the inception of human cognition: *Who are you? Why are you here? What is the nature of your soul?*

Walker stared into the flames as man had done from time immemorial.

Maybe he would only have answers when he pressed the trigger for the last time.

You are struggling. Make it stop.

Sensing his unease, Paladin thrust a nose into Walker's armpit, bringing him back, grounding him.

"Okay, boy," Walker said, looking around at the landscape, gray in the starlight. "If you really want me to. There's no one around."

He stood up and unstrapped his Martin six-string acoustic from the ceiling of the Volkswagen and returned to his camp chair, tuning the guitar in the pale moonlight. Paladin sat beside him, wagging his tail, his eyes glowing with the reflection of the embers.

"What'll it be?" Walker asked, strumming a few simple chords to warm up. Paladin lay directly on top of Walker's feet, as though intentionally keeping him in place.

The former SEAL reached down and rubbed his dog behind the ears.

"What do you feel like tonight, boy? How about one of your favorites?"

He dropped the guitar pick into his shirt pocket and used his fingers to pluck out notes of "Oh, Bury Me Not—A Cowboy's Prayer" by Johnny Cash.

After mastering the riff through the introductory bars, Walker took one last look around. He guessed there wasn't another living soul within ten miles. It was safe to play. Paladin's tail thumped. Walker hummed until he found the right note, and then, while his fingers danced over the strings, he sang to the dog and the stars:

> *Lord, I've never lived where churches grow . . .*
> *I loved creation better as it stood . . .*
> *Oh, bury me not, on the lone prairie . . .*

———

North of Denver, at Medicine Bow, Walker and Paladin watched a spread of towering cumulus clouds march over the plains from the west, its base as flat and forbidding as the iron skillet he had used for the trout. Walker thought briefly of the clouds from the Pacific and the rain that had hammered him at the Quinault Reservation. Invariably, that led him to think of the letters that were beneath the foam that held the weapons.

He shook it off. The guns and the letters weren't going anywhere.

Finish the mission. The final mission. Return Staub's favor.

He ejected the Led Zeppelin cassette in the eighties-era Blaupunkt stereo and tried to find something more upbeat. He ended up with his favorite Rolling Stones album, *Sticky Fingers*, which lasted forty rumbling miles.

That evening, he cooked a pot of beans with bacon on the galley stove and slept in the rooftop tent because the clouds had thickened and a gentle rain was falling. The sealant he'd applied back in Sisters to cover the crack made by the bullet held. No leaks.

While rain thumped the roof, Walker delved back into philosophy beneath his battery-powered reading lamp. Since it had been a while, he focused on pre-Renaissance thinkers, starting with Socrates, who tutored Plato, who in turn influenced Aristotle. He was soon swept up in a direct translation of Plato's ancient dialogues, a collection of philosophical texts that featured Socrates as a central character who argued various points about government and ethics. This led Walker to consider Plato's view that democracy was ultimately a flawed concept and that the only way to govern a nation was through an oligarchical or aristocratic elite.

He thought of the chaos that had accompanied the rise of social media, the deterioration of civil discourse, logic, and reason, and the creation of platforms that had turned a republic into a democracy.

"Maybe Plato was right. What do you think, Pal?"

Hearing Walker's voice over the raindrops, Paladin thumped his tail. Walker turned off the light and closed his eyes dreaming of ancient Athens with his dog curled at his feet.

The mountains gave way to hills and then to fields as Walker drove the van south along Route 385. When he finally arrived in Amarillo, Texas, he turned on his flip phone to update Leigh Ann and triple-typed a text message on the keypad: *Two or three days out. See you soon.* After that, he powered the phone off and left Amarillo in the rearview.

He found a different kind of beauty in Texas. The landscape was flat and treeless for miles, but not featureless. The tan concrete road, tilting telephone poles, and endless farm fields had a certain unity of form that reminded him of Edward Hopper paintings. A girlfriend had taken him to a Hopper exhibit while he was at NYU, introducing him to the intersection of art and philosophy, disciplines now inevitably linked in Walker's mind. He had admired Hopper's eye for early American industrialization and the changes it made on the landscape, and, most of all, the feelings of loneliness evoked by the artist's silent figures, who so often faced into the sunlight, alone and quiet. Like Hopper, Walker found something beautiful in the desolation.

With his hands on the wheel and his eyes focused two miles ahead, his mind wandered as he mentally debated the nature of beauty. One of the most lasting themes in Western philosophy was whether beauty was subjective, in the eye of the beholder, or objective, inherent in a thing itself. Making matters more complex was whether it applied only to the senses, like physical beauty, or to the abstract, such as the beautiful ideas of justice or truth.

Walker turned the debate over in his head to pass the time, arguing both sides in the style of Plato's dialogues, remembering the things he had learned from his professors and presented in his papers at NYU. When the current cassette, a Who album, clicked and stopped, Walker drove on in silence, continuing both sides of the debate until fatigue weighed on his eyelids.

He pulled over to the side of the road to stretch his legs and fired up the coffee percolator using the LP gas in the port galley stove. A little caffeine would keep him going. Well past midnight, he found a dirt road in the middle of a cattle ranch and, for the first time since Colorado, slept outside by the fire, stargazing while Paladin's ears twitched at the sounds of unfamiliar animals and night birds.

The next day, as he crossed the state line between Texas and Louisiana, he recalled how he had told Staub that he thought the entire state of Louisiana was one long bridge. Surveying the hazy skies and green fields through the windshield, he now understood that he had formed that idea during a drive across the South, skirting the Gulf Coast. Approaching from the northwest through the top of the state's boot-shaped outline, however, he saw dense trees, corrugated farm fields, and scattered towns that might have kept Edward Hopper busy with his paintbrush.

He replaced a Moody Blues cassette with Lynyrd Skynyrd and fast-forwarded until he got to "Sweet Home Alabama." It wasn't quite the right state, but Mobile was only a few hundred miles down the road. In Baton Rouge, he stopped for gas, bought a map of Louisiana, and plotted the route to New Orleans. At Vanagon speed, Leigh Ann Staub's home was just under three hours away.

"Last chance to back out, buddy," Walker said to Paladin as he pulled the van to a stop looking left down the frontage road.

Paladin barked.

"Not sure what that means."

He looked back at the vault under the rear seat where the .45 waited.

"Soon," Walker said, turning to the dog in the passenger seat. "Now, it's time to return a favor."

CHAPTER SEVEN

WALKER'S VAN RATTLED down Prytania Street, its patched roof catching glints of sun between the oaks. Paladin sat upright in the passenger seat, ears perked, nose twitching at the new scents.

Walker slowed as he passed rows of antebellum homes with white columns, wrought-iron balconies, gardens blooming in colorful symmetry. The Staub home was close, but he had a stop to make first.

He turned onto Washington Avenue and pulled up to the curb outside Lafayette Cemetery No. 1. The gates stood open. Inside, rows of above-ground tombs stretched in solemn order, their stone faces arranged like the temples of ancient Greece. New Orleans was a city reclaimed from swamp, and the tradition was to bury the dead above ground.

But nature refused to be outdone. Ivy crept along the masonry walls and curbs. Ferns sprouted through cracks. The tombs of the long-forgotten were streaked with mildew and moss, their inscriptions softened by time.

Walker stepped out, made sure his window was cracked, and turned back to Paladin.

"*Blijf.*" Stay.

Paladin sniffed the air and then lowered his head and let out a soft whine.

Walker wondered if Paladin could sense the death.

"I'll be right back."

As Walker made his way into the cemetery, he heard the thump of a bass drum, followed by the rich tones of tubas and, finally, trumpets. On the far side of the cemetery, a brass band emerged. The musicians wore black suits with white gloves. They carried polished horns. Behind them, mourners followed dancing slowly between the tombs in flowing white linen, bright parasols twirling. Handkerchiefs fluttered in the humid air like birds in flight.

The solemn dirge of the jazz funeral shifted as the band struck up a celebratory melody, horns bright, drums rolling. The second line came alive with dance; feet stomping, umbrellas spinning, limbs moving with joy.

Walker watched, transfixed by the celebration of life, a celebration in stark contrast to his dark mood. He was not there to celebrate. He was there to visit a dead friend.

He passed under intertwined sycamores, magnolias, and hickories, careful not to trip over the roots, and as the sounds of the band faded, he found himself standing before the two raised graves of John and Connor Staub.

Fresh white lilies had been laid on Connor's tomb.

Did Leigh Ann put those there?

He removed his ball cap and held it in his hand by his side.

"I'm sorry, John. I let you down twice," he whispered, his eyes moving from John's grave to Connor's.

He didn't know why he needed to see them, only that he felt it necessary.

Are both of these men dead because of me?

"There is no making this right, but I'll do what I can before I join you."

Not knowing how to leave them, he reverted to what he knew.

"'After your death, you return to what you were before your birth,'" he said, quoting from Schopenhauer, which he regretted as soon as he said it. Arthur Schopenhauer was an atheist, after all. That did not seem quite right, so he added, "That'll remain a mystery to me for a little while longer."

The band stopped. Walker bowed his head.

"I'll take care of Leigh Ann," he said quietly. "I promise. I still owe you that favor."

Then he turned back toward the van.

––––––

The girl with short raven-black hair watched him from a distance, perched on the hood of an aging BMW produced three decades before she was born, cigarette dangling from her tattooed fingers. He seemed too preoccupied to notice her. People were like that in cemeteries. Her arms were inked with serpents, constellations, and fragments of poetry. She wore jeans and a gray tank top, her Doc Marten boots laced tight.

He returned to his van, head down. Even as far away as she was, she could hear the vehicle take three tries to start.

She took a drag of her Marlboro and watched him through a veil of smoke, squinting as she memorized his license plate.

————

Walker had been to New Orleans twice. Once during Jazz Fest when his SEAL platoon was training at Fort Polk, but their time had been confined to Bourbon Street in the French Quarter. The second time was a more somber occasion. When they laid John Staub to rest.

When he turned onto Leigh Ann's street, he slowed the van to a crawl, looking from the address on a scrap of paper in his hand to the homes, searching for numbers.

Walker was familiar with the history of New Orleans from a paper he had written on Voltaire's influence on the French Revolution. This had led him to study the governing philosophies of that era, particularly the debate between royalists and republicans, a debate similar to the one that had shaped the country he had just crossed.

Louisiana and New Orleans were founded by the French in the seventeenth century. The state was named after King Louis XIV and the city for the governor of Orleans. However, in the 1760s, the ruling Bourbons gifted the city to their relatives on the Spanish throne to settle a treaty, making it a Spanish colony for the next forty years. In the late 1700s, fires raged through New Orleans and destroyed most of the French structures. They were eventually rebuilt, but the city's most famous architecture was Spanish, even in the French Quarter.

A few miles southwest, Walker found himself looking at a white two-story Spanish colonial house that would not have looked out of place in old Seville. It boasted a balcony, floor-to-ceiling windows with black hinged shutters, and a wide front porch behind tall columns. Like the neighbors on either side, the entire property was enclosed by an ornate wrought-iron fence.

Walker parked across the street, his old van looking a bit out of place in the neighborhood known to locals as the Garden District. He double-checked the address and compared it to the numbers under the gaslight lantern on the gatepost, thinking he had arrived at the wrong place.

Nope. This was it.

"You ready?" he said to Paladin as much as himself.

Sensing his handler's impending action but confused by the lack of an accompanying command, Paladin barked.

"My thoughts exactly."

Walker swung open his door and stepped down to the road. He glanced up and down the quiet street before looking back to Paladin.

"*Heir*." Here.

Paladin sprung from the passenger seat to the driver's seat and then to the ground at Walker's side.

Walker locked the van.

"*Volg*," he said. Heel.

The pair crossed to the house, and Walker pressed a button on the intercom built into the pedestrian gate.

"Hello?" the female voice said.

"Leigh Ann. It's Chris," he said.

"Chris! Come on up."

The gate buzzed.

Wearing teal surgical scrubs, Leigh Ann Staub greeted them at the front door.

"It's so good to see you," she said, stepping forward in a welcoming embrace. "And who is this?"

"Paladin, but you can call him Pal."

"Can I pet him?" She had been around enough working dogs to know that it was best to ask.

"He'd love it."

She let Paladin smell the back of her hand and then ran her fingers along the top of his head and scratched him behind the ears.

"Come in," she said, stepping back and holding the door open for them.

"Thank you. It's good to see you, Leigh Ann."

"You too," she replied, closing the door and locking the dead bolt.

As Walker followed her into the house, the first thing he noticed was the fine Persian Tabriz carpet on the floor, maroon with navy-blue geometric shapes. A remnant of a past life.

CHAPTER EIGHT

Asadabad, Kunar Province, Afghanistan
2020

THE MI-17 HELICOPTER shuddered, not from turbulence, but from the bite of a sharp banking turn. They were descending.

"Three minutes out," the Afghan pilot called out over comms in English.

He had been trained to fly the Soviet-designed helicopter on night vision at Fort Rucker in Alabama under a nonstandard rotary wing aircraft project called the Mi-17 Aviator Training Program. The Agency-run Afghan Counterterrorism Pursuit Teams used them for air assault operations. Walker trusted them. As much as he trusted anyone.

He reached down and ran his fingers over the six mags in his chest rig.

"Copy," he replied. "Do you have a visual?"

"Affirmative. I have visual on IR strobe. Raptor says the landing area is clear."

Raptor was the call sign for the MC-12W Liberty twin-engine turboprop with electro-optical infrared sensors providing ISR to the assault force and the Zero Unit close target reconnaissance team already on the ground.

Walker removed the headset that connected him to the pilots and put on his Peltors and Ops-Core helmet, switching on the four-banger NODs before leaning over to Staub.

"About two minutes," he shouted over the roar of the rotors. "Pilot has visual."

Staub nodded and tapped the Afghan commando next to him.

"Two minutes," he shouted to their terp, Ali, who passed the information in Pashto on the Afghan inner squad radio frequency.

The tan, brown, and green painted bird was one of two, each carrying fifteen Afghan commandos and two Americans toward their insert.

All wore desert tiger-stripe uniforms with the black, red, and green flag of Afghanistan on one shoulder and their unit flag, consisting of a shield with crossed swords and wings, on the other. They were similarly kitted out in plate carriers, body armor, mags and mag pouches, blow-out kits, and radios. They each carried the ubiquitous black M4 rifle. All wore black balaclavas to cover their faces. Revenge, after all, was a concept deeply rooted in Pashtun culture.

They would land in a clearing and meet up with an element from the Afghan surveillance and reconnaissance unit that would lead them the ten kilometers to the target, where the other half of the surveillance team had eyes on the target building, the house Naji had taken photos and video of weeks earlier.

Naji had sold a large, expensive Tabriz rug to a courier for Hamid Abrar, the Haqqani commander who controlled the Taliban resupply routes in Waziristan. A miniature sensor developed by specialists from the Agency's Office of Technical Service had been woven into the fabric, tracking back to Abrar's suspected safe house outside of Asadabad. It had been proven to be a valuable asset.

The helos touched down moments later, unloaded the assault force and then once again clawed skyward, vanishing into the darkness as the teams formed hasty perimeters.

"Raptor, this is Viking, how are we looking?" Walker said into his mic as he pressed down on the transmit button of his radio that was linked with their overhead ISR asset.

"Viking, Raptor, you are clear. We'll be with you all the way."

"Good copy."

Walker turned to Staub and Ali.

"Looking good. Let them know."

Most of the Zero Unit operators spoke English, but using an interpreter was still the most effective way to communicate. Having a trusted and tactically savvy terp like Ali had become invaluable.

"Yes, sir. Moving out," Ali said after a brief exchange with the Zero Unit commander.

After all these years of conflict, each Zero Unit operated as a finely tuned instrument. As they were ostensibly an independent host nation force, they did not have the red tape attached to missions that most of the U.S. military did. When night raids were curtailed by the American flag officers in favor of a kinder and gentler approach to counterinsurgency, an approach that put the tactical-level soldiers at higher risk, the Zero Units could still operate with impunity, guided by the technical intelligence of the CIA.

Walker and Staub would advise the assault element while two other Agency GB contractors would advise the blocking and containment element. Nate was a former Marine sniper turned cop turned GB operator, call sign Psycho, while Dave was a retired sergeant major out of Delta Force, call sign Grouper. They had all worked together for years.

The Americans each wore two radios, one linked to the Zero Unit tactical frequency and one tuned to their own so they could communicate in English to coordinate command and control without stepping on the Afghans' communications.

"Let's go," Walker said to Ali, who whispered to the Zero Unit commander.

A brief exchange in Pashto was communicated over the radio, and the two elements moved toward the tree line to link up with their recon unit.

They all knew their mission. They had done it a thousand times.

The team would be able to cover the ten klicks to the target quickly with overhead ISR. Two Zero Unit recon team members had stayed on target to ensure that Abrar was still inside. They would provide a quick update when the ground force arrived. Then Team One would assault the house while Team Two held security, with Nate and his snipers moving onto predetermined rooftops and Dave managing the overall blocking and containment. Walker and Staub would enter the building with the assault team. If things went sideways, a Marine combat outpost thirty klicks to the southwest was on standby as a QRF.

Walker felt at home in the Afghan mountains at night. The stars were the brightest he had ever seen. He found himself thinking of the armies that had marched through Afghanistan over the centuries under these same stars, from Genghis Khan to Alexander the Great to the Brits, the Soviets, and now the Americans. Afghanistan had the ill fortune of being geographically vital to moving goods through Central Asia. That curse had resulted in a culture in which war was a constant.

Ideally, they would make a surreptitious entry, grab Abrar out of his bed, patrol to a nearby field, and call in the helos for extract. The problem with the plan, as with every plan, was that the enemy got a vote.

Walker was also worried that Naji would be burned with this mission coming so close on the heels of his association with Abrar and his courier. That could not be helped now. When they got back, Walker would make the pitch to get Naji and his family out of Afghanistan. The flip side of being useful was that the Agency would want you to keep being useful.

Intel indicating that Abrar served as the liaison between compromised elements of the Pakistani intelligence service, the ISI, and Taliban military commanders was overwhelming. The intent of the operation was to snatch Abrar and interrogate him in the Salt Pit. Zero Unit interrogators were not under the same constraints as were officers and contractors of the CIA. Abrar could provide valuable insights into how high the ISI was compromised and into the active militant cells in this geographic division of the Haqqani network. He was a big catch.

Even in the darkness, the force covered ground quickly. Without the recon element guiding them and the overhead ISR asset to clear their path, they would have been lucky to make it before sunup. With those advantages, they patrolled quickly. Even with M4s and decked out with the latest and greatest technical hardware available, and with Rhodesian vests loaded with grenades, smokes, extra magazines, body armor, NODs, trauma kits, and water, they were not quite as light as the enemy they fought, but they were lighter and faster than any other allied force on the battlefield. The exceptions were Nate's snipers, who carried the heavier 7.62 autoloading rifles.

At the edge of the village, the point and command element dropped behind a rusting Soviet-era bus, the steel frame giving off the oily scent of decades-old diesel.

Ali entered and conferred with two members of the recon team using it as a hide site. He exited moments later.

"Abrar is still in the compound. No movement for the past couple hours."

"All right, let's do this," Walker said, checking once again with the air asset above, confirming all was quiet on the objective.

Nate and his snipers moved out to two nearby rooftops, giving them a commanding view of the compound and surrounding area.

"This is Psycho. Both overwatch elements in position."

"Roger, Psycho," Walker replied.

"Three, in position," came Dave's whisper in their headsets. Containment was set.

Walker double-clicked his mic, then looked to Staub, who was conferring with Ali and the Zero Unit squadron commander.

"How's that door looking?" Walker asked.

"We'll soon find out. Going to try to avoid going kinetic and waking up the neighborhood."

Walker nodded. *Nice and quiet.*

Staub moved past Walker and peered around the bus, eyes tracing the contours of the compound's entrance.

"Ready?" Walker asked Ali.

The interpreter and the Afghan commander conferred briefly in hushed tones.

"Ready," the interpreter confirmed.

The breaching element moved across the street through the darkness, the point man passing the entrance and holding security down the street while the next man went to the gate, a set of lockpicks already in hand. The explosive breacher was prepared with a charge just behind him. Assaulters were stacked and ready to flow into the structure.

Including the Americans and the surveillance element, they had thirty-eight operators on the ground, ISR above, two helos ready for extraction, and a QRF on standby. They had stacked the odds in their favor, choosing the time and place of the engagement. Now, if they could just stay dark and quiet.

"Moving," Walker said.

The two Americans ran across the street, the hard-packed dirt absorbing the sound of their footsteps. At the wall they joined the assault stack in the shadows. A lone dog barked in the distance, then fell silent.

I wish we had dogs on these ops, Walker thought. That was one of the negative cultural nuances of working with the Zero Units: no dogs.

Walker heard the creak of the gate as it swung open. Would that wake anyone inside? An unseen guard or security element?

He felt the assault train begin to move and knew that the man who had picked the lock and the explosive breacher had moved to the side, allowing the stack to push into the courtyard. Walker and Staub followed and covered the ten yards to another door on the inside of the compound in seconds. The assaulter with the lockpicks moved back to the front of the train and put his skills to use. With Staub on rear security, Walker stepped out to watch the breacher work.

The door cracked open, but it was not the result of a surreptitious entry. Someone inside had opened it. A man in a white robe. He was carrying an AKM rifle.

Just as he had been trained, the breacher pivoted to the side of the door and the Zero Unit assaulter behind him put three suppressed rounds into the chest of the man with the AKM, immediately flowing into the structure, followed by the assaulters behind him.

The enemy had gotten their vote.

Had anyone heard? Suppressed weapons like the M4s carried by GB and the Zero Units were just that, suppressed, not silent.

Pashto language from the assaulters came over Walker's headset, still measured and controlled, professional.

Walker knew they were pushing through the bottom floor of the two-story structure, just as they had done time and time again at the behest of the Central Intelligence Agency, hunters searching for their prey.

Walker and Staub trailed.

Front room, clear.

Second room.

Clear. No movement.

From the third room, Walker heard the unmistakable sound of suppressed gunshots. The Zero Unit was stacking bodies.

More Pashto over the radio.

Walker did not need their interpreter to know what was being said. *Ground level secure, moving to second floor.*

Walker and Staub entered the room of the engagement, now being held by one of the Zero Unit shooters. They knelt and checked the faces of the dead men; military-age males with AKMs. They were all too young to be Abrar.

More suppressed shots from the upper deck.

As Walker and Staub turned to reenter the hallway, Ali came over the radio to let the Americans know that there were two more dead tangos upstairs. Target was secure. Negative on Abrar. It was a dry hole, but they had one prisoner. Both men knew what that meant. The Zero Unit would conduct a quick battlefield interrogation, something American units had been directed to call "tactical questioning." This was the gray area in working with host nation forces in a sovereign country. Both Walker and Staub knew better than to insert themselves into the Zero Unit interrogation. Zero Units could be extremely persuasive when left to their own devices.

"What the fuck?" Staub said. "After all that, did we hit the wrong house? Abrar should be here."

"Where's the rug?" Walker asked.

"I didn't see it," Staub said. "Maybe upstairs?"

"It was delivered here, but the tracking device either died or couldn't transmit inside. But it was here."

"Let's look upstairs."

As they turned toward the staircase, Nate's voice came through their headsets.

"Movement in the house across the alley."

Walker paused and looked at Staub.

"Could just be neighbors," Walker said.

"Then where did Abrar go? He didn't just disappear."

"Unless our recon team missed him leaving."

"Possible, but unlikely."

They stepped into the room with the prisoner and were not surprised to see that he was stripped naked and bleeding from the head. He was being held down by four Afghan operators while a fifth had a gloved hand around his genitals, a blade pressed into the soft flesh. The prisoner was talking.

"What's he saying?" Walker asked Ali in a hushed voice. Walker did not want the prisoner to know that Americans were on target. He was more apt to talk if he thought he was solely in the hands of Afghans, who would not hesitate to separate his manhood from his body.

"There's a tunnel connecting the two houses. Abrar is next door."

"Where's the entrance?"

The Zero Unit men were already hoisting their prisoner to his feet.

"He will take us to it."

The prisoner was marched down the stairs naked and crying. Walker almost felt sorry for him.

He led them to a living room with *toshaks*, floor pillows, and back pillows lining two of the walls. A large iron chest was against another wall. It had been opened by a Zero Unit operator in a quick clearance. It held plates, bowls, mugs, and utensils.

"Show us," Ali said in Pashto. They had learned the hard way that anything could be rigged to explode.

The naked man bent forward and grabbed a handle on one side of the iron box. He struggled to lift it and pull it aside to reveal a hinged wooden trapdoor.

Ali looked to the Zero Unit squadron commander, who nodded.

"Slowly," Ali said in Pashto, indicating that the prisoner should open it.

Shaking, the man knelt and dug his fingers into a groove cut into the floor on the side opposite the hinge, and lifted.

Unsuppressed, the rifle firing from below on full auto seemed to shake the room as the 7.62x39 rounds tore through the naked prisoner, stitching him from his groin, up his torso, and into his head, which snapped back. He then fell forward, gravity pulling him into the underground shaft.

Two Zero Unit operators began firing back through the top of the wood door as another pulled a grenade from a pouch and crept forward. As the two shooters ran dry, he pulled up what was left of the trap door and tossed the grenade into the darkness, letting the door fall back into place. An explosion followed.

The squadron commander told his shooters to hold on the door and turned to the two Americans.

"Flexing to new target," he said, in broken but understandable English.

As Walker opened his mouth to respond, they heard the unmistakable sound of suppressed 7.62 rounds of Nate's snipers.

Nate's voice cracked through the Americans' headsets, still calm but now with added edge. *"Tangos inbound from the house to the east. Dropped three. Others took the alley, coming at you."*

"Shit!" Walker said.

"Here we go," Staub responded.

Walker turned to the squadron commander. "Snipers took out three tangos moving on this house."

"We will reconstitute in the courtyard and break out under the cover of our security element."

That would have been Walker's call too.

The Afghan officer moved toward the front of the house barking orders in Pashto into his radio.

"A little spicier night than we expected," Staub said.

"No shit," Walker replied.

They exited into the courtyard with the assault force. They had left two men behind to hold on the trapdoor, another two in the hallway leading to the front. Two more would stay in the courtyard.

With a clear line of sight to the heavens, Walker keyed his mic. "Raptor, what do you see?"

"Three dead tangos in the street to the east. Security element has pushed and taken up positions on the new target house. No squirters."

"Roger. Psycho, you copy that?"

"Loud and clear. We are spread pretty thin, but have both houses in an L. Move when ready."

"Good copy."

Staub was conferring with Ali and the Zero Unit commander.

"They're ready, boss. They are going to do a dual entry, front and rear. I'll go with Team One to the front. You go with Team Two to the rear."

"Wish we could soften this place up with some 105 rounds."

"Well, we don't have an AC-130."

"No, we don't. Let's grab this fucker and get back to base."

The two Americans broke out of the courtyard with their respective elements, sprinting along the street to their breach points, with Zero Unit security sending rounds through windows to keep anyone from shooting out.

Cover and move.

Walker was second to last in the line of march so he could coordinate with the snipers and air ISR asset.

As a Zero Unit breacher knelt to place a charge on the rear door, bullets zipped through the wood just above his head. The point man returned fire.

Walker heard the breaching charge from Team One detonate at the other side of the structure. There was a split second when he was aware of another explosion. His mind briefly wondered what it could be because his Team Two breacher had not yet placed his charge on the rear door. As the building came down on top of him, Walker had one final thought before he was consumed by darkness, fire, and dust: *What the hell are we doing here?*

———

Walker awoke to the rhythmic *whomp* of rotor blades.

"Glad you're alive, partner," a dirt- and grime-covered John Staub said from the bench seat above him.

"What happened?" Walker asked, attempting to push himself to his elbows, wincing in pain at the effort.

"Stay down, brother. We're en route to Bagram."

"Did the whole fucking house come down?"

"It should have, but the booger-eaters fucked it up and the explosive went low-order. Only took down half."

"How many did we lose?"

"Eight that we know of. Two unaccounted for. Probably dead. QRF inbound. Zero Unit was not leaving until they had all their men."

"Site secure?"

"As secure as you can be in Afghanistan."

"Dave and Nate?"

"They stayed with the unit to coordinate. Standby Zero squadron is inbound to assist."

"Abrar?"

Staub shook his head. "He was in the half that came down. A wall collapsed on you. Your body armor and helmet saved your life. The boys were using carpets as stretchers to move the wounded to the HLZ. We found you in the rubble and carried you to the helo in that fucking carpet from Naji."

Walker turned his head to the side, aware that he was lying on a maroon rug.

"It was in a part of the house that didn't come down," Staub continued. "And, I'm fine, by the way. Thanks for asking."

Walker leaned his head back on the floor of the fuselage and closed his eyes.

"Don't you go dying on me," Staub said.

"I wouldn't do that to you."

Walker thought of the absurdity of it all; an American on a Russian helo flown by an Afghan in a war with no end.

"Camus," he said.

"What was that?"

"Albert Camus."

"Who's he?" Staub asked.

"A philosopher."

"Of course he was."

"*The Myth of Sisyphus*."

"I don't want syphilis."

"Not syphilis, Sisyphus. The absurdity of pushing a boulder up a hill only for it to roll back down."

"I'm thinking maybe that helmet didn't work so well after all."

"Maybe not. Just feels like that's what we are doing here. 'Destroying the village to save it.'"

"You're an odd bird, Chris."

"I know."

Staub paused and evaluated his friend.

"And another thing," he said.

"Yeah?"

"You're welcome."

"Shit. Guess I'm going to owe you favors forever."

"Not forever, just for a very long time."

CHAPTER NINE

New Orleans
Present Day

"BEAUTIFUL HOME," WALKER remarked, unsure of exactly what to say to the wife of his dead friend.

"Thank you," Leigh Ann replied, brushing a piece of lint from her scrubs. "The first-floor rooms are original lathe and plaster. I remodeled upstairs and moved some walls around, so those are drywall."

Where uncovered by Persian carpet, dark mahogany floors gleamed. Leather sofas absorbed the last of the late-afternoon sun, shining like polished armor. Though the home's bones whispered of age, its decor was sleek, restrained, contemporary.

Walker tilted his head to take in the high ceilings.

"That has to do with the heat," she said, leaning down to stroke Paladin's thick coat. "Most of these old turn-of-the-century places have tall ceilings to let it rise." She looked up at him, hand still resting on the dog's back. "Take a seat, won't you? Can I get you something to drink?"

"Water's fine. A bowl for Paladin in the kitchen would be good too, if you don't mind."

Walker circled a low-backed leather swivel chair and settled into it slowly.

"Of course not. Be right back." Leigh Ann disappeared through the kitchen doorway.

Alone, Walker let his gaze travel. The fireplace was framed in white-painted brick, matching the home's exterior. A mahogany mantel jutted above it, bearing a single silver-framed photo. Walker rose and approached it. His fingers hesitated near the edge of the frame, almost touching the chilled metal. John, Connor, and Leigh Ann stood on the back deck of a boat at sunset, grins caught mid-laugh. John looked exactly as Walker remembered, weathered and steady. Connor must've been twelve. Time had turned the image into a relic. He leaned in closer, comparing the Leigh Ann of the photo to the one who had met him at the door. Now closing in on fifty, she still maintained her strawberry-blond hair of a decade prior, though it was now cut a few inches shorter. It took him a second to recognize what was missing: the twinkle in her eyes, the life, the vitality. That spark was gone. The natural smile in the photo had been replaced by one that was different, obligatory.

He turned from the photo and looked past the dining table, through a set of French doors onto a shaded patio and into the garden beyond.

Leigh Ann returned, glass of water in one hand. Ice clinked gently. She passed the water to Walker, who nodded in thanks.

"I set a bowl out for Paladin," she said.

With a quick command he sent Paladin padding toward the kitchen.

Leigh Ann sank into the leather sofa with a soft sigh. Walker did the same. The fabric of her scrubs bunched around her knees as she curled one leg beneath her. In her hand, she cradled a glass of white wine. "I know," she said after a sip. "It's early. But it's been a day."

"I'd imagine you have a lot of those in the ER. Days, I mean. Not wine."

"You'd be right on both counts." She smiled. "I've got a good crew, though, and I'm not usually wrist-deep in blood anymore. Management's its own kind of headache." Her hand reached up and undid the hair tie holding her ponytail, allowing her hair to fall to her shoulders. Walker noticed the Tudor Sub on her wrist. John's watch.

Walker nodded. "Management is overrated, isn't it?"

"Lord, yes."

"You sorry you went into it? Would you rather be walking the hospital floor? Like the Dam Neck days, over at the Portsmouth Naval Hospital?"

She looked toward the far wall, exhaling through her nose. "Tulane Med Center is a well-funded hospital, so we're staffed. I'm the charge nurse in the ER. Questions from interns and residents keep me young, sort of." She forced a smile. "This job allowed us a better life, which matters now. Or, it did."

"Looks like you found the right spot."

Paladin returned from the water bowl in the kitchen and sat by Walker, who reached down to scratch him behind the ears.

"Ah yes, the Garden District." She pronounced it with a genteel drawl, *Gahden*. "I remodeled this place after John died. I think I needed a project. I ended up doing all the things John always promised he would, 'just after one more deployment.'"

"I like the old homes," Walker said, bringing the conversation away from his intruding memories of John dying in agony. "So much history."

She smiled and tilted her head. "John always said you were into that. I saw your van out there. Looks like it's seen some miles."

"Yeah." He rubbed his neck and looked down. "My fatal flaw. I've always been an analog guy. It took me twice as long to get here as I would have preferred."

The words were barely out before he regretted them—*fatal flaw*. He'd nearly died in that van only a week ago. To cover, he pivoted. "How long have you been here?"

She took another sip and rested her glass against her thigh. "We moved in when John was with the Agency." She paused before continuing. "Everything in New Orleans bends around the river. That's where the name comes from, the Crescent City. Because of the way the Mississippi curves. Once you know that, you start noticing crescents everywhere. We wanted this neighborhood for Connor."

She paused. Her posture crumpled slightly. "Ah, Jesus," she said, voice raw. "Sometimes it catches me off guard. Seeing you. I thought I was grieving Connor. But maybe, maybe it's John too."

"I'm so sorry," he said gently. "Leigh Ann, what can I do?"

She studied him through glossy eyes, fighting through the emotions.

"We can't make small talk forever. There's something I want to show you. My office is up front."

Walker followed her down the hallway, Paladin at his side.

The office echoed the rest of the house in tone and restraint, classic colonial lines with a touch of elegance. Narrow windows stretched from floor to ceiling, admitting pale daylight that filtered through porch columns and landed in slants across the polished dark wood floor. White shelves lined the walls with carefully spaced books and framed photos, while an ornate French-style desk sat squarely at the center facing the street. Leigh Ann gestured for Walker to take the guest chair as she sat behind her desk and unlocked her Mac with a press of her index finger.

Paladin curled into a watchful arc near the door, resting his head atop crossed paws, eyes tracking his master's every shift.

"Connor's journals," Leigh Ann said. She had regained her composure between the living room and her office.

She opened a desk drawer and drew out a large, black Moleskine notebook. It was battered, its spine softened, the corners rounded. The second was cleaner, less seasoned, though still worn.

"I've scanned everything for digital copies," she continued, sliding the notebooks across the desk's glossy surface, "but these are his raw notes. I prepared a USB drive for you with the digital version."

"I don't have a computer," Walker said, running his palm slowly over the first notebook's battered cover as though reading the texture.

She studied him for a moment. Then she nodded. "Then the hard copies will do."

Walker cracked the older journal open. Rows of compact, precise handwriting stacked one atop another filled the pages, dark ink absorbing the light. Few breaks. No wasted space. A mind running hot.

"He was obsessed with Moleskines," Leigh Ann said. "He was an analog guy, like you. Used them all through LSU and prep school."

Prep school, Walker noted. Not high school.

"What prep school was that?"

"An all-boys Jesuit academy. About three miles from here."

Walker nodded. Skeptics and philosophers disguised as priests.

"You know, he was on his way to get his graduate degree in journalism at Columbia." Her tone dipped. "Dying in Afghanistan is one thing, Chris. Dying on the streets of New Orleans, working on a story, that's another. He wanted to start Columbia with some experience."

"Leigh Ann, what happened?"

Her face hardened, jaw set, eyes focused.

"He got to the wrong people."

"What do you mean?"

"Let me show you." She turned her monitor toward him and opened a file.

It was a scanned version of the journal, annotated in soft red ink. Passages were highlighted. Some sections were tagged with dates, others with clipped Post-its in digital yellow.

"He started a year ago," she said, scrolling to a specific entry. "These two ODs, Marcus and Lisa, they were Louisiana kids. One from here, one from Baton Rouge." She pointed with the back of her pen. "Then more names follow. Each with details."

Walker flipped through the notebook in parallel, turning pages beneath callused fingers. "Did he ever discuss any of this with you?"

"He kept it to himself. Said he was working on something big, 'a story on the Big Easy,' he would joke. Looking back, I think he was trying to protect me."

"It's hard to make sense of these entries," Walker said, eyes narrowing.

"That's the code Connor was using. I couldn't crack it, not entirely. But I had access to death certificates through the hospital, for the local cases at least. Some of the details matched what's in here."

"You used your credentials?"

Leigh Ann shrugged, pragmatic. "I had access. The investigators were not giving me anything." She tapped a page on the screen. "What I've learned so far is that Connor was trying to map opioid-related overdoses, figure out where the supply was coming from, and who was moving it. He focused in on a particular drug he called 'Snowball.' It's the new popular pill out there."

"How'd you get that far?"

"I gave myself a crash course in code breaking online. There's a printed legend taped to the back cover. It's a start."

Walker flipped to the rear flap of the older notebook. A taped sheet of paper bore a cipher legend alongside a printout of Leigh Ann's cross-referenced notes.

"I see."

"Connor found patterns in the overdoses. All tied to a network operating out of a section of town called the Ninth Ward, which is where he thought this Snowball was coming from." She opened Google Maps and pulled up an overhead view. "The Ninth is east of us, on the same bank. Right along the canal."

An image of roads, grids, and waterways appeared on her screen.

"It was nearly wiped out during Katrina. That levee," she tapped the canal, "broke wide open. The entire area was submerged fifteen feet underwater. It's never really recovered. The vacant homes became a magnet for gang activity. My ER gets constant GSWs, gunshot wounds, coming out of the Ninth."

"And Connor was doing research out there?"

"I think he was out there asking questions. I didn't know at the time. If I had . . ." She trailed off. Her shoulders slumped. "My schedule at the ER is chaos. I wasn't always here for him."

"What evidence do you have that there was police involvement?"

"As you read through the journals, you will see there is a code name, 'Slate.' Some of the people he interviewed mentioned a cop involved in the trade. Connor calls him Slate. I did some Google searching and asked a few police officers at the hospital but have not found anyone with that name. Could be code for someone or maybe a nickname."

"You said drugs were found in his car?"

"That's what the police report says. Heroin bricks in the trunk. They said he was a dealer, that he OD'd on his own stash."

"Where is the car now?"

"In the garage. Cops impounded it for a month. I just picked it up a few days ago."

Walker raised an eyebrow.

"Can I take a look?"

"Sure. Come on."

Outside, the light had softened to gold. Leigh Ann led him through the yard to a detached garage where a late-model Range Rover Sport with a few dings sat beside a green Jetta.

"It's open," Leigh Ann said. "He loved this car. Took it apart more than he drove it."

"Man after my own heart," Walker offered.

He leaned inside. The air was tinged with age, dust, and vinyl, and something faintly mechanical. The stereo was original. The glove box door was loose.

Walker grabbed the keys from a tray in the center console and then walked around and used them to unlock the trunk. He lifted the lid. The interior was lined with clean black carpet. He folded it back to find the spare tire.

"Their evidence photos showed five bricks of heroin around that tire," Leigh Ann said.

Walker ran a hand along the inside edge of the trunk before shutting it gently.

"Did Connor have friends, maybe a girlfriend I can talk with?"

"There was a girl that he saw from time to time. She was trouble. His friends had scattered, different schools, jobs. He was focused on this story and getting ready for Columbia."

Leigh Ann looked him in the eye. "I want justice for my son. But I need help. If John were still alive, it would be different. Everything would be different."

"I know."

"So, what now?" she asked.

Walker studied her face, finding resolve behind amber bloodshot eyes. He thought of his friend, the barrel-chested man with the huge smile and even bigger heart, the man who would have been around to raise and guide Connor had it not been for the philosopher standing in his garage.

He took a breath.

"I pick up where Connor left off. Find out who Slate is. I finish what your son started."

"You think you can do that?"

"I'm not a cop, Leigh Ann, but I'll do what I can."

"My husband always told me you were, well, different."

"I'm guessing that wasn't a compliment."

"No, it was. John said you were a good man."

"Leigh Ann, your husband was the best I ever worked with."

She considered him intently, choosing her words.

"Chris, New Orleans is not like anywhere else, which I think is how they got away with this. Connor uncovered corruption in the department, and they killed him for it. I know that with every fiber of my being. When you start asking questions they are going to react. They will come after you, hard."

"Well then," he said, voice low but steady, "I'll just have to go at them harder."

CHAPTER TEN

"WHERE HOPE MEETS *healing,"* Derek Matheson read aloud, squinting at the banner strung across the barricade as the black Suburban crept past a traffic cop. "Who came up with that?"

In the front seat, Carolyn Boyle, his executive vice president of marketing, half turned. He could see her blond hair against her dark pantsuit. In her mid-thirties, she had been on board for five years. With the pace he set and demanded from those around him, Matheson thought she would have burned out by this point. He often wondered when she found time to keep so fit and toned.

Her mouth curved into something between a cautious smile and a bracing wince. "I did."

The founder and CEO of Genyra Pharmaceuticals didn't nod. Didn't thank her. Instead, he glanced down at the sleek white dial of his Breitling Navitimer Chronograph, its 18-karat red gold case and bracelet catching a glint of sunlight through the tinted glass. Matheson wasn't a pilot, but he owned a jet.

"And the logo," he said. "Green and gold? Why not red? Genyra's branding is red."

Carolyn held her reply for a moment, eyes forward as she considered her answer. "It's Tulane's palette," she said. "And the city favors gold: saints, the Joan of Arc statue, the old flags—"

"We'll fix it," interrupted Genyra's chief commercial officer from the opposite leather captain's chair. Walt Kimbel's tone was smooth, automatic. Before jumping into the more profitable world of pharmaceuticals, he'd been a public defender with a law degree from LSU. "Carolyn, put it on the docket for Tuesday's marketing huddle."

"Of course," she murmured.

Matheson's eyes cut toward the window. He scratched at the stubble on his chin, carefully maintained at a millimeter or two for just the right look.

"It's nearly five. Why the hell aren't we there yet?"

He knew why. His jet had been an hour late taking off out of Atlanta thanks to a detour to drop his most recent girlfriend off before heading to New Orleans after their extended weekend in Turks and Caicos. The two-hour meet-and-greet with hospital staff had been scratched entirely.

"Cops are rerouting everyone. VIP parking's in the back," the driver said, eyes hidden behind mirrored wraparounds that looked too small for his face. Dale Harris's frame was linebacker-solid, his neck like a fire hydrant. He was an ex-cop from Baton Rouge, sidelined into the personal protection game after an excessive force charge caught on a body cam had bounced him from the department.

Matheson didn't respond. He was still hung up on the color scheme. The heat. The rush.

He turned sharply back toward Carolyn.

"Who's confirmed for media coverage?" he asked.

She perked up. "Actually, good news. Pushing the ceremony to five helps us. Local affiliates will catch the story right before prime time."

Matheson's jaw flexed. "Local. Not national."

"There's syndicated coverage, freelancers filing pool copy. Might get picked up wider."

"Might," he repeated, turning back to the window.

Silence mounted. Dale adjusted his grip on the steering wheel. Walt turned his head and feigned interest in a hot dog vendor on the sidewalk.

"No CNN, no Fox, no MSNBC?" Matheson asked.

"I haven't . . ."

"What about at the gala tonight? Any coverage?"

Carolyn's lips parted. "They . . . haven't confirmed."

"But you called them. We sent the press kits. You followed up."

"I did. Yes."

"So why aren't they here?"

"They thought the opening of the center was a local story."

"This isn't about the opening. This is about Genyra breaking boundaries. The opening was just supposed to be the visual."

"Yes, I understand that, sir. But we . . ."

"A drug that reduces end-of-life suffering in terminal cancer patients, extends lives, gets full FDA approval, and that's not a national story?"

She stiffened her back and sat up straight, putting on her executive armor.

"Goddamn it, Carolyn," he snapped, his voice booming through the cabin. "We used to push harder. You hit a voicemail and quit? You lob one idea over the net and then put down the racket?"

"Sir . . ."

"You didn't go to the top? You went to the gatekeepers and let them gatekeep. That's not the Genyra way. How many times have I preached our core values—tenacity, determination, *pugnacity*?" He shook his head when she didn't respond. "So here we are, draped in Emerald City colors, about to hand over . . . Walt, what was it again?"

"Sixty-three million," Walt said, without looking at him.

"Sixty-three million dollars for university research," Matheson said. "For people who can't return a call. For a media apparatus that doesn't think it matters. It's your job to tell them why it matters and make them believe it."

Carolyn swallowed and Matheson continued. "You didn't *sell* it. My job was research. Now it's leadership. Yours is sales." His voice dropped and his eyes shifted outside, looking at the green and gold banners set up for the event. "Not a national story. *Fuck.* Whole thing is a wash. Not even sure I should have come back for this."

No one spoke. The car slowed.

"We're here, boss," Harris said.

Matheson grasped the door handle as a man in an old-fashioned seersucker suit approached, hand raised, smile strained.

"Who is that?" Matheson barked. "Carolyn?"

She blinked at the bright light outside, groping for an answer because she didn't have an angle. Kimbel cut in smoothly. "That's Dean Avery. Tulane Medical."

Matheson thrust the door open without another word to his staff, leaving the air-conditioned confines of the Suburban and stepping into the damp heat of a New Orleans evening that enveloped him like a shawl. He squared his shoulders and buttoned the single clasp of his jacket, no tie, grinning.

"Mr. Avery, it is such a pleasure to see you."

He grasped Avery's hand with a firm grip and continued on with how honored he was to be there, to be dedicating this wing, his life's work. His eyes swept the crowd and saw a few cameras. Too few. Local.

He smiled and waved at them anyway.

CHAPTER ELEVEN

DEAN AVERY'S INTRODUCTION was measured, if a bit long for the heat, but flattering in the right places. Standing off to the side of the stage, Derek Matheson listened and approved.

Carolyn had written the intro. Maybe she earned a half point for that.

The dean highlighted Matheson's dual degrees from Tulane, his early vaccine research, the fifteen-year arc that led to Genyra's founding. He referenced "The Cancer Answer," the TED talk that had rocketed Matheson into the technocratic elite, where he played in the brighter lights among the tech bros.

The crowd laughed where they were supposed to. Applauded on cue. When Matheson finally took the microphone, tanned from the Caribbean, smiling, dressed to kill in tailored Tom Ford, he spoke with humble warmth.

He opened with a joke, Carolyn's. It landed. Light laughter. Just enough.

By the end, the standing ovation didn't surprise him. He nodded once, briefly, a man allergic to humble brags but addicted to applause. He stepped off the stage before the audience sat back down. *Always leave them wanting more.*

Matheson exited behind the stage, where Carolyn and Kimbel were waiting to shower him in compliments.

"Thank you. Let's go before I get caught up in a conversation that I don't have time for."

Their next stop was the gala at the Four Seasons. He had been invited to speak there too, but declined because his ex would be on the dais and he didn't like the optics. Better to be in the audience, comfortably disdaining that limelight because it shot below his orbit. Still, he wanted to look rested and at his best to impress her, which meant getting out of here now so he could change into a tux.

"One thing," Kimbel added smoothly, lightly touching his elbow. "Mr. Vargas watched the livestream. He wants a word."

"*Now?*"

"Upstairs. Carolyn got us permanent office space in the new wing. Fourteen stories up. The least Tulane could do for our sixty-three million. There's a video-call ready for you."

Matheson sighed.

"We'll keep it quick, sir. I promise."

———

From the top floor looking south, the haze that hung over the city resembled breath on a mirror, blurring the jagged towers of the Central Business District into the leafy sprawl beyond. Farther still, the Mississippi cut a rust-colored path past cranes and drifting freighters.

Matheson stood with his shirtsleeves rolled. The room was cold at sixty-six degrees, just how he liked it. Still, beads of sweat lingered along the bridge of his nose. He checked the Breitling, wiped his brow, and stared through the tinted panes at the Big Easy.

"Feed is up," Kimbel said, already seated. "He'll join in a moment."

Matheson turned and took his seat. No prep notes. No talking points. Just a businessman waiting to speak with someone who could have him flayed alive.

The screen flickered and the voice came through.

"*Hello?*" The deep voice was heavily accented Spanish.

"Hello. Can you hear us?" Matheson asked, his tone polished and clipped.

"Ah. There you are," the voice replied. "I can see you now."

Fulgencio Vargas was known to those who dealt with him on the shadier side of the ledger as *Cuchillo*, "Knife." His heavily pockmarked face appeared on the screen. It was lit from one side, shadows clinging to the crags. Behind him, the rolling green hills met the cobalt blue of El Salvador's Pacific coast.

"You look well," Matheson said.

A pause.

"It's bright behind you," Cuchillo responded with a squint. "Are you still in my new center?"

Matheson twirled a cuff link engraved with his company's logo.

"Yes. Top floor," he replied. "They've dedicated an office to Genyra."

"I'll bet that makes you feel important," Cuchillo said. "Did you get one too, Kimbel? Going to run your empire from a glass fishbowl now?"

Kimbel chuckled with performative warmth that was a bit too loud and eager. It translated as nervousness.

"No, sir," Kimbel said, in response to Matheson's death stare. "Business as usual."

Vargas shifted in his leather chair. "I had eyes on your little show today, Derek. The one with the flag waving and the white coats clapping. You've gotten better at pretending to be charming. Oscar-worthy performance."

"Thank you," Matheson replied. "But it was the FDA approval they cared about, the improvements in patient survival rates, the lengthening of lives."

"Oh, yes. And also the building they have no idea came from me."

Matheson's jaw clenched. "The building is a starting line," he said mildly. "The research that comes next, that's the real investment."

Vargas stared into the camera. "Don't forget that it was my intervention, my investment, that saved Genyra from bankruptcy and kept you afloat through the FDA approval process." He paused. "Your stock closed down point-three today. Wall Street doesn't love you as much as Tulane does."

"It was up five points last week," Matheson shot back. "We crossed five billion in market cap. That's very good for all of us."

Vargas's lips curled. "Kimbel, tell me, are we going to blow out the quarter? Or are company earnings meetings in New York next week going to involve apologies?"

Kimbel hesitated. "Sir, it's probably best if Dr. Matheson steps out for this part. He's the face of the company. Better to have him prepped with just the right information for the earnings call."

Vargas laughed softly, eyes glinting coolly. "Ah, yes." He leaned closer to the screen. "We can't have the doctor's hands getting dirty, now, can we?"

"None of us wants that," Kimbel said, desperate to extract Matheson from further haranguing. "We also have the gala tonight. It's important to get Mr. Matheson there on time. There'll be civic leaders and press. Good optics."

Matheson rose slightly in his chair, smoothing his expression into a mask of tired diplomacy. He felt it was time to reclaim his dignity. Kimbel was right. They had a schedule to keep.

"Wait." Vargas's order sounded like a gunshot on a crisp fall morning. "I'll have someone there tonight. Watching."

Kimbel offered a reassuring nod.

"I have many investments in this hemisphere. I look after them." Vargas straightened, casting a long shadow across the screen.

"Of course," Matheson replied.

Vargas tilted his head. "My people are nervous. They think the woman may not play ball and that the cops might double-cross us."

Matheson and Kimbel traded a glance.

"I want to assure you," Kimbel said, leaning forward in his chair. "We will deal with her."

"Oh, yes we will," Vargas responded. "Get a handle on this. That woman better not get all high and mighty on us."

"She won't, she's . . ." Kimbel didn't finish the rest of his point. The screen had gone dark.

Matheson exhaled through his nose and stared a moment longer at the blank screen. It was always easier when the devil wore horns. Harder when he wore a linen shirt. He turned toward Kimbel.

"Take me home," he said quietly. "I need a minute to think before the gala."

CHAPTER TWELVE

BY THE TIME Walker rolled into the Lower Ninth Ward, the sun was slouched low against the rim of the levee, casting long amber fingers through a lace of broken shingles and hanging trees. The light gave everything an eerie warmth, the same sensation he felt when studying the Hopper paintings.

Much of the Ninth, Leigh Ann had explained, was still condemned. But as his van rattled down the mostly empty streets, it seemed to Walker that the Ninth didn't resist the condemnation. It wore its wounds plainly and proudly, daring the observer to look away.

Walker eased the van along Reynes Street, tires crunching on gravel and windblown glass. Around him rose the aftermath of a storm that had blown out over twenty years ago. Leigh Ann had called it poor, but *poverty* didn't feel like the right word. This was something more elemental, quieter, crueler. In Kandahar, poverty screamed. Here, it whispered.

He passed a car that looked more like a battle wreck, its hood tilted like a broken jaw, wheels stripped bare. Windowless shotgun homes leaned at odd angles, craning toward the street, weary of what they had experienced. One porch held the husk of a rusted tricycle with a wheel missing. Everything living had either fled or was growing through the wreckage.

Walker slowed near what might once have been a store. The faded sign read *Buy Rite*, though only half the neon sputtered in pink light. A pay phone dangled nearby, its cord twisting softly in the breeze like a pendulum without a clock.

He stared at it for a long moment. *When was the last time I saw a pay phone?*

On his drive from one corner of the country to the other the week before, he had seen manicured avenues, majestic mountain passes, cornfields that stretched to the horizon, light reflecting off grain silo, the geometry of a well-kept ranch, the pastel hues of morning sun chasing away evening showers.

But not here. Here, the world had stopped being beautiful.

This wasn't poverty. This was neglect, institutional and generational, a spiritual rot as thick as the Spanish moss on the branches. A war zone, like Afghanistan. Not the firefights, but the blank spaces between. The way a bombed-out village looked two years after it stopped making the news.

Paladin stared out the window. He too knew a war zone when he saw one.

If Leigh Ann's decoding of Connor's journal was correct, it meant that Connor had dug through the bones of this neighborhood, peeling back layers of corruption in search of the rot at its core. An aspiring journalist working on his first story with a Moleskine and an inconvenient conscience, asking questions no one wanted answered, perhaps in a quest to connect a modern chemical weapon, fentanyl and Snowball, to floodwaters and failed promises.

And if Leigh Ann's theory was correct, someone killed him for it.

Walker passed a house that had had its front door torn off the hinges. A spray of yellow insulation clung to the threshold, fluttering like a moth's wing. Another's roof slumped inward, the siding buckled, stained with black mold.

"My God," Walker breathed as he maneuvered around a pothole.

It wasn't that it was unlivable. Some people still tried. He could see them, shadowed figures in doorways, shirtless boys leaning against porch railings, watching the stranger in the faded blue van. But it wasn't living, he thought. It was resisting death with dignity.

His inward philosopher reawakened.

Is resisting death with stubborn grace what I'm doing?

The nightmares did not care about intent. The cold sweats didn't respect strategy. And John Staub, his friend, his brother, was still dead because of what Walker had done. Or failed to do.

"Good men die," he whispered, answering the voice.

Paladin shifted on the passenger seat, watching him.

"Don't worry, boy, we're going to set up shop," he said, voice steadier. "Somewhere quiet." He reached across and scratched the dog's ear.

Paladin's tail tapped the seat twice in agreement.

Walker shifted into third and continued forward, deeper into the decay. Maybe he was still alive so he could finish what Connor had started. And maybe, in doing so, find one small answer to the question that haunted him.

Not whether he was good, but whether, with what time he had left, he could do something that was.

CHAPTER THIRTEEN

FBI SPECIAL AGENTS had varying reasons for requesting transfers. Jarrett Stanton was looking for a city that needed his help.

That's what had landed him, two years ago, in a trim Creole townhouse two short blocks east of the French Quarter, close enough to hear the late-night trumpets floating through the alleyways, but far enough not to smell the slushy hurricane cocktails spilled on Bourbon Street.

Like Stanton, the house was dignified and symmetrical. Four bedrooms, a wrought-iron balcony that draped over the sidewalk, and, most critically, no yard to upkeep. Instead, he'd overseen the construction of a square, brick courtyard laid in a herringbone pattern.

Inside, he was hardly the lord of the manor. The house hummed with the friction of female energy: three daughters in various stages of childhood with obsessions ranging from Disney princesses to gymnastics to ninth-grade debate club, all shepherded by Alma, his wife, his rock, and the only person who could conduct this family ballet in time with the Bureau's demands.

For all that, Stanton had methods to tune the girls out when he needed to, one of which was to open the windows that faced the street and listen to the jazz filtering over the rooftops while he dressed.

Tourists might call the Quarter a theme park, and they weren't wrong. But Jarrett didn't live for Bourbon Street. He lived for the undercurrent, the quiet hiss of buskers rehearsing near the golden Joan of Arc statue, the smell of chicory from the French Market, the way jazz didn't just echo here, it *lingered*. He would miss it one day. He had come here to help right wrongs, to fight corruption. And yet the city had seduced him too.

He checked his Apple watch. The gala at the Four Seasons would be starting soon. He wanted to walk. The device on his wrist told him he was barely above eight thousand steps, not nearly enough.

Come on, Jarrett.

He stood in front of his bedroom mirror. The stiff white collar of his tuxedo shirt flared awkwardly at his neck like the wings of a startled gull. In one hand, he held a black bow tie, a strip of silk that may as well have been a Rubik's Cube. He turned it over in his fingers, looped it once, and frowned before exhaling a sharp breath.

Alma moved behind him with the silent efficiency of a mother of three and the steady patience of a kindergarten teacher. Her own dress hung half-zipped, height elevated by heels. "You're making that face again," she said lightly, smoothing his shoulders. "The one you make before dental appointments."

Jarrett offered a lopsided smile. "You ever think it's a little ironic that I can take down a wire-fraud ring in Baton Rouge, but I can't figure out how to tie this thing without Googling it?"

"You're not allowed to mention federal investigations and internet tutorials in the same sentence," Alma replied, plucking the tie from his fingers. "You're more interesting than that."

"Tell that to the kids."

A raucous argument echoed down the hallway from a playroom that was a minefield of glitter hair clips and half-dressed dolls.

"That's *my* Snow White headband!" Veronica shouted.

"It is not! Eloise found it in the car!"

"In *my* booster seat!"

Alma winced. "Okay, that's escalating."

Audrey, the eldest and the self-appointed house diplomat, poked her head in. "Do I have to start confiscating the princess gear again?"

Jarrett raised an eyebrow. "Is that a thing now?"

"I have a whole drawer of mouse ears, wands, and pixie dust," Alma whispered, looping the tie with deft fingers. "It's starting to look like the Orlando TSA station's lost and found."

Outside the window, the indigo dusk of New Orleans stretched across the skyline. Jarrett's gaze flicked to the digital clock on the nightstand. Sixty-seven minutes until cocktails. Forty-seven minutes until he stood in a ballroom of state troopers, DAs, city officials, politicians, and the urban elite. As one of five assistant special agents in charge, his competition to make it to the next level—special agent in charge—was fierce. Jumping from ASAC to SAC was not just a matter of moving from GS-14 to GS-15. It was politics, and tonight was an opportunity to show his boss he was comfortable operating in and around those who filled the New Orleans society pages.

A knock on the front door cut through the chaos like a conductor's baton. Then a chorus of little voices: "She's heeeeeere!"

The babysitter barely had time to slide inside before the girls flung themselves at her in joyful greeting. Alma took a few steps into the hall and called down the stairway to the landing, "Brush teeth in twenty! No glitter on furniture! The babysitter's in charge if anything catches fire!"

And then it was quiet.

In the mirror, Jarrett adjusted the now-perfect bow tie. "How do I look?"

"Like a black James Bond," Alma said, slipping her arm through his.

"Does that make you my black Moneypenny?"

"I don't think they were married, or even romantically involved."

"You really think I need to go to this?"

She laughed at him. "Darling, for the past three weeks *you've* been telling me you need to get better at this kind of thing."

"It's ridiculous to me that with both the criminal branch and national security branch as part of my ASAC duties, I still have to hobnob."

"And why did you take the job of multiple people?"

"Because Cappy retired and someone had to do it while they transfer a replacement."

"And because Augie Lloyd knew you could handle the double duty. You can navigate these waters. Zip me," she ordered, turning.

After he zipped his wife's dress, she added, "There's going to be a whole lot more of this in your future, Mr. Bond."

He smiled. Her banter had taken the edge off.

She reached up and kissed him. "And, don't forget," she added.

"What?"

"Shaken, not stirred."

CHAPTER FOURTEEN

THE LIGHTS SHIMMERED like constellations over the ballroom. Three stories above the Quarter's clamor and a few miles upriver from the Ninth Ward, the gala at the Four Seasons radiated luxury with velvet chairs, monogrammed menus, and white-jacketed waiters.

Beyond the glass windows, the Mississippi moved without urgency, wide and dark and meandering through the hundred miles of swampy, unusable land until it reached the Gulf. Inside, New Orleans's elite drifted from bar to banquette, each step choreographed, each smile stage-lit. There were judges and socialites, donors and retired generals, tech founders and law enforcement officers, all under the bright lights of the Crescent City.

Derek Matheson preferred the views from the thirty-third and thirty-fourth floor event spaces because he equated elevation with power, but the third floor ballrooms could accommodate more guests. Tonight was about quantity.

Nominally, the gathering was to benefit a charity called New Leaf NOLA, a youth initiative whose mission focused on mentorship, education, and opportunity. But nobody in that room had shown up to save children. They came to be *seen* saving children.

That was especially true of Matheson, who believed he was the only one who could claim to have actually saved children with the products he created in his labs. He leaned against the white-linen edge of a sponsor's table, swirling a Topo Chico sparkling water in his hand. As a physician, Matheson eschewed alcohol, reminding anyone who asked him that the liver worked overtime to remove it precisely because it was a toxin. Moreover, his body was a temple. He liked his suits tight. Alcohol was empty calories.

At his side, Walt Kimbel tapped his arm.

"See those two by the bar?"

"I do."

"They're the local Bureau honchos."

The word *local* rankled Matheson, reminding him of the screwup with the media.

"The one with the white hair's Augie Lloyd. He's the SAC."

"What's that again?"

"The special agent in charge. The head FBI guy in town."

Matheson surveyed the lawman.

"He looks a little old to still be in the job."

"He looks even older than he is. Fifty-seven is mandatory retirement, but he's asked for and been granted several extensions from headquarters."

Lloyd sipped bourbon with a man who looked to be roughly his junior, a tall black man with a cropped haircut and classic horn-rimmed glasses. His jacket was buttoned like a military tunic.

"And the other?" Matheson asked.

"Jarrett Stanton," Kimbel replied. "ASAC, assistant special agent in charge, New Orleans Field Office."

"You call Lloyd the S-A-C but the A-S-A-C, A-sack?"

"Yeah. It's a Bureau thing."

As a young lawyer, Kimbel had battled the Bureau in court on occasion. The experience had made him valuable to Matheson when it came to fighting through government red tape.

"Why did Lloyd bring his number two?"

"Stanton runs the criminal branch and is also heading up national security. I hear he's being groomed for the top spot."

"Is he a problem for us?"

Kimbel grinned. "Not if he's here."

Matheson nodded, only mildly soothed, then noticed an impressive figure across the room, a black man, tall, broad-shouldered, his scalp not only shaved but polished. He was talking with a statuesque woman in emerald, Matheson's ex-girlfriend Irene Isaacson, now the district attorney of Orleans Parish.

Kimbel saw his boss looking at the woman. "She's talking with Cornelius Bates."

"FBI?"

"New Orleans PD. Rising star. You watch, she'll mention him from the dais tonight. Bates works out in the Ninth, a special division that does outreach. He wants to be chief. The most dangerous position in the city is to stand between Bates and a TV camera. Do me a favor, don't get near him. I'm meeting with him after the event tonight."

Matheson turned slightly. "Noted."

Kimbel knew how to stage-manage the boss. There could be myriad reasons why he did not want Matheson meeting with an NOPD police lieutenant.

"I'm pretty much going to steer clear of everyone," Matheson said. "Not even sure it's worth it to be here."

"You had two solid interviews on the way in," Kimbel said.

"Local TV. Not the best optic. I should go."

"No, you shouldn't. We need to stick around through Icy's speech," he said, using the district attorney's nickname.

Isaacson was the keynote speaker. It would not be a good look to leave before she spoke.

"I don't want to give anyone the impression I'm avoiding her," Matheson acknowledged.

The lights dimmed by a degree. The jazz band in the corner struck up a smoky swing, clarinet tight as a wire, bass murmuring underneath. Bartenders in ivory tuxedo coats flamed sugar cubes for Sazeracs, the scents of lemon and rye wafting through the room.

Carolyn materialized beside them, tablet in hand. "Icy's on in five minutes," she said, referencing the digital agenda. "Time to take our seats. The media's expecting her to announce something big tonight."

Matheson exhaled through his nose. He was still irritated with Carolyn over the logo and local media, but he had to keep up appearances. It wouldn't do to look sour with one of his employees in public, especially one as visually stunning as Carolyn.

"Where's our table?" he asked.

"Near the back. Just like you asked so you can slip out whenever you like."

They moved among the crowd, the room thick with conversation. Matheson offered tight smiles and firm handshakes, oiled enough to appear gracious, yet indifferent enough to feel powerful.

At the table, Matheson introduced himself to the guests with polished charm. They were pleasant but forgettable: an energy consultant, a foundation director, and someone with a yacht.

Sipping his sparkling water, he scanned the room. The partygoers' smiles were tentative. The laughter arrived late. Somewhere beyond the stage, a shift was pending, and every person there, from the judge on his third gin to the chief of police by the punch bowl, was bracing for it. The music faded and the spotlight flared to amber at the podium.

As the room light dimmed, so did the conversations.

Matheson shifted his gaze toward the side of the stage as Irene Catherine Isaacson entered, not like a guest but like the reason the room existed. Her tan skin glowed under a gown of green sequins, designed not to shimmer but to strike. Her dark hair had been swept to one side, gleaming under the lights. At forty-five, she still had the athletic good looks of the tennis star she had once been at Tulane. And those legs. Matheson remembered them well.

Theoretically, this was a night to talk about resurrecting the portions of the city that still needed attention after years of neglect. That meant respectful applause instead of wild cheering. The audience was in on the charade as much as the speakers.

While she smiled and thanked the crowd, Matheson felt a flicker of something that lived somewhere between nostalgia and dread.

Matheson had hired her before she became Orleans Parish district attorney, back when she was fresh off a stint as an assistant U.S. attorney arguing federal appeals before the Fifth Circuit. Even then, she knew how to work Washington and how to navigate the FDA. It was Kimbel's idea to hire her. It was Matheson's idea to sleep with her.

He had paid her a fortune to push that HPV drug across the finish line, and like she was stewarding her own investment, she'd reeled him in too. They were both married, but that hadn't mattered until the spouses found out. Icy's husband left without a fight, knowing better than to take on the shark that she was. Matheson had enough money that he raised the white flag. His wife had taken her newfound fortune to Europe.

Isaacson waited until the last clap died. "Thank you," she said into the mic, her voice low and deliberate, a slow-burn drawl, velvet over steel. She'd always known how to play up her southern roots.

"Let's skip the pleasantries, shall we?" A ripple of amusement moved through the room. "Yes, we'll get to the auction. Yes, New Leaf does vital work. And yes, I'll be asking you to open your wallets, your calendars, and your reputations for this cause. Of that, I give you fair warning."

Laughter.

"But first, let's talk about progress."

A few people in the audience exchanged glances.

"Our partnership with the NOPD and the Orleans Parish Sheriff's Office has brought the city's homicide rate down 31 percent over the last three years," she began. "Though our shared dedication to this mission has lowered crime, drug addiction, and homelessness, we are not satisfied, nor near the goal we have set for ourselves. The work is not even close to being done. But I do think it's fair to say that we've laid the foundation for what we must now build."

She didn't just scan the crowd, she measured it. Calculated it. Matheson could picture her rehearsing this speech in her head while running five miles before dawn, while reviewing the attendee list, while slipping into her designer gown and string-thin underwear. Every word was a move. Every pause, a trap.

" . . . armed robberies down 15 percent. Assaults down 22."

Matheson thought of the quote often misattributed to Twain: *There are lies, damned lies—and statistics.* Icy knew that. She'd once explained to him the anatomy of persuasion: *ethos, logos, pathos.* Credibility. Facts. Emotion. Aristotle's formula, sharpened to a blade in her hands.

She already had the *ethos*, the credibility, partially inherited, partially earned. Here she was delivering the *logos* through the numbers. And now, finally, came the *pathos.*

"I met a mother in the Ninth Ward," she said. "In 2003, she had twin boys. One was lost in Katrina. The other, she nearly lost to the silence that followed, the abandonment, the despair. Until last year, when her son met an officer from Lieutenant Bates's COPE unit."

She paused, letting the acronym settle.

"For those unfamiliar," she said, "COPE stands for Community Outreach through Police Engagement. A specialized unit created by Superintendent Franklin and led by Lieutenant Cornelius Bates, both of whom are with us tonight, and both proud supporters of New Leaf. Supe. Lieutenant. Please stand."

Bates rose, all toned muscle and high-wattage smile. The applause was warm, practiced. Kimbel leaned toward Matheson.

"She's laying it on thick," he whispered. "She and Bates must have a deal."

Matheson nodded, though he saw it differently. Kimbel was a technician, good at execution, blind to the architecture required to build an enterprise. He didn't see the scaffolding beneath the speech. The ethos. The logos. The pathos.

But as Bates soaked in the spotlight, Kimbel caught on. "That's smart," he murmured. "Depending on where she goes next."

And on Isaacson went, slicing through the crowd, name by name, favor by favor. She knew who she owed. She knew who would owe her. She recognized judges and clerks. She recognized Augustus Lloyd, the FBI New Orleans SAC and his deputy, Jarrett Stanton, both of whom stood up, claiming a share. It was a neat trick, Matheson thought. She had managed to make it look like they all worked for her.

She recognized the key sponsors of the event: hoteliers, restaurateurs, the New Orleans Saints football team, and finally, Genyra Pharmaceuticals. Pointedly, though she knew Matheson was there, she didn't call him out, a calculated slight, he thought. *All's fair in love and war.* This was New Orleans, where the rules were fluid and the game was rigged, but only if you didn't know how to play. Isaacson competed at a master-class level.

Matheson watched her, his mind drifting as she spoke. These days, the wealth ensured that when it came to women, he had his pick of young, eager ones who didn't ask questions. But none of them could match Icy. His hubris had driven her away. And suddenly, he regretted it.

Would she take him back?

No, he concluded. She knew him too well.

"We'll get to that auction in a moment," she said.

The crowd was glowing now, lubed up by alcohol and admiration. The pathos had lowered their guards. The jokes had landed. Someone new to the game might have guessed Isaacson's act was meant to increase the haul for New Leaf. She had been a lobbyist once, after all. But Matheson knew Icy did not work like that. The speech was too good. Something bigger was coming.

"Before we all start shaming each other with bids," she continued with an enchanting smile, "I thought I would address something to avoid the distraction, to keep the attention on New Leaf. You know how it is here in our beloved Crescent City. Nothing can distract like rumors and gossip. Sometimes I hear gossip about myself that I find so delicious that I even wish it was true!"

After the laugh, she turned serious, the killer prosecutor who never lost. Depending on the stakes and the juice that flowed between the state and defendant, she might take the case, she might not. But when she did, the result was never in doubt. "So let me say what some of you have been expecting of me for some time."

Her words drifted outward, landing in silence. No clinking glass. No coughs.

"This city raised me. It shaped me. And it taught me that our problems are never solved in one night. Or at one gala. Or by one worthy organization. Those can all help, but real systemic change can only come through force of will, with clarity of purpose, and above all, accountability. So let me take accountability right here, right now."

Matheson gauged the pause before her next sentence, created to maximize the yield for whatever was to come.

"My name is Irene Catherine Isaacson. And tonight, I am announcing my candidacy to be the next governor of the great state of Louisiana."

Silence turned to thunder.

Matheson didn't clap. He didn't breathe. His hyper-intelligence kicked into gear as he thought through the innumerable angles of what he had just heard. Favors and secrets would be turned around, new ones created, old ones betrayed.

Beside him, Kimbel muttered, "Well, no need to report this to Vargas. He's got eyes in the room, right now."

Matheson thought through the repercussions of Icy's announcement, hoping the drug lord's eyes weren't focused on him.

CHAPTER FIFTEEN

WALKER HAD CONSIDERED camping behind an abandoned two-bedroom house in the Lower Ninth to get a feel for the place. He even tucked his van beneath the drooping arms of a weeping willow with branches that shielded him from the street. His VW bus was well hidden, but not invisible, and in a place that looked dead but wasn't, movement drew attention. The slow-rolling cars, the flickers of light in otherwise dark homes were signs, territory markers. And Walker could not shake the feeling that he might have parked on someone's invisible line. A gang leader's turf. A dealer's drop zone. A place where strangers weren't just noticed, they were shot.

This is a bad idea. You need a FOB, a forward operating base.

He decided to drive it at night before conducting a foot patrol. Many of the houses that looked abandoned during the day weren't empty. Walker saw flashlights flickering behind boarded windows. He witnessed fires in barrels. In some houses, he caught the dull glow of a phone screen or a lighter's spark betraying the presence of squatters or addicts. A few blocks had vehicle traffic, cars creeping up, idling, pulling away.

By day, the Ninth was a graveyard of broken promises. By night, it was something else, feral and alive.

The district stretched wide, hemmed in by the Mississippi to the south, a twelve-foot levee wall to the west, and swamp to the north. Leigh Ann had managed to decode street names from Connor's notes, but no addresses. Walker still had ground to cover before he could pinpoint the drug houses Connor had written about, those tied to Officer Slate.

He noted white NOPD vehicles with crescent-star logos and *COPE* on their doors. He thought they might pull him over as the van looked out of place. He was prepared to tell them he was driving from Washington to Florida and had gotten lost without a GPS.

Having pushed his frogman luck enough for one day, he steered the van north, hugging the edge of the swamp along Florida Avenue. He rolled over a crumbled curb, tires crunching over a broken sidewalk, and picked up a dirt track that snaked across rusted rail lines and into a patchwork of neon-green grass and stagnant brown water. Out here, cover came easy: switchgrass towered like sentries, and shaggy gum trees leaned in like they were listening. It was just what he was looking for.

He fed Paladin and boiled water to make ramen noodles before cracking Connor's journal and going to work, his finger tracing over the smeared pages.

Leigh Ann had already mapped out some patterns: phrases, symbols, fragments of street names. Walker suspected a Vigenère cipher, the kind that needed a key, maybe a book or phrase.

He fell asleep in the roof tent, the journal open on his chest, the swamp air drifting in through the mesh triangle of the pop-top. It might've been a decent sleep, the air cooled by the swamp, if Paladin hadn't nudged him awake.

The dog was rigid, ears forward, eyes locked in silent alert. Walker knew that posture all too well. He had seen it in a hundred bivouacs across Iraq and Afghanistan.

Walker stayed still on the elevated mattress, hand on the dog's flank. The van was locked, but the windows were cracked for airflow. He listened.

A rustle in the brush.

His first thought was wildlife. The swamp was alive after dark with animals that might be unfamiliar to Paladin. Earlier that evening, Walker thought he had seen the glint of alligator eyes floating offshore while Paladin drank. He had stood watch with a pistol in hand, just in case. Maybe it was an animal now. Maybe.

Then the rustle shifted and he heard a whisper. Two voices. Trying to be quiet.

Fuck.

If he killed someone, even in self-defense, he would have to answer weeks of questions, maybe even be charged with something in the process. That would defeat his purpose for being in New Orleans. If he could, it would be best to defuse this situation. And if he had to kill, then he would find out if those eyes in the water really belonged to gators.

Maybe the locals did not like a strange van parked on their turf.

Their attempt at stealth and the time they chose to visit said it all—they weren't here to talk.

Walker slipped his hand around the grip of his Glock 19 and rolled to the side, careful not to silhouette himself. Through the mesh, he caught the silver glint of moonlight on swamp water. Then, across Paladin's back, he saw an old Chevy Blazer on the other side of the train tracks. Eighties-era, fat tires.

He whispered a command to Paladin, instructing him to stay still. Then, like doing a dip in a gym, he positioned his arms on the sides of the hatch and lowered himself into the van. The shift in weight made the vehicle shake.

An audible laugh from outside. "Guess he heard you. He's up!"

A shout very close to the van. "Ay, man! Get out here! Let's go!"

Walker pulled on his jeans so he could holster the Glock and quickly pulled on a T-shirt to conceal it. He didn't want to kill anyone. He had done enough killing.

Walker saw the 12-gauge shotgun barrel poking through the cracked window on the driver's side. A light shining down its barrel as the gunman scanned the inside of the van.

He spotted another gun barrel at the window on the starboard sliding door, one that belonged to an AKM. It was like seeing a ghost.

"Get the fuck outta there!" one shouted. "Come on! Move!"

They were young, mid-twenties. The one with the shotgun had a slack mouth, ribbed black tank top, Florida Marlins hat, and a gold chain. The other, wielding the AKM, wore a beanie and sported a wispy beard. The way they held their weapons told Walker that they were amateurs. Still, he remembered an adage from one of his instructors at the Farm: a bullet from an amateur will kill you just as dead as one from a professional. If they knew the area and were looking to score, maybe they could be useful.

"Get out here!" Beanie yelled. "Hands where we can see 'em! Don't fuck with us!"

"What do you want?" Walker called out. "Just camping here for the night."

"Whatever you have. Now get your ass out here, bitch!"

"Negative," Walker said. "You come in here."

They hadn't expected that. The pair traded a look. Tank Top tried the sliding door and found it locked while Beanie cupped his hands to the window. "It's just him!" Beanie called.

"Open it," Tank Top shouted. "Do anything else, and we splatter you all over this piece of shit."

Walker leaned forward, unlocked the van door, and slid it open.

"This is a classic," he said.

"Out!" Tank Top called.

Walker stepped through the door and stood barefoot on the dirt. Tank Top's slack mouth twisted into a sneer. "Cover him!" he said to Beanie before stepping inside the van.

Walker waited for Tank Top to cross the van's rear quarter. He would be blind in that moment. Only for a half second, but enough. Three steps . . . two steps . . . one.

"*Fass!*" Walker shouted. Bite.

Paladin leaped down from his roof perch, a hundred pounds of muscle and fury. He flew into the man with the shotgun. Paladin compressed his jaw over the gun arm, snarling, teeth flashing, neck thrashing. The shotgun fell to the floor of the van.

Walker lunged at Beanie, spinning him into the corner of the van with bone-jarring force. The rifle was trapped between them, barrel pointed skyward. Walker's knee shot up, slamming into his assailant's groin, and as Beanie doubled over, Walker ripped the weapon free. In one fluid motion, he reversed it and drove the stock into Beanie's face with a sickening crunch.

Beanie screamed, hands clutching his shattered nose, blood pouring through his fingers as he crumpled to his knees. Walker hit him twice more in the face with the butt of the rifle before turning to Tank and smashing it into his jaw.

"*Los,*" Walker barked. Let go.

Paladin backed off as Walker snatched up the shotgun and pulled the man out of the van. His Marlins cap was gone, his cheek torn open in a ragged flap that exposed the gumline, an ugly wound, bleeding like a spigot.

Walker delivered a Thai kick to the side of Tank Top's leg, causing him to buckle and drop to the ground. Both assailants lay bleeding and moaning at Walker's feet.

"You broke my jaw, man," Tank managed.

"Consider yourself lucky."

The AKM had a sling, so Walker ran it over his shoulder and press-checked the shotgun, a Mossberg pump-action. A shell was chambered.

"What did you two think you were doing?" he asked Tank Top.

"Scoring, asshole."

"You thought you'd rob me?"

The man didn't answer. He cupped his hand to his cheek. Blood poured through the fingers. Walker asked a different question. "Where's a good place to get Snowball around here?"

"He's a fucking narc!" Beanie yelled. "Don't answer him!"

Walker whirled around and bashed the shotgun stock into Beanie's neck.

"Fuck!" Beanie screamed. "Get that shit anywhere. This is the Ninth."

"Dealers pay off any cops?"

"What the fuck are you talking about?"

Walker lowered the shotgun barrel. "Give me your wallet." The man dug into his pocket and tossed his nylon-Velcro wallet to the dirt.

"You too," he said to Tank Top.

Walker picked up the wallets and ensured they had IDs.

Then he pointed the shotgun directly at Tank Top's head. "Take your buddy to a hospital. Remember I have your wallets. If you talk about this to anyone, I'll hunt you down and kill you."

"You're fucking crazy!"

"Maybe. But if I ever see you again, I'll skin you alive before I feed you to the gators."

CHAPTER SIXTEEN

WALT KIMBEL WASN'T about to meet with Lieutenant Cornelius Bates in the bar at the base of the Four Seasons, a few stories beneath the ballroom where the city's elite continued to drink and celebrate while the media snapped photos.

Instead, he chose the back bar at the Rusty Nail in the Warehouse District, a shadowed haunt on the edge of the Quarter.

Kimbel ordered a Sazerac, both because he liked the drink and because it looked like the kind of choice a man in a tuxedo would make this close to Bourbon Street. He was two sips in when Bates sauntered through the door.

"You look like you could use one of these," Kimbel said as Bates slid into the booth, the width of his bow tie perfectly aligned with the outer edges of his penetrating eyes.

"That's tourist shit, Walt."

"Then what can I get you?"

"Since this is on Genyra and we're all dressed up, let's go with a bit of Pappy."

"I should have guessed."

"I'll take it neat. A double."

The order grated on Kimbel as trendy and needlessly expensive, but he fetched one from the bar anyway. Bates was vital to the operation and had a direct line to Vargas.

"So," Kimbel said as Bates took his first sip, "Icy's going to be our next governor."

Bates lowered the glass and smiled. "Maybe your boss shouldn't have dumped her."

Kimbel shrugged. "I stay out of my CEO's romantic life."

"Well, you screwed up mine tonight. Her name's Cecily, by the way. She took an Uber to my place. What the hell am I doing here, Walt?"

Kimbel picked up the iPhone on the table, unlocked it with his face, tapped a few numbers, then tilted it toward Bates.

"Still the account you want me to use, right?"

The slightest hint of a smile fractured Bates's poker face when he saw seventy-five thousand dollars in the app's transfer column.

Walt stabbed the button and waited for a response from the man across the table. A normal person would have expressed gratitude. Not Cornelius Bates.

"That's just a little bonus to make sure our arrangement doesn't change once Icy gets into the governor's office in Baton Rouge," Kimbel said. "We wanted to let you know what a valued partner you are."

Kimbel caught the subtle shift in Bates's posture, the way his mouth sucked his cheek. The trouble with dirty cops was that they never knew where to draw the line. Their egos always took over, incapable of the cool detachment needed to keep an operation running smoothly. Then again, that's why they were cops, not businessmen. Kimbel knew what was coming.

Bates leaned in close, his voice nearly drowned out by the piano playing on the far side of the bar. "You think I'm fucking stupid, Walt? That I'll keep doing this for scraps? I know you have your big product launch coming up."

"Which one is that, Bates?"

"Xylaxyn."

"You read the business section, congratulations."

"I also know the ties between Xylaxyn and Snowball."

"The hand that feeds, Cornelius," Kimbel said, holding up his palm. "Watch those big teeth of yours."

Bates sat back and laughed, sipping a little more bourbon, regarding Kimbel with a slit-eyed stare before leaning in again. "Xylaxyn will replace fentanyl. That's your plan, right?"

"It's possible. Fentanyl's tainted even though it's a bona fide cancer treatment."

"What would your board, hell, what would the FDA do if they found out that your business partner in El Salvador was taking the precursor chemicals for Xylaxyn, which are every bit as potent as fentanyl but not on the DEA's radar, and cutting them into the white pills the kids call Snowball?"

"You are playing a dangerous game, Bates."

"If that fucking Staub kid figured it out, someone else will too."

"You took care of that."

"He figured out that Cuchillo's legitimate sugarcane freighters were bringing it in. Now, how do you suppose a kid who was not even a journalist worked that out?"

"I think it started with your crew, Bates. I told Vargas that selling it in New Orleans was a bad idea."

"I know you think you are hot shit, Walt. Even Cuchillo thinks you're the whiz kid who masterminded a way to use Genyra's pharmaceutical distribution network to move Snowball around the country and then launder the money to make the earnings reports shine. I understand all that, but with Genyra's growth I want points on this."

"That's not how it works."

"It is now. And until you figure how to make it work, you can keep the skids greased with another little bonus."

"I just gave you seventy-five grand, Bates."

The lieutenant was a shark that smelled blood. Kimbel didn't mind. Bates just needed time to realize that threatening to blackmail Genyra was mutually assured destruction. Maybe he would take it up with Vargas.

"We have a profitable arrangement for all of us," Kimbel said. "We should aim to keep it that way."

He lifted his phone, tapped on the screen, and turned it to Bates. "Another seventy-five headed your way. Good?"

Bates nodded.

"For now."

The Genyra executive pressed the blue button and shot another seventy-five thousand dollars over the wires.

Bates finished his Pappy and set the empty glass on the table.

"I'm glad I swung by for this little chat," he said, getting up to leave. "I've kept Cecily waiting long enough."

Kimbel watched him leave and took a deep breath, wondering how long they would be able to keep their enterprise alive.

CHAPTER SEVENTEEN

THE TULANE MEDICAL Center cafeteria was never truly quiet, but just now, things were deceptively mellow. Walker was always in tune with rhythms. Over the buzz of the overhead fluorescents, he listened to the soft clinks from vending machines, a nurse flipping through chart printouts, her pen tapping in tempo at a nearby table. The air was heavy with the aroma of burnt coffee and grilled cheese sandwiches.

Leigh Ann sat across from him next to the window. The sleeves of her scrubs were rumpled. Her hair was pulled back in a loose braid, clipped hastily and starting to fray. A paper cup of black coffee sat untouched on a napkin.

"You didn't bring Paladin," she said, glancing at the empty spot near his boots.

Walker shook his head. "Didn't want him picking up the wrong scents."

He took a bite of his turkey sandwich, chewing slowly. The artificial chill of lettuce met the faint bite of mustard. "I've been watching the Ninth for the past four days," he said after swallowing. "Connor's journal is starting to make a little more sense."

"You've cracked his code?"

"Not quite. I've started working up a few notes on the typewriter. He used a cipher that requires a key we don't have, but like you, I see context. Now that I've been out there a bit, I recognize some of the place-names."

Leigh Ann leaned in, one hand wrapped around her coffee cup. "How about Officer Slate?"

"I've seen multiple police patrols. One cruiser lingered near a stash house on Clouet for twenty minutes. It's not exactly damning."

She sipped her coffee at last. It had already gone cold. "Be careful, Chris."

"I'm careful," he said. Then added, "You should be too. Vary your routes to and from the hospital. Lock your doors. And I'd recommend a security camera setup that you can monitor from a mobile device."

She shook her head. "I know. I need to do that."

"Make time," he said, voice low but firm. "You're not invisible in this."

She gave a small nod, her eyes serious.

"Do you have a firearm in the house you are comfortable with?"

"I have John's Glock. He taught me to shoot but I'm not any good."

"We'll find a place and get you back up to speed."

"We probably should," she responded in resigned affirmation.

"And, while we're talking about them, I've seen a few cruisers with the acronym COPE on them. Do you know what that is?"

She tapped the table with one nail, thinking.

"I've heard of it. It's some special unit within the police focused on drugs, I think. Not really sure. Probably a political tool, something to look good. Down here, symbolism matters. Hang on, I'll look it up."

After a few seconds on her phone browser, she nodded. "It stands for Community Outreach through Police Engagement. The law down here doesn't have the best reputation, so they invent things like this as window dressing."

"Maybe even as cover," Walker added.

"It's possible."

"When John and I were in Afghanistan, we knew a DEA guy who would pass through the CIA station for intel updates. Ramirez . . . Sanchez . . . Vasquez. Something like that. I remember that he was from New Orleans. You don't happen to remember anyone like that, do you?"

Her eyes assumed a distant look. After a few seconds, she offered a close-mouthed smile. "I bet he meant Javier Gonzalez. John invited him to a Fourth of July barbecue we hosted a few years ago."

Walker snapped his fingers. "Yes. That's it. Speedy Gonzalez. Gonzo. John saved him a couple hundred bucks when he was about to buy a fake 1860s Enfield rifle as a souvenir. The real ones went quick at the beginning of the war, but there was a market, so a ton of fakes flooded it. DEA is federal. It would be good to talk with a familiar face, someone who knew John and what he did overseas. Might be a good source of intel on local PD. You don't have contact for him, do you?"

"I'm sorry, I don't. There is a federal building. Maybe start there?" After tapping her phone screen, she flipped it to show the Google Maps reference. Walker scrawled the address down on a napkin.

Just as he finished, Leigh Ann's pager buzzed on the table, jumping once, then again. She looked at it and frowned. "Sorry, Chris. Drive-by. Multiple GSWs incoming."

Walker stood with her.

"Can I help?"

"This is my job. Come back by the hospital when you are finished in town. I'll be close to the end of my shift by then."

Her pager buzzed again. She looked down and, without another word, ran from the room.

———

Paladin was happy to see Walker when he got back to the van, which he'd parked in the shade of a garage with a window cracked and the K9 cooling fan engaged. The dog thumped his tail while the former SEAL fired up the old beast.

He studied his paper map carefully, thinking through the route, before exiting the hospital area. He drove beneath the skybridge that connected the main building to the new Tulane-Genyra Cancer Research Center. The skybridge was still emblazoned with a green and gold poster from the grand opening. *Where hope meets healing.*

The drive took him into the heart of city traffic before spitting him out onto a freeway with a view of the Superdome. He was soon on a tall bridge crossing the Mississippi, its brown water snaking its way south, dotted with barges.

All federal buildings looked bland, Walker thought on arrival. But after the stunning architecture of the Garden District and the dazzling sensory assault in the French Quarter, this building looked particularly boring, four stories of beige concrete with a square sign out front.

In the lobby, he saw metal detectors and a guard in the dark blue uniform of the Federal Protective Service. Anticipating that, Walker had left his pistol in the van. He made it through security and studied the directory on the wall. There were entries for the United States Attorney's Office, the Health and Human Services Department, and the Department of Homeland Security.

Though there was no entry for the DEA, Walker approached the front desk.

"Hey, I'm sorry to bother you but I'm looking for an old buddy who works at the DEA," he said. "Is there a way to leave him a message?"

"Name?"

"Javier Gonzalez."

The man scanned Walker's bearded face, dirty ball cap, untucked button-down shirt, and jeans streaked with road dust. "You can submit a general meeting request through the DOJ."

He handed Walker a clipboard.

Walker studied the form. The questions were innocuous but probing: Social Security number, full name, date of birth, legal residence, phone number, reason for the inquiry.

While reading, he heard the metal detector beep behind him. He noticed the cameras in the corners of the room. The memories the form conjured were not pleasant: the board of inquiry, the threat of prosecution, the warning never to speak of his last mission in Afghanistan.

He wondered what his Social Security number might trigger in some nameless, faceless database in Washington. Then again, it said right there on the form that lying about the information or omitting it would be treated as a felony. Walker's head throbbed. *Fuck.*

He returned the clipboard without writing anything.

"I'm not big on paperwork. I'll connect with him through Facebook. Thanks anyway."

"Oh yeah?" the marshal said, staring intently at Walker's face as though memorizing every detail.

"Appreciate your time," Walker said as he turned back toward the exit.

Coming here was a mistake. The final link in a long chain of them.

CHAPTER EIGHTEEN

Kabul, Afghanistan
2021
Two Months Before U.S. Withdrawal

AFTER THE SOVIET occupation, before the Taliban swept through like a sandstorm, the Ariana Hotel had been the closest thing Kabul had to a Western outpost.

Ten stories of brown masonry, it looked more like a college dorm than a hotel, but in a city where the power grid was a suggestion and plumbing a luxury, the Ariana had become a beacon for diplomats, journalists, and spooks after the Soviet withdrawal.

When the Taliban rolled in with black flags and Kalashnikovs in 1996, the Ariana had been seized within hours. They turned it into their de facto seat of government. The bar was shuttered. The satellite dishes ripped down. The pool filled with sand.

After 9/11, the reversal was swift and surgical.

American Special Forces, working with Northern Alliance fighters, retook the city in weeks, and the Ariana was among the first objectives, with Taliban ministers slipping out the back as U.S. operators breached the front. Within days, the building was rebranded as the "U.S. Embassy Annex," a name that meant nothing and everything. In reality, it became a CIA base of operations.

The Agency wasted no time. They set up a bar in the basement, an unofficial morale booster in a dry country. They called it the Tali-Bar, a dark joke in a war full of them. General Order Number One of the United States Central Command forbade alcohol for U.S. troops, but the CIA didn't answer to CENTCOM. The alcohol flowed freely.

Walker found Fisk in the back corner, nursing a drink under the dim glow of a bare bulb. The walls were lined with graffiti, messages left by those passing through over the past twenty years of misadventure, including Kipling's warning from "The Young British Soldier." A Soviet RPG launcher was suspended from the ceiling, a scorched fragment of the Twin Towers bolted to the wall near a framed photo of the CIA team killed at Camp Chapman.

"What are you drinking?" Walker asked.

"Manhattan," Fisk said, though his glass was nearly empty.

"Want another?"

"Better not."

Walker ordered a Foster's oilcan-style beer and poured it into a frosted mug. The bar was loud with operators, contractors, and case officers blowing off steam. In the next room, pool balls cracked and laughter echoed through the haze of Cuban smoke.

Fisk drained the last of his drink. "I'm headed back to Langley. Orders came through. Gave up my quarters yesterday. Can't say I'm going to miss that container."

Walker wasn't surprised. Fisk would be reassigned to a desk, maybe a liaison role. Something cleaner.

"Where you headed?"

Fisk gave a tight smile, his cheeks ruddy from the bourbon. "Need to know."

Even after serving together, Fisk maintained the divide between his job as a case officer and Walker's as a Ground Branch paramilitary officer. Different tribes in the same war.

"We've got a gap coming," Fisk said, perhaps realizing he'd sounded like a dick. "I'm recommending you take over handling duties for Mongoose."

Walker raised an eyebrow.

He had been the one running brush passes in the bazaar, keeping eyes on the source, making sure Mongoose had not been burned. Fisk approved extra surveillance, but Walker and Staub had been doing the legwork.

"Mongoose is still viable," Fisk said. "Langley wants to keep him in play."

"I thought his deal was a year."

"It was. We extended the timeframe. That's how it works."

Walker leaned back. "Mongoose is jumpy. After all the Haqqani pricks he's given us, they've got to be putting things together. If I tell him you're out, he might bolt."

"Bolt. Please. Where would he go?"

"I don't know. Maybe he'll just go dark."

"Then don't tell him. Give him what he needs to hear."

"Come on, Lenny."

"Relax, Chris. Mongoose will get his payout. It's in the files."

Fisk lit a cigarette, exhaling toward the ceiling, the smoke wrapping around the RPG launcher above.

"I didn't smoke before this place," he said. "Now look at me."

"We all leave here with something," Walker replied.

Fisk reached into his pocket and slid a folded scrap of paper across the table. "That's the case file number for Mongoose. You can access it from the SCIF at Eagle Base. Keep tabs from there."

"If something goes sideways?"

"Mongoose is compartmentalized. He's run out of headquarters now. Use that cryptonym. They'll help."

Walker tucked the paper into his shirt pocket. "That it?"

Fisk stood and offered his hand. "That's it. See you around, Chris. I should roll. I'm out in a few hours."

Walker shook his hand, then watched Fisk disappear into the smoke and noise of the Tali-Bar.

———

Walker sat at a hardwired terminal in the SCIF at Eagle Base, the glow of the screen casting shadows across his face. He had already pulled the Mongoose case file, what little of it was not redacted.

Redacted. Such bullshit. Walker put it out of his head, thinking instead of Mongoose. The next time Walker met Naji, the first question would be about the visas. Walker would lie if he had to, that was part of the job, but he didn't want to. He would do as instructed and contact the counterterror center at HQS. Maybe he could get the visa expedited.

The door hissed open. Staub entered, fresh from a briefing, still wearing the chalky white gypsum of the compound on his boots.

He kept his voice low. "The meeting I just came from? You are not going to fucking believe it."

Walker didn't look up. "What's up?"

Staub leaned in, even though the SCIF was hardened against every known form of surveillance, analog, digital, or otherwise.

"The chief read me into a new SAP," he said, pronouncing the acronym like the stuff of pine trees, short for special access program. "We're planning to shut this place down."

Walker looked at Staub. "Define shut down."

"Evac," Staub whispered. "It's not just the military like we thought. Extraction routes. Safe houses. Contingency plans for certain assets. The kind of thing you do when you're pulling stakes."

Walker's stomach tightened. "A full withdrawal?"

"The chief called it a contingency, but yeah, and it already has a code name, 'Sable Wind.' He wants the plan finalized in under two weeks."

Walker sat back. The quiet in the SCIF. The empty cubicles. The silence before the storm.

"No Agency presence?"

"Doesn't look that way. We all thought we'd keep a small footprint here if we stuck to the political drawdown timetable, but it looks like everyone is pulling chocks, to include us."

"When do we leave?"

"Nothing official, but unofficially, we're out of here in a month. Maybe less."

"You get a list of asset evacuees?"

"Eyes-only file. Chief said it's in the system. I can pull it from here."

Walker slid his chair aside. "Well, here's the system. Let's see the list."

Staub logged in. It took five minutes of multifactor authentication, biometric scan, and rotating encryption keys appropriate for SAP-level access. Finally, a list populated the screen. No names. Just six-digit identifiers. Roughly a hundred of them.

"Just numbers," Staub muttered.

Walker leaned in. His eyes scanned the list, looking for the cryptonym Fisk had given him that represented Naji. He walked through the first three digits of all the lines.

"They're leaving Mongoose behind," he said. "Those fuckers."

"That can't be right. After everything he's given us?"

Walker pulled a folded slip of paper from his shirt pocket, double-checking the alphanumeric string. He held it up to the screen. "This is Mongoose. He's not on here."

Staub reviewed the list and cursed under his breath. "That's low. Even for Langley. Why would they leave him behind? A mistake?"

Walker's voice was flat. "I don't know, but if we leave him, he's as good as dead, and so is his family."

"The chief said to keep all assets in place, but maybe we can find a way to get him out sooner," Staub said.

"We could ask him to get some intel in Pakistan, tell him to take his family, something like that."

Staub looked at him. "You're talking about a black extract. Off the books."

"Maybe we just give him a little help to make it to the other side of the border." Walker gestured to the screen. "No one at Langley is going to notice that he's gone anywhere. They're not tracking him and with a withdrawal coming things are going to get fast and loose. I saw it when we left Iraq. We can take advantage of that."

"Taliban might be watching to see who moves. They are going to note a change in our posture, no way around that. If they want to know who turned, they will be watching for people and families trying to get out before we leave."

"Then we protect him."

"Fuck, for all we know, Langley sold him out," Staub said.

"Why would they do that?"

"I don't know, some backroom deal? Whether intentional or an inadvertent oversight, I'd say Naji is cooked."

"He's our responsibility."

Staub exhaled slowly. "You want to whisk Naji and his family out of here. No Agency support. No air cover. No backup. Just us."

"*Tertio optio*," Walker said, invoking the Latin phrase for "third option," the motto of the covert Special Activities Division of the CIA. The first option was diplomacy. The second was war. They were the third.

"I think your math is off," Staub said. "The system has failed and we are on our own, which makes us—you and me—*quattro optio*, the fourth option."

Walker stared at the screen, then back at his friend.

"We owe Naji," he said.

"You make this shit personal and bad things happen," Staub responded.

"Think of it as a favor, then."

"To you? I'm really racking them up."

"Not to me. To Naji."

CHAPTER NINETEEN

New Orleans
Present Day

WALKER PULLED INTO the hospital parking lot and was directed to a spot by a uniformed police officer. There was something happening in front of the facility that had caused an increase in security and a crowd of press to gather.

Leaving Paladin in the van with the window cracked and the K9 cooling kit turned on, Walker approached the police officer on parking lot duty and asked him what was happening.

"DA's making an appearance," he said.

"That would do it. Thank you."

Walker approached the front of the hospital just in time to see Irene Isaacson duck into a black Suburban as press snapped photos and shouted questions. He couldn't help but think that she looked like a movie star surrounded by paparazzi.

Walker weaved his way through the throng of reporters and entered the emergency room.

The smell of blood caught him off guard. He felt the familiar yet faint surge of dizziness that had plagued him since Afghanistan. The odors, the atmosphere, the noise of the ER reminded him of a combat hospital. For a moment it felt like his brain hit a pothole.

I'm worse than Paladin in a thunderstorm.

He stood to the side and took in the scene; reporters were interviewing some of the hospital staff while a few police officers remained behind in the DA's wake.

He spotted Leigh Ann down a corridor. She was talking to a man in a suit and seemed to be on the receiving end of the conversation.

He waited until they parted and caught her eye.

She smiled and walked to him in the lobby.

"What happened here?" Chris asked.

"The DA stopped by for a photo op."

"Because of the gang shooting?"

"What better way to make a point?"

"I guess that's what they do."

"Where are you parked?"

"Far end of the lot."

"Give me a few minutes and I'll meet you there."

———

"So, this is home?" Leigh Ann asked, looking around the confines of the van.

The AC along with Paladin's fan maintained the interior at a comfortable temperature compared to the heat beyond the doors.

"I guess so."

"That's what you have been doing the past few years? Traveling?"

"I spend most of my time in the Pacific Northwest. I like it up there."

Leigh Ann sat in a padded chair on one side of the swing-out table in the van's main space while Walker sat opposite on the fold-down couch atop his cache of weapons. Paladin stayed in the passenger seat up front, nose protruding around the side.

"Who was that guy in the suit you were talking with?"

"Hospital administrator. He was a little upset with me."

"Why?"

"Well, as you saw, the DA was here."

"Isaacson?"

"That's her. People here call her Icy."

"Icy?"

"Nickname, based on her initials. I think she likes it. She's made her mark in local politics and is now taking the next step. Her father was a judge, then mayor. She was a prosecutor who went to work in Washington, then came back to New Orleans to run for DA. I'll bet she's going to be our next governor.

"The kids that came in were from Chalmette, downriver, outside Orleans Parish. Icy's rise to prominence is tied to reducing the murder rate here in the city. She's campaigning on the idea that she'll work her magic outside it in the rest of the state too.

"In fairness, she didn't stand around wounded kids. She interviewed the hospital staff. After all the noise made about the abandonment of hospitals during Katrina's long flood stage, hospitals are a regular route for politicians."

"What happened?"

"She wanted to speak to some of the staff. That's one of the things that they do. It shows they really care."

"Like a general sitting down with privates and sergeants at the mess hall in Afghanistan to get the 'ground truth.'"

"Similar, I'd think."

"Only to go back in front of Congress to say the same things as every other flag officer. Politicians. Sorry, you were saying?"

"She took a private audience with a group of nurses in the break room to discuss the gang shooting and some more general health-care-related issues. I scratched out a note as she was fielding questions."

"A note?"

"It seemed like an opening, an opportunity to let her know about Connor."

Walker raised his eyebrows. "What did you say?"

"Just that I had questions about my son's case and suspected police involvement. I gave it to her as she was leaving. I told her it concerned my son's murder and asked her to please read it as soon as she could."

"How did she respond?"

"She handled it like a politician. She's smooth. She said she was so sorry for my loss and that she would read it."

"You believe her?"

"Who knows, but I had to do it."

The pager clipped to Leigh Ann's scrubs buzzed.

"I've got to go but I'm off tomorrow. How about you stop by the house for dinner, and we can go over next steps? And I can try to convince you to stay in the guest room, as nice as this van is."

Her pager buzzed again.

"See you tomorrow," she said as she reached over and pulled the handle on the sliding door.

Paladin lifted his head.

"*Blijf*," Walker said as he followed her outside.

"And Chris."

"Yeah?"

"Thank you."

They embraced, and as he watched her walk away he found himself in another memory, watching someone else walk into the dust of Afghanistan, the weight of the past rising to meet him in the present.

CHAPTER TWENTY

Afghanistan
2021

WALKER GLANCED IN the rearview mirror of the Toyota Hilux truck as he sped along the dirt road toward Torkham on the Pakistan border just west of the Khyber Pass, watching the dust swallow up the Mitsubishi Montero that followed.

He turned his head to see the young girl, Naji's daughter Zahra, asleep in the back seat with a blanket, astonished at how relaxed she looked. Her father sat next to Walker, in the passenger seat. He wore a white-collared shirt, pressed slacks, and the haunted look of a man on the run. The word from Langley was that Naji was to stay in place as part of a stay-behind covert intelligence network and continue to pass information to the Americans on conditions in Afghanistan. They had set up a way for him to communicate by shifting his business to focus on areas near Pakistan where he could meet American intelligence officers, trusted agents in the ISI, and cutouts from the Turi tribe in the months and years ahead. Walker and Staub were instead using that same route to get him and his family out of the country for good.

They had enough money, CIA contingency funds Walker had liberated, to live on in Pakistan while they pushed the special immigrant visa through proper channels. Naji and his family would get to the United States; it would just be from Islamabad instead of Kabul. In their infinite wisdom the Agency had put Naji on a terrorist watch list and multiple coalition High Value Individual target lists to make it appear as if America considered him an enemy. The intent was to protect him from Taliban death squads killing all those who had worked with the United States. Someone in an air-conditioned office at Langley had come up with that idea. Whoever it was didn't know the Taliban. One consequence was that he could not board any of the flights leaving Kabul. They had to get him out another way—through Pakistan.

The country was deteriorating quickly. The Mansour family needed to get across the border while they still had a chance.

Walker had driven these roads many times. His low-profile Velocity body armor was hidden beneath a loose button-down shirt, sleeves rolled, sweat already soaking through the fabric. His M4 was on the floor behind him, his Glock 19 holstered at his side.

Naji's wife, Rina, along with their eldest daughter, Fatima, were in the trail SUV driven by Staub. Both vehicles were thin-skinned, meant to blend in with local traffic.

Walker's eyes scanned the terrain as he went. Even with the Taliban taking Afghanistan back province by province, the IED threat was still prevalent.

Ahead, the road narrowed between two low ridgelines. Walker brought the Hilux to a stop. Staub's Mitsubishi skidded to a halt behind them.

"What's wrong?" Naji asked, voice tight.

"Stay put," Walker replied, reaching for his rifle and stepping out into the dry and alkaline Afghan air. He grabbed a set of Vortex binos from the door-panel pocket and walked back to Staub, who rolled down his window.

"How's everyone doing back here?" he asked, trying not to alarm Rina and Fatima.

"I think we have two ladies who could use a bathroom break," Staub responded.

"Okay," Walker replied. "This is a good place for it."

Staub turned to Rina and said "bathroom" in Pashto, indicating a patch of nearby boulders just off the road.

As Rina and Fatima exited the dirty SUV, Staub picked up his rifle and binos and joined Walker.

"See them?" Walker asked.

"Where?"

"Dark boulder at the turn about five hundred yards ahead."

"Got it."

"Okay, come back toward us about thirty yards. There's a mound of dirt."

"On it."

"Just behind it. See the yellow?"

"Motherfucker."

It had been common practice for insurgents to use yellow plastic water jugs as part of IED construction. Most civilians used them to haul water. The Taliban filled them with aluminum powder and ammonium nitrate.

"Rocks on both sides," Staub added, eyes still pressed to the binos.

"Yep."

"Wish we had assets up telling us if there are any active cell phones in play."

"Yeah."

"We are pretty remote out here. Might be a pressure plate that the Taliban knows to drive around."

"Or this is an obvious ploy to get us to drive around and right into an actual IED."

"Could be. Maybe we wait and see if a vehicle comes by and either drives around or goes right through."

"Could. Or we could go take a look," Walker said.

"We?"

"I could go take a look."

They turned to see Rina and Fatima returning from behind the rocks.

"Have Rina take Zahra from my vehicle to the bathroom. I'll leave the family with you."

"Where are you going?"

"I'm going to go defuse a bomb."

CHAPTER TWENTY-ONE

New Orleans
Present Day

IT WAS FOUR-THIRTY in the afternoon, the end of the workday for many in government service. But not for Jarrett Stanton.

Inside the sterile, fluorescent-lit conference room on the third floor of the Federal Building, the air was cool and dry, humming with the low buzz of a ceiling vent. The walls were bare except for a whiteboard filled with color-coded charts and a corkboard pinned with maps of the great state of Louisiana, each one marked with pins and string like a spiderweb of crime.

Stanton stood at the head of the table, sleeves rolled to the elbows of his crisp white shirt, tie loosened, correctly indicating he had been at it since dawn. His dark eyes scanned the room like a hawk circling a field. He was in his element, his weekly Trends meeting, where data was gospel and patterns were prophecy.

The room was quiet, professional, anodyne. Two rookies sat stiffly at the far end of the table, trying to fit in.

"He always like this?" one of them whispered.

"Oh yeah," came the reply from a grizzled agent with a coffee-stained tie. "We do this every week."

The door creaked open, and Augustus Lloyd, the special agent in charge of the New Orleans Field Office, poked his head in. He was a big man with a double chin, a slow drawl, and a thinning hairline in sharp retreat, his face aged with sunspots.

"We've got that call with the DA," Lloyd said.

Stanton checked his smartwatch. "Trends meeting, sir. Just finishing up."

"I'll get us dialed in." Lloyd gave a mock salute and disappeared down the hall.

Stanton had near-religious reverence for the Trends meeting. This was how you fought crime, not by chasing rumors or gut feelings, though those could help, but by amassing data, spotting patterns, and digging in. He believed in numbers. Numbers didn't lie.

Analyzing data was the most efficient way to do their jobs, and if he was going to get on the phone with a former federal prosecutor who was likely to be the next governor of Louisiana, he wanted to have his trends buttoned up.

Opioid deaths were picking up across the state, and with the DA running for governor she was going to want to know more. That might be so she could pin it on her opponent, the current state attorney general, or it might be so she could do something about it.

He clicked a remote, and a projector lit up the wall with a spreadsheet of calls, arrests, and incident reports.

"We're seeing a spike in opioid-related calls upstate," he said, tapping the screen with a laser pointer. "Synthetics. Same pattern as last quarter, but the clusters are tighter. Someone's moving product again. Showing up in Baton Rouge, also some in neighboring states. Thoughts?" Stanton's voice was calm, clipped, precise.

The agents scribbled notes.

Stanton was about to encourage the team to voice theories based on data when a voice piped up from the far end of the table. Scott Abrams, one of the rookies. Eager. Sharp and still green enough to think initiative was always rewarded.

"Not sure if it could be related, but we had a visitor yesterday," he ventured.

"You were on complaint duty?"

"Yes, sir."

Complaint duty was a rite of passage for the new guys. Nine or ten crackpots a week drove out to the FBI district HQ on Lake Pontchartrain to talk about UFOs, Elvis sightings, and the Trilateral Commission. But every now and then, a walk-in said something useful.

"A walk-in? Here?" Stanton asked.

"No, sir. It was down at the Federal Building. U.S. marshal reported a strange encounter with a walk-in. Drug-related."

Stanton turned his head slightly. "Okay, Agent Abrams. What do you have?"

"A man came in looking for a specific DEA agent. When he was asked to fill out the usual forms for the request, he bolted. The marshal thought he got spooked by something."

"ID? Video surveillance?"

"No ID. He was wearing a hat, pulled low. Bearded. I saw it, which is why I bring it up."

"Where are you going with this?"

"I'm not sure. Something stood out about him. He was a rough-looking character. I saw a still photo first and pegged him as homeless, but on the video he sure didn't walk like a homeless guy."

"What does that mean?"

"Just seemed like he walked with purpose. Like a cop."

His voice lowered, steamrolled by the scoffs from saltier agents.

Stanton waved them down.

"Who was he looking for?"

"A UC," he said, using the acronym for undercover. "Javier Gonzalez."

"Can we enhance the video, maybe do a facial pattern search, find out who this guy is? The man wants to meet with the DEA. Let's give him the FBI."

"Yes, sir. I'll check."

Stanton's watch buzzed. Time to talk to Icy.

CHAPTER TWENTY-TWO

Afghanistan
2021

WALKER DROVE SLOWLY ahead thinking about fate and stopped the Hilux a hundred yards shy of the yellow jug concealed behind a pile of rocks. This close, he was able to see the det cord running through a hole punctured in the five-inch-diameter white screw top and ran his eyes to a flat spot in the road in line with where a vehicle would cross it.

There's the plate.

He had seen this type of pressure plate a dozen times before. Most setups were made up of three components: switch, battery, and electric blasting cap. The pressure plate, or switch, was usually saw blades separated by a nonconductive material and placed in the road where a vehicle's wheel or wheels would most likely roll, thus creating the "pressure." Wires would be connected to each saw blade, and when a wheel ran over the pressure plate, the saw blade would bend, touching the other saw blade to complete the electrical circuit, which set off the electric detonator. The bulk explosive was usually buried on the side of the road or directly underneath the vehicle.

If Walker had the right explosive charge, he could have blown it in place. Too bad he didn't.

There was also the possibility that this was a hoax IED, set up to get them to drive around and over a more cleverly camouflaged device.

He looked back at Staub, who was watching his every move through binos. He had left his radio with his partner as radio frequency transmissions and IEDs did not play well together.

He turned back to the device.

It was time.

He lay on his stomach and crawled forward, carefully inspecting and probing the ground as he went; one doesn't want to inadvertently set off a pressure plate or secondary IED.

Sweat from heat and nerves dripped from his pores as he approached the yellow jug.

There was no way to tell from outside of the makeshift bomb how much explosive was inside. The standard insurgent ratio was nine parts ammonium nitrate and one part aluminum powder, and the jugs were usually close to forty pounds, which was more than enough to destroy a Hilux truck or midsize SUV.

Or one dumbass messing with it.

As he got closer, Walker could see the det cord poking out of the lid, attached to a blue wire. If he could sever the wire, he would render the whole thing inoperable.

Well, you haven't blown yourself up yet. Keep going.

Walker slowly opened the small hook and line kit he had taken with him. He focused on slowing his breathing as he used a "pull line" to attach a "hook knife" to the detonator wire.

Still have all my fingers and toes. That's a good sign.

Walker slowly backed out the way he had come with the pull line in hand, careful not to inadvertently jerk or pull too soon while still exposed to the blast. When he was about seventy-five yards away he crawled behind a boulder. He looked back toward Staub but couldn't see him, which meant he was far enough away and behind cover.

Moment of truth.

Three, two, one.

Walker pulled the line attached to the hook knife, remotely cutting the detonator wire.

Nothing went boom.

Have to check it.

Walker moved back to the IED, slowly and deliberately.

The wire was cut. The explosive was still there, half-buried against the boulder, but Walker verified the electrical circuit to set off the IED was disrupted.

Next, he conducted a quick secondary search to verify there were no other explosive devices.

All clear.

He turned and signaled to Staub that it was safe to drive forward with the family.

He stowed his kit and made his way back to his vehicle thinking that had he been a smoker, now would have been a good time to light one up to calm the nerves. Instead, from a Nalgene bottle he downed most of his lukewarm water flavored with powdered orange Gatorade.

"You good, brother?" Staub asked, exiting the Mitsubishi to check on his friend.

"Yeah. Taliban must know to drive around it. This was set up recently as I don't see any tracks veering off the road yet."

"Maybe there's a route to bypass that starts back the way we came, and we just missed it."

"Could be. Let's get Naji and Zahra back in the Hilux. We're getting close."

The two-vehicle convoy continued on, slower this time, the four-wheel-drive vehicles eating up the miles to the border.

"You have the papers handy?" Walker asked Naji.

Naji patted a worn leather satchel and smiled faintly. "Right here."

The road ahead shimmered with heat.

Three klicks later, Walker squinted at the horizon and keyed his radio.

"Checkpoint up ahead. Panel van."

"*Baksheesh*?" Walker asked his passenger. Gift?

"Most likely," Naji said. "They know there will be a surge of traffic to the border with the Americans leaving. They're going to want to capitalize on it. Opportunists."

Let's hope so, Walker thought.

"What do you think?" he asked Staub over the radio.

"*I think it's time to pay up.*"

Walker keyed his mic twice in response, then reached into the center console and pulled out a white pillowcase and a thousand dollars in U.S. hundred-dollar bills.

As they approached, two men carrying AK-type rifles stepped out of the van. They were dressed in black.

Walker rolled down his window, slowed the vehicle, and held out the white pillowcase.

"Just be calm," Walker said as he brought the Hilux to a stop about ten yards from the checkpoint. "Give me your papers."

He stuffed the money into the pillowcase and stepped out, one hand raised with the white pillowcase, which doubled as a truce flag, the other holding the Agency-forged Taliban travel papers at shoulder level. The fighters watched him advance.

Walker only knew a few phrases of Pashto, which he hoped would be beneficial in this situation. He was counting on the cash and documents to speak for him. He was also counting on human nature. If the travel documents were real and these bandits killed people traveling under Taliban protection, they and their families were as good as dead. Better to accept a "gift" and err on the side of caution.

"We're leaving the country. Per the agreement," Walker said in barely passable Pashto. He said it in a way that assumed everyone knew about the agreement, playing on the intellectual vanity of human nature.

The lead fighter, a hawk-faced man with a black beard, nodded slightly.

"Exit papers," he said.

Walker handed over the forged documents.

"You are a soldier," Hawk-face replied, in heavily accented English.

"Just a security guard. We are only assisting in the withdrawal from your country."

The fighter barked something in Pashto that Walker couldn't follow but he understood the hand signal to mean *pay up*.

Walker handed the pillowcase to the lead man.

The bandit pulled the money out and seemed to weigh it in his hands. Then he handed it to his partner.

"Go with God," the man said, throwing the pillowcase back at the American. "And never come back."

Walker kept his hands up by his shoulders.

"Don't you worry," he replied, before turning back toward his vehicle.

CHAPTER TWENTY-THREE

WALKER PULLED INTO the run-down service station and pre-paid for gas in cash through a sliding drawer to a man with hollow eyes sequestered behind thick glass. He then began fueling his faded blue van and took Paladin to a nearby patch of weeds so both man and beast could stretch their legs.

Parts of the Ninth Ward had clawed their way back from the brink, pockets of resilience scattered among the wreckage. Here and there, clusters of retail shops stood like outposts, their windows scrubbed clean, their signage defiant. Some homeowners had fought to reclaim their blocks, painting trim, planting flowers, polishing their porches like armor against the decay.

The ward wasn't rotten to the core. In fact, its core was the part still holding on. It was the fringes, the outer edges, where the rot had taken hold. That's where the streets turned quiet in the wrong way, where the houses jutted like broken teeth, and where the criminals dominated the night.

Walker was surprised at how inexpensive the fuel was in this part of the country. New Orleans was home to a number of petroleum-related businesses along the Mississippi Delta, which must have helped reduce cost of fuel.

The gas pump clicked off with a *thunk* while Paladin sniffed around a patch of weeds near the curb, tail twitching, ears perked. Walker wandered over to the dog and stood with his hands in his pockets, feeling the sun on his face.

He turned to the sound of a green seventies-era BMW 2002, patched with Bondo and coughing smoke, that had lurched into reverse and backed up in front of the van. Walker's spine stiffened. There were other pumps open, so it was odd that this driver had chosen the one directly in front of his. His hand instinctively went to the Glock beneath his shirt.

The car looked familiar. He had noticed a similar vehicle when he exited the Federal Building.

The instinct faded when the driver's door cracked open and a girl stepped out. She was young and wiry, a pale waif with thick mascara-framed eyes. Her dark jeans were torn at the knees and tucked into black Doc Martens. A crucifix tattoo, medieval and jagged, clung to the side of her neck. She looked like she weighed ninety pounds soaking wet.

She put the nozzle into her car, punched the buttons, and, while waiting for the tank to fill, ambled to Walker's van. She must have assumed he was inside, paying the bill, because she kept to the driver's side and peered through the windows, standing on tiptoe.

Walker calmly approached out of the dead space. "Can I help you?" he asked, careful to keep his voice neutral.

"Oh," she said, turning. "Sorry, I . . ."

"You like old cars?" he asked, looking at her vintage Beamer.

Her pale face flushed.

"Sorry. Yeah, I was just checking it out," she said, backing toward her car.

Walker wasn't buying it. The way she had pulled in and immediately checked his van suggested that was her intent. He wondered if she might be related to the guys who had tried to rob him at his campsite on the swamp.

She removed the nozzle and hung it back on the pump.

Walker moved to his van's driver's-side door and opened it for Paladin.

"*Dein Platz*," he said. The dog jumped into the van and across to the passenger seat, staying upright and watching through the front windshield.

"Platz? What the fuck language is that?"

"German."

"Cute."

"*Blijf*," Walker said to Paladin.

"German?"

"That was Dutch."

"A multilingual dog?"

"Kind of. The commands are more of a mash-up of Dutch, German, and a little English."

"That's weird."

"You wouldn't happen to know a couple guys who tried to break into this van the other night, would you?"

"What? No. What the fuck is wrong with you?"

She placed her hands on her hips, defiant.

"You know, I think I've seen your car before," he said.

She studied him up and down, contemplating what to say next.

"What's your interest in Connor?" she asked abruptly.

"Connor who?"

"Don't give me that. I've seen you around."

"Who says I have any?"

"I do. I saw you visit his grave. This van of yours was parked on Connor's street. You were at his mom's hospital and at the Federal Building. You a fucking cop? Undercover or something?"

Shit, I better up my game if I only caught her once.

"Cop? That's a new one."

"Like I said, what's your interest in Connor?"

"Why are you following me?"

"Question with a question. Fine. It's not like you're hard to find," she said, inclining her head at the van.

It was a fair point.

"I'm a family friend of the Staubs."

"You knew Connor?" she asked, arms tightly crossed over her chest, fingers tapping against her elbow.

"I met him when he was young. I was tight with his father." He stepped forward and offered his hand. "My name's Chris Walker. That's Paladin. He goes by Pal."

She hesitated, then reached out and shook his hand.

"And I would guess you are Connor's girlfriend."

"I *was* Connor's girlfriend," she replied. "But we weren't into labels."

Walker noticed she hadn't led with her name.

"I'm sorry for your loss."

"Yeah, well . . ."

"You hungry?" He gestured toward a greasy spoon diner across the street, its neon sign flickering like a dying star.

"You creeping on me?"

"No." Walker held his hands up. "I'm here helping Connor's mom tie up some loose ends. I owed her husband a favor."

"A favor?"

"I'm really just here to help."

"What does that have to do with buying me lunch?"

"Who said I was buying?"

———

The grill was a time capsule from a happier decade. Cracked vinyl booths, yellowed menus laminated with grease, and a jukebox in the corner flipping vinyl. The scent of stale beer and burnt fried chicken lingered in the air.

They slid into a booth in the back, while Paladin waited in the van. Walker had parked it so the dog could see into the diner.

"You live around here?" he asked.

"I thought you said you weren't creepin'."

"Isn't that a normal question?"

"You don't talk to girls much, do you?"

"I mostly talk to my dog."

"I always attract the crazy ones."

Walker shook his head. "Listen, I just want to find out a little more about Connor."

"Yeah, well you could start by asking me my name."

"Okay, what's your name?"

"Mirabelle. Mirabelle Travois, but I go by Belle."

"Nice to meet you, Belle. How's that?"

"Better."

A waitress who could have been anywhere from forty to seventy took their order and then disappeared into the kitchen.

"And do you live around here?" Walker tried again.

"No. I live east of the Quarter."

"What do you do?"

"Day job? Tattoo artist. Shop's a block off Bourbon. Drunk college kids and men having a midlife. You have any tats?"

"Are you implying I'm having a midlife?"

"If the shoe fits."

He laughed.

"I do," he said, tapping his ribs. "A little something from my Navy days."

"You don't look like a military guy."

"Thanks, I guess."

"I was going to say you look homeless."

Walker ran his hand through his greasy blond hair and beard.

"Yeah, I guess I could use a trim."

"Are you and Leigh Ann involved?" she asked.

"You mean *romantically*?"

"Hey, I wasn't accusing you of anything."

"Well, the answer is no. Did you have a good relationship with her?"

They were interrupted as their burgers and soft drinks arrived.

"Hardly," Belle continued when the waitress was out of earshot. "She thought I was a bad influence on her son."

"Were you?"

"Guess so. Connor's dead."

Walker studied her with fresh eyes. She was hurting.

Her eyeliner was smudged, and her black nails were chipped. She sat with one leg tucked under the other. She picked at her burger, took a few bites, then pushed the fries around her plate.

"I saw the guitar in your van," she offered, distant eyes gazing out toward the parking lot. "Nice vintage Martin."

"You play?"

"I dabble, but not acoustic. Industrial punk."

"Well, that's a bit of common ground."

She grunted and stuffed a ketchup-covered fry in her mouth.

"I go to LSU Extension. Got my bachelor's in accounting. Working on my master's in management information systems."

"What's that?"

"How old are you?"

"I'm not much of a computer type."

"Well, it's like the technical infrastructure of the business world."

"I have no idea what that means."

"Doesn't much matter. I ink people up to pay for school. Live with my grandmother to save money and help look after her."

"How'd you meet Connor?" he asked.

"A show at the Dungeon."

"Dungeon?"

"Punk venue. Connor was different. Smart. Angry, but in a good way. He had a kind of . . . coyote energy. He was a doer, wanted to fix things. Found out we both went to LSU."

"Did Leigh Ann think you got him into drugs?"

She dropped a fry. "Fuck you, man. You think just because I look like this, I got a clean kid from the Garden District to OD?"

He had pushed too hard.

"If the shoe fits," he said, echoing her words from moments earlier in a bad attempt at a joke. "Hey, I'm sorry. I didn't mean anything by it. Most everyone, like you, correctly assumes I'm homeless."

"Well, get a haircut and take a shower," she said, settling back down.

"Maybe I will."

"And for the record, I don't do the hard stuff. Connor lost a friend to some synthetic hard shit. He hated the drugs that ripped this town apart. That's one of the reasons he was going into journalism. He wanted to bring a light to it. He was different than other kids from the Garden District. Guess I was attracted to the contrasts."

Walker took a breath.

"Belle, I wonder if you can help me."

"Help you with what?"

He reached into his bag and withdrew Connor's journal, the leather cover worn and creased. He laid it on the table and opened it to the center. "You recognize any of this?"

She leaned in and froze for a moment when she saw Connor's handwriting. "Let me see that." She flipped through the pages. "So it exists."

"You've never seen this before?"

"No, but I knew about it. Connor told me he wrote in code."

"He did. He used some sort of a cipher, a key book that I don't have," Walker said.

"I know it had something to do with his dad's old work."

"Old work?"

"Military stuff."

"That's helpful."

The waitress stopped by to check on them. Belle was still picking at her food. Walker asked for coffee.

"He was looking for Snowball," she said.

"Do you know it?"

"*Of* it."

"Leigh Ann thinks Connor was framed by the cops for digging into this. Would that make sense to you?"

"You're kidding, right? In this town, cops and criminals work together. Connor wanted to blow the lid off something like that, make a difference."

"How do you know?"

"Know what?"

"That he found a connection between law enforcement and this Snowball drug."

"I was his girlfriend. We talked a lot, but when I asked too many questions about this story, particularly around cops and the drug trade, he would tell me the less I knew, the better, at least until his story broke."

The waitress set down a coffee and the check and walked away.

"Another dead end," Walker said to Belle as much as to himself.

"We're in the Lower Ninth, Chris. New Orleans kids hit the Ninth to score pills. All those empty shacks after Katrina have turned into a drug mall."

"I'm noting the police activity out there."

She closed the journal and slid it back across the table. "You some kind of private detective or something?"

"More of an 'or something.'"

"How did you say you knew Connor's dad?"

"I didn't."

"Did you work together?"

"We did."

"At the CIA?"

"Why do you ask?"

"Connor didn't know much about what his dad did, but he knew it had something to do with the CIA. It was another reason he was so motivated to become an investigative journalist. I think he intended to investigate his father's death one day, even talked about going to Afghanistan."

Walker's eyes fell to his coffee cup.

"Hey, what time is it?" she asked.

Walker turned up his left wrist. "I don't know."

"No watch?"

"Homeless, remember."

"What's your phone say?"

"I have a flip phone in the van."

"What century do you live in?" she asked and dug into her pocket, pulling out an Android with a cracked screen.

"Didn't realize it had gotten so late. I've got to get going," she said, pulling the check to her. She flipped it over and wrote her phone number on the back of the receipt with the waitress's pen. "Call me if you think I can help. Connor deserved better."

"I will. And, he did."

"Thank you for lunch." She began to gather her things and then stopped. "What are you really doing here, Chris?"

He hesitated. "Like I said, I owe Connor's dad a favor."

CHAPTER TWENTY-FOUR

Afghanistan
2021

THE HILUX RUMBLED over the rutted dirt road, dust clinging to the windshield like a second skin. The Pakistan border was close, though as everyone working in this part of the world knew, borders here were merely a suggestion, arbitrary lines drawn through tribal lands at the height of the Great Game in 1893 meant to create a buffer zone between world powers. Durand's ghost haunted them still.

Walker adjusted his grip on the wheel, steering the smoothest course he could while constantly checking the rearview mirror to ensure the green Montero was still behind him.

His eyes were on that rearview when Naji hit his shoulder and pointed ahead.

Walker braked and snatched the binoculars from the door pocket.

Ahead, he saw the familiar outline of a Toyota Land Cruiser. He adjusted the focus through the glare and identified three armed men in mismatched fatigues and scarves, black flags fluttering on a whip antenna at the back of the truck. The terrain on their left was a rocky embankment, high ground. To the right was a boulder field that gave way to a wadi beyond.

"Fuck," Walker said, handing the binoculars to Naji and keying his radio.

"Three MAMs visible," he transmitted, using the term for military-aged male. "Probably at least one more in the truck. I'd say they are Haqqani Network."

"How much money do we have left?" Staub asked over the radio.

Walker opened the center console to look at the remaining cash.

"Enough," he said.

"I hope you're right."

"Ask Mr. John how Rina and Fatima are faring," Naji requested.

Walker keyed his radio. "How are your passengers?"

"All good here," came the reply.

"They're good, Naji. We will be across the border soon."

"You know as well as I do that the border means nothing here."

"It means something to Pakistan. We're linking up with a contact my organization has in the Turi tribe. They are fiercely anti-Taliban and anti-Haqqani. They are going to see to your safe passage farther into Pakistan."

"How do you know they just won't kill us?"

"We are going to give them ten thousand dollars."

"Why wouldn't they just take it and kill us anyway?"

"Because with America leaving, they want to continue to be paid. They will pass us information in exchange for compensation. They don't want to jeopardize that relationship."

"And you will leave us with the Turi?"

"I'm sorry, Naji. That's the best we can do. They shouldn't be much farther past this checkpoint."

"It is in the hands of Allah."

"Chris," came Staub's voice over the radio.

"Go."

"These guys are getting the deal of the century out of our withdrawal. I don't see why they'd fu—" Cognizant of the child in the back seat, he corrected his language. *"I don't see why they would jeopardize the deal. They want money, not heads."*

Staub made a good point. Why would the men in the truck screw up this truce? In another week, the Americans would leave everything. That was the dirty deal the U.S. government had made with the Taliban. The soon-to-be-rulers of Afghanistan were getting what they'd always wanted, foreigners out and a modern army's abandoned equipment. The old Tali-Bar at the Ariana Hotel would probably be their cabinet room again in a matter of weeks.

Walker wanted to believe it. The simple fact was, they had already moved through one checkpoint and had been spotted by this one.

"Good copy. Let's buy our way through," Walker replied.

He turned to Naji's daughter in the back seat. Her eyes were wide, not with fright but with wonder.

The vehicles continued forward.

They rolled to a halt and switched off their engines.

The checkpoint ahead was a bleak reminder of what America had accomplished in its twenty-year war: rusted oil barrels, a pile of yellow plastic water jugs, a makeshift gate of strung barbed wire, and three men with AKMs across their knees on the open tailgate of the Cruiser.

"These men look different than the last ones," Naji said. "They have the look of the devil. Let me come with you."

"No. Stay here with Zahra."

"I am a rug salesman. We have a reputation for a reason," he said. "This close to Pakistan they might speak Urdu. How's your Urdu?"

"Shit."

Naji turned to smile at his daughter. "I'll be right back, dear child," he said, switching to Pashto. He kissed his hand and leaned back to place it against her forehead.

"Okay," Walker consented. "You have your papers?"

"Yes."

Walker stepped out slowly, hands raised with the white pillowcase filled with cash in one. These were fighters, not opportunists like the last checkpoint. Walker's gift was therefore a few thousand dollars more. Naji followed, his steps cautious. He was ready to translate, to warm them up just like he had learned to do with customers in his shop. He forced a smile.

The leader of the group was a squat, thick-waisted man with a cheek distorted by an old wound. He hopped off the tailgate and stepped forward, muttering something in guttural Urdu.

"Border tax," Naji translated, voice tight, nodding and smiling.

Border. That was good news.

"Does he want to see your exit papers?"

Naji said something else in Urdu, his tone almost playful, his smile broad.

The thick man barked something back, indistinguishable to the American.

"No, he just wants to know how much money we have."

"Tell him I can show him."

Naji spoke again and the leader stepped forward holding out his hand.

"Give him the money," Naji said.

Walker very deliberately reached into the pillowcase and handed over the cash, keeping his eyes low, his posture respectful.

Naji and the leader exchanged a few clipped words in Urdu as the man ran his fingers through the bills. Naji's smile never wavered.

The man said something else, short and clipped.

"He said we can go," Naji said.

The man jerked his head in a reluctant nod.

"Back away slowly," Walker said.

Naji pressed his palms together in a slight bow, then began stepping back toward the vehicles.

When they were twenty yards from the truck, eyes still on the gate-keepers, high-pitched static pierced the air.

The radio on the leader's hip crackled to life, barking something urgent in a dialect Walker didn't recognize. The leader's face changed. His eyes sharpened, his mouth tightened, the wound near his nose twisted. Naji froze.

"They know who I am. They're looking for me," he whispered, voice hollow.

"What are they saying?"

The voice on the radio was shrill and tense.

"The radio! They are going to kill us!"

One of the men on the tailgate raised his AKM.

Walker's hand flew to the Glock, indexed the grip, cleared leather, and fired three times at the AKM-armed man on the tailgate. All struck center mass. He pivoted and went for the second target, who was now scrambling from the rear of the truck, fumbling with his weapon. Walker fired again, hitting the man in his chest, neck, and head.

"Get down!" Walker screamed at Naji.

The leader had moved to the far side of the truck with surprising quickness, stuffing the cash in his tunic while shouting orders in Urdu.

A driver opened the door, stepped out, and raised a Kalashnikov.

Walker crouched and fired as Staub's rifle erupted behind them, sending rounds through the Land Cruiser's window and door, shattering the glass and punching through the thin steel, taking the man in his stomach and chest. He fell to the ground in a heap. Walker finished him with a head shot.

"Move!" Staub yelled from the rear vehicle.

Walker grabbed Naji by the arm and hauled him to his feet as Staub's rounds tore through the Land Cruiser. The leader tried to run up an embankment behind it, but took six rounds of 5.56 in his back. He continued to claw his way up as two more of Staub's rounds caught him in the head.

Walker could hear the voice on the radio and didn't need to speak Urdu to understand what was being said, but there was no one left to answer.

He heard the Montero approach, engine racing.

"Naji, let's get to the truck," Walker urged.

Naji stumbled and fell. Walker was hauling him to his feet when the unmistakable shriek of an RPG ripped through the air overhead. The rocket-propelled grenade nicked the top of the Mitsubishi's roof like a stone skipping on a pond, then slammed into a boulder on the far side of the road, detonating on impact.

Where the fuck did that come from?

Gripping Naji's arm, Walker yanked him toward their vehicle. They had to get off the X. They had to move. Hitting a moving target was much more difficult than a stationary one.

"Go, go!" Walker yelled at Staub as he passed in front of the approaching Montero, catching Rina's eyes behind the burqa as she looked past him to her stranded daughter in the Hilux, the eyes a mix of terror and rage.

Get to the truck. Get to my rifle.

The sound of the second RPG was more sickening than the first. It came from the outcropping above them. It had targeted the Hilux, the truck with Zahra inside.

Walker was only two steps into his sprint when the RPG hit.

The warhead impacted just in front of the driver's-side door and detonated with an intense flash followed by an instantaneous plume of black smoke that engulfed the front portion of the vehicle, the shock wave and rapid combustion of gases throwing the hood skyward.

Zahra.

Walker turned and dropped to a knee. He caught sight of movement in the rocks above and returned fire with the pistol. The slide locked to the rear as he heard Staub's rifle pick up cover from just outside the SUV. He pulled the Glock into his workspace and pressed the magazine release with his thumb, stripping the magazine. His hand continued to the pouch on the left side of his belt, grabbing a full one and slamming it home. He then pulled back on the slide to release it and chamber a round.

Get to Zahra.

He heard Naji scream his daughter's name as the older man scrambled to his feet and stumbled toward the wreckage. Walker saw movement from the back side of his truck. Zahra had escaped the vehicle and was running toward her father.

There is a distinct difference between the sound of an AK-type rifle and the larger-caliber PKM belt-fed machine gun.

It was the man behind the general-purpose machine gun who took Naji's life.

The first rounds fell short, eating into the hard-packed dirt between Walker and his source, then adjusted. The first round caught Naji in the leg when he was mere feet from his daughter. As Walker ran, he watched Naji stumble, the projectiles taking him in the hip and lower back and working their way up the right side of his spine, neck, and finally his head. He was dead before he crashed atop his young daughter.

Staub's rifle picked up again, sending rounds up at their assailants, providing cover fire as Walker slid to a stop in the dirt and rolled the rug salesman over.

Zahra was still, and for a moment Walker thought she was dead too. There was blood trickling out of one ear and her face was dirty and dark from the explosion. Her eyes blinked. She was in shock.

Walker threw his hands under her neck and legs, scooping her from the ground and sprinting to Staub's vehicle as his partner continued to send rounds into enemy positions in the rocks above.

He threw open the right rear door and pushed Zahra in with her sister, jumping in after her.

"Go! Go! Go!" he yelled over Staub's gunfire and Rina's screams.

Staub ducked back into the vehicle and slammed the door, then threw it into drive and smashed his foot on the accelerator. As the SUV surged forward, he looked back at Walker and past him at the crumpled figure in the road.

"Fuck!"

He turned back to the obstacle ahead, yelling, "Hold on," and crashed the vehicle through the makeshift barbed-wire gate. The vehicle ripped the gate off a wood pole on one side where it was haphazardly attached and pulled the other pole directly from the ground. The barbed wire wrapped around the front grille of the SUV as it careened down the road, gunfire continuing to erupt behind them.

Walker threw his body over the kids in the back and felt a round impact his rear plate, just as the SUV careened around a bend, putting them out of their enemy's line of sight.

"We're clear," Staub shouted.

Rina continued screaming and moaning in Pashto, reaching back to her daughters, whom Walker was checking for gunshot wounds.

"Kids are okay!" Walker shouted over Rina's screams as the car bounced over ruts in the unpaved road.

"Give me your rifle," Walker said.

Staub slipped the sling over his head and handed it back. Walker performed a tac reload to top it off.

Neither of them noticed the plastic yellow water jugs camouflaged on the roadside.

CHAPTER TWENTY-FIVE

THE EXPLOSIVE CHARGE detonated beneath the speeding SUV. Its blast created an inverted cone of gasses and pressure that ripped upward, carrying with it dirt, rocks, IED components, and pieces of the vehicle. The Mitsubishi was thrown onto its side, sliding into a ditch on the far side of the road.

For Walker, it was darkness, followed by pain, and a subsequent intense ringing that sounded like it was coming from the deepest recesses of a cavern.

Is this death?

Walker came to on his back, ears ringing, vision blurred and spotty. He rolled to his side. The world seemed tilted. He noticed the hard dirt of the road seemed to have loosened into sand. He wondered why. The answer came a moment later. Bomb.

> *When you're wounded and left on Afghanistan's plains,*
> *And the women come out to cut up what remains,*
> *Jest roll to your rifle and blow out your brains*
> *An' go to your Gawd like a soldier.*

He blinked his eyes, bringing Staub into focus. He was dragging himself through the sunroof and onto the road.

How the fuck did I get here in the middle of the road? Must have been blown through the rear passenger door.

Walker pushed himself to his knees. Where was his rifle?

Staub was shouting something he couldn't hear. Blood ran down Walker's temple. His head throbbed. He tasted dirt and blood in his mouth.

The ringing in his ears shifted to an angry hissing. He touched one. His hand came away with blood and mucus.

Gunfire cracked from the ridgeline. A few fighters were shooting at them from behind rocks, but they were still too far out to be effective.

The Montero was on its side, smoke curling from the engine block. One of the girls was screaming.

Walker scrambled to his feet and ran to Staub, taking a knee next to his battered friend.

Staub's baseball cap had been blown from his head, as had his sunglasses. Blood ran from his nose and ears, mixing with that from the glass shards in his face and neck.

The ringing in Walker's head became the screaming of one of the children.

"You're okay, buddy," he said. "Let's get the girls."

Staub's eyes looked glossy.

"Can you move?"

The big man shook his head.

"Get the girls, Chris. Rina's dead." He drew his pistol. "My legs aren't working."

Walker stared at his friend.

"You get the girls and get to the Turi contact," Staub said, his breathing labored. "We've got to be close."

"Fuck that, you're fine. Let me help you up."

"Hey! Chris, I'm not. You get the girls and get the fuck out of here. We didn't get very far. Those shitheads will be on us soon. Now fuckin' go!"

"I'm not leaving you."

"Hey, you owe me a favor, right?"

"What?"

"You owe me. Now get the girls. And hey," he managed a smile through labored breathing, "if you make it out of here, look in on Leigh Ann and Connor."

He slipped the Tudor Submariner from his wrist. "You know what to do with this," he said, handing it to Chris.

Walker reluctantly slid it into his pocket.

Staub set the Glock across his chest.

"I'll blast anyone that comes down the road," he said, now coughing up blood.

"I'll get the girls, but then I'm taking you with me."

They heard the unmistakable sound of an incoming mortar.

"I said go!" Staub shouted.

Walker ran to the back of the overturned SUV and grabbed the screwdriver from his plate carrier as a mortar landed and exploded fifty yards long.

They are bracketing us in.

He tried to pull up on the liftgate, but it was jammed from the crash. The rear window had been blown out but splinters of glass were held in place by the weather stripping, which Walker scraped away with his screwdriver. He then crouched low and crawled into the toppled SUV.

The interior was still filled with smoke and dust. Walker could feel it burning his lungs. His left shoulder bumped the back of the rear passenger seats. He reached toward the screaming.

"It's okay, I've got you," he said, trying to calm the hysterical child as he dragged her past the rear seat. It was the youngest daughter, Zahra.

He looked back and could see Fatima through the smoke. She appeared to be breathing.

"Can you crawl?" he yelled at her. "Crawl. Come to me."

Nothing.

"Shit! I'll come back for you!"

He grabbed Zahra under his arm and hauled her through the SUV.

A second mortar landed twenty yards short of the vehicle.

"Hurry, Chris!" Staub yelled.

Once outside the SUV, Walker threw the small girl over his shoulder and sprinted for a mound of rocks down in the wadi.

The girl had stopped screaming. She was breathing but her face was pale. He set her down on the far side of the rocks and turned back to the SUV. He was halfway there when he heard the whistling of a third mortar.

Please, dear God, no.

The prayer failed.

The earth rose up as if a volcano had erupted beneath the Montero. When it cleared, the SUV lay on its back. It was burning. Fatima's body had been ripped in half. It had been blown through a side window. The vehicle had rolled over onto Staub's upper torso, and one of his legs was missing.

They're gone. All gone.

He had started to run to his dead friend when a fourth mortar hit the SUV, covering Walker with debris, smoke, and dirt.

You owe me. If you make it out of here, look in on Leigh Ann and Connor.

He gazed at the burning heap, then back at the rocks where he had left Zahra.

"I'm so sorry," he whispered.

Go, Chris!

He turned and sprinted to Zahra, lifted her into his arms, and set off into the wadi.

An' go to your Gawd like a soldier.

PART TWO

*"The greatest conflicts are not between two people
but between one person and himself."*

—Gaius Musonius Rufus, Roman Stoic philosopher

CHAPTER TWENTY-SIX

WHY HAD HE survived?

Is that me wondering or the philosophers?

He drove through the night from the Ninth Ward toward the Garden District, crossing bridges and waiting at stoplights with Paladin in the passenger seat.

Leigh Ann had never heard the whole story. Neither had Connor. And now he never would.

She deserved to know how her husband had died as a hero, a protector, a guardian.

That the incident happened across the wrong border and threatened a fragile truce meant it had been classified. Leigh Ann and Connor were told that John had died in service to his nation in Afghanistan, in an engagement with insurgent forces. There was truth to the lie. It was lying by omission. Those lies continued even when John's star was chiseled into the CIA Memorial Wall at Langley.

The Agency lawyers had threatened Walker with prison for executing an illegal mission and stealing contingency funds. They hung John Staub's death around his neck, where it weighed like an albatross. About that, they were right. They were right about all of it.

Because of the border issue and classifications involved, there would be no formal trial. The brokered deal allowed Walker to medically retire with a combination of his years in the military and at the CIA, a victim of traumatic brain injury. If he ever spoke or wrote of the rogue incident that resulted in the death of John Staub, they would come after him, take his retirement, and prosecute him for his crimes.

Perhaps Walker had agreed to the deal so he would not have to face

John's wife and son with the truth; the truth that he was the man responsible for the death of Leigh Ann's husband, Connor's father.

Isn't philosophy fundamentally a search for truth?

Then why are you running from it?

He coasted to a stop and parked along the street a few blocks from the Staub residence. After Belle had so easily placed him at Leigh Ann's, he decided to at least not park directly in front.

You need to tell her.

What good will that do?

Truth.

If you make it out of here, look in on Leigh Ann and Connor.

You owe me.

Walker had failed his friend on the battlefield and then failed him again in death.

He exited his van onto the dark street and called for Paladin to join him.

"Good boy," Walker said as he locked the vehicle.

Would Irene Isaacson really look into Connor's case as she had promised Leigh Ann? Doubtful. Isaacson was a politician, and politicians told people what they wanted to hear.

You can still honor Staub and return that favor.

If you want to avoid suicide, find something to do.

Who said that? Voltaire?

Maybe.

His encounter with Belle was encouraging. After all, she might be the key that unlocked Connor's journal. Maybe Walker could crack the code and complete Connor's work on the Royal De Luxe in his van. Connor couldn't continue investigating, but Walker could. Maybe that, in some small way, would help fulfill the promise he had made to a dying man.

Paladin looked up at Walker as they made their way under the classic streetlamps, past the ironwork, gardens, and columns of the grand, historic homes, as if to ask why his master was walking so slow.

"Don't worry, partner. Just thinking."

It was nearly nine. Leigh Ann's ER shifts made for late nights.

His conversation with Belle had reminded him that he needed to vary his routine so instead of using the main entrance, he passed the front gate and decided to use the driveway that led to the detached garage.

He heard jazz floating through the humid air. It seemed louder than he remembered but maybe that was how Leigh Ann liked it when she was alone. Nothing the neighbors would complain about. He stepped past the hanging tropical plants between the garage and house, noting that Leigh Ann needed better perimeter lighting. As he was about to take the steps up to the side door, Paladin froze at his side, silently alerting, just as he had done a thousand times in Iraq and Afghanistan. Walker stopped in his tracks.

Paladin alerted when he smelled certain explosives or precursors common in IEDs: C-4, TNT, Semtex, ammonium nitrate, RDX. But there was another odor that also triggered him.

Blood.

CHAPTER TWENTY-SEVEN

MAYBE IT WAS nothing, but Walker had learned long ago that primal instincts should not be ignored, especially those of a multipurpose canine.

He stepped off the path and into the garden shadows between the detached garage and the main house, drawing his Glock.

"*Stil,*" he whispered, ordering Paladin to stay silent.

Maybe it's nothing.

The side entrance led into a room just off the kitchen, warm yellow light emanated through sheer curtains.

He watched for shadows, listened for footsteps, voices.

Nothing but jazz.

Paladin stood rigid beside him, silent but alert. The dog's body language was unmistakable—something was wrong.

Walker leaned in and murmured, "*Volg.*" Heel.

He kept to the garden, pushing to the back of the house to get a good angle on the kitchen through a window that allowed someone at the sink to look out over the flowers.

Oversized Edison lights hung above the island, where he noticed an open bottle of wine and an empty platter. The swinging door that separated the kitchen from the dining room was closed, unlike on his first visit.

He turned back to the street, which was now partially obscured by a southern magnolia. Had there been any suspicious vehicles parked on the street? Had he not been so consumed with thoughts of Belle, John, and the CIA, he might have noticed. Or maybe not. Parking on the street was common in this neighborhood. His van was probably the most suspicious vehicle out there.

Damn it! Get your head in the game.

He thought he heard a male voice inside the home, but when he stopped to listen, all he caught was jazz over the chirping of crickets and the long rattle of cicadas.

A thousand thoughts swarmed in his head, but an overriding one was that of Leigh Ann's meeting with Irene Isaacson.

Still might be nothing.

Then what of the male voice? Leigh Ann hadn't said anything about having another guest.

Maybe it was the TV.

You could just knock on the door.

You could call the police.

Leigh Ann reached out to you for a reason, and it wasn't so you could call the police.

She was afraid of the police. She was convinced they had killed her son.

Staying low, Paladin at his side, he wound his way along a garden path and covered the rear corner to the home in a few seconds, maneuvering through the landscaping lights over a small patch of grass and around fluted canna lily buds, angular bird-of-paradise flowers standing five feet high, and the leafy hostas and ferns hanging over fine-grain cedar bark. He paused near the side of the house, next to a shovel, bucket, rake, and pruning shears.

Paladin wasn't interested in the plants. His snout pointed like a spear at the rear porch, utterly silent, a predator on the hunt.

Stop. Look. Listen. Smell.

Walker heard a door swing open and saw a shadow fall across the back porch.

The shadow took the shape of a man with a slung weapon. A guard? Lookout? Just like Afghanistan and Iraq. Why was his weapon slung?

The man walked across the veranda, briefly illuminated in the light. He was mid-twenties, maybe thirty, Hispanic, shaved head, neck and face covered in tattoos. He walked to the far edge of the porch, unzipped his fly, and began to relieve himself.

There is not going to be a better time. He's at his most vulnerable.

What if this is a mistake?

It's no mistake.

Kill him? Question him to get intel and find out how many more are inside?

Take him with the Glock?

That warns anyone else on-site and gives up the element of surprise.

If there were more, Walker needed to stack the odds in his favor.

Send Paladin forward?

Too noisy.

Blade?

Maybe there was a better way.

Walker holstered his Glock and grabbed the shovel.

"*Blijf,*" he whispered. Stay.

Kill or capture?

Leigh Ann made the decision for him as her voice, twisted into an unmistakable scream, echoed from the recesses of the home.

Execute!

The man must have thought Walker's footsteps came from a comrade because he finished shaking the last of his urine into the bushes before turning with a look of annoyance that altered to disbelief as the full force of Walker's baseball swing with the shovel connected with his face.

His neck snapped back, his brain reverberating against his skull.

If Walker had any thoughts about keeping him alive, those thoughts faded when he heard Leigh Ann's next scream.

As the man collapsed to the deck, Walker smashed the shovel into his head once again. He then placed the flat cutting edge of the tool against his unconscious opponent's neck, and as if he was about to start digging into hard dirt, he slammed his boot down onto the footstep. He adjusted the shovel's angle and brought his heel down twice more in quick succession, almost severing his enemy's head from the body.

"*Heir,*" Walker said.

Paladin vaulted onto the porch and crossed the deck to his master, sniffing the body at his feet.

The dead man's weapon was slung over his shoulder, so Walker set the shovel aside and worked the sling down his arm, prying his left hand from the lower wood handguard, noting the man's fingernails were stubby and embedded with dirt.

What the fuck is this?

It looked like an AK-type weapon but with a short barrel and without a stock. It had the standard banana-shaped magazine and felt heavy, which meant it was probably loaded with thirty rounds. He pulled the charging handle back slightly to confirm there was a round in the chamber, then ensured the selector lever was in the top position.

I'll be more accurate with my Glock.

Handguns were often referred to as defensive weapons, but as an instructor at the Farm had told him, it was all about how you used it. Walker was going on the offensive.

As he slung the AK-style pistol, he became aware of a peculiar, almost sweet odor with a tinge of sickness coming from the dead man. Cologne? Aftershave?

"*Zoek*," Walker said, pronouncing it *zook*. It was a command for Paladin to search based on the smell.

Speed. Surprise. Violence of action.

If we still have surprise.

At least you have speed and violence of action.

The man had left the door open when he exited to take a piss. His friends would be expecting him back. They would get Walker instead.

The hunter-killer part of his soul was firmly in the driver's seat. The philosopher was relegated to the passenger side.

He entered the house pistol up and ready, searching for targets, sacrificing security for speed, Paladin slightly ahead of him off to his right side.

The screams sounded like they had come from upstairs.

He stepped into a hallway lined with the Tabriz carpets John had purchased at Pan Arabian Rugs in an alley in Kabul.

Walker heard footsteps upstairs. The screaming had stopped. Now there were voices, guttural, too muffled to make out what they were saying but it sounded like Spanish.

He turned a corner and looked up the stairs into the eyes of a soon-to-be dead man on the landing.

In the confines of the house, Walker's gunshots sounded like cannons as he put four rounds into the chest of a man with a tattooed face, in jeans and a checked shirt, a man who didn't even have time to raise the gigantic stainless Desert Eagle pistol in his right hand.

Surprise is gone. Push the speed. Lean into the violence.

Walker sprinted up the stairs, putting another round into the head of the man holding the Desert Eagle as he gained the top landing with Paladin off his right knee.

There were two options at the top of the staircase, but it was clear that the dead man had come from the left.

The sisal carpet Leigh Ann used as a runner over the dark mahogany was crooked. A blood streak ran down the ivory wall below the family photos.

A tattooed face emerged from the room at the end of the hallway.

Walker's 9mm round caught him in the chin and sent him stumbling back into the room. The former SEAL followed him in, quickly scanning for additional threats and putting two more bullets into the man's head.

The bedroom was spacious with a high ceiling rimmed with ornate crown molding. A fan rotated above a king-sized bed. One of the French doors leading to a small balcony was open. The drawers of both bedside tables had been pulled out and emptied onto the floor, as had the drawers from the dresser and armoire.

Leigh Ann sat slumped in a chair, tied, gagged, her blouse torn, hair tumbling around her face. Before Walker checked her pulse, he knew that she was dead. The claw hammer on the floor, covered with matted hair and blood, spoke to how she met her end.

The mother. The son. The father. All dead.

Walker took his fingers from the side of her neck and quickly cleared the attached bathroom and balcony. He heard tires squeal in the street and unsuccessfully tried to make out the type of vehicle that was so quickly departing.

Walker rushed back into the room, holstered his pistol, and reached for his blade to cut Leigh Ann from the chair.

It was Paladin who saved his life.

The Malinois leaped toward the bedroom door, attacking the arm holding the weapon, which in this case was another AK-variant pistol. Paladin's teeth tore into the forearm of the overmuscled man in the black T-shirt, who squeezed the trigger and sent a round into the floor while he continued toward Walker, a primal scream emanating from his tattooed lips. The man towered over six feet tall and looked like he had ingested a steady diet of steroids, growth hormone, and testosterone since birth.

He dropped the AK, hurled Paladin into a wall, and pressed his forward charge at the SEAL.

Walker went for his pistol, but the large man barreled into him before his hand could index the grip. Walker heard glass break as they crashed through the pane on the French door that was still closed. He felt a shard slice through his skin as the big man took him to the ground.

Walker was pinned to the deck by his throat, the man's massive left hand cutting off his air supply as his right rose up to strike.

With his pistol and the slung AK trapped beneath him, Walker went for the Regiment Blade at his appendix, drew it, and punched it into his attacker's left pubic bone, slightly below the man's left hip.

The banger howled in agony, his hands instinctively going to the source of the pain. Walker attempted to call Paladin, but even with the pressure released from his windpipe his voice was temporarily stifled. In this case he didn't need to say a word. The dog knew his job, and had a running start. He hit their aggressor at full speed, attacking the bicep of his right arm, teeth crushing through skin, muscle, tendon, and into bone, a growl emanating from his throat, ancient in origin.

That was the opening Walker needed. He twisted the blade in the man's pubic bone and used it as a lever as he trapped the giant's left hand while also ensnaring the man's left leg with his right. He then thrust his hips up and bridged to the right, taking the tattooed man with him.

With the man now on his back, Paladin clamped onto his chest, tearing through the meaty flesh before moving to the throat.

A dog biting and tearing near one's neck triggers the most primal of fears, harkening back to the days when wolves hunted in packs, subduing and consuming their prey in a bid for survival.

The big man's eyes were wide with fright, and a guttural howl escaped his lips as he thrashed, wanting nothing more than to be rid of the devil upon him.

Walker rolled away from his assailant to make sure he did not accidently cut his dog. He sheathed his blade, and brought his hand to his pistol as he stood, gasping for breath.

"*Los*," he shouted, giving Paladin the command to release.

Immediately Paladin let go of the man's bleeding neck and returned to his handler's side.

The man struggled to his knees, bringing his hands to his larynx as blood poured from the wounds.

"*Hijo de puta*," he sputtered.

Walker heard sirens in the distance.

"Speak English?" Walker asked between breaths as his eyes found the Trijicon HD night sights of his Glock 19. "*Hablas Inglés¿*"

"*Me cago en la puta madre que te parió,*" the man spat back.

Walker glanced at the dead woman tied to a chair in the bedroom behind him and then back at the man on his knees.

"Guess not," Walker said.

He shifted his focus to the bright orange glow of his tritium front sight, aligned it with the man's head, and pressed the trigger.

CHAPTER TWENTY-EIGHT

LIEUTENANT CORNELIUS BATES had visited the Garden District many times in the past few weeks, though for reasons not related to police work. He was in the market and had found himself a real estate agent.

He liked this neighborhood because the homes were more than houses. They had *personalities*. Bates thought these homes fit *his* personality: good-looking, classy, charming. With their Greek Revival, Italianate, or Spanish architecture, one might even call them seductive, a word that had always appealed to him. Moreover, these homes had stories to tell, and where there were stories, there were secrets.

Bates had walked with the agent down this very street, Prytania, right before they stopped at the bar near the Irish Channel, where he worked his charm, getting her tipsy enough to agree to go out with him the following week.

It did not bother him that the Irish Channel was not an actual waterway. He had been raised in New Orleans, a product of the Ninth Ward, where there really *was* a canal, one that had broken. Over here where the elite had put their stamp on the river lands, the canals had never been connected to the Mighty Miss. Had they known?

Bates wouldn't have been surprised.

The police cruisers parked at the corner of Third and Prytania formed a phalanx around the wrought iron, playing a red-and-blue light show on the neighbors' walls. A handful of people were out in the street wearing robes and slippers.

He thought that was good. One never knew who might be watching. This was an area that was home to judges, politicians, and the executives who funded their campaigns. Icy herself lived a few blocks down on Third. He had attended an event at her home a few months ago. The charm hadn't worked that time. Icy was as good as her name.

Shoving thoughts of that rebuff aside, Bates decided it would be better to walk through the cordon of policemen rather than drive through as he would have in the Ninth. Here in the Garden, it was better to be seen, to show up as the man in charge.

He stopped in the middle of the street and shifted his beefed-up Dodge Charger into park. When he stepped out, he straightened his tie and adjusted his shirt. Unlike other ambitious detectives, he rarely wore a suit jacket, even in the cool evening air or during the brief New Orleans winter. Bates preferred to show off his narrow waist and well-developed shoulders that came from pumping iron and working the heavy bag at Le Boxeur gym in the heart of the French Quarter.

"Crime scene secured?" he asked a patrolman near the yellow tape. Clearly, the scene had been secured. Why else was the tape there? But Bates could sense as well as see the onlookers within earshot. It was important that they knew a leader had arrived.

"Yes, Lieutenant. We've got the perimeter set up."

Bates nodded his shining bald head. He put his hands on his hips and took it in. Five cruisers had responded. Good. It was necessary to provide a show of force here in the Garden. One of them had the letters on the trunk of his specialized unit, the one that would elevate him to the top job: COPE. He wished that cruiser had been parked closer to the onlookers.

"Any media?"

"Yes, sir. Three broadcast channels. We're holding them down the street for now."

Now, that was a rookie move. Under Icy's sharp leadership, the NOPD budget lines had been increasing over the past few years. That funding came from the property tax dollars of the parish, much of it from this neighborhood. It was important for these people to see a swift and heavy police response.

"Go ahead and let them bring the cameras up," Bates ordered. "We want to display full transparency."

The patrolman nodded. Like all NOPD officers, he understood the force's reputation. Citizens didn't always trust the department.

"I'll let them through, sir. We'll set them up on the far sidewalk."

"Perfect," Bates responded.

With his badge exposed on his belt that matched the leather of his holster carrying his Glock 22, Bates ducked under the rope. He preferred to carry the .40-caliber full-sized Glock like the patrolmen. The smaller Glocks he was now authorized to carry as a lieutenant looked too small and unimpressive against his muscular body.

Detective Howard Gormley stood at the wrought-iron gate, his round belly casting a shadow on the home's brick path. "Hey, boss," he said when Bates approached.

"Place is a friggin' zoo."

"Yeah, I know."

"Who all's in the house?" Bates asked.

Gormley tugged at the double chin beneath his stubble. He was in his mid-fifties with pale skin that looked as if it had never seen the sun. His hair was full but gray, and his eyes were so droopy that the other cops called him Bloodhound, shortened to Hound. Gormley chose to believe they were complimenting his investigative skills.

"Detective Kile along with CSI techs, checking out the vics."

Kile's already in there? Shit. And the vic's a Ms. Staub? Whe else?" Bates asked, noting the patrolmen within earshot.

"A couple of John Does so far. Look Hispanic."

Because he worked in Bates's COPE unit, Gormley wore a tie without a jacket, just like the boss, though he had violated the dress code by choosing a short-sleeved shirt.

"I'll take a look," Bates said, snapping rubber gloves over his hands.

NOPD had eight districts, the equivalent of precincts, that covered the greater New Orleans area. Technically, this crime scene should have been processed by the head of the Sixth District, since they were in the Garden, but Bates had made a few calls and talked with the superintendent of police. He explained that the principal victim and homeowner, Leigh Ann Staub, was the mother of a stiff they had picked up over in the Ninth tied to the heroin trade. With what was reportedly a shoot-out at her home, Bates suggested it might have been retaliatory gang activity. The supe knew Bates had the ear of the DA and agreed with his assessment. Bates was going to make this his scene.

He slid cloth booties over his shoes and crossed the mahogany foyer with the Persian rugs. Phillip Kile, a detective with the Sixth, was standing there, eyeballing the scene and taking notes.

"What's up, Kile?" Bates said as he approached.

Detective Kile flipped his notebook closed and stepped forward carefully, staying on the wood floor so as not to alter the impressions in the carpet.

"Fucking mess, I'll tell you that."

"Looks that way, but let me make your night. COPE is taking this one."

Kile studied the man who had intruded on his scene.

"We're in the Sixth, Lieutenant."

"COPE follows the leads wherever they go. That's here. We got this."

"I can't agree to that. Not unless I hear from my squad. Or maybe Homicide."

Kile had been an Army Ranger and still had the haircut. He wouldn't respond to intimidation but did understand the chain of command.

"This is coming from the supe," Bates replied.

Because he thought this might come up, he had asked the superintendent to send an authorization on the secure text circuit. Bates handed his phone to Kile.

"Yeah, okay," the detective responded after a few seconds, handing the phone back. "Scene's yours. You want me to stick around and help? I don't mind. There is a lot to process here."

Bates shook his head. "I've got Gormley and a COPE patrol unit here, but if you could assign your Sixth officers to the cordon, I'd appreciate it."

Bates paused and scanned the rest of the room. Two crime scene techs were at work taking photographs of the dead man on the back porch, just past the open French doors.

"Have the techs been upstairs?" Bates asked.

"Just a quick cursory scan to confirm the vics. They haven't processed anything yet. One of yours was first on scene, an Officer Dupuis. I have him securing the second floor."

"Any security cameras in this house?"

"Negative."

"Too bad. Anything else stand out to you?"

"No, Lieutenant."

"Okay. Thanks for the head start, Detective."

Kile remained standing for a few seconds, as though imprinting the scene on his memory. Having lost the pissing contest, he nodded at Bates and pulled off his gloves as he headed for the door.

Gormley entered, grinning.

"Did old Kile take that hard?" he asked.

"He took it as an order."

"Army boys are good that way."

"Hound," Bates began, speaking softly, careful to keep his voice lower than those he could hear on the front porch. "Go grab Rayne. He's outside somewhere. Sixth is taking cordon."

"I'm on it."

"And, make sure the guys from the Sixth are set up in a way that allows media to see the house, but that's it. We all circle up here. This is our show. Nobody else."

"Damn straight, Corn."

Cornelius didn't like his name shortened to Corn, but this was the NOPD, and when you had a name like Cornelius, your nickname was preordained.

With Gormley out of the house Bates quickly scanned the pantry and then stepped outside to speak with the CSIs. Just as he had with Kile, he asked them to give him some time on-site to process. When they shot him a puzzled glance, he smiled and explained that he preferred the crime scene to be free of investigators when he arrived. "I like to see it just as it went down," he told the two women, one young, the other middle-aged. "No distractions."

Finally, alone with the dead man on the back porch steps, Bates knelt, backlit from the kitchen, casting a shadow out over the garden.

He snagged a penlight from his shirt pocket, clicked it on, and used it to check out the dead guy's face.

The cause of death was obvious; someone had almost chopped off his head with a shovel. Rigor mortis hadn't yet set in, which suggested he had been killed less than two hours ago.

Bates had been on a date, enjoying a whiskey over at the Carousel Bar in the Monteleone when Gormley called. Desiree had worn that plunging number, teasing him whenever she leaned forward, touching his arm and laughing at whatever he said. Maybe he would take her out again tomorrow and ask her to wear that same dress.

He ran the light over the man's body and noted a patch of clothing had been seemingly cut from his shirt.

Strange.

Bates clicked off the light and turned it around. He used the narrow end of the device to pick through the dead man's clothing, finding a chain on a belt loop that disappeared into a pocket. Bates carefully tugged the chain and found a wallet attached to it. He flexed the D ring at the belt loop and set the wallet and chain to the side. In the dead man's other pocket, Bates found a set of keys. The man's fingernails showed residue of a light brown substance. That would have to be cleaned.

He glanced around to ensure he was alone. Detective Sergeant Gormley was back in the main living room talking with Officer Tim Rayne. Rayne wore the blue shirt and tie of the NOPD, crescent-shaped badges on his chest.

Bates jerked his head, beckoning them outside.

He stood up and handed the wallet, chain, and keys to Gormley. "Get rid of this."

"You got it."

Gormley and Rayne followed Bates inside and up the stairs. All three policemen had to step carefully on the polished wood to avoid slipping in the cloth booties that covered their shoe soles.

At the top landing, they stopped and looked down at a man holding a Desert Eagle pistol who had taken multiple gunshots to the chest and at least one to the head.

"Notice the grouping," Bates said.

"Tight," Gormley said.

"Yep."

Bates looked both ways down the hall.

"Otis!" he shouted for Dupuis.

"Down here, sir," came the reply from the left.

Bates turned and saw the tussled sisal carpet and blood streaks on the wall. He had done five years in Homicide. While the other two cops waited behind him, he lowered himself to a crouch like a baseball catcher and shined his penlight along the floor molding, where fibers tended to collect. Five feet forward, he noticed something on the molding. He got to his feet and moved carefully down the hall. Gormley and Rayne waited. They had seen their boss at work and knew when to shut their mouths.

Bates bent down to examine what appeared to be dark animal fur, bunched up, atop a slight film of dust on the floor, which meant it was recent. It was too coarse to belong to a cat.

"Did anyone mention a family dog?"

"There wasn't one," Gormley said.

"Maybe she got one a week ago or something?" Rayne offered. "You know, because she was nervous after the kid thing happened."

"Yeah?" Bates asked, turning slightly. Rayne was young, had a lot to learn. "Then where is the damn dog?"

"Gunshots could have scared him off?"

Gormley took it as an opportunity to correct the younger officer. "No dog toys in the yard, dish in the kitchen, or kibble in the pantry."

"That's why he's the detective," Bates said. He jerked his chin at Gormley. "Bag that fur, Hound. We should check it out before the CSIs do."

Bates stood and entered the bedroom, his eyes drawn to the dead woman on the floor beside a chair in the room's center, a bloody hammer beside her.

What a way to go.

Beyond her on the balcony was a massive body with a gunshot wound to the face.

Sergeant Otis Dupuis stood to the side of the dead woman with his thumbs in his belt loops. Bates didn't like that and nearly told the patrolman to stand up straight. He was a COPE man. He had been Army, hadn't he? Airborne or something? He should look like a COPE man. Then Bates reconsidered. He needed Dupuis for this. No sense in pissing him off right now. Might even be good to give him a little positive reinforcement. Dupuis had promise and it was important to build a base of supporters.

"You keep the CSIs out of here, Swampy?" Bates asked. Dupuis was from Jean Lafitte, Jefferson Parish, down Highway 45. The hardscrabble town was built on fill dirt poured into the swamp, named for an infamous pirate. Thus the name.

"Yes sir, Lieutenant," Dupuis said, syllables softened by a lazy Cajun drawl.

"Nice work. Talk us through what we got here."

Dupuis hitched his pants, removed his thumbs from his belt loops, and pointed out the features of the scene. "We have two deceased males and one female. Windows are smashed on the door that was locked in place, glass outward on the balcony. Wood splintering in the corner. I think it will match the brass casing from the Draco AK pistol over there," he said, pointing at the weapon on the floor.

"Those fucking things," Bates said. "What else?"

"Foot scuff on the sill, outside, like somebody hopped it."

"And?"

"Room has been tossed. The way these books and papers are knocked all over the floor suggests the perps were looking for something. Contusions on the woman's hands and feet indicate torture, sadism, or an interrogation."

"And the rest of the house?"

"Upstairs rooms are tossed like this one. Downstairs doesn't show signs of a search, so either they knew what they were looking for was on the second floor or they did not have time to toss the lower level."

"Let's talk about the vics. Start with this guy," Bates said, pointing to a man in the corner whose face was a mess of bone, blood, and brain matter.

"Latin male, hard to tell how old he is. Face caught at least two rounds, maybe more. Tats visible on his arms and neck. Still holding the Draco."

Bates walked past the dead woman and pointed his penlight at the muscled Hispanic man on the balcony. His face was blotted with tattoos.

"And him?"

"Latin male, about thirty, maybe a little older," Dupuis continued, looking at his notepad. "There are bite marks on his right forearm, bicep, neck, and even the right side of his chest around the armpit."

"Dog. What did I tell you?" Bates said, looking back at Gormley and Rayne.

"You knew there was a dog?" Dupuis asked.

"Dog hair in the hall," Bates explained.

"Looks like the guy downstairs, just bigger," Rayne offered. "Same kind of shirt and tattoos."

"Same smell too," Gormley added.

"I was getting to that," Dupuis said.

"So, who killed him?" Bates asked.

Dupuis flipped his notebook closed and looked at the other officers.

"Same person who killed the dude on the landing and downstairs on the back porch?"

"Why kill downstairs man with a shovel and these three upstairs with a firearm?"

"He wanted to keep it quiet downstairs," Gormley offered.

"Why didn't the John Doe downstairs have a piece?"

"Excuse me, sir?" Dupuis said.

"Draco AK pistol on the floor over there probably belongs to the stiff who got chewed up by Cujo. This poor fucker without a face is still holding his. Dead asshole at the top of the stairs has the Desert Eagle cannon. But the guy outside is unarmed?"

"Maybe our perp killed him with the shovel and took his weapon, used it on the rest of the crew," Rayne said.

"Maybe. But who does something like that? Did you find any brass?"

"Just one casing from the Draco so far."

"Think this guy cleaned up after himself? Grabbed his brass?"

"A more thorough search will tell."

He lowered his eyes to the dead woman, her hair matted and tangled in a drying pool of blood. "What about her?"

"Multiple contusions to the feet, shins, knees, hands, and wrists," Dupuis said. "Will probably match the bloody hammer on the floor. Ligature marks on her limbs and the plastic ties indicate she was zip-tied to the chair at her ankles, arms behind her back."

"Until someone cut her out," Rayne said.

Bates turned to Gormley. "What did you find in the kitchen?"

"Open bottle of red. Some sort of roast in the oven. Very well done when I got here. The chrome faceplate was smeared with blood."

"So, she had invited someone for dinner."

"Yeah," Gormley said. "That someone killed the rest of these fucks."

Even though they were inside with the lights on, Bates examined the woman with his penlight. She was dressed up in a silky blouse and nice pants. She was also barefoot, which to Bates's way of thinking meant she was probably comfortable with whomever she had invited over. He let the light linger a little too long over the thin silk concealing her breasts.

The three subordinate men exchanged a look.

Bates shook his head. "Looks like Mrs. Staub had a date. He interrupted a robbery. Whoever he was, he cut the zip ties and tried to revive her. That's why she's out of the chair. He took at least one weapon from the man he killed on the back porch."

"And why did he leave? Why not call 9-1-1 and wait for the cops? Be a hero?" Dupuis asked.

"Maybe he knows how we treat heroes?"

"What?"

"Never mind. Maybe he spooked or maybe he's on probation, doesn't want to get caught up in some shit. Who the fuck knows."

"How you want to handle this?" Gormley asked.

Bates spotted the vintage Tudor dive watch on Leigh Ann's wrist. He remembered when it was on Connor's.

"Did anyone else come up here?"

"Just Detective Kile, but he took a quick glance and told me to secure it."

Bates knelt down, removed the watch, and slid it into his pocket, noting how loose it was on her wrist. It had been sized for a man.

"She must have a jewelry box in here. Take everything shiny."

"That the story, Lieutenant?" Gormley asked. "Robbery?"

"Connor Staub lived here. He OD'd, so we have a direct drug tie, but maybe he was also dealing to kids in the Garden. This could be a hit from a rival in the Ninth, looking for Connor's stash. They tied up poor old Mama Staub and asked where she hid her valuables. When she didn't deliver, they tortured her and killed her either on purpose or by accident. In the middle of all that there's an argument or somebody on the crew gets greedy. He turns on the others, takes the jewelry, splits it with the getaway driver. I'd buy that. We've seen shit like this before."

"That works. But what about her dinner date?" Gormley asked.

Bates thought for a moment.

"That guy could be a problem."

"What do you want us to do?"

"Find him. Then eliminate the problem."

CHAPTER TWENTY-NINE

WALKER TWISTED HIS shirtless torso so that Belle could better see the wound on his upper back.

"You are going to need stitches," she said.

"No stitches. Just pour some peroxide in, cover it with gauze, and tape it up. If we need to, you can squeeze in some superglue. I wouldn't have called you if I could reach it myself."

They were in Walker's van parked at a new location along the river, sitting on the bench seat in the back. Paladin watched them from the passenger chair.

Walker grunted as Belle poured the peroxide into the wound.

"Oh, don't be a baby."

"You are supposed to warn me first."

"Sorry," she said. "I've never picked glass out of someone's back before."

She was dressed in her uniform: Doc Martens, dark jeans, and black tank top.

"I think there might still be some shards in there," Walker said.

"I'll get them," she said, blowing a strand of raven-black hair away from her eyes.

Belle set the bottle down on the swing-out table and picked up the tweezers. She adjusted the headlamp Walker had given her and pulled the wound apart with her left fingers, probing for glass shards.

"Take your time," Walker said with a hint of sarcasm, focusing on the ticking of an old clock by the bookshelf.

"Fuck you, I'm doing my best."

"I'm just kidding, but really, try to get them all."

"You Jacques Cousteau?"

"What?"

"What's all that SCUBA stuff in the back for?"

"Breathing underwater."

"I know that. I'm just trying to keep your mind off the pain."

"That's thoughtful of you."

"Ah, there's one," she said, picking at it with the tweezers.

Walker winced.

"Stay still," she warned. "Almost got it."

"Damn it!"

"There, see? I got it."

She dropped the glass shard in the bowl with the others, poured a little more peroxide into the wound, covered it with gauze, and then taped it in place.

"Just like bandaging a large tat. Like that one," she said, touching the bone frog tattoo that covered Walker's right rib cage.

"I remember," Walker said, turning to face her.

"The artist did a good job. What is that thing anyway?"

"It's a Bone Frog."

"What's a Bone Frog?"

"Like a frog, but just it's bones."

"Why?"

"It was a military thing."

"I don't get it."

"It's a tribute to those we've lost."

"Like Connor's dad."

"Yeah, like Connor's dad."

"Well, that's depressing."

"Says the woman dressed in head-to-toe black."

"Fuck you. I thought you were going to take a shower, but it doesn't look like you have one. You smell worse than you did at the diner."

Walker smelled his armpit.

"I guess I do."

"And hey, you owe me for a couple tats I would have done tonight. The Quarter was full of drunks looking to make some bad decisions."

Walker laughed.

"I got you, don't worry," he assured her.

Walker had escaped out the back of the house and through the garden as the first squad cars arrived, bolting through a neighbor's yard and working his way to his van, which was parked well outside the initial cordon.

With the wound on his back unreachable, he called the only person he thought he could trust in New Orleans. He had told her about the evening's events as she pulled glass from his back.

"So, what now?" Belle asked.

"Now, I pay you for the tats you missed out on tonight along with a healthy tip for patching me up, and you go back to your life."

"The fuck I am. Chris, whoever killed Leigh Ann was looking for those journals," she said, pointing to the leather notebooks on the van's sink.

"We can't be sure."

"I thought you were in the CIA."

"I never said that."

"Yeah, well, you didn't have to."

She rubbed her eyes, smudging her thick mascara further. Despite the outside veneer, there was a frailty to her.

Walker turned his head and looked at the notebooks.

Maybe the best thing to do is burn those things and get out of town before anyone else dies.

"Earth to Chris," she said, reaching out, gently touching his chin and turning his head back to hers.

"Sorry," he said. "I just don't know what else I can do here."

She crossed her arms.

"I thought you said you owed Connor's dad a favor."

"I do."

"Well."

"Well, what?"

"Well, stop feeling sorry for everyone, especially yourself, and let's get to work."

"Belle, this isn't a game. This is serious business."

"You don't have to tell me that. I fucking know it."

"I just don't want to see you get hurt."

"I'm already hurt, Chris. And guess what? You come to town and next thing you know, Leigh Ann is dead. If these assholes who killed Connor are willing to kill his mom to find those journals, how long do you think it is before they come looking for me? Maybe they track me down to my grandmother's, do to me and her what they did to Leigh Ann."

Take a breath. Think this through.

"Chris, the only way to protect me is to decipher those journals and print Connor's story. Otherwise, I think whoever killed Leigh Ann is going to keep tying up loose ends."

His head ached as his internal philosopher began to stir.

Was the DA mixed up with corrupt cops? Could the information in Connor's journals keep her from becoming the next governor of Louisiana?

You lit the fuse. You knew the risks. You chose to act.

Next came the darker voice, the one shaped by years of reading Schopenhauer. The one whose internal voice was more whip than whisper. The old question of misguided actions from free will. Walker's dissertation had argued that Schopenhauer's will was not moral, not rational. It simply was. A blind, ceaseless force that drove all beings to act, to strive, to suffer. And if that was true, then what of guilt? What of responsibility?

If I am merely the puppet of a blind will, then am I not absolved?

But he didn't believe that. Not really. Not anymore.

You knew what you were doing when you came here. You knew what would follow. You didn't act blindly. You knew.

He exhaled sharply, frustration boiling over from the endless loop of philosophical self-condemnation.

Get it under control.

The guilt, the grief, the circular logic.

"Stop!" he barked.

Paladin's ears perked. Belle's mouth opened slightly.

Walker swallowed hard, embarrassed. "Sorry," he muttered. "Sometimes I overthink things. I need some fresh air."

He moved to the sliding door and pulled back on the handle.

"Put some clothes on. The mosquitos will eat you alive," she said, grabbing a denim shirt from a pile of dirty clothes and throwing it at him as he stepped from the van.

"Thanks," he said, slipping into the worn button-up.

"Now, build us a fire," she said. "We need to plan."

"You don't take no for an answer often, do you."

"I don't even know what that means. Camping means a campfire. And it means bourbon. You have any bourbon in this relic?"

"Yeah, in the galley."

"Okay, get a fire started."

Maybe she was right. Maybe the only way to end this was to finish

Connor's story and expose the corruption. If not, anyone who knew about the journals remained a threat.

"And stop feeling sorry for yourself," she added.

She was perceptive.

"*Heir*," Walker called. Paladin bound from his seat.

"Hey, while you are out there, grab my leather jacket from my car."

His eyes flicked to the Martin guitar in its ceiling rack. Belle caught him looking.

"I'll even let you play for me."

He pressed his lips together.

"I don't really play for anyone but Paladin."

"You are a strange character, Chris. Hot tip: when a girl asks you to play for her, play for her. Now, start a fire. I'm going to find that bottle."

———

Perched on a hunk of driftwood, Walker gazed at the faint glow of the city beyond the swamp, where the haze blurred the stars and the skyline shimmered like a mirage. Belle poured two fingers of whiskey into the only two cups he kept in the van.

With Paladin curled at her feet, Belle sipped the whiskey and stared through the leaves at the ink-black water.

"I've lived my whole life in this city," she said, her voice low over the crickets. "I've heard stories about when it was grand. You can still see it; the bones of something beautiful. People used to take pride in what they built. Now?" She shook her head. "Now it's partiers on Bourbon Street looking for their next high. Addicts in the streets. We call them homeless, but most of them are just lost in a fog. The city's rotting from the inside out. And the people in charge? They're selling it off piece by piece. That's the bullshit Connor was trying to expose," she added. "The rot."

She glanced at him over the rim of her cup, one leg bouncing on her knee. "You're into philosophy, right? I mean that's what the rolling library is about, isn't it?"

"I studied it for a while."

"Where?"

"NYU."

"You know," she continued softly, "people love to get philosophy quotes inked on their skin. I did a bad hand of cards across a guy's back once."

"What does that have to do with philosophy?"

"I asked him the same question. He said it was from Voltaire. 'Each player must accept the cards life deals him. But once they are in hand, he alone must decide how to play them.'"

"It's not really Voltaire," Walker said.

"I looked it up. Google says it's Voltaire."

"Google's wrong. It's from a book about Voltaire."

"Oh well, somebody has a 7-2 off-suit tattooed on their back for life and is telling people it's because of an eighteenth-century philosopher."

They both laughed.

"You're not cursed, Chris," she said. "You're just someone who's been dealt a brutal hand. But you're still here. Still choosing. That means something."

He looked away, but her words lingered. Voltaire's words. Not guilt. Not fate. Choice.

"Philosophy is about how we, well, human nature, doesn't change. Isn't that the gist of it?" Belle asked.

"Some people think so."

"What you are is what you were when," she said.

"Massey. Impressive," he said.

"What is?"

"That you know Massey."

"I went to college."

"Though he's a sociologist not a philosopher, but yeah, I'd say that's it."

"So, what were you doing 'when'?"

"Is this where we get to know each other?"

"This is what normal people do, Chris."

"Okay. My 'when' stage. I was with my mom in the van behind you. She wanted me to see the country."

"That's it?"

"Well, there's more."

"Spill it."

"She was my foster mom, and she was dying."

"What?"

"The doctors gave her a year to live. She never told me. She took me out of school, and we traveled the country in the van. She didn't want our last trip together to be overshadowed by her diagnosis."

"How old were you?"

"Eleven. We were on the road for two years before going back to Oregon. She made it until I was sixteen. The doctors couldn't believe she survived as long as she did. Then I was on my own."

"Chris, I am so sorry."

"I didn't know any different."

"And your dad?"

"I'm adopted, but the guy who would have been my dad split early on. I don't even remember him."

"So, you joined the military to find a family?"

"You are perceptive, aren't you?"

"It's not a big leap, Chris. Well, did you?"

"Did I what?"

"Did you find the family you were looking for?"

Walker thought of the SEAL Teams, the CIA, and the man who bridged them both: John Staub.

"I guess I did," he said, feeling the alcohol warm his system.

"Then why did you leave? I mean, you are *old*, but not that old." She smiled.

"Afghanistan. I lost Connor's dad and then we lost the country. Abandoned so many people who helped us fight a lost cause over all those years."

"So, it's about abandonment?"

"What?"

"For a philosopher you are not very observant. You have abandonment issues. So do I, so cheers."

She leaned forward and touched Walker's cup with hers.

"Every generation thinks the next one's doomed," she continued. "That they're soft. Lost. Hopeless. You think the world's gone to hell and that we're all just dancing on the ashes. But you've got it backward."

He raised an eyebrow. "Enlighten me."

She tilted her head, studying him by the firelight, petting Paladin, who had taken a liking to her.

"You got screwed," she said, slicing through him with surgical precision. "You were told to fight for a country, and instead of finishing it, they let you wallow in shitholes around the world while defense contractors got rich and you got hollowed out. And now you think the whole thing's beyond saving so you want to leave it behind."

Who is this girl?

She sipped her whiskey, eyes on the water. "But it's not. You don't see the ones who are still trying. People like Connor. People like me."

Paladin shifted beside her. She reached down and ran her fingers behind his ears.

"Connor was trying to make a difference," Walker said quietly. "Is that your point?"

"Yeah," she answered. "That's my point. He saw his dad fighting for a sinking society. Leigh Ann was doing that too, working in that ER like it was a battlefield hospital. Connor wanted to fight, but he was different. His weapon was a pen, not a gun. And he saw the enemy for what it was: corruption from within. The ODs made it personal. We can finish what he started. You can still make a difference."

"How old are you again?"

"I'm wise beyond my years," she said, taking another sip of bourbon.

She leaned toward the fire, elbows on her knees. Her eyes were sharp.

"We're not going to let these bastards get away with this, are we?" she asked.

"No."

"What's next?"

Walker looked at the thin young woman across the flames of the fire, a girl he was now responsible for protecting.

He bent forward and met her gaze.

"We finish Connor's story."

CHAPTER THIRTY

AN HOUR AFTER leaving the scene of Leigh Ann Staub's murder, Lieutenant Cornelius Bates leaned back in his Aeron office chair, cracked his knuckles, and cursed the city manager for the thousandth time. The air-conditioning in the NOPD headquarters on Royal Street had failed again. Typical. The building—a peach-colored Greek Revival wedged between antique shops and tourist traps—was beautiful, historic, and utterly dysfunctional. An uncharitable observer might consider it a metaphor for the city it served.

Bates, however, was not an uncharitable observer. He loved the location. A block from Bourbon Street, across from the famous Café du Monde that served beignets and lattes 24/7. A dedicated parking spot and the Carousel Bar at the Monteleone just steps away.

Tonight, the heat was a slow, sticky crawl. The window was open, the ceiling fan spun lazily, and Bates fanned himself with a manila folder, muttering about bureaucratic sabotage. In New Orleans, even air-conditioning was political currency.

A knock at the door.

"You ready for me?" came the female voice.

"Yeah," Bates said, rising to shake her hand.

Tilda Marchand, the department's public relations officer, stepped inside. Sharp-eyed, sharp-tongued, and always two steps ahead. She took the seat across from him, smoothing her crisp blouse.

"You can hear the music from here," she said, nodding toward the window. A trumpet wailed over the humid air, followed by the thump of a bass drum.

"Perks of the downtown office," Bates replied. "Be nicer if I could close that damn window. Maybe we should leak that to the press."

"Don't bother. They'll just cut the power."

He forced a smile, but his mind was elsewhere. Bourbon and a sixty-two-degree thermostat were calling.

"All right," he said. "What are you hearing?"

Tilda tapped her pen against a yellow legal pad. "That reporter, Evan Greer, he's been calling every ten minutes. Says he's got sources in the Garden District. Bloodbath, he says. Wants to run with a gang angle. He's pushing for home invasion. You know how they love that phrase. Sells papers."

Bates didn't respond. He reached for his glass of Diet Coke, condensation causing it to weep, took a slow sip, and let the silence stretch.

"Icy's office called too," Tilda added. "They're nervous. This kind of thing, in that neighborhood? Not good for her campaign."

Bates nodded slowly. Isaacson had built her platform on a cleanup narrative: crime down, streets safer, the city reborn. A massacre in the Garden District didn't fit the script. He could already see the headline: *BLOODBATH IN THE GARDEN.* Icy would lose her mind.

"Greer said he's going to print by two a.m.," Tilda said.

"Then we don't have time to clear this with anyone else."

"Your call, Lieutenant. I'll spin it however you want."

Bates rocked in his chair, eyes narrowing. In New Orleans, everything was connected: departments, favors, secrets.

Manus manum lavat.

One hand washes the other. Year one Latin class, ninth grade.

"Tell Greer it was a cartel hit," he said. "Mexicans. Probably came through Eagle Pass, Texas. Shift the blame. Make it sound like a turf war that spilled the banks: Sinaloa, Jalisco, Gulf. Let Homeland Security take the heat."

Tilda raised an eyebrow. "You sure you want to throw shade at DHS?"

"Not shade. Context. Four of the vics looked like cartel guys. They were in the home of a woman whose son died of an overdose a month ago, meaning there were drug ties. Don't give Greer the name, just hint at it. Let him think he's cracked something."

"Greer's already got an angle on the woman. Nurse at Tulane. Good rep. He wants to paint her as a martyr."

Bates hesitated. Based on the narrative he and his crew had set up, Staub was the mother of a junkie who brought this mess to her door. But martyrdom had its uses. If the public saw her as a victim, Icy could spin it as sympathy by association.

"Let him run with the martyr angle."

"And the brutality? That's the obvious question. He heard she was tortured. Somebody said a hammer was involved."

Bates swore inwardly. Someone had already leaked something to Greer. One of the CSIs? Detective Kile, pissed off that he'd been bounced from the case?

"Cartels were looking for something," he said. "Kid's drugs, maybe cash. The house was torn apart. Jewelry was gone so at least one perp got away with it."

A buzz in his pocket. Not the phone on his desk, the other one. The one that never left his side.

Tilda glanced at the desk. "That you?"

Bates stood. "Confidential informant. I take these outside. Don't want them hearing police chatter."

He buttoned his collar, tightened his tie, and stepped into the hallway. The building was quiet, the fluorescent lights humming. He took the stairs two at a time and pushed through the rooftop door.

The night hit him like a warm wet towel. From here, he could see the Mississippi, dark and slow beyond the rooftops. He dialed the missed call.

"It's me," he said.

"I call, you answer."

"I was in a meeting. About the thing."

Cuchillo's voice came through like a blade. "The *thing*," he seethed. "Four men gone. Do you have a leak? You got my men the address and now they are dead. You said it would just be the woman."

For all the clinging heat, Bates felt a chill. "There's no leak. We think she had a date, someone we didn't know about."

"Some random date didn't kill four of my men. This was a pro."

"We have not ruled anything out yet."

"Did one of my competitors hire someone to send me a message?"

"We don't have a complete picture. The press is hungry. For now, I'm feeding them Mexican food."

Cuchillo liked that, Bates could tell. The silver lining might just be some added heat to his competition over the border.

"We have a good thing, you and me. We have for a long time."

What was that he heard in the background? Bates wasn't sure whether it was the ocean outside one of Cuchillo's El Salvador homes or simply the static of a satellite bounce.

"What do we know?" the drug lord asked.

Bates felt better. What most people didn't understand was that those who ran complex cartels were thoroughly talented managers. Sometimes that meant checking emotion at the door and getting to the facts. Not dissimilar to police work.

"We have a witness report from a neighbor. Saw a white guy. Described him as 'homeless looking.' Longer hair and a beard. Thinks the dude was blond but wasn't sure. Had a dog with him. About all we got so far."

"Unbelievable! My two men who got away thought a SWAT team was in the house. Are you sure it was one man?"

"That's what it looks like."

"Regardless of who it is and who they work for, it's not good for my reputation. You need to find him."

"I will."

"I've got a boat coming upriver tomorrow," Cuchillo said. "More of my people. Use them to help."

Bates stiffened. He didn't need a war in New Orleans. "We'll find him."

"Good. When you do," Cuchillo added, "my men need to be the ones to kill him. And it needs to be visible. Ugly. It must send a message. Reputation is everything in this business."

The line went dead.

Bates stood there for a moment, the phone still pressed to his ear, the sweat on his brow cooling in the night breeze. Below, the city pulsed with life; drunks shouted, sirens wailed, streetcars clattered.

He pocketed the phone and turned back toward the stairwell.

Cuchillo had it right. Reputation was everything.

He was also relieved not to have been pressed about the way in which Cuchillo's men were dispatched. He did not want to be the one to tell the drug lord that one of his hitters was almost decapitated by a garden shovel.

CHAPTER THIRTY-ONE

THE CALL CAME at 2:41 a.m.

Jarrett Stanton's phone buzzed once on the nightstand. He stirred beneath the cotton sheets, the ceiling fan above him spinning shadows across the plaster. Alma lay beside him, one arm flung across the pillow, her breathing slow and even. Stanton reached for the phone, squinting without the aid of his glasses: *AUGUSTUS LLOYD*. He silenced the phone and slid out of bed like a man defusing a bomb, careful not to wake his wife.

The floor was cool under his bare feet as he padded down the hallway, past the girls' rooms. Veronica's door was cracked open, a faint glow from her night-light spilling into the hall. He descended the stairs and stepped into the kitchen, where the scent of jasmine from the courtyard still lingered in the air.

He called his boss back.

The SAC answered on the third ring. "Jarrett, sorry to wake you."

Stanton rubbed his eyes. "What's going on, sir?"

"Icy just called me. Direct. At home. She's pissed."

That woke Jarrett up. "What happened?"

"Local PD is reporting a federal crime. A cartel hit on a home in the Garden District. Tortured and killed a woman. A nurse from Tulane."

"Why is a cartel killing a woman in the Garden District?"

"Apparently her son was mixed up in the trade and OD'd a month ago. But there is something else that doesn't make sense."

"What?"

"Four of the hitters were killed on scene."

"By the cops?"

"No. They were dead when they got there, likely Mexican nationals according to NOPD. Media's already up and running. That reporter, Greer, pinged Icy's office for a comment. They're saying it's a drug war that crossed borders, maybe from Mexico to Texas to here. Sinaloa, I think."

Stanton blinked. "I haven't seen any data that suggests Mexican cartel activity in New Orleans."

"Doesn't matter. What matters is the narrative taking shape. Icy's office is in damage control mode. She's worried it's going to blow up, maybe go national, generate political interest on the Hill. If it's true, it's a juicy story. You can understand why she'd try to get ahead of this."

"Politics," Stanton said. "We're short of facts."

He shook his head briskly, rattling the cobwebs in faint disbelief. *Didn't truth matter anymore?*

"The nurse's son was Connor Staub. NOPD said he was an addict and a dealer, which is how he got mixed up with the cartels. We have any touch points on that case?"

Jarrett's mind was still catching up. As a numbers man, he had a good memory for qualitative details. He didn't recall anything about a Garden District kid involved with cartels. "Not familiar with it. NOPD must've handled it."

"Yeah. I figured. For what it's worth, Icy's already all over this. She wants us to find the link to the Mexicans, which is federal jurisdiction."

"Assuming there is one, you mean."

"Where there's smoke. No need to make this complicated."

Stanton leaned on the kitchen island. "I'm not making it complicated. Things get that way naturally."

The SAC exhaled sharply. "I probably don't need to say this out loud, but a story like this will probably get interest from the deputy director."

Stanton remained quiet.

"You don't want to turn lemonade into lemons," Augie went on. "Icy's critics are going to have a field day with a Garden murder and with the victim being an ER charge nurse at Tulane. It's bad. Find the link to the cartels and get me something I can use with Icy. See you at the office."

Stanton stared at the phone for a moment and then set it aside, flipping on the coffee maker, which he had set up to brew the night before. He propped open the tall French doors that went to the hardscape and let the cool night air inside.

The city was asleep in the dark; no trumpets, no grind of garbage trucks, no inebriated revelers hollering in the alleys. He listened to the hum of the refrigerator as the coffee dripped into the decanter.

He was so deep in thought that he didn't hear his wife approach. He gave a slight jump when she wrapped her arms around him.

"Did I surprise you?"

"Just thinking."

The coffee ready, Alama poured them two cups, yawning in her silky robe and fuzzy slippers.

"Everything all right?" she asked.

"I got a call from Augie Lloyd."

"Is it bad?"

He took a few seconds before replying. "Yes, just not sure how bad. Not yet."

"I'm sorry."

"I need to get to the office. I need more data."

CHAPTER THIRTY-TWO

IT WAS STILL dark when Jarrett Stanton walked down the front steps in a blue tropical wool suit.

It was already shaping up to be another scorcher, but Stanton was used to it. His father had been a law professor at the University of Georgia and later at Auburn, which meant the family was accustomed to the heat. And at his level, FBI agents wore suits. This one concealed the Glock 19 he carried in a black leather holster on his belt. Handcuffs were in a matching leather case at the small of his back, and a spare magazine rode on his left side. Like most FBI agents, he had never fired his weapon in the line of duty. He was prepared to do so if necessary, but he believed that if you worked the data, you could build cases and make arrests without having to go to the gun.

A tanker truck contracted by the city roared into view, spraying water through nozzles on its front bumper with the force of a fire hydrant. Stanton breathed through his mouth. The water was infused with lemony detergent, which helped freshen the streets throughout the Quarter, but early in the morning, it was like a big dose of the Lemon Pledge his mom used to spray all over his childhood home. Still, he noted the morning procedure with approval. Another sign that this city was cleaning up its act.

One disadvantage of the neighborhood was that he had to deal with street parking, specifically a reserved parallel spot in front of the house. The lemony foam was still draining into the gutters by the truck as he approached with a computer bag slung over his shoulder. When he was a few feet from the vehicle, he checked his watch. He expected to do a lot of driving around the city and knew it would be tough to hit his step goal when stuck behind the wheel.

He opened the rear liftgate of his Bureau-issued Chevy Tahoe and removed his jacket, laying it down in back so it wouldn't wrinkle. The truck's rear cargo area was dominated by a three-foot-high TruckVault that created a raised, false floor beneath the carpet.

Every FBI special agent across the country carried tactical gear, often stored in their vehicles to minimize response time to a crime scene. Stanton had more gear than most because of his SWAT qualification. The back of the TruckVault was secured by a cipher lock that opened to reveal two long storage drawers: one held his raid windbreaker and vest with ceramic plates; the other contained his M4 and four loaded magazines.

The FBI New Orleans Field Office was eight miles from the Quarter, a drive that took him twenty minutes. He drove in silence to make sure he could hear the encrypted radio traffic.

As the sun clawed its way over the eastern edge of Lake Pontchartrain, Stanton flicked the windshield wipers. The humidity near the lake was so thick that it condensed in droplets on his air-conditioned windshield. He slowed to turn off Downman Road as Lakefront Airport came into view.

The terminal was in the distance, a faded Art Deco gem with bones of marble and steel, its elegance dulled by time and the damp swamp air that drifted off the shallow lake. Once the crown jewel of New Orleans aviation, it now resembled an abandoned movie lot.

A few years ago, he had talked Alma into watching all four seasons of *The Untouchables*, the Eliot Ness TV series starring Robert Stack, in which the legendary Prohibition-era FBI agent took down Al Capone. To Stanton, the airport looked like a set from the show. The only spoilers were the corporate jets sitting idle on the apron, their white skins catching the golden morning light.

He passed the airport and turned toward the Field Office a few blocks away. The building loomed behind a perimeter of vertical iron fencing, each bar rising like a spike from a medieval palisade.

Stanton slowed as he approached the gate, eyeing the security cameras and the reinforced concrete barriers. The place didn't look like a federal office; it looked like a prison or a fortress. Maybe that was the point. He parked the SUV in the spot reserved with his name, worked his way through security, and navigated the hallways, saying his compulsory hellos before taking his position behind his desk. He had called ahead for Connor Staub's case file. It was sitting on his desk.

STAUB, CONNOR. Male. Age 21. Deceased. Cause: Overdose.

He read through the NOPD report. Even though it described the tragic death of a young man, the initial field report was as impersonal as a traffic ticket, with checked boxes, a date and time, and a signature. A few pages down, Stanton saw the final report, typed, but essentially saying the same thing. Connor Staub was found in a 1993 Volkswagen Jetta in a vacant lot in the Ninth. DOA. Overdose. Heroin in the trunk.

Stanton leaned back, the springs in his antique oak desk chair clicking. He was picturing the scene. A cop sees a car. Shines a light in the window. Sees a dead kid. Doesn't bother to call EMS but searches the trunk first.

That might make sense. The kid might have been blue, stiff as a board.

But what about the vehicle search? The officer just happens to pop open the trunk before another unit arrives? The report did not indicate that it was a canine unit. A dog could have smelled drugs in the trunk.

By the letter of the law, he didn't need a warrant. It was a homicide and NOPD was seizing the vehicle. They would search it once impounded, though they usually got a warrant to remove one argument from the defense attorney's playbook.

Stanton filed away the NOPD officer's name: Officer Tim Rayne. The report was countersigned by his supervisor, Officer Otis Dupuis.

And that was it, until the kid's mom was murdered along with four gangbangers in her Garden District home.

Stanton lifted the phone.

"Morning, J.J. You dig up anything on the Staub case?" he asked Agent Jennifer Jimenez.

"Yes, sir."

"Bring it over, would you?"

Stanton hung up and swiveled behind the capacious desk, neatly arranged with a clean blotter, a Bureau cup with a dozen black government-issued Skilcraft ballpoints, and a brass desk badge Alma had given him when he was promoted: "JARRETT STANTON, ASAC."

He checked his watch and shook his head. Less than a thousand steps. Not good. He swiveled to the display case behind him, a horizontal shadow box topped with glass, and with four metal feet, about the size of a coffee table.

Stanton stood up. The watch would buzz soon to tell him to do it anyway.

He looked through the glass at the sacred object, a hunk of parchment paper with faded ink, twenty-eight by twenty-four inches. In artful cursive script, the first paragraph read:

We the People of the United States, in Order to form a more perfect Union, establish Justice, insure domestic Tranquility, provide for the common defence, promote the general Welfare, and secure the Blessings of Liberty to ourselves and our Posterity, do ordain and establish this Constitution for the United States of America.

Stanton knew it by heart but liked to read it at the start of every working day.

After the original Constitution was signed in 1787, the official printers of the new Congress, John Dunlap and David Claypoole, created five hundred copies for review by the delegates. Less reported were the additional copies the printers sold to citizens of Philadelphia for the next ten years.

Jarrett's grandfather had purchased it at an estate sale in Buckhead, where it was assumed to be a handsome yet insignificant copy. It was later verified to be a surviving souvenir from around 1790. It wasn't worth as much as any of those first five hundred, but it was still worth as much as Stanton's house. If it wasn't safe inside these four walls, the document wasn't safe anywhere.

Two quick raps at the door broke his concentration. Stanton turned. "Come in."

"Good morning, sir," J.J. said, walking forward in dress pants and a tucked blouse, Glock and badge on her belt, folder in her hand.

"Close it, please."

J.J. had been in the district office for just over a year. She had transferred from Miami, where she had spent eight years as a special agent assigned to the criminal drug squad. An attentive, observant, athletic former Chicago prosecutor turned agent, she was objectively good-looking, with the dark features and black hair that streaked naturally brown in the summer. Stanton was not concerned with her beauty; he was interested in her intellect, dedication, and investigative instincts, which was why he had called Augie Lloyd on the way in and requested that J.J. be assigned to the Garden Murders and report directly to him.

She shut the door, and Stanton waved her to the chair in front of his desk.

"Okay," he said. "What did you find?"

"The Staub kid's OD was handled by the COPE squad at NOPD."

"Lieutenant Bates's unit."

"They do a lot of work in the Ninth. Not surprising they got the call."

"Do we know how the call came into dispatch?"

"It didn't come into dispatch," she answered. "Records indicate it was a routine patrol. I have inquiries into the NOPD vehicle pool to see if they match up. Also checking the standard routes that they drive over there."

Stanton nodded his approval. *That* was why he had chosen J.J. "What else?"

"Like you said when you called earlier, sir, no probable cause listed when the officer, Rayne, opened the trunk, but as it was a homicide he didn't need one."

That had been nagging at Stanton. The drugs found inside the trunk had informed the cause of death. An open-and-shut case. Too simple? Sometimes, cases actually were exactly what they seemed. But not always.

"The car is a '93 Jetta, base model," he said. "I looked it up and, at least according to what I could find, that model didn't come with an inside trunk release."

"Meaning Officer Rayne would have had to reach across the dead kid to grab the keys from the ignition or search his pockets for them to open it," she said, completing his thought.

"That seem strange to you?"

"Not necessarily. They were in the Ninth. High crime area with a dead kid. I don't think it would be all that unusual to search the car. Inventory exception allows him to do it since they were seizing the vehicle, though it is a little odd that he did it alone."

He tented his fingers before his face and rocked in his chair. "And the tox screen?"

She glanced at her papers. "A smorgasbord of opiates."

"Do you mean opiates, as in truly derived from the opium poppy plant? Or opioids, as in synthetics?"

"Both, according to the tox screen."

"Fentanyl?"

"No."

"What drugs exactly, then?"

"Like often happens, the OD was a result of a drug cocktail. There were elements of opiate-based heroin, but also synthetic opioids. When they intermingle, the lab techs can't attribute the lethal chemicals back to individual drugs."

"Any of that drug we've been hearing about from up north? Snowball?"

"There's no telltale chemical signature to Snowball. It reads as another synthetic opioid. I can say that there were no pills at the scene. Just the heroin bricks."

"So, he took pills somewhere else?"

"It happens. Or he had some leftover pills in his system and shot up with heroin before he crashed and burned."

"Track marks on his arms?"

"None noted in the ME report. But that's not all that unusual. He could have cooked the heroin and smoked it elsewhere. Or injected it in hard-to-detect locations."

"Can we check out the heroin stash to see how it might have been accessed?"

"We can, but I would need to get it from the NOPD evidence locker."

"Hold on that for now," Stanton said.

The normal way for him to handle this would have been to start a PI, a preliminary inquiry, to officially look over the NOPD's evidence records. But after studying the case files in his home office early that morning, his gut told him to poke around a little first, quietly. The politics on this thing were too explosive for someone to start shouting that there was an FBI investigation in the works.

"Tell me about the mother," he said to J.J.

She flipped a page vertically, folding it over the file folder. "Leigh Ann Staub. Forty-eight years old. Long career in nursing, some of it on naval bases in Virginia. For the past few years, she worked at the Tulane Medical Center ER as a charge nurse, a senior position."

"Record?"

"No criminal record."

"What about professionally?"

"She was a star, well respected at Tulane," J.J. said. "At least with what I've been able to uncover so far in interviews and personnel files."

"Finances?"

"She had a 401(k) worth about three hundred grand and thirty-five thousand or so in the bank."

"That's a good chunk but not enough to afford a house in the Garden. How'd she get it? Divorce?"

"This is where it gets a little murky."

"How so?"

"Her husband had a business that did well for a few years."

"What type of business?"

"That's the murky part. Final Options, LLC. He was the sole employee. I did some digging. Want to know where it led?"

"I do."

"Langley, Virginia."

"He was CIA?"

"A contractor. Former SEAL. Worked overseas, so it looks like he collected a few years of tax-free dough that helped purchase the house. He was killed in Afghanistan in 2021. Not much information other than that. Wife got a USAA life insurance policy. Enough to pay down the home loan but not enough to be able to stop working."

"Interesting. I may reach out to Langley. I worked with a guy there after the terror attack in the Quarter last year," he said, referring to ISIS-inspired former Army serviceman Shamsud-Din Bahar Jabbar, who in the early morning hours of New Year's Day 2025 rammed his Ford truck into partiers on Bourbon Street. He then unloaded on the crowd with a rifle and pistol before being shot by police. Jabbar killed fourteen people and wounded almost sixty others. He also had a detonator in his truck connected to two pipe bombs in coolers on Bourbon Street, bombs that did not detonate.

"How about media?"

J.J. set her phone on Stanton's desk and turned the screen to face him. "This is online and will be in the morning papers."

The headline read *Massacre in the Garden.*

"This the crime beat guy?"

"Evan Greer. The article says it was a cartel hit linked to the son. Greer is connecting his OD to the drug world. He doesn't come right out and say it, but he sure connects enough dots between what happened in the Garden and Connor Staub's OD."

Stanton took her phone and perused the article, thumbing all the way to the bottom before handing it back.

"What's NOPD saying about the scene in the Garden?"

"Officially? Or what I could dig up on my own?"

"Both."

"Their story tracks with the reporter: drug hit, four dead guys in the morgue, Hispanic, John Does, zero identifying information other than a lot of tattoos. The NOPD is waiting on the coroner's report, but that's just to stall. One had his head almost taken off with a shovel."

"A shovel?"

"Yeah."

"That's a new one."

"The others were shot, according to the admitting tech I talked to. Three Draco AKs and one Desert Eagle were found at the scene."

"AKs?"

"Well, AK-type pistols. They have become quite popular after their appearance in rap videos."

"Seriously?"

"Soulja Boy? He's not on your playlist, sir?"

"I prefer jazz."

"Are you going to meet with DEA on this?"

"I'll touch base with Mendez and link up with him as soon as he can cut away."

"Want me to tag along?"

"Maybe for a follow-up. So, what's the part that the NOPD *isn't* talking about?"

"It's more of a sense, really," she said.

"I tend to listen to those too. Paired with data, of course. What's yours?"

"That the NOPD is moving fast with the cartel angle. The CSIs are already done at the house. Evidence is bagged and tagged."

"All of that in less than twelve hours, you mean."

"Feels a little rushed. Then again, nobody wants flashing lights in the Garden."

"The DA is going to want to put a bow on this quick," Stanton said, tapping his fingers on his desk and thinking about Isaacson's announcement at the gala, the run for governor, the spotless record. The cartel message was just what she needed. *Not on my watch*, she could say. *This is a failure of the federal government.*

"J.J., you remember in the last staff meeting, when the rook on complaint duty mentioned a walk-in at the federal building who wanted to talk to someone at DEA but left?"

She smiled and flipped another page over. "I certainly do. In fact, I was about to mention that. I interviewed the U.S. marshal who was at the desk that day. He said the walk-in was blond, bearded, fit. Described him as a tough guy. I verified the description with the lobby cams, but there's not a good shot of his face. He was in a ball cap, eyes down the whole time, almost like he didn't want to be seen."

"Anything we can run through facial recognition?"

"No, but we have the next best thing."

"Tell me."

"The marshal said he felt weird about the encounter, so he followed our mystery man out and saw him drive off in a beat-up VW camper van, eighties era, faded blue with a white roof. It caught his attention because it was raised on its tires, like a four-by-four."

"Plate?"

"It was too far-off for him to get a plate, but he thinks the colors were Oregon."

"So, a few days before we see a cartel battle play out in the Garden, a guy shows up, asks to talk to the DEA, and takes off because he got nervous. Pretty thin."

"Agreed, sir."

"Let's look into it anyway. At least we can cross him off the list."

"Do you want me to have NOPD put out a BOLO?" she asked, using the term for "be on the lookout for."

"Who's working this homicide? Kile from Sixth?"

"He should be, but because this looks gang-related it's going to the COPE unit."

"Bates. Direct report to the superintendent."

"That's right, sir."

"And let me guess, before you look, the case has been assigned to . . ."

J.J.'s cheeks flushed as she flipped through her hastily assembled file.

"The officer who processed the original Connor Staub crime scene," he continued. "Officer Tim Rayne."

She sighed. "Yes. Rayne. I should've caught that."

"You've been on this for two hours."

"You're seeing a potential conflict of interest."

"Why assign it to the same guy?"

"Because he's already familiar with the case?"

"Maybe," Stanton said, tapping his fingers again.

"You're not going to want to run the search for van-man through NOPD, are you?"

"No," Stanton said. "Let's take a drive."

"What are you thinking?"

"Let's talk to some of these neighbors in the Garden and walk the crime scene. I'd like to drop by the morgue and talk with that marshal over at the fed building. If the NOPD is going to make this federal to deflect blame from the DA, we best have our ducks in a row."

"If we do all that, we're going to kick up a lot of dust. NOPD's going to know we're looking into this. It's going to make a lot of people uncomfortable."

Stanton stood and put on his jacket.

"The day you get comfortable in this job is the day you should hang it up. Plus," he looked at his watch, "I need to get my steps in."

CHAPTER THIRTY-THREE

DEREK MATHESON DIDN'T like waiting. But if he had to, there were worse places than the leather-wrapped cabin of his Bombardier Challenger 3500.

The midsize business jet was four years old. It had a few creases in the upholstery and scuffs on the trim that went with the miles it had flown before and after its acquisition by Walt Kimbel from a distressed leasing firm.

He finished off the last of his kombucha. No coffee. No alcohol. He didn't touch drugs of any kind. *Drugs will kill you,* he liked to say with a smile, a line that always landed well coming from the founder of a cutting-edge pharmaceutical empire.

He checked his Breitling, cuff link flashing with the Genyra logo. Kimbel was late. Not like him. The longer the delay, the more Matheson's mind wandered to the headlines, the fallout, the implications. The murder in the Garden District had already made the front page of *The Times-Picayune.* The narrative was forming. And if they didn't control it, someone else would.

The cabin door hissed open, and a gust of Lake Pontchartrain's humid air rolled in. Kimbel stepped aboard, tie loosened, bag in hand. He stuck his head into the cockpit to tell the pilots they could take off, then dropped into the seat opposite his boss.

The engines spooled up, and the jet began its slow taxi. Matheson leaned across the aisle.

"So?"

Kimbel exhaled. "It's not good."

"Why?"

"Vargas is furious."

"At us?"

"No. At our friends."

Matheson relaxed slightly. "The NOPD?"

Kimbel nodded. "They botched it. Or someone interfered."

Matheson gestured to the phone on the tray table. "I read the article. Sounds like a drug war."

"That's the line."

"Is it true?"

"Could be. Either way, it's the perfect note for Icy. She'll have both senators screaming for action. Divert blame to the administration and it plays right into her law-and-order platform. She can claim that she cleaned things up locally and that it was the feds who screwed up; promote her and she'll clean up the state the way she cleaned up New Orleans."

Matheson faced the window as the jet bumped toward the runway. He thought of Icy on the dais at the Four Seasons, announcing her run for governor. She had looked unstoppable. Now she was pulling strings behind the scenes, shaping narratives, bending institutions to her will.

Goddamn, she was good.

He should have married her.

"She's going to win this thing," Matheson said.

"I've been thinking the same."

"We need to get on the record. Donate to her campaign. Possible?"

"Can we afford not to?"

Matheson shook his head. That's why he had Kimbel. He had a good team paving the way for him these days, making his job much easier than it used to be. His CFO was already in New York prepping the shareholders. Carolyn Boyle was spinning the press. The machine was humming.

"How much?" he asked Kimbel.

"Five million."

Matheson raised an eyebrow.

"Off balance sheet. One of the partnerships. Vargas will fund it as a pass-through. He's vested in us. We're vested in Icy. It's a smart investment for him. And he's a shrewd businessman."

How much deeper can we go with Cuchillo?

"And the FEC? Won't the feds be looking into campaign contributions? Isn't that a problem?"

"The Federal Election Commission doesn't have jurisdiction over a governor's race. State-level. Louisiana Board of Ethics handles it. And they refer criminal cases to the local DA."

"Icy."

"Exactly."

"But the attorney general, her opponent, could override that. He'd hit her hard with the conflict of interest."

"Which is why we're going to contribute legally. She's set up a 527 political action committee. T-JAW."

"T-JAW?"

Kimbel grinned. "Truth, Justice, and the American Way. No campaign limits on a Super PAC, provided they operate independently."

"I thought Super PAC contributions were disclosed to the FEC?"

"They are, but we won't give directly. We create a 501(c)(4) group to run educational issue ads."

"And since they do not have to disclose their donors, they make the contribution to T-JAW."

"Exactly; for general welfare and educational purposes. And sir, there are some things best left to me."

The jet braked at the hold-short. Kimbel tightened his seat belt.

"Get some rest, sir. We want you fresh in New York."

The engines roared, the wheels thumped, and the jet lifted into the sky.

As they climbed, Matheson looked down at the lake, the city, and the low-slung brick buildings of the FBI's New Orleans Field Office. The place looked like a prison: intimidating fences, squat architecture, black SUVs crawling in and out. One of them exited the gate as he watched.

Get your head straight.

He forced his thoughts to the investor meeting. Today was the day he would unveil his forecasts for Xylaxyn, a revolutionary anti-inflammatory and synthetic painkiller for cancer patients. Among its other benefits, it eliminated the need for fentanyl, the legitimate opioid for stage four cancer sufferers that had become politically radioactive thanks to Chinese knockoffs and overdose deaths.

Matheson's line was ready, drafted by Carolyn, just waiting for the press release: *Not only are we enhancing lives—we're eliminating the need for fentanyl. My competitors like to say it's a controlled substance, but is it, when we've lost so much control?*

That sound bite would echo across CNBC, ripple through trade journals, and land like a sledgehammer on his competitors. Kimbel would make the calls. Senators would listen. The pressure would mount. Fentanyl would become a drug of the past. And Xylaxyn, his drug, would be the only alternative.

Ten years on the patent. Ten years of dominance. He wouldn't just be a multibillionaire. He'd be untouchable.

He glanced around the Bombardier's cabin, at the worn leather and scratched chrome.

Fake it till you make it.

The old mantra flickered in his mind like a neon sign. He'd faked it once upon a time. Everyone had. But then he met Fulgencio Vargas—*Cuchillo*—and everything changed. Vargas had made him an offer he was not strong enough to refuse. Vargas had offered him the world.

As much as he knew he needed to stay focused on Xylaxyn, his mind was drawn back to the Garden District.

"Is the story true?" he asked. "Was it a rival cartel hit?"

Kimbel hesitated, then leaned closer. "You really want to know?"

Matheson raised an eyebrow.

"Word is that some guy with a dog showed up and took out most of the crew like a pro. Bates said they're keeping it quiet."

"A professional?"

"Current theory is he's a *sicario*. Maybe hired by a rival. No one knows who. But it's not in the reports."

"Come on. Even I don't buy that."

"It won't matter for much longer."

"Why?"

"Because our friends are going to find him before he can talk."

"Bates?"

"Could be Bates. Could be Cuchillo's people. Could be both. Regardless, he's not going to be around much longer."

"Meaning the official story sticks and Icy can spin it right into the governor's mansion."

"Exactly. One guy and a dog against Bates's COPE unit and Cuchillo's assassins? Shit, sir. I wouldn't want to be him."

Matheson leaned back in his seat and closed his eyes.

Neither would I.

CHAPTER THIRTY-FOUR

WALKER DOWNSHIFTED TO second gear to slow Belle's old BMW, killed the headlights, then stepped on the clutch, allowing the car to coast slowly to a stop along the curb.

"Nice," Belle said. "They teach you the silent approach in the CIA?"

He glanced at her in the passenger seat, her face illuminated by the glow of Google Maps.

You sure this is a good idea? You thinking straight?

He checked the rearview. Clear.

Ahead, a few streetlights, leaning on crumbled foundations, still tilted in the direction Katrina's floodwaters had forced them twenty years earlier. Walker had once read about an old mining town in the California Sierra foothills that had been forcibly abandoned to make way for the Folsom Dam. Later, during a drought, the reservoir got so low that the old buildings were visible again. In the pitch black of 1 a.m., this section of the Ninth looked like that; a city of ghosts.

"Learn what in the CIA?" he asked her.

They had spent the past four days poring over Connor's journals in the van. When she went to work at the tattoo shop, he remained behind, clacking on the old typewriter, connecting dots and thinking through the plan. Then, in darkness he surveilled their target.

"Rolling to a stop in the shadows, Jason Bourne. What did you think I meant?"

"I knew what you meant. Let me see the SAT photo."

She handed him the phone. He pinched in on the satellite overlay.

"Is that where you set up the past few nights?" she asked.

"Yeah. It really wasn't enough time to establish patterns."

"And that's where you'll be on overwatch?"

"Overwatch? Where'd you hear that one?"

"*Call of Duty: Modern Warfare Three.* Like a decade ago."

"No. I won't be able to get to you in time if something happens. I'll be closer."

"I told you, Chris. Kids score here all the time."

She reached to release her seat belt.

"No. Not yet," he said. "I want to make sure nothing's changed."

"Get some G-2?" she asked, smiling.

"Yeah. G-2, intel. *Call of Duty*? Get in the driver's seat. I'll be right back."

The interior light on the old car had failed years ago, so Walker didn't need to worry about that. The door, however, creaked like a rusted ship hatch when he opened it, making him wince.

"Sorry," she said from inside the car.

He pulled up the collar on an old surplus Army jacket and kept to the shadows, walking past graffiti-marred homes with plywood-covered windows, to an abandoned store that had been his hide site for the past few nights. He checked out the interior through the broken windows to be sure no one was inside, noting the empty overturned racks were positioned just as they had been twenty-four hours earlier. A few faded posters for liquor sagged behind the register.

At the edge of the building, he paused to observe the street. The only cars were abandoned, missing wheels and any semi-valuable parts. They were now just hunks of rusted metal with rotting seats, some providing shelter for the homeless or giving addicts a place to shoot up.

He found the overstuffed dumpster by the shop. It had been there so long that it was recognizable from the satellite image. Walker dug the toe of his boot onto a hinge and hoisted himself up. He jumped and caught the edge of the roof, pulled to his elbows, swung a leg up for leverage, and rolled over the lip.

Knowing that he might present a silhouette, he stayed low, moving past a long-dead AC unit, vent pipes, and a giant hole with jagged wood splinters. When he'd asked Belle about the hole after his first night of surveillance, he learned that a lot of people in New Orleans kept axes in their attics. When the storm waters surged, those who had heeded that advice had chopped holes in their roofs and waited for help, help that often took days to arrive.

He stopped at the far corner and swiveled his ball cap, so the visor faced backward, and dug a monocular night vision optic from his jacket pocket. He turned it on and brought it to his eye.

Sure enough, as with the past three nights, the same two military-aged males were at the front of the house, one in a yard chair out front, another on the porch.

Stop thinking of them as military-aged males.

That's exactly how you need to think of them.

The man in the chair was black, shirtless. Even from here, Walker could see that he was jacked. His chest and shoulders were wide and chiseled, a bandana tied around his head. He rested his feet on a full-sized cooler while he screwed around with his phone. His friend on the porch looked younger, skinnier, and wore a flat-brim ball cap on his head.

No lights escaped the house. Like most of the others in the area, it was still without power.

Walker shifted his focus back to the street as a car approached.

A modern Jeep Wrangler with Arkansas plates pulled to a stop in front of the house, a Razorback mascot sticker on the back window.

The guy by the cooler gestured and the Jeep's headlights blinked out. A blond male, also military-aged, in shorts and a T-shirt, stepped out of the car, thick neck, clean-shaven. Walker could see there was a passenger in the vehicle.

The transaction went smoothly. Razorback walked up to Muscles, handed over some cash. It was hard to see what, if anything, was exchanged. Then Razorback returned to the Jeep and drove off. Walker had seen similar transactions over the previous nights.

Connor's journal indicated that this was a known trap house. Though there were still blanks without the cipher key, they had figured out that the pills had colorful names: Yellow Jackets, Queenies, Pez, and Snowball. Connor was focused on Snowball. There was something different about it.

No sign of cops. The two guys out front were the same two that he had seen in his earlier observations. The op was a go.

After climbing down, he returned to Belle's BMW, opened the passenger-side door carefully, trying to avoid the squeak, and slid into his seat.

"You happy?" Belle asked.

"Not happy."

"Why?"

He glared at her. "Just nervous."

"Oh, come on. Girls buy out here too. They're often the ones who show up with drugs at the pill parties. Dealers are in it for money. They want repeat customers. And besides, I totally look like a junkie."

Belle had played up her makeup, giving herself a sickly pallor. From his research on the opioid epidemic, he knew that the drug created an immediate physiological dependence. That was what drove the business. For increased highs, pills were cut with fentanyl. One or two grains too many and the powerful painkiller designed for cancer patients would stop the heart. Addicts continued to service their physiological cravings, and as the government had cracked down on fentanyl, a new drug had appeared on the scene. It was called Snowball.

"We talked about this," Belle said, reading the doubt in his eyes. "Even though you look homeless, you move like a cop. Like you're on a mission or something. They'd peg you for a narc in a heartbeat. You don't know the language. I do, trust me. They won't sell to you. I can handle this."

During his surveillance, Walker had noted a derelict vehicle in the front yard of a vacant house from where he could observe Belle's buy and act as a quick reaction force if necessary.

"I don't like it."

"They want the money, Chris. Come on, let's do this. Hand it over. All we need to do here is confirm that they sell Snowball. The only way to do that is to buy some. Let's go."

Walker handed her eight hundred bucks pulled from the stash in the van.

"Give me five minutes to get in position," he said. "Then drive up, make the buy, and get out. Anything looks off, trust your gut, don't push it."

Walker turned around and slid a wool military surplus blanket from the back seat, revealing his Bravo Company AR and Ops-Core helmet.

"Jesus, Chris, we are not here to kill everyone."

"Sometimes your adversary has other ideas. I'll be close if you need me. Make the buy. Don't loiter. Then meet me back here when it's done."

Walker stepped from the car and slid the sling over his head. He then attached his monocular NOD to the helmet, again wishing he had liberated a bino or quad NOD from the Agency instead of the monocular, and adjusted the helmet and optic on his head. He tested his IR laser. It was working. He then removed the helmet, tucked it under his arm, and wrapped the wool blanket around his shoulders to obscure the helmet and weapon.

"What do you think?"

"This tactical homeless look is surprisingly similar to your normal everyday homeless look."

"Perfect. Remember. The buys I've seen go down this week are quick and smooth; cash in exchange for what I think is a small Ziploc bag of pills or powder."

"Stop worrying. I've got this."

"Give me five mikes."

"Five mikes?"

"Five minutes."

"Roger, good buddy," she said, in an attempt to take the edge off.

"Dial me in."

He wore a wired earbud that was plugged into the flip phone in his pocket. Belle dialed the number and established the comm link. She zipped her phone into the breast pocket of her leather jacket and adjusted a Bluetooth earpiece.

"Say something," he said.

"Uh, read you loud and clear?"

"Can you hear me?"

"Yes."

"Okay. Stick to the plan."

Walker shut the door and moved off into the night.

CHAPTER THIRTY-FIVE

WITH HIS JACKET collar turned up, helmet in his armpit, and suppressed rifle pulled tight to his body beneath the blanket, he walked over the cracked, dilapidated sidewalk toward the eighties-era Cadillac Sedan DeVille propped on cinder blocks in the driveway of an empty house. Good concealment. The passenger-side door was missing so Walker slid into the seat without excess movement. From here it was seventy yards to the dealer's house. He pulled the blanket from his shoulders and adjusted the helmet and NOD on his head. He then deliberately loosened his sling and set the rifle's handguard on the dashboard with the suppressor protruding just over the hood. The DeVille was missing its front window, so Walker had an unobscured line of sight to his target.

It's not a target.

Yes, it is.

"I'm in position," he whispered into the built-in mic of his earbuds. "Go off Bluetooth and switch to speakerphone."

"*Okay,*" she responded. "*Going off Bluetooth.*"

Walker heard rustling as she unzipped her pocket and switched her phone to speaker so the earbud wouldn't draw attention. He heard the zipper close.

"*How's this?*" she asked.

"I got you. Remember, I won't talk but I'll be able to hear the exchange."

"*I know. Okay, I'm going in.*"

"I've got you, Belle."

"*Quit worrying.*"

He could hear the BMW's engine whine as Belle fired it up and made her approach. Her headlights illuminated the green glow of his night vison monocle. A moment later the car drove into view and pulled to the curb in front of the trap house.

He watched her exit the vehicle and heard her via comms.

"Hey, can I come up?" she asked.

He couldn't hear the reply, but watched the broad-shouldered dealer wave her in. She stopped a few feet in front of the cooler. Walker scanned the porch. The young man with the flat-brim hat said something.

"The Garden," Belle replied. They'd rehearsed that she was a failure-to-launch, entitled Tulane dropout who lived with her parents in the Garden District, just in case she was questioned, though they hadn't thought it would really come up.

The responding tone of voice suggested the dealer was telling Belle to get lost. The flick of his wrist suggested the same thing. Interesting. Why didn't they want her money?

Don't push it, Belle, get out of there.

"I need it," she said. *"Dying, man. Come on. I'm looking for Snowball."*

Again, the answer was no, the body language telling her she was not welcome.

Walker tensed and adjusted his grip on the rifle.

"Beat it, bitch," Cooler said.

It looked like Flat Brim was typing something into his phone.

What is going on?

She pulled out her roll of cash.

"Six hundred," she said.

The man with the flat brim was coming down the porch steps. He wore high-top sneakers, a New Orleans Pelicans T-shirt, and shorts. He was still on his phone.

Come on, Belle, time to go.

Flat Brim circled around Belle, focused on his device.

Shit.

Now, with his back facing the street, he could see that Flat Brim had a shiny pistol jammed in his shorts. His hands were occupied with the phone.

"My girlfriend told me I could get Snowball here," Belle said.

"Get outta here, girl," Cooler said, his voice taking on a brasher tone.

Take his advice, Belle. Get out.

"Nah, hold tight, pretty girl," Flat Brim said. *"Why you so interested in Snowball?"*

Damn you, Belle.

Walker pressed the pressure pad on the rail of his rifle, and an IR beam visible only to him cut through the night. He centered it on Flat Brim's upper back.

"*Fine, fuck you. I'll get it somewhere else,*" Belle said, stuffing the cash back in her jacket pocket and turning to go.

Flat Brim grabbed her arm.

"*Don't rush off,*" he said. "*Maybe we can hook you up. Then you hook us up.*"

Walker flipped the selector from SAFE to FIRE and brought his finger to the trigger.

As he started to exert pressure, his NOD lit up from the headlights of a fast-approaching vehicle that screeched to a halt behind Belle's BMW, blocking Walker's view.

He studied it through his night vision. New-model Dodge Charger. Black. The silhouette of a male head in the window. He was wearing a hat and appeared to have short hair. The car had thick tires over plain wheels.

Cops?

Walker tried to look through the Charger's windows, but the tint prevented it.

If these were cops, then she would not get into trouble if she kept her mouth shut. She had no drugs on her, just money. She wasn't in possession. Maybe this was a good thing. It would settle matters peacefully.

The man in the undercover police car stepped out, his interior light off. He was tall and thick, dressed in civilian clothes but wearing a black plate carrier with a Velcro badge. Walker could see there was someone else in the car. A partner?

The dealer by the cooler stood up for the first time. Flat Brim made no attempt to hide his gun.

What the fuck is going on here?

He listened to the interchange through Belle's phone.

"*She's looking for Snowball. Says she's from the Garden.*"

"*The Garden, huh? Where?*"

"*Why the fuck should I tell you, Sasquatch?*"

"*Because, honey, I'm the law.*"

Belle went quiet.

"*Let's figure this out inside,*" the cop said. He touched something on his belt.

Must have been a radio, Walker thought, because the other man in the police vehicle got out and approached. He was thinner than his partner but wore the same jeans, shirt, hat, and gun belt along with a plate carrier clearly identifying him as NOPD.

"Let go of me," Walker heard Belle shout over comms.

Cops. Dealers. Shit.

"Inside," the cop ordered, marching her up the steps and into the house.

"What the fuck is this!" Walker heard a man yell in his earpiece. The line went dead.

They had found her phone.

Belle screamed.

Walker sprang from the vehicle, weapon up, thumb of his left hand on the IR pressure pad. He moved into the street toward his target.

He would have entered the gate while Cooler was still looking back at the house had it not been for the headlights of a passing car that swerved around the corner. The Honda Accord accelerated away, undoubtedly freaked out by the sight of a man with a rifle in mid-stride closing in on the house they were probably about to approach for a drug buy.

Damn it!

The man by the cooler stood up. He reached behind his back.

Walker depressed the pressure pad. An IR laser appeared on Cooler's chest.

Cooler's hand holding a Glock 17 was rising when four of Walker's bullets tore through his chest. His body contorted around the wounds, and he fell forward into the weeds. Walker put another round in his head as he passed by.

Had Flat Brim and the cops heard the gunfire? Even though suppressed, his shots were not completely silent. Whether or not they heard would depend on how loud things were inside the house.

He climbed the stairs, crossed the rotting porch, and put his hand on the knob. He doubted it was locked with a sentry out front.

He paused for a moment. Were they waiting for him inside, weapons trained on the door? Maybe.

He thought he heard Belle's voice telling someone to "fuck off" coming from deeper inside the house. She was probably loud enough to have kept them from hearing the suppressed shots.

There was no time for a safer, deliberate combat clearance. This was hostage rescue and required a more dynamic approach. Walker turned the knob and entered, breaking left to clear the corner and then sweeping back to the right as he continued out of the doorway's fatal funnel. The room contained an overturned card table and a couch with springs exposed. Insulation drooped through gaping holes in the drywall.

As he moved down the wall of what was once a living room, he tripped over something at his feet. He regained his balance, confirmed the room was clear, and then looked down at what he thought was a pile of old blankets to find that he had stumbled over a skinny naked black woman. Now awake, she looked up at him, her eyes wide with annoyance and confusion.

"Just a bad dream," Walker whispered, pushing across the room to a threshold hung with strings of Mardi Gras beads.

He could hear the woman muttering behind him.

The house was dark, which still gave him the advantage.

He pushed through the beads, this time going right.

He was in a kitchen filled with trash, smelling of rotting food, decay, and mold. The counter was cluttered with cardboard boxes filled with plastic bags. He stepped closer. The Ziplocs contained pills and small sealed pouches that he didn't recognize. The pouches were about the size of ketchup packets at a McDonald's.

A stairway was to his left. He heard male voices and stepped past the still-swaying Mardi Gras beads.

I'm coming, Belle.

The blow landed on the back of his helmet, which took the brunt of the hit. Walker staggered forward and spun to see the naked woman he had left behind holding a wooden Louisville Slugger. Her scream was almost as painful as her first hit.

As she wound up to deliver another home run, Walker rotated and drove his rifle into her chest, reset, and slammed it into her neck. She paused the bat mid-swing, like she was checking up on an outside ball, allowing Walker to pivot his feet and send her careening through a flimsy plywood-covered window with a spinning back kick.

With that scream, they know I am here.

He heard footsteps on the stairs. A second later Flat Brim appeared, stainless Beretta 92FS in his right hand.

"Patricia, shut the fuck up, girl!" he shouted.

Walker's first three rounds ripped through the Pelicans logo on Flat Brim's chest. A fourth found his forehead, knocking the hat free. As gravity took hold of his body, he tumbled down the narrow staircase, coming to rest in a heap at its base.

"NOPD!"

The shout came from the top of the stairs. It was followed by the beam of a flashlight.

"Drop your weapon and show me your hands!" Same voice. Commanding, with a tinge of arrogance like it came from someone whose orders were usually obeyed.

"Coming up. Don't shoot," Walker said.

"Hands!"

Walker stepped over the dead body at the base of the stairs, pressing the IR pressure pad twice in quick succession, which engaged the IR laser's constant mode so that it stayed on without the pressure of his left hand. He lifted his left hand high above his shoulder so it would be the first thing someone at the top of the stairs would see. He dropped the rifle to his right side, angled up, on fire, finger on the trigger.

Through his monocular NOD he saw the beam of light coming from the top of the stairs. He took a step, then another.

"Don't shoot," he said again, trying to make his voice as feeble and weak as he could.

He took another step and saw the top of a ball cap, the same one worn by the two men who had exited the Charger. With his weapon still below the officer's line of sight, the IR laser landed on the man's forehead just below the brim of his NOPD hat. Walker pressed his trigger to the rear.

The single shot broke the sound barrier and caught the officer in the forehead, the bullet splitting the hemispheres of his brain in two down the medial longitudinal fissure.

He was dead before his body collapsed at the top of the stairs.

Walker performed a tac reload, ejecting the depleted magazine and exchanging it with the full magazine in the back pocket of his jeans. He then cautiously worked his way up the staircase. It was a small house. There were not many places Belle could be.

He stepped over the dead man.

You just killed a cop.

You killed an enemy combatant.

The short hallway was clear.

Walker slipped into the first room on his left.

It had once been a bathroom. A sink was on the floor next to a hole where the toilet should be. He glanced into a filthy bathtub as he passed and saw that a body was curled up in it. The smell conjured images of the dead.

Keep pushing.

The bathroom had a second door that was partially closed. He stepped to the side to get an angle on the room, a bedroom with peeling wallpaper. He could hear whimpering. Female. It didn't sound like Belle. He decided to slow his clearance, the thought being that Belle was now the cop's bargaining chip. *He won't kill her,* Walker hoped. Hope is not a solid course of action. He combat-cleared from the bathroom and discovered the source of the crying: another woman, white, short hair, skinny, sitting on the floor, her face between her knees.

He moved swiftly and silently across the room to a door that led back to the short hallway. A closed door was directly across the hall. Last door on this level. A master bedroom?

He moved into the hallway and listened. He thought he heard mumbling and the scuffling of feet.

Go through the door?

Odds are the cop has his weapon trained on it.

Has he called for backup?

Other corrupt cops?

He doesn't need corrupt cops. He can just call for backup saying they interrupted a deal gone bad.

Maybe he should just leave? *No way, then he kills her. They know she pieced enough together to come here asking for Snowball. They found her phone. She's a liability. No way he lets her live.*

You need to interrogate this guy.

No, you need to save Belle.

Walker looked down the hall. The same rot and decay that infected the lower level was just as prevalent upstairs, including the holes in the walls spilling insulation.

He turned to his left and studied the drywall.

The first hole did not penetrate through to the room beyond.

Walker kept moving.

The second hole was smaller. Made by a hammer? A fist?

He reached out and, as quietly as he could, pulled the remaining insulation toward him.

Slowly.

He tugged a little more and heard feet shuffling beyond the wall.

The hole was small, but it was a through-and-through, and in the green phosphor of his Harris monocular, he saw the police officer. He had Belle's neck in the crook of his left arm, pulled tight to his chest. She was on her tiptoes, fingers clamped on his forearm. A human shield.

The cop was whispering in her ear to stay quiet. His right arm was extended and his Glock 22 .40 pistol was pointed at the door, the door that Walker had almost entered moments earlier.

The hole in the wall was just small enough that Walker could see into the room or feed his rifle into it, but not both. He needed the barrel of his rifle and the IR laser on its rail to have a perch along with a clear line of sight from his NOD so he could align the laser with his target's head.

Think!

What the 2005 floodwaters had not destroyed, they had left to rot. That rot had infected everything. He reached out and felt the drywall in front of him. It crumbled in his hand. The other side must be the same. Hope again? No, it had to be.

He heard sirens.

Shit.

Walker positioned his suppressor on the edge of his side of the drywall.

One punch and start sending rounds, or slowly work it through so there is enough room to see the target, align the laser, and take the shot?

Slowly, that should work. With the cop's and Belle's heavy breathing and elevated heart rates, and the physical exertion of holding her in place, Walker figured he could maneuver his rifle into position. All he needed to do was push out a piece of drywall just below the already existing hole, making it larger.

He took one last look and was about to exert pressure against the inside of the wall when the cop let Belle go, pushing her onto the floor in front of him. Walker watched as he shifted the Glock to his left hand and reached for the inside of his left ankle. He was going for a drop gun. There was only one reason for him to do that. To kill a witness.

Change of plan.

Walker punched his rifle forward, but it didn't penetrate the drywall.

The cop heard the sound and spun in Walker's direction, raising the Glock and a smaller revolver from his ankle, pressing both triggers in wild abandon.

With Belle on the ground, Walker's shot required much less precision. It didn't need to be an accurate head shot. All Walker needed was rounds on target.

His finger found the trigger, and he sent round after round through the drywall. His first shots impacted the wall to the cop's left. Walker quickly adjusted. He continued to fire, his bullets finding a knee, then a thigh. As the cop stumbled, Walker pressed his attack, sending rounds into the officer's pelvis, then into the body armor that protected his stomach and chest, then through his exposed neck and face.

Walker pulled his rifle from the hole and sprinted down the hall to the bedroom door. Throwing it open, he marched past Belle and put another round in the cop's head before rushing to Belle's side.

"Are you okay?"

She looked at him.

"What took you so fucking long?" she asked.

"You're okay. Let's get out of here," he said, dragging her to her feet and toward the door.

"Wait."

She broke away from him and ran to the dead police officer. "This bastard has my phone, car keys, and cash."

She pulled them from his pockets and ran back to Walker.

The sirens were getting louder.

"Let's go," he said, leading her into the hallway and to the stairs, where they stepped over the dead body of cop number one. They rushed down the steps and over Flat Brim.

Walker turned left.

"That's not the way," Belle shouted.

"I know," Walker said, stepping into the kitchen, toward the counter.

Belle followed.

He pressed the button on the back of his Scout light and illuminated the cardboard boxes on the counter with white light. They were marked with different names in thick black pen: "Yellow Jacket," "Pez," and "Snowball."

Walker reached in and grabbed a handful of plastic baggies from the Snowball box and stuffed them into his jacket pocket.

"Now we go," he said, grabbing Belle by the arm and hurrying through the Mardi Gras beads into the living room, out the front door, past dead Cooler man to the BMW.

"Get in," he ordered, running to the driver's side and jumping behind the wheel. "Give me the keys."

The sirens had to be just blocks away.

Walker stepped on the clutch and turned the key. The engine sputtered.

"Oh, come on," he said.

"Pump the clutch twice, and then slowly give her gas," Belle advised.

Walker followed orders and the car rumbled to life.

He sped from the curb and kept the lights off until they were two blocks away, at which point he slowed to the speed limit and turned on the pale, yellow beams.

"You ever meet anyone you didn't kill?" Belle asked.

Walker ignored her, making sure to obey all traffic laws as he made his way back to the river.

CHAPTER THIRTY-SIX

THE RAIN CAME down in sheets, hammering the slate rooftops and turning the cobblestones of Jackson Square into a slick, glistening mirror. It was the kind of rain that made tourists duck into galleries and locals pull their hats low. But Jarrett Stanton didn't mind. He liked the rain in New Orleans. It washed the city clean, or at least it tried to.

He sat alone at a corner table in Genevieve's, a small café tucked just off the square. The windows were open despite the storm, and the scent of chicory coffee mingled with the ozone tang of wet pavement. If his table had been six inches nearer to the sill, the rain might have splashed into his cup. Genevieve's was a few blocks from the French Market, where he and Alma took the kids for ice cream treats on Saturdays.

Across the square, a jazz quintet played under a sagging awning, their brass instruments gleaming. The drummer tapped out a quick rhythm, unfazed by the weather. The band played on, dancing, moving, performing with gusto.

He checked his watch. 12:04 p.m. Two thousand steps. Long way to go.

A man in a colorful shirt hurried over the bricks, anxious to get out of the downpour.

"Alvaro," Stanton said, rising as the DEA agent shook water from his shoulders like a golden retriever coming out of a pond.

"Looking dapper as always, Jarrett," Alvaro Mendez said, running his fingers along his two-day-old stubble. His Hawaiian shirt was half-buttoned and speckled with water marks. The chains that held the badge around his neck somewhere below the shirt were tangled in his chest hair. He wore grungy Chuck Taylors and faded jeans.

Special Agent Alvaro Mendez reached into his back pocket and withdrew a brass case. At first, Stanton thought it was a flask. Mendez snapped it open. Cigars. He offered Stanton a stogie.

Stanton waved it off.

"Really?" Mendez said, surprised. "It's a Cuban."

"Perk of the job?"

"Straight from Havana."

Mendez struck a match against a book from a bar in Juárez. The logo, a jaguar lounging in a tree. Puma Club.

It took the DEA agent three matches to get the cigar lit. The breeze off the square kept breaking the flame.

As in the rest of the country, smoking was prohibited inside restaurants, but the Big Easy was just that, lax on rules. The waitress said nothing as she took their orders—Mendez, a double cheeseburger; Stanton, a garden salad.

"I appreciate you meeting in the Quarter," Mendez said, puffing smoke toward the slowly turning ceiling fans. "I got in late."

"Mexico?"

A shrug.

Stanton knew better than to push. DEA agents lived in shadows and sometimes they forgot how to step into the light.

"Have you seen the local news?" Stanton asked after a sip of water.

Mendez puffed and blew. "What story?"

Stanton pulled out his phone and opened the *Picayune* article. The latest headline showed the Staub home wrapped in yellow tape. The headline: *GARDEN DISTRICT RESIDENTS SHOCKED BY DRUG VIOLENCE.*

"A month ago," Stanton began, "a kid named Connor Staub OD'd in the Ninth. NOPD found bricks of heroin in his trunk. Now, a few nights ago, his mother, Leigh Ann Staub, a charge nurse at Tulane, was murdered in her home. Garden District. Four Latin males found dead at the scene."

Mendez read the article, cigar clenched in his teeth, his eyes narrowing. When he finished, he stubbed the cigar out in a spoon with a sharp twist, preserving three-quarters of it for later.

"A turf war between Sinaloa and Jalisco? In the Garden District?"

"Maybe."

Mendez snorted. "The article plays into Isaacson's hands."

"The DA favors that narrative," Stanton agreed. "I'm sure you can imagine why."

"It's bullshit. There's no cartel activity in town. I'd know."

Stanton paused and looked at the rain, thinking.

"The cartels have been cooking Chinese fentanyl into opioids and smuggling them in through Texas, New Mexico, Arizona, and California," Stanton said. "We are not that far removed."

"There has been a huge crackdown on fentanyl. Deaths nationwide are down."

"Fentanyl deaths are down but overdose deaths overall are not. Something new is coming in to take its place."

"There's always something new," Mendez said. "Keeps us in business."

"Bureau is getting reports on a drug called Snowball. Could be coming in from the cartels."

"We aren't seeing anything like that in this district."

"No one from the DA's office reached out to you about this cartel angle?"

"Not to me, but I'll ask around. Fuckin' politics. It's not about compromise. It's about blame and division. Fuck these people."

The waitress returned with their food. Genevieve's was quick, which was one of the reasons Stanton had chosen it. Between his official responsibilities as ASAC and this investigation into cartels operating in New Orleans, he was short on time.

The DEA man wrapped the dead cigar remnants in a napkin and popped it back in the brassy case before attacking his burger.

They ate in silence for a minute. The rain drummed steadily on the awning over the open windows. The jazz band played on, hitting the standards when a knot of tourists showed up with umbrellas.

"Oh when the saints . . . Go marching in . . ."

"There's more," Stanton said, dabbing his mouth with a napkin. "Not in the papers yet, but it will be."

Mendez looked up from his meal.

"Another hit," Stanton continued. "Ninth Ward. West end. Abandoned home over by the old levee."

"Those bangers can't go a day without killing each other. Usually low-level street stuff. Meth."

"This was different. Two dead NOPD officers. An officer named Tim Rayne and a rookie named Keith Hendrick. They were both COPE unit patrolmen, but here is where it gets odd—Officer Rayne was the responding officer to the Staub kid's OD."

Mendez paused and dropped a fry back on his plate. "How were they hit?"

"Waiting on the ballistics."

"The dealers in that area tend to move around those houses a lot, staying nomadic. Does NOPD have a line on them?"

"That's the question," Stanton said. "For now, we are keeping Bureau interest as quiet as we can."

"Who's read in?" Mendez asked.

"Agent Jennifer Jimenez."

"J.J. She's solid," Mendez said, going back to his fries.

"The investigating detective, Gormley, hasn't shared much. Agent Jimenez tracked down the CSI techs who worked the scene. They told her something noteworthy."

"What's that?"

"They think the scene had been cleaned up."

"Cleaned up?"

"Yeah, either two wounded individuals left the scene, or someone removed two dead bodies; one from outside and another from the base of the stairs inside."

"Now, why would someone remove two bodies but leave two dead cops?"

"That's what I'm asking you."

Mendez set the burger down.

"Weird shit happens around here all the time, Jarrett. You know that."

"Yeah, I do. But this time, that 'weird shit' is being manipulated to fall back on the Bureau and DEA."

Mendez pushed his plate to the side and leaned back. He might play the burned-out fed, but his mind was razor sharp.

"So, the story's going to be that the drug war's escalating," he said. "The media will make it sound like New Orleans is the new Medellín because the feds aren't doing their job. That's Isaacson's play."

"It seems so," Stanton said. "But here's the thing: though it's a convenient narrative for her, it doesn't mean it's wrong."

"At the Staub house, the four Latinos working on the mother get iced by someone with sharp pistol skills," Mendez said, walking it through in his mind. "Similar MO to what goes down a few nights later in the Ninth. Dealers, users, cops, and an unknown party crasher who doesn't leave witnesses."

"That's the thing, we do have a witness."

"Yeah?"

"No one saw anything the night of the murders."

"Let me guess: J.J. presses."

"She pounded the pavement, knocked on doors, and tracked down a junkie who claims to have been in the trap house. Girl. Seventeen. High as a kite."

"Strong witness," Mendez said, his tone thick with sarcasm.

"She's not credible enough for a jury, but she saw something. She was crashing when Jimenez found her and called EMS. Paramedics gave her naloxone in the ambulance. Probably saved her life. J.J. interviewed her in the hospital."

"Does NOPD know about her yet?"

"Not yet. It looks like she wandered into a neighboring house and collapsed in a drug-induced haze until Agent Jimenez found her."

"If this girl is telling the truth."

"That's right, but she did say something, well, different . . ."

"What?"

"She said the shooter looked like a cyclops. One eye. Killed everyone with, in her words, 'a gun that made no sounds.'"

Mendez raised an eyebrow.

"A cyclops with a silencer?"

"Yeah."

Stanton pulled a folder from his bag and slid it across the table.

"Best sketch artist in the district," he said.

Mendez studied the pencil sketch, looking at a man in a tactical helmet, a monocular night vision device over one eye, and a long-barreled rifle.

He let out a low whistle.

"Helmet. Mono NOD. Suppressor. Looks like something out of a fucking Clancy novel."

"What do you think?" Stanton asked.

"I can see why you have questions."

"*Sicario*? Some sort of contractor? He looks military."

"We have reports of former U.S. mil selling their training to the cartels for top dollar."

"We've seen those too, but this feels different."

"*Feels?* Jarrett, you're not going soft on me, are you? What about your data?"

"Try this on for size: A few days ago, a guy walked into the federal building, looking to talk to the DEA. When he was given the appropriate forms to fill out for a contact, he got spooked. Bolted. The U.S. marshal on desk duty said he drove off in a blue VW camper van."

"*Sicarios* don't drive VW buses. And they don't ask to talk to the DEA. Who was he looking for?"

"Javier Gonzalez. You know him?"

"Gonzo? Yeah, I know him. Hasn't worked Cajun Country for a few years. Not sure where he is now, but I can find out. Did some interagency time back in the day."

"What kind of interagency work?" Stanton asked.

"The CIA type. In Afghanistan."

"No shit?"

"No shit, Jarrett. That's not unusual. You Bureau guys did a lot of that too."

Stanton lowered his voice.

"Do you know what Leigh Ann Staub's husband did for a living?"

"I have a feeling you are going to tell me."

"Former SEAL who worked for the CIA."

"Now it's my turn: No shit?"

"No shit."

"Where's he now?"

"Lafayette Cemetery No. 1. Killed in Afghanistan."

"I'm not as smart as you Bureau guys, but I'd say that constitutes a clue."

"Agreed."

"You got video of this DEA visitor from the Federal Building?"

"Yes, but it's not great. Back of his head. He wore a hat. We know he's white, bearded, with long blond hair."

"There's something else, isn't there?"

"There is. NOPD has a statement from a Staub neighbor saying they saw someone matching that description in the area the night of the murder."

"And?"

"And we have Ring doorbell footage of a VW van parked a few blocks down arriving before the first calls came in and leaving before the cops arrived. Too far away for facial recognition."

Mendez leaned back and interlaced his massive fingers behind his head.

"Is this where you tell me you don't believe in coincidences?"

"I do believe in coincidences. I see them all the time."

"And the dead cops? What were they doing there?"

"Department is hailing them as heroes. Rushing into a violent scene. Could be. We don't know."

"Somebody knows."

"Somebody always knows."

"And in this case, that 'someone' is skilled in the art of snatching souls."

"It would appear so."

"I need another burger. What's your theory?"

Instead of answering right away, Stanton tapped his foot to the beat. The tourists were clapping. Stanton liked tourists. They were a sign the city was healthy.

"Do cartels ever hire people on this side of the border? Hitters?"

"They might. They're very results-oriented, but they tend to keep that kind of talent in-house."

"I see," Stanton said.

"My gut is that there's no cartel war here in New Orleans. Nothing's come out of Venezuela since January. We've got the Gulf locked down. Coast Guard, DHS, and the Texas border's tighter than it's been in a long time. We're shutting down fentanyl and precursor labs internationally. Now, if we were in El Paso or Brownsville, maybe I could see a cartel war shaking out, but here?" He shook his head. "This is Isaacson trying to shift blame so she can keep her hands clean on the way to the governor's mansion in Baton Rouge."

Stanton knew that Mendez had run ops in Mexico and countries farther south for years. If the man said there was no spillover, then he was inclined to believe him.

"There is something, though," Mendez said.

"What is it?"

"You buying lunch?"

Stanton nodded.

"We have someone on the inside, so high even I don't know their identity."

"A CI in the cartel?" Stanton asked, using the acronym for "confidential informant."

"I don't know, but I have my suspicions. My point is, I can file a query through HQ. With moms, kids, and cops dying in New Orleans, they just might tap him for information. We would at least know if what is happening here has a Mexican cartel connection. No promises but I can give it a shot."

"Thanks, buddy."

"Can I keep this?" Mendez asked, holding up the cyclops sketch.

"Yeah."

"And Jarrett, be careful. I know I don't need to tell you this, but these people don't fuck around."

Stanton stood and dropped three twenties on the table.

"Get that second burger and do me a favor; you hear anything about that van, give me a call."

"Because you want to talk to your man before NOPD?"

"I have a feeling that if NOPD finds him first, we'll never get the chance."

Stanton buttoned his jacket and stepped back into the rain, his mind cycling through data as the jazz band continued to play, their notes rising above the gurgling gutters and the applause of tourists.

CHAPTER THIRTY-SEVEN

FIFTEEN MILES AWAY as the crow flies, twenty-two by riverboat, Detective Howard Gormley felt the vibration of his burner phone against his hip. He shifted on the slick aluminum bench of the airboat, rain pelting his poncho like buckshot, the wind clawing at his soaked gray hair. The flat-bottom boat was propelled through the night by a large, caged propeller at the stern that looked like it belonged on a vintage aircraft, allowing the boat to navigate the shallow marshes and swamps of the bayou. The Hamilton Standard propeller screamed like a B-17 over Berlin.

Otis Dupuis sat behind Gormley on the elevated helm, in waterproof Helly Hansen rain gear and Xtratuf fishing boots.

Gormley's rubber muck boots rested on the backs of two corpses. One was shirtless, muscles still taut in death. The other was a wiry man in a Pelicans T-shirt and sagging gym shorts, his face blue, tongue swollen, eyes bulging. Gormley pulled the phone from his poncho pocket.

"Kill it!" he barked over the roar of the Lycoming O-540 engine behind him, slicing the air with his hand.

Officer Dupuis eased off the foot throttle and flipped the kill switch. The propeller spun down with a metallic whine. The rudders behind it shifted as the airboat coasted into a slow drift across the marsh, gliding over sawgrass and shallow water, the sound of the engine replaced by the hiss of rain and the distant croak of bullfrogs.

Gormley pressed the phone to his ear. "Okay. I can hear you now. What's up?"

"*Jesus, Hound,*" came Bates's voice. "*You sound like you just drove through a hurricane.*"

"Feels that way."

Gormley could picture Bates sitting dry in his corner office on Royal Street, probably sipping chicory coffee while the Quarter buzzed outside his window. Meanwhile, he and Dupuis were out here on an airboat, doing the wet work.

"*How's the boat?*" Bates asked.

"Solid. This rig is a beast. Got a six-cylinder Lycoming, fast as fuck."

They had launched out of Jean Lafitte and taken the long way through the Barataria. They were looking for a suitable location to dispose of their cargo.

"I had to listen to Army boy go on and on about his weapons collection," Gormley said, looking back at the younger man.

Dupuis laughed as he scanned the waters ahead.

"*Listen,*" Bates said. "*You sure there were no witnesses at that house in the Ninth where Rayne and Hendrick bought it?*"

"Took us fifteen minutes to get there, so I can't be one hundred percent, but I don't think so."

"*That chick with the bat you put down with Rayne's drop gun was the only witness?*"

"Yeah. There was that kid upstairs in the tub, but he was out cold. He didn't see shit."

Steam hissed off the engine cowling as rain hit the hot metal. Gormley glanced at Dupuis, who gave a subtle nod. It hadn't been the easiest cleanup, but they'd seen worse.

Gormley didn't like Bates's long pause back there in his comfy office. It felt like a rebuke he didn't deserve. "We cleared the scene," he said. "Bodies, brass. Why? You nervous?"

"*Got a call from the Bureau. That agent, Jimenez. She wants to talk to me.*"

"Jennifer Jimenez?"

"*Yeah.*"

Gormley wiped the rain from his eyes. "She came sniffing around me too. I told her it looked like a cartel war—no witnesses, no leads, our jurisdiction."

"*Think she bought it?*"

"What else can she do? Now, if they'd identified these two boys at my feet and found out they were our informants, that would look suspicious as fuck and could have led back to us, especially with someone like Jimenez on it. This way, that connection disappears. We did the right thing, boss."

Dupuis tapped Gormley's shoulder. "Hey."

Gormley cupped the phone. "What?"

"Gator nest. See that mound? Mama's guarding it."

A low rise of mud and reeds sat just off the bow. A pair of amber eyes glowed above the waterline nearby.

"There's the bull floating off the bow," Dupuis said. "Twelve-footer, easy."

Gormley nodded. "Perfect."

He brought the phone back to his ear. "Gotta go. We found a good spot."

"All right. Make sure they don't float."

"They won't."

Gormley ended the call and slipped the phone back into the pocket beneath his poncho. He stood, the airboat rocking slightly beneath him. The bull gator's eyes didn't blink at the waterline.

"Come and get it," Gormley said into the storm.

They reached for the first body.

CHAPTER THIRTY-EIGHT

THE BOMBARDIER ROLLED to a stop among the other private jets, *PJs* as Matheson's friends called them, at the New Orleans Lakefront Fixed Base Operator flight line. Matheson looked out the window and admired the other planes: their size, livery paint, and parking positions. The FBO managers parked the jets in order of size and Matheson's was at the far end; the wrong end.

Not for long.

The earnings meeting with the shareholders and analysts at the Plaza's Grand Ballroom had gone well. Interviews were conducted by reporters from national outlets, and all of them led with Genyra Pharmaceuticals exceeding earnings targets and had developed a radical new treatment for suffering cancer patients to replace fentanyl. They explained that fentanyl had become a controlled substance in 1968 as a powerful opioid analgesic for palliative care and that other derivatives like Actiq followed, but even that drug needed a trace of fentanyl to be effective. As Matheson had described it in multiple interviews, with Carolyn Boyle sitting somewhere behind him, the whole country had suffered through an opioid crisis, with fentanyl-laced pills killing more Americans than had been killed in all wars since the end of World War Two. Fentanyl was snuffing out America's youth. Matheson would be their savior. Xylaxyn would change the industry by improving patient care while eliminating the poison seeping into American communities. As he had repeated in one closing line after another, *Genyra is about saving lives, and not just those of cancer patients.*

As Kimbel had flown back earlier to prep the New Orleans team after the successes in New York, Matheson immersed himself in the business pages throughout the flight. His stock was surging. More satisfying, the reporters were calling him both a business wunderkind and a leader in cancer care research.

About damned time.

The co-pilot opened the door and heavy salt air rushed in off Lake Pontchartrain. Though called a lake, the enormous body of water was a shallow marsh estuary, connected to the Gulf via the Rigolets and Chef Menteur passes. Matheson was born in Louisiana, to unknown parents, adopted and raised by a kind couple who still lived on the far side of the lake. His adoptive father, an HVAC dealer, insisted they fish together for speckled trout on this estuary, dropping lines from a steel boat. Matheson had never been interested, waiting out his father's lectures and provincial career advice with silent irritation. The old man wanted Derek to join him in the air-conditioning business. "People always need to be comfortable," he'd say. "There's a future in that." A future of shitty houses, bland women, and Chevrolets, Matheson would think to himself. When he returned from an exotic vacation or an important meeting, that swamp air remained a salient reminder of his roots, taunting him that no matter how hard he tried, his feet would always remain stuck in the thick swampy mud.

Today was different. Matheson welcomed the thick air. He was returning triumphant.

Carolyn had told him that now was the time to play up his modest *N'awlins* background, his working-class roots, the Budweiser to Moët story. She had remained in New York, making sure the previous day's sound bites stuck. As he descended the stairs and felt the heat on his shoulders, a familiar wave of irritation washed over him. She better make that story stick. This was the moment, the golden opportunity. In the interval between the FBO lobby and the driveway, he developed a scowl, annoyed by the smell of the baking asphalt.

His mood changed when he saw his driver standing in front of a new Tesla Cybertruck, the angular stainless steel body glinting in the sun. If he were to be seen as a tech disruptor, he needed to upgrade from black SUVs.

While Dale stowed the luggage in the truck's bed, Matheson admired the vehicle in the warm breeze. This was his day. But just as every rose has its thorn, every cherry has its pit. Matheson found his when Dale opened the rear door revealing Walt Kimbel, his face creased with worry.

"Problem?" Matheson asked, knowing the look all too well.

Kimbel answered by jabbing a thumb at the flight line. "See that last Gulfstream over there?"

Matheson slid inside and looked through the tinted glass. "What about it?"

"It belongs to Vargas. We're on our way to see him."

———

"Please inform Mr. Vargas we're here," Kimbel said to the woman behind the desk at the New Orleans Four Seasons Hotel.

Matheson lounged in the plush seating area, suit jacket on, no tie. Harris had taken a standing position where he could see the revolving doors and most of the lobby. A tan line outlined his eyes and the bridge of his nose where his wraparounds usually rested.

"Someone's coming down," she replied.

Someone turned out to be a Latin man with spiky black hair and a goatee wearing a loose, short-sleeved button-up with a wide collar. "Let's go," he said.

Kimbel signaled Harris to step forward.

Vargas's man shook his head. "He stays here."

In the elevator, Kimbel and Matheson were subjected to a frisk.

"Is this really necessary?" Kimbel asked.

The man didn't answer. He simply went about patting them down, checking their pockets, treating them like they had been selected for secondary screening at a TSA airport checkpoint.

"Well, well," Vargas said when the door to the presidential suite opened. "It has been a while, hasn't it?"

Matheson was forced to squint to get a good look at him. The far side of the room was nothing but glass, a view over the Mississippi River and the flat marshlands that stretched for miles to the south. The clouds had thickened with the afternoon heat. Some of the flat, gray bottoms beneath them showed dark streaks, stretching down to the ground like the tentacles of a jellyfish.

"This is a very pleasant surprise," Matheson said.

Kimbel was equally gracious.

"Leave us," Vargas said to his security man as he poured two fingers from a bottle of Patrón en Lalique Serie 2 into a glass at the bar.

Fulgencio Vargas was a legitimate, self-made businessman, presiding over a business that exported sugar from San Salvador to the U.S. and Europe. He was also an increasingly ruthless drug boss who went by the name *Cuchillo*. As the value of the latter business had grown, Matheson was increasingly uncertain as to which of those personalities would show up whenever they met.

Matheson led with cautious solicitude. "I saw your new jet on the tarmac."

Vargas waved at a room service table with ice buckets. "Drink?"

Kimbel took a beer from the ice, relieved that the Central American sugar-magnate personality was presiding and not the terrifying drug lord. Matheson snatched a Topo Chico sparkling water and popped the top.

The two Americans settled onto a sofa. Vargas took a chair, his back to the windows, his hands resting comfortably on the squared-off armrests.

"I watched the earnings call," he said. "Good numbers."

"Not bad," Matheson said with obvious satisfaction.

Kimbel stepped in. "We are forever in your debt. Long-suffering cancer patients will soon have the pain relief they require. Xylaxyn really has a chance to change things."

"I stopped by the Tulane wing," Vargas answered, his face shadowed and hard to read against the white sky behind him. "My mother."

"She's on the Xylaxyn protocol," Matheson said. He received regular reports on Vargas's mother, one of the first to get the treatment during the clinical trial phase. "I think I can honestly say she's getting the best palliative hospice care in the world."

Vargas sighed. "She's dying. She looked gray."

"Conscious?"

"Yes."

"Comfortable?"

Vargas offered a rueful half smile and shook his head. "You're not selling, here, Derek. There are no cameras."

Matheson felt a pang in his gut. "I want to do everything I can for her. You know I mean that. I mean it as a physician and a friend."

"Thank you." Vargas sipped his drink. "How long does she have?"

"I'll check with the team tonight," he replied. "It could be as long as six months."

In truth, she might have a month. Xylaxyn could make her comfortable. It could lessen the worst symptoms of her liver cancer and buy her a few extra weeks. Matheson was not eager to be the messenger of that news.

Vargas swirled the liquid in his glass.

Matheson looked past him at the distant rainfall. What was he supposed to say? How do you make small talk with a volatile psychopath drinking tequila and contemplating his mother's death?

"On to business," Vargas said, leaning forward, eyeing the two men across from him.

"What can we do for you?" Kimbel said a little too quickly.

"You know, Mr. Kimbel, Matheson here is a doctor, and doctors plunge their hands into blood and guts."

"We can speak plainly here," Matheson said. "Transparency among business partners is a sign of health."

Vargas laughed. "You are such an American. So high-minded. So condescending. So full of shit."

Matheson desperately wanted to reach for his sparkling water but remained frozen in place.

"My grandfather," Vargas said, "owned a sugar plantation in Cuba, back in the days of Batista, *Fulgencio* Batista, my namesake. Did I ever tell you that?"

"I thought your family was from San Salvador," Matheson replied.

Vargas tossed back the remaining ounce of tequila.

"No. My father lost everything when Castro came to power. He held on for a long time, fighting for his land. He thought the Americans would save us. 'They hate the *Comunistas* and the *Marxistas*', he told me. But the Americans didn't come. Castro's people did. They took the cane fields, killed my grandfather, many of our family. My parents made it to Nicaragua. And there, my father said, 'The Americans will protect us here. They love Somoza.'"

He stood, re-upped his drink at the bar cart, and sat back down. "In 1979, when I was eleven years old, Somoza fell. We crossed the border to El Salvador, fleeing the *Sandinistas* because once again, the Americans didn't come. Instead, they were pouring money and guns into El Salvador, letting the *contras* do the dirty work."

"I see," Matheson said, desperate to offer some understanding. "So that's how your family ended up in San Salvador?"

"My father had learned; it wasn't so much that he hated Communists or even the Americans. He now saw them as two sides of the same coin. The ideological struggle of the Cold War was really just a fight over money. The governments, whether American- or Communist-backed, fought for the fields. In our case, the sugarcane fields. That's when my father taught me how to play this game, how to get a business off the ground. It has nothing to do with transparency."

He set his glass on the coffee table between them.

"Be careful about how you speak to me, Dr. Matheson. Your company crawled out of the same swamp as mine, a benefactor of powerful people in the government who profit from the rise. *You* think you're a genius. *I* think you're smart enough to know that when you need someone like me, you jump at the chance. I kept you afloat when you were on the verge of losing it all. That makes us partners for life."

Vargas grabbed his drink and sat back.

"Do we understand each other?"

"We do."

The gangster's demeanor shifted. "Good. So let's talk about the logistics of our business. Dirty hands and all."

Vargas stood up and turned his back on them, surveying the river, a meandering white ribbon reflecting the milky overcast sky. "I can see my refining plant from here," he said. "Two ships unloading today, direct from San Salvador. You know we process more than a million pounds of sugar per day?"

"You've tapped the right market," Kimbel said, attempting to relieve the tension. "Americans love sugar."

"My more profitable business, the one we share together, however, is in trouble."

"How so?" Kimbel asked.

"These attacks on my, *our*, people."

"Fulgencio, we—"

"Did I not just give you five million dollars for that Ice Queen's campaign? Does she not run the police department? What the hell are they doing? What the hell are *you* doing? Can't you get control of her?"

"I'm working on it," Kimbel replied as coolly as possible. "The good news is that Bates's people recovered everything from the Staub house. These murders, these attacks, are being spun the right way as Mexican cartel spillovers. It's not touching Genyra. If you look through all the papers, you'll see no mention of Snowball. We're keeping that out of New Orleans. Bates only lets dealers sell Snowball to out-of-towners, and the murders sound like the usual cross-border mayhem."

Vargas rolled his head on his neck as though limbering up. "Be that as it may. Someone is killing my workers. My men. Someone knows."

"The police think it might be a *sicario*," Kimbel offered.

"*I* think it might be a *sicario*!" Cuchillo shouted. He closed his eyes, regaining his composure. "These men he killed were Barrio Eighteen. Do you know what that is?"

Kimble nodded. "A gang."

"Not just a gang. It's a fucking army. Your State Department just designated them a foreign terrorist organization, a label they wear with honor. My sources tell me they were killed by one man with a dog?"

"That's what we understand. Bates has the resources of the NOPD at his disposal. Whoever this is, he won't be around much longer, that I can assure you."

"Let me make this perfectly clear to you, both of you, Bates, your Ice Queen in the DA's office: You find him and make him suffer. If not, my associates from Barrio Eighteen might just pay you a visit."

CHAPTER THIRTY-NINE

LIEUTENANT CORNELIUS BATES didn't like the idea of the FBI poking around his case in the Ninth, until he saw Special Agent Jennifer Jimenez walk across the threshold of his HQ office on Royal.

She wore her hair back in a tight ponytail, but Bates was already imagining what it would look like tumbling forward as his eyes passed over the rest of her body. She even made the gun and badge on her belt look good.

"To what do I owe the pleasure?" he asked, approaching her from around his desk, smoothing his tie over his snug shirt.

He reached out to shake her hand. Firm.

"Thank you for meeting with me, Lieutenant Bates. I have a few questions on the murders in the Garden and any connection to those last night in the Ninth."

Bates returned to his position behind his desk. She took the chair facing him, jazz drifting in through the open window behind her. Royal Street was one block over from Bourbon and it was nearing twilight, which meant happy hour was in full swing.

"What's the FBI's interest in my case?" he asked.

"International drug trafficking."

He knew the superintendent would play this however Icy wanted. The DA did not like the idea of runaway crime on her watch, but if a drug war was heating up, she intended to lay that culpability on the feds. Bates needed them to stay out of his way, chasing shadows, especially after his recent call with Walt Kimbel.

"What are you offering?" he asked.

"The Bureau can lean in with federal resources."

"We've got adequate resources on this thing. We know the area. And I don't have to remind you: we lost two of our own."

She nodded, her hands resting on her knee. "Sincere condolences on the loss of your men." After a respectful beat, she added, "You think this might be spillover international cartel activity?"

"I would work with the DEA on that," Bates said. Over the years, he had discovered a little trick when dealing with the feds. He could play one off the other when he needed to.

"We're discussing a task force," she responded. "Pooling resources from DEA, FBI, ATF, and NOPD to explore any cross-border connections."

She was good, Bates thought. She recognized his tactic and had countered it with the right bureaucratic maneuver.

"We appreciate that, but it may be premature. Task forces make a lot of noise. Let my people work their sources. We're stalking, not flushing. Give me a few days," Bates said. "I'll get you a briefing on the latest developments and we can go from there. Maybe we could meet up and discuss it over at the Carousel Bar?" Bates jerked his bald head toward the Hotel Monteleone. There was no ring on her finger. Why not?

Special Agent Jennifer Jimenez stood up to leave, offering her hand across the desk. "I'll be in touch," she said.

She exited the peach-colored edifice three minutes later, pulling out her phone. She waited to initiate the call until she was a half block up Royal. The rain had let up, but the streets were still wet, a patch of clearing pink showing behind gray cloud wisps. She ducked into a cobblestone alley beside a souvenir shop.

"How'd it go?" Stanton asked after the first ring.

"I'm not sure yet."

"Did you show Bates the witness sketch?"

"No."

"Reason?"

"Not sure. Just a feeling I got from him."

"What feeling was that?"

"My skin crawling."

CHAPTER FORTY

THE NINTH WAS bordered on three sides by water—canal to the west, swamp to the north, and the Mississippi River to the south—and, after the drug house hit, Walker had lit out in search of a better forward operating base.

He drove his van through neighborhoods near the Mighty Miss and then bumped over a railroad frontage road. Killing his lights and investigating with the monocular NOD on foot, he found a long-forgotten meter-wide, litter-strewn trail, overgrown with buttonbush shrubs and cattails. It led to the river, where the ground turned muddy and lumpy with sinewy roots fighting to push clear of the damp soil. An oak grove stood in silence, rings on the trunks marking the river's seasonal reach. For Walker's purposes, it was perfect.

He had killed two cops and, dirty or not, the counterstrike would come.

Walker was on the clock. It was only a matter of time before they found him. Maybe the cops would do the job of his 1911 pistol for him, though they might do it out of rhythm. Either way, his fate was preordained: suicide by cop or by his own hand.

He spent the day comparing Connor's journals with the take from the trap house, to piece together the network that the young man had been investigating. In the SEAL Teams and in the CIA, he would have turned everything over to a team of analysts. Here, he was the analyst.

He left the two dead officers' phones behind so the police or another federal agency couldn't track them, but he had grabbed their badges and wallets, which now lay on the van's retractable table. Officers Tom Rayne and Keith Hendrick.

He matched Rayne to Connor's code: "Slate." Hendrick was a match for "Chestnut." Connor had used off colors with the requisite number of letters. He tied both officers to trap houses in the Ninth and documented that they were part of the COPE unit.

As the sun neared the horizon, Walker called Belle and arranged to meet her at a pickup location about a mile from his current position. As much as he hated to admit it, he needed a computer. He then showered with sun-heated water from tanks replenished by the Mississippi and did his best to trim his hair and beard. He changed into a set of fresh clothes, stuffed his dirty ones into a laundry sack, and locked the van.

With Paladin at his side and his Glock tucked in its holster, he walked over the train tracks to the position he had passed to Belle. The sun cast long shadows across the cracked pavement and gnats swarmed as Walker watched the sparse traffic on Almonaster Avenue. Nothing seemed out of place.

With the BMW possibly burned, Belle told him that she would borrow her grandmother's car. When he asked what it was, she just said he would appreciate it.

Walker was watching a container truck bang along toward the city when a dark blue AMC Eagle wagon with wood paneling rolled to a stop on the shoulder.

Walker opened the rear passenger door and Paladin jumped inside, leaning forward to lick Belle's cheek.

Walker slid into a cracked but still plush leather passenger seat.

"What do you think?" she asked.

"A Wagon Queen Family Truckster on steroids."

"I don't know what that means," she said.

"Never mind. It's an eighties classic. I can see Grandma has taste."

"Her name's Gloria," Belle said as she merged back onto the road.

Rolling at sixty, pointed into the setting sun, Belle glanced sideways at him. "You clean up nice. I didn't realize you had a neck under there."

"I didn't want to scare Gloria."

Belle smiled. "She doesn't scare easy."

———

Gloria Travois lived in a weathered Creole cottage on Kerlerec Street, a half mile from the French Quarter. The house, built in 1910, wore its age well. Its white clapboard siding had faded to a soft gray, and the wrought-iron railings on the porch bore flecks of rust, but the windows were clean, the shutters freshly painted, and the flower beds were well tended. Every third or fourth house on the street was run down. One was boarded with vines crawling up the siding. Another had a tarp for a roof.

Belle parked the AMC on the cracked driveway.

"Where's the Beamer?" Walker asked.

"Garage."

They climbed the steps and Walker looked around while Belle worked the keys on the iron security door.

"Half the block's gone to hell," she said, noting Walker's apprehension.

Inside, the floorboards groaned beneath their feet, the sound echoing faintly through the quiet house. The walls were a gallery of distant worlds, decorated with sepia-toned portraits of tribal elders, close-ups of wild-eyed predators mid-hunt, and sweeping vistas of jungles shrouded in mist or deserts cracked and endless. One photograph caught Walker's attention: a tight shot of an alligator, its yellow eye sharp, the rest of its body submerged in dark water. The image was intimate, almost confrontational, like the creature had been watching the photographer as much as the photographer had been watching it.

"Her work?" he asked, voice low.

"Every shot."

Walker followed Belle to the kitchen, where Gloria was finishing rolling out a pie crust. She was small and wiry, her silver hair pulled into a bun. Coke-bottle glasses magnified her brown eyes. She wore a linen blouse and slacks. Her hands were dusted with flour.

"You must be Chris," she said, extending a hand after wiping it on her apron.

"Yes, ma'am. It's nice to meet you."

"And this is Paladin," Belle said. "He answers to Pal."

Gloria bent down and stroked the dog behind his ears.

"Hope you brought your appetite."

The dining room glowed with warm light, the kind that softened edges and made the world feel safe. The table was set with mismatched china and cloth napkins, each piece looking worn but cherished. In the center, a cast-iron pot of *coq au vin* steamed, its aroma rich with wine, garlic, and herbs. A basket of fresh baguettes sat beside it, their crusts golden and crisp, still warm from the oven.

Walker sat across from Gloria, Belle to his right. Paladin lay under the table, tail thumping now and then, content in the way only a dog can be when surrounded by family.

Gloria bowed her head. Walker and Belle followed suit.

"Dear Lord," she said. "Thank you for this food you have set before us. Please bless my granddaughter and her new friend Chris. Keep them safe on the road ahead, and I implore you, dear Lord, please impress upon my granddaughter the importance of a good, hearty meal. Amen."

"Amen," Walker said.

"Amen. That wasn't embarrassing at all," Belle said.

"Well, eat something, my dear."

Belle rolled her eyes.

"So," Walker said, breaking off a piece of bread, "you were a photographer?"

Gloria nodded. "For twenty years, before I settled down. I worked for *Life* and *National Geographic*. Traveled more than I stayed put."

"The portfolio in the entry hall is impressive."

She cut a piece of meat and chewed slowly. "Mementos," she said. "I hold on to things."

"So do I. Was it always wildlife?"

"No. I did some slice-of-life work here in the city. There were so many photographers back then. You had to find your own angle."

"She's being modest," Belle jumped in. "Her work's in galleries. She shot the Preservation Hall Jazz Band in the seventies."

Gloria waved a hand. "That was luck. I happened to be there. My most popular photographs were of the Mississippi River; people on the boats, wildlife in the inlets and swamps."

"I saw the alligator picture. And the blue heron."

"Good eye," she said. "Most people think it's a crane. That was for a piece on the Bayou. New York sent me down for it, but it was easy with our place out there."

"There's a family place out on the water," Belle explained.

"It's not one where you'd ever want to swim, but my husband, God rest his soul, hunted and fished out there. I took photos. It's rustic. No power, no plumbing. But peaceful."

"Your husband sounds like my kind of guy."

"We had some times out there, Alexandre and I. He ran a bakery on

Royal Street. We sold it years ago, but I still bake. These baguettes were his recipe."

Walker chewed slowly, savoring the crust. "Delicious."

The conversation softened into the kind of respectful quiet that settles over a table when the meal is nearly done and the company is good. How did he end up here? A retired military working dog, a goth girl, her grandmother, and a man who had spent most of his adult life looking over a gunsight, sharing a meal like family.

"You'll stay with us tonight," Gloria said.

"Oh, I couldn't," Walker replied, shifting uncomfortably in his chair.

"You certainly can. Belle tells me you live in your van. You'll stay in the room over the garage. Belle tells me you have some work you need to do together."

"Belle tells you a lot," Walker said, glaring at the young woman in black.

"She tells me everything," Gloria said playfully.

"I do not, Grandma."

"Did you or did you not ask me to fix his haircut?"

Belle dropped her head, face flushed red.

"This is mortifying," she said.

"Then it's settled. I used to cut Alexandre's hair. I'll fix you up. Then you and Belle can get to work."

———

The room above the garage was small and smelled faintly of cedar, old paper, and the remnants of chemicals that contributed the sour tang of peroxide. A table sat beneath a shelf of white ceramic jugs. Neat, clean, and tidy, everything had its place. It was warm, but a window AC unit tried its level best.

"She used to string sheets across the rafters to make a darkroom," Belle said. "Connor and I would hang out up here."

Walker examined the space, taking in the slanted ceiling, the single lamp, the twin bed with pillowcases still showing fold creases. A black Gibson electric guitar was on a stand, plugged into an amp.

"Want to play me some of that industrial punk?" he asked.

"My music drives Grandma a little batty. You are welcome to give it a strum."

"Okay, no music."

She crossed her arms. "You know, you look like a shorter, skinnier Thor with your new haircut, like after he gets cleaned up to be a gladiator in that one movie."

Walker ran his fingers through his freshly cut hair. "Thanks?" he ventured.

Below them, the washing machine in the garage hummed and churned.

"Looks like we missed that one," she said, pointing at a piece of flannel shirt in a Ziploc bag.

"That's something else."

"As in?"

"I'll explain later."

"We need another seat," Belle said, already halfway out the door. "Be right back."

Walker moved a wooden spindle chair to the desk, its legs uneven on the warped floorboards. The lamp cast a warm cone of light over the workspace, illuminating Connor Staub's battered Moleskine journal and Walker's typewritten pages, smudged Courier font on crisp paper, punched out by his Royal De Luxe on the van's swivel table.

Belle returned with a folding chair, set it up, and sat forward, inspecting the pages Walker had laid on the desk.

"So," she said, "you've cracked Connor's cipher?"

"That would be overstating it," Walker replied. "But I've definitely made progress."

He tapped the edge of the journal, then gestured to his typewritten notes. "Connor used a Vigenère cipher. It's an old-school polyalphabetic substitution with extra letters thrown in. Looks random unless you know the key word."

Belle leaned in. "And you figured out the key word?"

"I figured out part of it. He embedded clues in the margins with little marks, almost like typos. Turns out they weren't. They correspond to phrases his father and I used back in the SEAL Teams. Figured that out thanks to you."

"What phrases?"

"Old mottos like *the only easy day was yesterday*. I tried that as a key, and a few of the entries started to make sense. He's got others, but I'm still working out the phraseology."

She raised an eyebrow. "So what did you get from the bit you've decrypted?"

"Fragments. Enough to confirm that he thought the cops were dealing Snowball and that a cop named 'Slate' and another named 'Chestnut' were involved. Slate has the same number of letters as Rayne, and Chestnut has the same number of letters as Hendrick. Rayne and Hendrick are the two dirty cops from the trap house. There are three other code names here. At least two appear to be higher up the chain than Rayne and Hendrick. Five letters, seven letters, and six letters."

"What's your IQ? You some Mensa genius or something?"

"I just connect dots."

Belle's eyes narrowed. "All these guys cops?"

"Unclear. The cipher's still holding back the rest. I think Connor layered it by using multiple keys. Maybe even used a book cipher on top of the Vigenère. He was smart."

"You mean paranoid."

"Not paranoid enough."

Belle dropped her head.

"I'm sorry, Belle. That didn't come out the way I intended."

"Forget it. So, we have the names of two dead cops who we confirmed were the two Connor had identified as being tied to the drug trade."

"For now," Walker said. "But there's more, and in this case, I think we need an internet connection to figure it out."

Paladin remained curled near the door, his head resting on his paws, nose twitching. Belle glanced at the bed, then at the dog.

Walker studied her in the lamplight. She was tough but there was something beneath it. Not weakness. Just wear.

"I screwed up the buy, my one job," she said. "Instead, I became a hostage, a liability. That wasn't the plan."

"You kept your head."

"You saved my life, Chris. I'm in your debt."

Favors. Just like with Staub.

"Let's review. That's always important after a mission."

"Sounds good. What would you have called this meeting in your SEAL Team days?"

"An AAR. After action review is the formal report. A hotwash is what we would do right after a mission while it was still fresh."

She offered a crooked grin. "Love it. Let's hotwash the shit out of this."

"Okay. We can start at the beginning. I heard most of what the guy in the yard said to you. He refused to sell you Snowball."

"It wasn't just a refusal. He wanted to know exactly who I was and where I lived."

Walker went to the bed and retrieved his duffel. Next to the flannel in the Ziploc he had laid out a white plastic trash bag. He returned to the desk, opened it, and carefully removed some of the contents, placing them on the desk: pills, capsules, and half a dozen clear packets.

"So that's the drug haul," she stated. "Eclectic mix."

Walker nodded. "Let's go back to the point where you spoke with the guy sitting next to the cooler in the yard. He asked you where you were from. I don't think he did that to the guy in the Jeep."

"So?"

"The Jeep had Arkansas plates."

"They only sell to people out of state? We've had deaths from Snowball in Louisiana."

"Connor's journal says not in New Orleans. It also says that opioid overdoses are climbing around the country."

"That's true but that's not attributed to Snowball."

"Based on what Leigh Ann said, labs have a hard time attributing overdoses to any specific opioid."

"Meaning?"

"They were trying to distance themselves from it. Maybe that's what Connor was trying to crack; connecting the cops to the next level in the network."

"The smugglers? You get all that from a dealer asking me where I was from?"

"He sold to someone with out-of-state plates and not to you with Louisiana plates. I'm just saying I think that could be significant."

"Maybe he was just sexist."

"Money has a way of overcoming prejudice."

Belle picked up one of the packets, turning it in the light. The label was as plain as a condiment package: "FENTANYL."

"I didn't realize until recently that fentanyl is an actual drug name," she said. "I thought it was some deadly poison the Chinese make."

"Check out the small print from the manufacturer."

"Prelaxo," she read.

"Fentanyl brought to you by the biggest pharma company in the world, right out of Minneapolis."

"Hang on," Belle said. "Let me check the web."

She thumbed her smartphone and read through a Wikipedia article.

"This says that fentanyl is a legit treatment, been around for fifty years. It's an opium derivative used for stage four cancer patients in hospice. Look at this image," she said, turning her phone so he could see the screen. "Some of what you picked up are dermal patches. Peel and stick."

"That trap house had quite the selection," Walker said.

He flipped through his typewritten pages, selecting one and placing it on top of the pile. "Connor referenced a 'corporate-sponsored hospital' in his journal. Did he ever mention that?"

Her eyes softened the way they always did when they discussed Connor. "He asked his mother questions about hospital procedures as background research."

"What did she tell him?"

Belle pressed her lips together tightly, shaking her head. "I got the idea that Connor didn't speak to Leigh Ann much." She paused for a few seconds. Walker waited. "To be honest," she continued, "Connor avoided talking about Leigh Ann with me. We both knew she didn't approve of us. His mom was kind of a forbidden subject."

"Well, what we know for sure is that Connor wanted to expose opioid abuse. Maybe he was starting with fentanyl origins in New Orleans? Like, who's really behind the trafficking."

Belle typed on her phone, studying. "Connor might have been trying to protect me, but he didn't mention fentanyl often. And, according to this, fentanyl-related OD deaths are down over the past year. Connor would have known that."

After reading her phone for a few more seconds, she went on. "I got the sense he was tracking an emerging epidemic. That was more his style. That would be Snowball, which isn't fentanyl."

"Drugs get laced with fentanyl. Maybe Snowball did too," Walker said.

They looked at the fentanyl packet on the desk, a narrow strip of foil wrapper separating them from the contents.

"Quite the selection," she said.

"Yeah, I'd guess the white pill packets are 'Snowball.'"

Belle frowned at her phone screen, still reading. "Most of the media coverage on fentanyl is about precursor chemicals from overseas and how those chemicals are laced into street drugs. Fentanyl is a synthetic opioid. The variability is what makes it so deadly. Just a little too much and it deadens the respiratory system, stops your heart."

"Raw, hospital-grade fentanyl in the kitchen. Maybe it was a pill factory, going about the work of lacing pills. Makes economic sense for them to do something like that."

"Remind me, it was dark and I was a little traumatized at that point. Did the kitchen look like a lab?"

"No. It was filthy. Garbage everywhere. I only saw it through night vision and we were in a hurry. I took what I could. Standard SSE."

She lowered her phone. "Jargon, Chris."

"Sorry. Sensitive site exploitation. That's where we grab everything after a raid: phones, computers, thumb drives, notes, whatever." He nodded at the pills. "I've documented everything I could about the cop identities and the drug haul."

Belle leaned in, reading Walker's typewritten pages carefully. "You put a ton of work into this. Are you trying to get into journalism school too?"

"I want to assemble everything into a logical package. We used to call them target packages. Connor's dad knew a guy in the DEA back in Afghanistan. After we build this out and make a few more connections, I'm going to take this to him. I'm not sure how to get in touch with him yet, but I'm working on it."

"Why not now?"

"Because it will end up back here with the local cops for further investigation, which means no justice for Leigh Ann or Connor."

Belle looked at the tops of her Doc Martens, her hair falling forward. "When Gloria said that her husband owned a bakery, she didn't tell you everything."

"No?"

"Back then, the Mafia moved in, forcing him to pay protection. He did it for as long as he could. Eventually, he lost the shop, turned it over to them in exchange for his life. He spent the rest of it out at the bayou cabin."

"Did he go to the police?"

She rolled her eyes at him. "Have you learned nothing about this city?"

The washer below stopped with a buzzing alarm.

"I'll go shove that in the dryer," Walker said. "Look through the rest of this and tell me what you think."

When he returned, Belle was comparing his typed pages to Connor's handwriting. "This is really good," she said. "If you're right that Rayne is Officer Slate and Hendrick is Officer Chestnut, then we know those two were part of this Snowball-dealing ring. Would have been helpful if Connor wrote in complete sentences instead of this shorthand."

"Rayne and Hendrick were just pieces of what Connor was trying to uncover. You can see that, here in the back of the journal, where he set up these diagrams. He was looking for the roots of the distribution, the way Snowball was getting into the city. That all seems to come through this entity."

"Marked by an X."

"Right. Either he didn't know what the name was yet, or X is the code name he gave it. Doesn't help us much either way, as it's just a letter."

"Or a symbol. See, the one over here is a plus sign." Belle pointed to another mark on the diagram.

"I think that the plus sign is likely a medical cross," Walker said, lifting one of his typed pages. "Earlier in the translation I came across this reference to 'corp hosp.' I think he probably meant a corporate hospital or hospital corporation, something like that."

"What's this box with the arrows going in? The hospice thing?"

"I don't know. I found another entity called 'dorado,' but I don't know if dorado is another layer, like the code he used for Slate. Not sure what it is. If it was a hospital, I would think it would have a cross. My thought is that it's the drug company that supplies the hospital. It could be the X."

"If it's the X, it sits in the middle of his diagram. Maybe it's not a color. Maybe it's money. My high school Spanish tells me that it means golden." She typed into her phone. "Google Translate says so too."

"Or the color. Could it be a pill mill?" Walker nodded toward the fentanyl patches. "That would make sense. The suspected hospital shoots over the fentanyl patches and those are converted into laced pills in a mill."

Belle's eyes brightened. "I once picked up a book for him at Faulkner House, a used bookstore on Pirate's Alley. It was about China's involvement in the opioid crisis. At the time, I had thought Connor's research was leading to an exposé of China's role in opioids, especially fentanyl. But he looked through it and said they had it all wrong. Something like that."

"We need to figure out what dorado is," Walker said. "That's the common denominator here, the known unknown."

"Known unknown. Not sure if that's jargon or just gibberish," Belle said. "But let's see what the internet has to say about dorado." She thumbed her phone.

"You trust that thing too much," Walker said.

She gestured to the smudged typewritten pages with a smirk. "We need to evolve if we are going to solve." Belle tapped her screen quickly, eyes scanning. After a few minutes, she turned it toward him. A blunt-nosed fish stared back, bright, iridescent, almost cartoonish. "Check that out."

"Your point?" he asked.

"Read the search bar. Dorado is also a fish. Gulf waters. Mahi-mahi. Like sushi." She swiped to another page. "Dorado, as in the fish, also happens to be the logo for a freight forwarding company on the East Bank. Dorado Freight. They handle imports from South America."

She pulled up the company's website. A stylized fish leaped over a wave, bold and clean.

"Maybe we should get you one of these," she said, waving the phone.

Walker accepted the outstretched device and read.

"This isn't far from my new camp, east side of the Mississippi."

He handed the phone back.

"Let's go check it out," Belle said, the enthusiasm rising in her voice.

Walker shook his head. "We're done with joint ops."

"What does that mean?"

"It means, get some rest, but before you do, does Gloria have a color printer?"

"Pretty much all printers are color these days, Chris."

"How about a scanner?"

"It's both."

"Good." He tossed Rayne's badge wallet to her. "Ever made a fake ID?"

CHAPTER FORTY-ONE

THE DISTRICT ATTORNEY'S Office sat on South White Street, a squat, beige building with narrow windows and a faded seal above the door. It looked more like a DMV than the nerve center of Orleans Parish justice.

The conference room was tucked behind a frosted-glass door. The walls were painted a cool, institutional gray, but Irene Isaacson had added a framed campaign poster from her first run for DA and a signed letter from a former U.S. attorney general prominently displayed in a gold frame. A flat-screen TV was mounted on one wall, muted, a national news channel running.

The table sat eight, with low-backed task chairs that had seen better days. Icy looked down the length of the table, Jarrett Stanton and Augie Lloyd on one side, Lieutenant Cornelius Bates on the other. She wore a cream pantsuit, her hair down, tapping a handcrafted NOLA pen made of reclaimed wood from the historic St. Charles streetcar on a yellow legal pad.

Bates sat under the clock, a thick case file open in front of him. He wore a tailored navy suit for the occasion, made of stretch fabric, athletic cut, tight at the shoulders.

"Let's start with what we know," the NOPD officer began, flipping a page in his thick file, one of two murder books he had brought with him in a silver aluminum briefcase. "First scene: Garden District. Homeowner and victim is Leigh Ann Staub, a charge nurse at Tulane Medical Center. Cause of death: blunt force trauma to the head, likely with a claw hammer that was used to torture her. Three unidentified Latin males also deceased, shot with nine-millimeter rounds. One additional deceased unidentified Latin male. Cause of death a combination of blunt force trauma to his head and sharp force trauma to his neck, likely from a shovel recovered next to the body. No signs of forced entry. No witnesses to the crime, but a neighbor reported a white male and a dog in the area at the time of the murders, and a Ring doorbell has a person of interest matching that description leaving in a blue VW camper van that was parked a few blocks away."

He looked up, letting the silence settle.

Stanton sat with his back straight, hands folded, a manila folder in front of him on the table.

Lloyd leaned back in his chair, his expression appropriately somber.

Bates slid the first murder book aside and opened the second.

"Second scene. Ninth Ward. Two of my COPE unit officers were surveilling a suspected drug house." He paused and looked up. "Officers Rayne and Hendrick, killed by someone using a rifle chambered in .300 Blackout. Also found: one black female. Killed with a shot to the head from a .38-caliber revolver."

"Were drugs recovered at the scene?" Icy asked. "Opioids?"

"The place was cleaned out."

"You said it was a known drug house," Stanton observed. "You must have records that suggest who the dealers were. And what they were dealing."

"That's exactly what Rayne and Hendrick were investigating," Bates replied. He paused as if conducting a moment of silence for his fallen officers.

"Continue," Icy said.

"Early read from ballistics is that we are dealing with one shooter."

"One shooter? With a .300 Blackout and a .38? That doesn't seem right."

"The rounds extracted from my officers appear to have come from the same rifle. The .38 is anyone's guess."

"That could suggest another shooter," Stanton offered.

"Anything's possible in the Ninth."

"And the killer?" Icy leaned forward, her fingers steepled. "You must have a theory, Lieutenant."

Bates nodded. "We think this is a cartel war. The two crimes are linked by this single shooter and the drugs, the Staubs' residence connection through Connor Staub, and the Ninth, well, we all know the Ninth."

"I'm not buying the drug connection in the Garden District," Icy said.

"Ma'am, the principal victim was Ann Staub. Her son, Connor Staub, died a month ago of an OD. That suggests a drug connection. Looks like the kid was doing more than using. The amount of drugs found in his vehicle suggests he was dealing. We think enforcers from a cartel were looking for money or drugs that Connor owed them when a hitter from a rival cartel showed up. Gunfight ensues. The place was ransacked. They were looking for something."

"And that led to the Ninth?"

"We caught a boot print. Size eleven Vibram sole boots. One set. Not the type of footwear usually associated with cartels. We found the same boot print at the shooting in the Ninth. And of course, there's the shot placement."

"What do you mean?" asked the DA.

"This guy knew what he was doing. He had training, experience, or both."

"And no direct witnesses to the Ninth murders?" she asked.

Bates glanced across the table at the two FBI men.

"We canvassed the neighborhood, but you know how it is over there. Bureau had better luck. Agent Stanton," Bates said.

"With the cross-border international drug trafficking connection to the murders, we opened an investigation," Stanton said. "Special Agent Jennifer Jimenez found a witness who had fled the scene in the Ninth, a homeless woman suffering from the effects of drug addiction. EMS took her to the hospital, where she offered information."

"What kind?"

"She claims to have been present in the drug house at the time of the murders. Claims that the shooter also murdered her two friends she called 'Gremlin' and 'Playboy.'"

"Did she get a good look at the shooter?"

"Special Agent Jimenez requested a Bureau sketch artist." Stanton turned his folder so Isaacson could see the composite sketch. "The witness called the shooter 'Cyclops.'"

Icy shook her head. "Is that a suspect or a hallucination?"

"That could be a monocular night vision device on the shooter's head. The place had no power, so it was dark. The sketch and the witness's description of the shooter as a cyclops makes sense in context."

"But no good in court," Icy said. "Any snot-nosed public defender in this building could get that testimony tossed."

Stanton nodded.

"We agree, ma'am," Bates interjected. "However, if the sketch is accurate, it illustrates the sophistication of the shooter. Based on the earlier point about this being rival cartels, we're thinking this all might be the work of a *sicario*."

"An assassin," Icy said.

"Yes. These hits were likely part of a special mission in whatever cartel war is going on. Shooter was possibly trained by some of our ex–spec ops boys now selling their training and experience on the open market."

"A specialist."

"Could be a contract killer, former Special Forces, something like that. Cartels have been known to hire hitters with that type of background."

Stanton cleared his throat. "Respectfully, Lieutenant, the DEA doesn't support the cartel spillover theory."

Bates swiveled to him. "Something I'm not aware of, Jarrett?"

"I caught up with Alvaro Mendez, DEA. He says there's no credible cartel activity in New Orleans."

"Mendez is DEA. Cartel involvement in the city would reflect poorly on him," Icy observed.

Stanton didn't flinch. "DEA has a high-level CI they are going to ping for us. Mendez will report back to me as the federal liaison on this case. But, for now, I don't think we should zero in on the cartel spillover theory until we have tighter evidence. Might lead to confirmation bias."

Lloyd interjected for the first time, his voice calm and reassuring. "We need to remain open to all possibilities. But one of them, it seems to me, is that this *is* cartel spillover. DHS thinks they have the Gulf locked down. Border Patrol and ICE have stepped up enforcement on infiltrations from the south. But, like Lieutenant Bates said, this might be a contract killer. The shooter could have already been in the States."

On edge, Stanton glanced at his boss. The narrative was forming. The facts were secondary. How many times had Alma told him that if he wanted to make SAC, he had to play the game? And here he was, witnessing Lloyd make everything fit the story Icy wanted to hear.

"Connor Staub was found with heroin in the trunk of his car. There's our lead," Bates said.

Lloyd shifted in his seat. "I agree. Sounds like the Staub family got in the way of a cartel. The mother was caught in the crossfire. Whatever ring the younger Staub was involved in was related to the activity in the Ninth."

"Or that's just a coincidence," Stanton said.

Icy's eyes narrowed at him. "Prosecutors don't believe in coincidences. You don't believe in them, do you, Special Agent Stanton?"

"It's not a matter of belief, ma'am," he said. "Sometimes facts just coincide. Correlation is not causation."

"In other words, *Post hoc ergo propter hoc*," she replied.

"Exactly," Stanton said. "'After this, therefore because of this.' Logical fallacy. These are two events, not necessarily related."

"Are you a lawyer?" Icy asked.

"Auburn Law."

"All right, Counselor. Let's review the facts. We have a lone wolf killer who has come out of nowhere, offing people connected with a drug ring associated with Connor Staub. We have a gunfight at the Staub home with four unidentified vics. That puts the Staubs at the center of this thing. Now, Agent Stanton, you're the ASAC for the criminal."

Lloyd cut in. "Actually, Special Agent Stanton is filling multiple ASAC roles." He cast Stanton an appraising glance. "He's running my criminal and national security branches, heading this investigation for the district precisely because of the dual roles. He was on the task force that investigated foreign links after the New Year's Day terror attack in the Quarter."

"Well, then," Icy responded. "Sounds like you're well equipped to check out foreign links here, Agent Stanton, and not just the narratives that the DEA might want to provide."

Careful, Stanton thought, thinking of Alvaro Mendez's take on Icy. *Stick to the facts and data.*

With his face neutral, he replied, "I will acknowledge it sounds like the work of a lone killer. But at this point, we don't have enough indicators of a cartel infiltration. I'm on it, though, ma'am. And if that's the case, we will liaise with DEA and NOPD to shut it down."

"And you'll keep this office informed," she added. "This is sounding more and more like a federal case, but this office still has jurisdiction on the murders."

Stanton nodded, realizing she had just maneuvered him into an accountability trap. With a federal case he would either solve it or look incompetent. If he made arrests, the narrative would be that it was done in partnership with the DA and NOPD. If not, he would be hung out to dry. He could see Bates across the table, looking down, hiding a smirk.

"We know about the Staub son," Lloyd offered, breaking the silence. "What's the deal with the rest of that family. Father? Siblings?"

"Connor was an only child," Bates reported, flipping through the files. "His father, John Staub, was killed in Afghanistan five years ago."

"Was he in the Army or something?" Icy asked.

"Navy. SEAL Teams. Switched over to the CIA. Detective Gormley hit a wall looking any deeper into him."

"Relevance?"

"It's not beyond the realm of possibility for servicemen or contractors to smuggle drugs back into the U.S.," Bates replied. "Brits have the same issue. It's almost always heroin. Back when COPE was first cracking down on drug infiltration, we saw packages that originated from Afghanistan. DEA confirmed it." He glanced at Stanton. "Did Mendez happen to mention the Central Asian angle?"

"No," Stanton admitted.

"Well," Bates continued, "could be that when Connor's father was over there, he set up a drug ring. That's how the kid got the heroin. Could be he recruited some of his operator buddies to work for the cartel. Maybe one of them is our *sicario*. Pays well enough, and God knows those boys got screwed working for Uncle Sam in that shithole. I'm surprised we don't see more of them going rogue."

Stanton looked at Bates in disbelief. "John Staub died in 2021."

"Could be an associate. Why else would the killers at the Staub home have sacked the place the way they did? I'm just saying, seems like an angle FBI ought to pursue. Like you said, Jarrett, keep all angles open. *Post hoc ergo propter hoc.*" He smiled. "I never heard that one before, but I wrote it down."

"Worth looking into," Icy agreed.

"We're on it," Lloyd said quickly. He turned from Icy to Stanton. "Dust off your CIA contacts and see what you can find."

Alma's voice rattled through Jarrett's head. *You need to learn to play the game.*

"I'll circle up with the Agency and check on the Afghanistan angle," he said.

"Thank you, Agent Stanton," Icy replied, with a pleasant smile. "That will help the parish a great deal. Please make sure the Bureau keeps Lieutenant Bates informed."

You need to learn to play the game.

CHAPTER FORTY-TWO

DETECTIVE HOWARD GORMLEY nosed the black Dodge Charger over the railroad tracks, his headlights sweeping the trees.

Night had descended on the river like a curtain falling on a stage. The boat traffic had stopped. There were no cars parked along the road. Even the freight trains were quiet.

This was the spot, Gormley thought as he put the Charger in park. This was where they said to look, down there in those trees.

The NOPD's tip line had gone digital and was state-of-the-art. Calls that came in were recorded and summarized by an AI agent in a speech-to-text procedure. The transposed data was then housed in the cloud, available for detectives' queries.

After the hit in the Ninth that left Rayne and Hendrick dead on a rotting floor, Gormley had ordered a surge of COPE uniforms into the streets. Bates wanted pressure, making sure the neighborhood knew that law enforcement was going to respond. Gormley was on board with that. He wanted answers. The boys wanted payback.

Most of the COPE officers were straight arrows. Gormley and Bates had pulled the ones with promise out for *special* training. With Rayne and Hendrick dead, they would need replacements.

Sure enough, one of those candidates, Officer Paul Nickerson, found a man with stitches in his face, who admitted to trying to rob someone in what he described as an "old shitty camper" by the swamp, only to turn around and get his ass kicked. A dog had mauled his face, and the guy in the van had snatched his shotgun. *A blue van.*

Gormley then set up an evergreen query in the NOPD automated tip-line system with search words equating to VAN + BLUE + WHITE MALE + DOG.

His phone had beeped a few hours later with an alert. The system was as good as advertised. Somebody walking along the river had seen a blue van in the trees and called it in as a homeless person setting up camp. The caller did not like the idea of homeless running roughshod over the river.

Gormley didn't mind homeless camps. They kept the drug trade going. Job security.

A blue van down by the river. He chuckled thinking of the old Chris Farley *Saturday Night Live* skit.

Ten minutes after the alert, Gormley logged into the system and marked the tip as cleared. No threat. No follow-up required. He might mention it to Nickerson, to test how he responded, see if he wanted in on a little extra money in the future.

Gormley killed the Charger's engine and stepped out, careful not to scrape his rubber-soled oxfords on the railbed gravel. The river whispered beyond the trees. He moved slowly, his Glock drawn and low. If the dog was still around, he would be ready. He tightened his grip on the pistol thinking of that dirtbag with the hole in his face.

The predawn air was cool with a slight breeze. Gormley paused, listening. No voices. No footsteps. Just the rustle of leaves and the distant hum of a barge.

Then he heard a scratch, a branch brushing against metal.

He froze.

There it was again.

Gormley crept forward, eyes scanning the shadows, pistol at the low ready in his sweaty hands.

His heart beat faster, and a few steps later he noted the absence of light, a void against the moonlit river. The shape was wrong for a car. Too tall. Too rectangular and something even stranger: a triangular pop-top, barely visible above the brush. Camper van.

For a moment he worried its occupant would be able to hear the pounding in his chest. He forced himself to turn and retrace his steps as quietly as he possibly could. On the other side of the tracks, he started up the Dodge Charger and drove a quarter mile down the street before pulling into an abandoned lot. He fought to control his breathing and only then did he call Cornelius Bates.

"I think I found our guy," he said quietly, passing along the plate number. "What you want me to do, Corn?"

Bates took a few seconds to answer. Gormley had woken him up, surely, but Bates sounded alert. *"Nothing. You and Dupuis keep an eye on* it. No reports. I'll run the plate quietly and find out who we're dealing with. Good work, Hound."

"You want to hit him tonight?"

"I want to see who else might be involved. See if he's got a network in play. Let's give it a day or two."

"You got it, boss."

Gormley hung up and stared into the darkness, suppressing visions of a dog attacking him from out of the night.

CHAPTER FORTY-THREE

STANTON'S CONFERENCE ROOM smelled oddly perfumed, a result of the carpet powder that the cleaning crew had used the night before. He had noted it in the past but hadn't really minded it. This morning, it bugged him.

Outside, the sun was rising over Lake Pontchartrain, chasing away the stars. Inside the FBI Field Office, the mood was grim. The special agents around the table read people for a living and they had caught the boss's mood immediately.

Twelve agents, each with a manila folder or a laptop open in front of them, stared at the big TV screen following the presentation. It was 6:30 a.m., and the meeting was already a half hour old. Stanton kept his hands flat on the table, fingers splayed, listening.

Supervisory Special Agent Kozinski, "Koz," was halfway through his summary. He was a data man, like Stanton, which was why he had been promoted to supervisory special agent, SSA. Koz was putting together probabilities based on data, forecasting crime trends, his eyes flicking between his notes and the screen behind him.

"You're saying opioid trafficking has actually been declining across the district," Stanton interjected.

The supervisory agent nodded. "Yes. Overall, opioid deaths from fentanyl-laced drugs are down nationally. My forecasting model suggests the trend will continue."

Stanton glanced around the table. "You're not looking closely enough," he noted, flipping through the document Koz had prepared in support of his presentation. "Fentanyl deaths are down, yes. But that's off a ridiculously high peak. Opioid deaths are rising."

He made his agents write their presentations out in a Word document, no longer than six pages. He had found that too much could be hidden in a PowerPoint.

Koz nodded again. "We're down 16 percent this year. Forty percent from the high."

"I'm looking at the national chart in the appendix," Stanton said. "Down from the peak, yes, but rising."

"Within the standard deviation," Koz offered. "Data smoothing suggests it's an anomaly."

"Not so."

Koz blinked. "I'm sorry, sir?"

Stanton held up the report. "I'm looking at your overlay, national versus our district. Our trend is outside the deviation band. Barely, but it's there. General overdoses are ticking up. Appendix D."

Chairs shifted. Pages flipped.

"That statistic includes all drug-related deaths," Koz said. "Not just opioids. It also includes violence associated with drug activity."

"Exactly," Stanton said. "Which means we're not just dealing with fentanyl. We're dealing with something else. Maybe a substitute, maybe a new precursor. If that's the case, then we need to figure it out so we can shut it down before it spreads. That's not in the model."

Koz stood silent. The other agents stared at their hands. Zero eye contact.

Stanton's watch buzzed. It was 6:45 a.m. If he didn't leave now, the traffic would double the trip to the airport. Time to wrap.

"Deeper dive, Koz. The drugs may change, but the demand for the high doesn't. You have to run more than one model to get ahead of that trend." He looked around the table. "No one gets comfortable. Not in this district. No normalcy biases allowed, understand?"

The agents nodded, murmuring acknowledgments. Stanton turned to his left. "J.J., step outside for a word."

Special Agent Jimenez followed him into the hallway. They didn't speak until the door clicked shut behind them.

Stanton moved to the coat rack, grabbed his long, black nylon jacket, and slung it over one arm. His weather app said it was raining up north.

"Anything else on NOPD and the Staub-related crimes?" he asked.

"Ballistics came back," she said. "Confirmed what Bates has been saying. A single rifle, .300 Blackout, was used on the officers in the Ninth Ward house. Boot prints between the Staub house and drug house are another link."

"And the junkie?"

"Killed with a .38."

Stanton paused, processing. "And the guy on the Staub porch? Another abnormality."

"If the blunt head trauma didn't kill him, the shovel to the throat certainly did."

He nodded, pulling his briefcase from under the desk. "What about van-man? You come up with any more leads?"

She shook her head. "Nothing solid. No plates. No hits on traffic cams. Whoever he is, he's careful. Or gone."

Stanton checked his watch again. "Keep looking. I'm going to be out of the office for a bit."

"D.C.?"

He gave her a look and turned away.

She smiled faintly. "Safe travels."

Stanton didn't hear her. His mind was already in the Beltway.

CHAPTER FORTY-FOUR

Washington, D.C.

STANTON BOARDED THE 9 a.m. American Airlines flight out of Louis Armstrong International Airport. His Bureau credentials got him through a side door at security with his pistol on his belt. There was a form to fill out so the plane's captain was aware. Stanton was familiar with the protocol.

The plane touched down at Reagan National just after noon. He moved fast, skipping the cab line and sliding into a waiting Bureau sedan. The driver knew the route, straight to a nondescript federal building near Foggy Bottom where Leonard Fisk, his contact from the Joint Terrorism Task Force days, was waiting in the lobby.

Fisk was in a fitted suit and striped tie, his hair trimmed and slicked back, looking like a mid-level business executive aiming for the top floor.

"Fisk, good to see you," Stanton said, extending his hand.

"Better circumstances than the last time, at least I hope so."

"So far," Stanton said.

Fisk did not offer any background on his latest assignment in D.C. and Stanton knew better than to ask. The CIA man led them through a labyrinth of hallways and buzzed them into the SCIF. "Put your phone in the box," he said.

Stanton slid his phone into a small locker and took the key.

The room was bare and boring, consisting of a few chairs and a table.

"So," Fisk said, settling in. "Trouble in the Big Easy? Our guy from the New Year's Day attack have associates looking to repeat?"

"Something else has come up, closer to your world."

"Important enough for you to fly all the way up here."

There was a natural rivalry between the FBI and CIA. Stanton respected the Agency and its people, but not its style. There were too many instances where the intelligence service had blurred the lines not just between right and wrong but between legal and illegal. From past experience, Stanton knew that Fisk liked to hang back and hold on to information. As a data man, Stanton found that counterproductive.

Play the game, Alma's voice whispered.

"A name came up in the federal employee database on a person of interest in an investigation in New Orleans. Drug related. He happens to be a former CIA contractor."

"That so?"

"When I dug into his background, I ran into a brick wall. A file that was there but not there. Redacted."

A faint expression of amusement curved Fisk's face, as if he was relishing the idea that a senior FBI sleuth had been frustrated by Agency protocols.

"And?" Fisk asked.

"All it said was that he served in Afghanistan with the Agency."

Fisk raised an eyebrow.

"From our conversations when we worked the Bourbon Street attack, I knew your Afghanistan time overlapped with his."

The mild smirk evaporated. "Who are we talking about?"

"John Staub. A contractor with Ground Branch."

Fisk shook his head slowly. "Staub's dead."

"I know."

Fisk tilted his head. "What are we doing here, Jarrett?"

"We have two crime scenes in New Orleans that seem to be connected. One of the murder victims was John Staub's widow, Leigh Ann Staub. Somebody killed four bangers at the scene. Then two cops were gunned down in a drug house in the same area where John's son, Connor, died of an apparent OD. We think it was the same shooter."

"I'm sorry to hear about John's family. He was good. But not *that* good."

"Meaning what?"

"Meaning he wasn't good enough to come back from the dead to avenge his wife and kid."

"How well did you know him?"

"Well enough, but we weren't tight. I'm not Ground Branch. I was a case officer, operational level. Staub was tactical."

"That's what I'm after."

"What?"

"Insight on his friends and associates."

"Like I said, we weren't close."

Stanton pulled a file from his bag.

"John Staub was an assaulter at SEAL Team Six for ten years. Tight community. When they get out, some of them find a home here."

"Here?"

"At the Agency."

"That's true," Fisk confirmed.

"I looked through Department of Defense records and compared them to the federal employee database. I was able to identify twenty-three operators that Staub overlapped with at SEAL Team Six who went on to work with the CIA."

"Like you said, it's not uncommon."

"But only one of them served in Afghanistan at the same time as Staub and you."

"Chris Walker," Fisk said.

"What can you tell me about him?"

"Some sort of amateur philosopher. We went through the Farm together, but he kept to himself. Issues with authority. He was always trouble."

"That so?"

"Jarrett, if you came all the way here to confirm that Walker was Agency and that he was a problem, you have it."

"I came all the way here to show you this." Stanton opened the file and pulled out a series of still photos from the surveillance camera at the Federal Building in New Orleans. He handed them to Fisk.

"As you can see, not enough for facial recognition. I have the video on my phone out in the lockbox in case that might help."

"I don't need it."

"You recognize him?"

Fisk dropped the photos back on the table.

"That's him. That's Walker. I can tell by his posture. He always moved like a fucking predator. I'm surprised he's not dead by now."

"Why do you say that?"

"He left the Agency under a cloud, angry. Operators like that with nowhere to go usually end up suck-starting a pistol. I figured he'd last a year on the outside, tops."

"Why did he leave the Agency?"

Fisk shook his head. "That, my friend, is above your pay grade."

CHAPTER FORTY-FIVE

WALKER SAT IN the front passenger seat of the classic AMC Eagle wagon. Belle was behind the wheel in her leather jacket, skirt, and Doc Martens, backing into a parallel parking space along Poland Avenue, a few miles downriver from the French Quarter. The streets were slick from a passing shower that had turned to mist. More rain was on the way.

"You sure you have everything you need?" she asked.

"I'm good," Walker said, patting his pants pocket with the forged ID.

"You sure you don't want me to take Paladin back to your van?"

"No," he said, holding up the Ziploc bag with the flannel. "I want Paladin to sniff this out. If he gets a good read, we'll know that this is the Dorado we're after. I might not even have to use the ID."

"The fake ID," Belle reminded him.

"Right, the fake ID."

Now that she was in the parallel slot, she threw the lever in park. "You never told me how you got that."

"It's from one of the guys at Leigh Ann's. I cut off a section of his shirt. They all had a weird smell to them, something dark under the fingers. If that smell is here, Pal's going to know it. Isn't that right, boy?"

Paladin barked once from the back seat.

Belle tilted her face toward the chain-link fence topped with concertina wire. Dorado Freight was tucked into what used to be a busy naval facility. It was abandoned in 2011. It featured wide concrete aprons and tan buildings, some with broken windows. The federal government had recently leased sections to the city, which then sublet a few warehouse buildings to companies, one of which was Dorado.

"I could wait," Belle offered. "You sure you want to walk back to your van from here? You know where you're going?"

It was a workday for her. She'd be at the tattoo shop by ten, working a longer shift because the shop owner was on vacation this week and had left Belle in charge.

"Don't wait. If this goes south, I want you as far away from it as possible."

"Hey," she said. "I was going to leave you a present as a surprise in your camper. But I'm going to give it to you now. It will help you fit in around here."

"A present?" He scratched his trimmed beard.

She opened the center cargo console and extracted a New Orleans Saints ball cap. "Your old hat is looking pretty ragged."

"I'm actually a Seahawks fan," he said.

"Now you're a Saint."

"Oh yeah?" he said, trying it on.

"Yeah. The patron saint of lost causes."

———

Before moving through the gate, Walker stopped at a bank of freight trailers without trucks in an asphalt parking lot. Some of the containers bore the names of shipping companies like COSCO and APL. Others were blank.

"*Blijf*," Walker commanded Paladin. The dog sat on his haunches.

He climbed onto the rear hinges of a cargo door to reach the corrugated roof of a freight trailer. From this vantage point, he had a clear view of the far edge of the former naval base.

He lay on his stomach, pulling a set of small Vortex binoculars from his coat pocket for a quick reconnaissance.

Ninety percent of the former naval base appeared abandoned. He saw hangars with broken windows, concrete overrun by weeds, and familiar painted lettering that had faded over time.

All empires eventually fall. Just ask the Stoics.

He shifted for a better view and surveyed stacks of containers. They called them Connex boxes in the Teams, a term left over from CONEX, a militarized abbreviation for Container Express. In addition, beyond the containers, the facility had three-wheel mounted cranes along the wharf.

In his earlier SEAL days, Walker had learned a lot about ports. The wharf-side equipment also included reach stackers and straddle cranes. He focused on the river and noted a protruding pier. There were no cargo ships there, but he saw a pleasure craft, a forty-something-foot sport fisher with a tall conning tower. Someone at the facility liked to fish the Gulf. Maybe that's why the place was called Dorado.

He moved to his side, checking on Paladin. The dog sat like a palace guard.

He pulled on the lanyard around his chest, freeing the slender plastic dog whistle.

He scooted himself to the edge and hopped down. "*Blijf*," he reminded Paladin. After walking a hundred yards down the street, he blew the whistle three times. Paladin sprang up and ran to him. As soon as he was at Walker's feet, Walker blew the silent whistle twice. He then turned his back and moved another twenty yards down the sidewalk. Paladin remained in place.

Good to go. That would have to do for the rehearsal on this reconnaissance op.

He blew the whistle three more times and continued forward with Paladin on his left side.

By the time Walker reached the road gate along Poland Avenue, the rain had started again in earnest. He pulled his Saints cap lower. Would a cop wear a Saints hat? Yeah, he thought. Probably. People in this town were nuts for sports.

The road narrowed, squeezed between another parking lot filled with empty trailer chassis and a building just around the corner that looked like the main office hidden among dozens of CONEX boxes and pallets. He pulled out the Ziploc from inside his coat and opened it. The shirt fragment was a foot long and three inches wide.

Walker knelt beside Paladin, carefully unzipping the plastic bag. The piece of fabric inside still carried the strangely sweet smell he remembered from Leigh Ann's.

He held the cloth to the dog's nose.

Paladin sniffed, nostrils flaring, ears twitching forward.

Walker pulled the cloth back and pointed toward the darkened wharf. "*Zoek*." Search.

As Paladin started to search, Walker's eyes caught the rear license plate of a Ford F-150 parked outside a construction trailer and amended the command.

"*Zit*." Paladin sat, awaiting his next command.

The specialty plate featured a bronze redfish arched across the left side, frozen in a splash of coastal blues. Its tail bore the signature black spot, and the water around it shimmered with hints of marsh grass. Above the plate number, the word *Louisiana* stood boldly, while a small line beneath read *Support Wildlife & Fisheries*.

He thought about the boat at the otherwise empty dock. Could it belong to Dorado's owner?

Stop. Look. Listen. Smell.

He heard the hum of a forklift fifty or sixty yards away, out of sight. Three separate naval warehouses sat with open doors. A stray voice, and then another. At least two male workers inside the warehouse. The air smelled of diesel and the thick tar between the concrete. He scanned the rest of the area. This was a reconnaissance, that's all. Get in, observe, get out.

Walker moved to the edge of the windowless construction trailer. From this angle, he could see what was on the pallets: piles of burlap sacks. Coffee? That made sense. Dorado's site had said it handled food cargo. New Orleans was a major port for goods coming up from Latin America.

"*Blijf*," he whispered.

Time to adapt.

He walked around the trailer and knocked on the door.

A man in his mid-sixties with a hefty gut opened it. He was bald with a gray beard, wearing Carhartt pants and a plaid shirt.

Walker flashed the NOPD badge. "Sorry to disturb you, sir. Investigating a crime, and hoping I might be able to ask you a couple questions."

"What kind of crime?"

"A kid robbed a house two blocks in from Poland Avenue."

"What's that got to do with me?"

"It was a few hours ago, before sunrise. We have officers canvassing the streets up there. Lots of places on this old base to hide."

"Not here." The man gestured to security cameras covering his warehouses.

Walker noticed the split images on a flat-screen TV on the far wall.

"Mind if I take a statement?" Walker asked.

"I'm pretty busy here." He took a breath. "All right. Let's make it quick, though."

The trailer was simple: a desk, computer, sofa, two chairs, and two filing cabinets. Walker took in the disorganized state of the desktop piled with papers, three used coffee mugs, and a *Saltwater Sportsman* magazine opened and folded back on an article featuring marlin. Beyond it, on a card table, he spotted a radio on a charger and a pair of clipboards. The interior walls were paneled in faux wood.

Walker flipped open a pad and hit the plunger on the end of his pen. "Name, sir?"

"Charles Babineaux," the man said, perched on the edge of his desk. "Where'd you park?"

"Outside the gate, searching the perimeter. Your role here, sir?"

"I'm the owner and president of this company. Dorado Freight. Can I see that ID again?"

Walker scribbled the name down and handed over the wallet. Babineaux inspected it for a few seconds and handed it back. To further sell it, Walker took off his coat so Babineaux could see the Glock. "You mind if I ask what the company does?"

"We offload freight and send it out to customer warehouses in the area."

"What kind of freight?"

Babineaux shrugged. "The kind that comes on ships up and down the river. Why is this necessary?"

"A lot of containers here. An ideal spot to hide. Is all your freight through containers?"

"That's the industry standard. Twenty-, forty-footers, occasional high boxes."

"Are most of them in the yard out there empty or full?"

"Empty. We drop 'em on trucks and off they go."

"Are the empty ones locked?"

"No."

"Was someone here this morning between two and four?"

"No."

Walker angled his head at the split-screen monitor. "Mind if I review the tapes?"

Babineaux lifted his iPhone from his desk and opened his security camera app. "If they had caught movement, I'd have a little clip right here. I also would have gotten a notice on my phone. As you can see, the last movement was last night at eleven, when we shut down."

Walker scribbled the detail down in his notebook and flipped it closed. "Okay. Thank you for your time. I'll transpose this and email it to you. Can I get that email?"

After a brief hesitation, Babineaux offered his company email address. Walker wrote it down, then asked, "You mind if I take a look around the property?"

"Like where?"

"Inside some of those containers."

"Tell you what. Head over to the middle warehouse. I'll call the foreman, José, and let him know you're coming. He'll show you whatever you need."

"Thanks," Walker said, moving to the door.

"Happy to help. The middle warehouse is that one there," Babineaux said, pointing to a nearby building.

Walker walked through the rain toward the warehouse where he had heard a forklift earlier. The door was ajar, so he entered, his eyes adjusting to the gloom. The metal structure had pallets stacked on racks holding the same burlap sacks he had seen earlier. Now that he was closer, he could see they were stenciled with a hummingbird logo. But that wasn't what drew his attention; it was the sickly-sweet smell.

He saw a man emerging from a small corner office.

"José?" Walker asked, approaching the man with a flash of his badge.

"Sí."

"What you got there?"

José was mid-thirties, with a crew cut and a tattoo on his neck. He gestured with his chin at the sacks. "Sugar."

"I didn't realize sugar has a smell."

"Sugar in the store doesn't. This is processed sugarcane, before it goes to a packaging company."

"It comes into the country by container ship?"

José looked at Walker suspiciously, eyeing the weapon at his side. Walker had put his coat back on but stood with his hands on his hips to reveal the gun and badge. "Sugar comes in via a bulk carrier to a refinery downriver. We send it off to manufacturers. I can show you."

"I just need to look around some of the empty, unlocked containers," Walker said. "We had a burglary not far from here this morning and just need to confirm our man isn't hiding in here."

"This way."

José led Walker across the spacious warehouse. They exited through a door on the far side.

Charlie Babineaux stood facing them, a sawed-off side-by-side 12-gauge in his meaty hands. Behind him stood two Latin men covered in tattoos, aiming AKMs at Walker's chest.

"I got some friends in the NOPD," Babineaux said. "Turns out, they've been looking for you."

CHAPTER FORTY-SIX

IF IT HAD been just Babineaux with a shotgun, Walker would have made a play. But two military-aged males with AK-type weapons were another matter.

José moved quickly, snatching Walker's pistol from his holster.

"That way," Babineaux said, gesturing with the shotgun. He pointed to an empty shipping container.

"Want us to tune him up?" José asked.

"Bates said not to get close to him. He's some kind of badass. That right, buddy?"

Walked remained silent. *Bates?*

"Move, hero," Babineaux said, chuckling.

One of the riflemen had maneuvered to the edge of the CONEX box, letting his weapon hang on its sling so he could wrestle with the notoriously difficult handles of the container.

"Get in the box," Babineaux ordered.

"I'm not getting in that fucking thing," Walker replied.

The butt of the AKM connected with his lower back, dropping Walker to his knees.

As he doubled over in pain, his left hand went to the lanyard at his neck, moving to the silent dog whistle. He blew four quick blasts. *Attack.*

His other hand went to the Regiment Blade in his waistband.

Come on, Paladin, come on.

"Get in," Babineaux ordered again.

Walker's back was to three of them. The man who had opened the CONEX box stood by the door, ready to close it once Walker was inside. The SEAL turned his head slowly toward his aggressors, his empty left hand indicating that he was getting up.

Beyond Babineaux, fifty yards away and closing like a torpedo, came Paladin.

Walker struggled to his feet still bent over in pain, his left hand now on his lower back where the AK had connected.

"Don't fuck with us!" Babineaux yelled. "Get in the damn container!"

Walker faked a stumble, hesitating, drawing the man who had hit him with the AK closer for another blow. He saw him turn the rifle around and rear back.

Walker met Paladin's fiery eyes. The dog ran silently at full speed, mouth open, tongue flapping. Fur missile inbound.

Three . . . two . . . Paladin was airborne.

Babineaux went down hard, the dog tearing at the arm still holding the shotgun.

Walker spun, knocking the butt of the AKM offline and thrusting the curved blade into his captor's stomach, then quickly extracting it and punching it in and out of his body, working his way up his torso. Three quick punches pierced his heart. Two more to the throat finished him, covering Walker's face in blood as he severed the carotid artery.

Trained to eliminate the next threat, Paladin was off Babineaux and ripping the arm of the man with the AKM at the CONEX box door to shreds.

José was raising the Glock he had taken from Walker when the blade sliced across his wrist. As the pistol fell to the ground, Walker reversed the direction of his attack and sliced through Jose's bicep, cutting to the bone. José's working arm flew to the site of the pain, leaving him defenseless. Walker jabbed twice. The knife was designed to function as a natural extension of the hand. The weapon punctured José's neck. He opened his mouth to scream but his larynx was already separated. Walker's hook, which sliced across his bloody throat, finished him off. José was dead moments after he toppled to the ground.

Babineaux was in bad shape, bleeding from his arm, chest, neck, and face; what was left of the skin on his jaw barely covered the bone beneath. He writhed in pain reaching for the shotgun as Walker passed him, kicking him full force in the head with the toe of his Iron Ranger boot.

Paladin continued to maul the man by the CONEX, who was doing his best to fend off the Belgian Malinois intent on subduing him.

"*Los,*" Walker ordered as he approached. Let go.

Paladin stopped immediately.

"*Fass,*" Walker said, pointing at Babineaux, telling the dog to bite the fat man on the ground.

Walker knelt and jabbed the blade into the AK man's lungs, heart, and throat. He was dead in seconds.

He stood and turned back to Babineaux, who less than a minute earlier had held the upper hand.

"*Los*," he ordered. Paladin took two steps back, mouth open, panting.

"Good dog," Walker said, as he knelt and switched his attention to the wounded man. "Tell me about Bates."

"Fuck you, soldier boy."

"I'm going to make this easy on you, Babineaux. Tell me about your arrangement with Bates and I'll let you live. If not, I'll do something our Afghan friends used to do to prisoners when we turned our backs. Do you know what that was?"

Babineaux spat blood.

"They would put a blade, not dissimilar to this one," Walker said, holding the Regiment Blade up for Babineaux to focus on, "up to a prisoner's cock and balls. If they didn't get a coherent answer, they would slice them off and go to the next guy. He was usually more co-operative."

"Cops will be here in moments. You're done, asshole."

"All the more important for you to talk quickly, if you want to keep your stones that is. Now what are you importing and what is your arrangement with Bates?"

Babineaux spat again.

"Fentanyl? Snowball?"

At the mention of Snowball, Babineaux's head jerked up.

"You are going to talk to me," Walker said, kneeling down, blade in hand.

As Babineaux opened his mouth to speak, his body spasmed and his eyes rolled back in his head, foam mixing with the blood coming from his mouth.

Heart attack? Stroke? Did he choke on something or bleed out somewhere?

Walker checked for a nonexistent pulse.

"Fentanyl, Snowball. You got off easy, you son of a bitch."

He stood and surveyed the scene.

Four dead bodies.

Bates was on his way. How long did that give him? Five minutes? Ten?

Should he stay and ask Bates the questions he was about to ask Babin-eaux? No, Bates would have backup.

Time to move.

SSE.

He sprinted to the trailer with Paladin at his heels. He turned over the wastepaper basket and dumped the trash on the floor, whipping out the black liner. He filled it with clipboards, notebooks, Post-it notes, un-opened mail. Remembering the cameras, he followed the HDMI cable from the TV to a low flat camera server box. Was it linked to the cloud? No way to tell. He yanked the electronic box loose and shoved the box into the bag.

What else?

There was a dock for a laptop, but no computer.

Get out of here, Chris.

The truck.

Keys.

They were on a magnetic hook on the filing cabinet, a big, fat, Ford-branded key fob.

"Let's go, boy," Walker said to his dog.

Exiting the trailer, Walker and Paladin ran to the truck. He opened the driver's-side door and hurled the bag across into the passenger footwell. Paladin jumped in after it and took his position on the seat, his mouth and fur wet with blood. Walker pulled himself in and fired it up.

Walker was half a mile down Poland Avenue when he saw the Dodge Charger roaring down the road, speeding in the opposite direction, a blue light flashing on the dash.

CHAPTER FORTY-SEVEN

THE TRUCK HAD to be ditched. All these modern vehicles had some sort of trackers installed.

Walker parked on the west side of the Ninth Ward, near the tall levee wall, one of the few improvements since Katrina. He found the same overgrown backyard he had used on his first visit to the abandoned neighborhood. The willow tree concealed the truck from the street.

Paladin sat up front, gazing through the windshield. Walker had cleaned the blood from his snout with some towels he had picked up at 7-Eleven. Only an extremely close inspection of the dog would reveal that he had maimed two men less than an hour earlier. He had used the inside of his jacket to wipe his own face. Even though he paid in cash, the man behind the counter hardly glanced up from his doom scrolling.

He killed the engine and leaned over to scratch his dog's ears. Paladin licked his chops as Walker surveyed the contents of the 7-Eleven bag.

"Sorry, boy. One burrito a day is enough."

He opened the door and stepped outside. Paladin followed, hopping over the center console. Walker dropped the SSE material on the far side of the willow.

"*Blijf*," he commanded.

He returned to the Ford and lowered the tailgate, emptying out the contents of the 7-Eleven bag. He smoothed the hand towel he bought from the automotive section of the convenience store and pumped hand sanitizer onto it until it was soaked. Then he opened the fuel door and stuffed the coiled rag into the tank. To ensure it reached the fuel, he unscrewed an antenna from the front fender and used it to push the rag deeper down the pipe.

When the rag hung six inches below the fuel door, Walker checked on Paladin. The dog was exactly where he was supposed to be, staring at Walker, his eyes bright.

He remembers what it was like to be a working dog. He wants more targets.

Walker flicked the lighter and touched it to the rag.

"Come on," he said to Paladin, slinging the trash sack full of SSE over his shoulder. "We need to hustle."

They moved out through the gathering dark.

Walker heard the explosion two blocks away.

———

"Where've you been?" Belle asked. *"I've been waiting for you to call all day. Are you okay?"*

"I'm good," Walker said into his burner phone.

She paused. *"Well, what happened? Did you get anything useful?"*

"I think so. Sorry I didn't call sooner. I had to take care of a few things. I could use a lift back to my van."

"Let me close up. Where are you?"

She rolled into the Ninth twenty minutes later in the AMC Eagle.

"Big take?" she asked as Walker climbed in and Paladin settled in the back seat.

"I don't know. I grabbed what I could. I'll go through it tonight."

"We can go through it," she corrected him. "Gloria is making her death-by-gumbo tonight. It's poured over a roasted quail."

"Can't do it."

"Why? Got a date?"

"Let's just say we poked the bear pretty hard today. I just want to protect you, Belle. Things are heating up."

She glanced sideways at him, accelerating toward the river.

"The best way to protect me is to let me help finish Connor's story and expose this thing so there is no point in silencing anyone else. Let's compile what we need and get it to that reporter, Greer, who's been covering the story on Leigh Ann's death."

Walker knew she was right.

"Rain check for tomorrow," he said. "I'll take a crack at this SSE tonight and brief you up tomorrow. Hopefully death-by-gumbo will keep."

When the Eagle braked near the railroad tracks at the southern reach of the Ninth Ward, Walker nodded to the SSE material. "A lot of the product at Dorado was refined cane sugar. The sacks had hummingbird logos on them. I think those binders are shipping records. I don't know if it'll be useful, but it's something."

"You look like shit, by the way. You need some rest."

"Thanks."

"I have an idea. Let's divide and conquer. Isn't that what you say in 'The Teams'?"

Walker rolled his eyes.

"You let me take a crack at the binders," she continued. "You go through whatever else is in your Santa garbage sack there. Tomorrow, we compare notes."

Walker paused. It wasn't the worst idea.

"Okay," he said. "Deal."

He removed the binders from his sack and set them on the back seat.

"Chris, take care of yourself tonight," Belle said, as he exited the vehicle. "Call me if you want to talk."

———

At midnight, Sergeant Dupuis rolled his 2007 Chevy Silverado 3500 dually to a stop near the railroad tracks, headlights off. He put the big truck, with its four wheels on the rear axle, in park and hopped out, approaching a black Dodge Charger through the rain. Its driver's-side window lowered.

"When do we do it?" he asked Gormley, who sat behind the wheel playing solitaire on his phone.

"I already texted Bates. He said to wait until three a.m. Shift change for the patrol units."

"Time for some payback."

"Fuckin' right it is."

———

Due to the weather, Walker had pulled the van's back seat down into a bed and was sleeping next to Paladin. The river passed by off his starboard side, unencumbered by the events of the day or any day.

Walker had not gotten much from his SSE haul, nothing he would have considered actionable intelligence in his former profession. A lot of bills and unintelligible notes and phone numbers on yellow stickies. He hoped Belle had fared better.

Earlier, he had pulled Jean-Paul Sartre's *Being and Nothingness* from his shelf. The pages were dog-eared, the spine cracked from years of use. Walker had read it countless times, but tonight, one line had held him captive: *Man is condemned to be free; because once thrown into the world, he is responsible for everything he does.*

As he shut his eyes, he debated the truth of Sartre's claim. Was he truly free? Or had his path been carved by trauma, war, the ghosts of men he had killed and those he had lost in battle? Men like John Staub.

Man is condemned to be free.

He thought of Paladin's utter lack of conscience. Was that what separated man from beast? The dog snored softly next to him.

It was then that his mental debates segued into determinism, the idea that every action was inevitable, shaped by prior causes. If that were true, then perhaps he was not to blame for the blood on his hands, John Staub's blood, and, by default, the blood of Connor and Leigh Ann. But Sartre wouldn't let him off so easily. Freedom, Sartre argued, was a burden, a responsibility that could not be escaped.

Walker's ruminations grew fuzzier until they morphed into his dreams.

Man is condemned to be free.

———

At 2:59 a.m., across the tracks, Detective Gormley checked his watch. He rolled down his window. "Let's go," he said gruffly.

Dupuis had been ready and waiting. He started the Silverado and shifted into drive. The heavy dually, fitted with a thick grille-guard bumper, nosed forward. When it was aimed at the leafy growth hiding the van, Dupuis shoved his right foot down, pinning the accelerator to the floor.

———

Walker felt the broadside hit before he heard the vehicle behind it.

His VW Westfalia van toppled sideways, slamming him against the sliding door's rectangular glass window. Paladin barked in the darkness. Walker felt the dog clawing to escape. He had just gotten to his knees when the van was bashed a second time.

An engine roared. The vehicle it powered backed up and then accelerated again, smashing into the van's undercarriage. He was thrown into Paladin, the dog's body shaking uncontrollably, clawing, barking.

This time their tormentor did not back up. Instead, the vehicle pushed them toward the river.

The van was sliding, moving over rocks and grass while the engine of the vehicle being used as a weapon thundered outside. Walker tumbled and smashed his head into the swing-out table when the van rolled again.

Maybe we can break the opposite side window and climb out.

The next roll felt different.

Rather than flip, the van dropped and hit the water, nose up, weighed down by its rear engine. Water poured in through the windows and jagged holes in the metal. Walker felt it rising all around him. Cold, fast, and dark.

The van rolled again before it submerged, becoming one more wreck headed for the bottom of the Mighty Mississippi.

PART THREE

"*Justice is the constant and perpetual
will to render to each his due.*"

—Ulpian, Roman jurist (third century AD)

CHAPTER FORTY-EIGHT

CHRIS WALKER'S HEART pounded against his ribs as the SEAL instructors splashed into the Combat Training Tank.

Less than a mile away, tourists sipped Bloody Marys at the historic Hotel del Coronado, while toddlers built sand castles, kids skim-boarded and surfed in the Pacific, and couples lounged on beach towels soaking up the Southern California sun.

Inside the enclosure of Naval Amphibious Base Coronado, a young Chris Walker, barely out of high school, stood on the pool deck with his SCUBA rig next to him, hoping he wasn't about to drown.

If Hell Week was the crucible that tested a candidate's mental fortitude, Pool Comp further culled the herd and tested their ability to remain calm in the water under stress, a hallmark of Navy frogmen.

After nearly four months of Basic Underwater Demolition/SEAL training, he was lean and strong; his damp brown cotton T-shirt, a sign of completing the arduous Hell Week, clung to his taut muscled frame. He was in the most uncomfortable shorts ever designed. Known as UDT shorts, they had not evolved since the early days of World War Two when the predecessors of today's SEALs had worn them on beach reconnaissance operations off Normandy, North Africa, and islands in the Pacific Theater.

Walker had survived First Phase of what was touted as possibly the toughest training ever devised by a modern military: surf torture, log PT, lifesaving, underwater knot tying, drown-proofing, freezing swims, long soft sand runs, the obstacle course, and the infamous Hell Week. But this was different. The Second Phase instructors did not care that you were tough enough physically and mentally to graduate from First Phase. They did not care if you were a great leader or if you had the "teamability" so crucial to success when operating as part of an elite unit. They did not care about your resilience. They cared only about finding out if you had the trait that differentiated the SEAL Teams from every other special operations unit in America's arsenal; they needed to find out if you were comfortable in the water.

In an enemy harbor in the dark of night, when placing a limpet mine on the hull of an enemy ship, could you deal with a malfunction in your rig—no light, no air, in the unforgiving medium of the ocean? Would you blow the mission and kill yourself and your swim buddy, or could you problem-solve in the most dire conditions? Pool Comp was that test. It determined if you would continue on to learn combat diving with a Dräger LAR V rebreather and then move on to the land warfare phase of training, or if you were packing your bags for the fleet.

Master Chief Clay Harlan stood at the end of the line of SEAL candidates, arms crossed, his face shadowed by the ball cap Walker had never seen off his head.

"Gear up."

The SEAL candidates donned their fins, hoisted the buoyancy compensators—twin 80 tanks they had been told to call "cylinders"—with hoses onto their backs, then tugged their masks into place, performing buddy checks and then dive supervisor checks.

"First three, prepare to enter the water," Harlan said.

Walker and two candidates made their way to the edge of the pool and placed one hand against their masks and regulators.

"Enter the water."

Walker stepped forward and splashed into the Combat Training Tank, entering another world. The tank had a military-sounding name, but in reality, it was just a big swimming pool, one where the candidates of Walker's BUD/S class would prove they had what it took to become frogmen.

Twelve feet down, the world was blue and cool. He calmed his nerves with slow deep breaths of the nitrogen-and-oxygen-mixed gas. If all went well, he would be under for about fifteen minutes. He settled on the bottom and began his crawl, focusing on the objective and concentrating on the rhythm of his breathing.

Rhythm.

Then came the first hit.

An instructor slammed Walker into the bottom of the pool, ripped his mask away, and yanked his regulator from his mouth.

Remain calm. Think about your procedures.

Another instructor tore his fins from his feet and then delivered two swift uppercuts to Walker's abdomen, forcing the air from his lungs.

Walker forced himself to relax as an instructor spun him around and slammed him into the deck while the second one delivered another punch to his gut.

Then it was quiet.

Procedure.

This was the test.

"If you can't get comfortable under the water," Harlan had said, "then you've got no business being a frogman. Panic is the enemy."

Panic is the enemy.

Then don't panic.

Air. That's the priority.

Walker moved to his knees.

Without his mask his sight was blurry, but he could go through the correct procedures in the right order with his eyes closed. He reached back for his hoses to find that they had been tied to the manifold at the top of the tanks.

That was to be expected.

He felt his heart rate slowing to conserve what little oxygen was left in his lungs, his body constricting the flow of blood to his extremities and directing additional blood to his vital organs.

He unclasped the nylon that harnessed the tanks to his back, reached behind his head, and grabbed the mess of hoses and manifold, pulling it over his head in front of him.

Work the problem.

He concentrated on the knot.

Some instructors saw their jobs as gatekeepers to the SEAL Teams. Others saw themselves as mentors. Master Chief Harlan was the latter. It was from Harlan that Walker first learned that the word *panic* was derived from the Greek god Pan, who was associated with nature, wild places, and sudden uncontrollable fear. Every Friday and before each major evolution, Harlan addressed the classes that passed through his phase of BUD/S. He was a warrior poet passing along what wisdom he had acquired via life experiences to the next generation of frogmen. He told the class that the Greeks believed Pan inflicted irrational fear in soldiers.

So much so that the words *panikon deima* meant "fear of Pan." Panic, he had told them, was not just fear; it was primal, internal, a fear of fear. Panic was the enemy, and that enemy came from within.

After that Friday sermon, Walker had taken to the web to research psychologists who had studied panic. He initially came across Freud and Jung, who explained that the physical symptoms—a rapid heartbeat, cottonmouth, and tingling—were a response to unresolved trauma and a confrontation with what they called the shadow self. Did panic come from within or without? Walker found that Stoic philosophers Epictetus and Seneca declared that panic was a failure of reason. If panic was a failure of reason, then reason was the antidote.

Trust in the procedure.

Trust in reason.

Walker untied the knot, brought the regulator to his mouth, and sucked.

Nothing came.

He felt his carbon dioxide levels rising, his brain telling his body to breathe. If he succumbed to that instinct, he would take water into his lungs. Here at BUD/S it meant failure. On a mission it meant death.

Reason.

He reached for the valve knob and twisted.

CHAPTER FORTY-NINE

DARKNESS. COLD. PRESSURE.

The river pressed in from all sides. Paladin clawed at his back. Objects tumbled, striking his head as the van rolled.

It was not so different from the test in the Combat Training Tank when he had employed his reason to visualize the problems and solve them step by step. He learned to prioritize, trust the procedures, work the problem, and fight the forces of irrationality.

His success in the pool that day kindled a lifelong passion for philosophy. It had also become a weapon.

Black water and chaos. The van was still moving; tumbling, scraping, groaning as it was dragged down by the current.

Panic is the enemy.

Walker was upside down, his shoulder jammed against the ceiling, water rushing past his ears, Paladin beside him thrashing, claws scraping at the walls, barks turned to bubbles, a piercing whine as the water filled the last pocket of air.

Reason. Then move.

The van's interior was a tangle of blurred shadows and shifting debris. Scrapes, bumps, and bashes echoed through the metal shell as it slammed against the massive, jagged rocks lining the river like the teeth of a bear trap. The Army Corps of Engineers had placed them there to armor the shoreline, to keep the Mississippi from swallowing the city whole. Now they were tearing Walker's van apart.

The van pitched again, tumbling over the underwater slope of stone and concrete. Glass shattered. Bent like a crushed soda can, Walker's vehicle rolled nose-first into the dredged channel, where the river ran deeper and faster for the shipping lanes.

Get Paladin out of here!

Walker grabbed his dog by the collar and found the edge of the sink.

That meant that the sliding door should be to his right.

He pushed off the refrigerator and propelled himself toward the door, felt for the handle in the dark, found it, and pulled.

Nothing.

The van was on its side. The door was on the river's floor.

Walker had a brief memory of being with his first platoon in the helo dunk tank at Marine Air Station Miramar. They had donned blacked-out masks and strapped themselves into a fuselage that was then dropped into a tank and rotated upside down. They had learned to find their way out using reference points.

Walker grabbed the back of the passenger seat with his right hand and, with Paladin's collar in his left, pulled his way diagonally into the driver's seat.

No way you can open the door against the water, but you can roll down a window.

He knew every inch of the vehicle. It was his home. As the van continued to slide, Walker rolled down the van's window and pushed Paladin through. Then he grabbed both sides of the window frame to heave himself upward, when the van rolled again, sucking Walker back inside. He felt something with his feet and pushed off, slamming his head into the floor.

What way is even up?

He felt dizzy, his body craving oxygen.

He had oxygen, a nitrogen-oxygen mix and it was feet away.

Out of both habit and necessity, Walker had organized the equipment in his van with extreme care. It served a purpose when living in such a confined space. Everything had its place, including his dive gear.

He twisted his body and groped through the dark, his skin scraping against torn metal, pulling himself along the inside of the van. His fingers found the tank first. The bag with his buoyancy compensator and regulator was secured in the cargo compartment with a cambuckle strap. He loosened it, found the bag's zipper, opened it, and felt for the first stage of his regulator. He attached it to the tank that was still strapped to the side of the van, turned on the air, and grabbed the second-stage mouthpiece, hitting the purge button to clear it of water before sucking in the life-saving gas mixture.

The van rolled again but Walker kept the regulator in his mouth as the vehicle lurched and slammed him into the opposite wall. He bit the regulator, and forced himself to breathe slowly, the dizziness subsiding.

Who hit you?

Cops?

The cartel?

Don't you fucking die.

Paladin. You've got to find Paladin.

And you've got to find the motherfuckers who did this.

The van smashed off a rock.

Get out of here.

Grab your AR.

No time to mess with the vault.

You need a weapon.

His hands reached up and found the Riffe speargun attached to the transition sill where the side of the van met the ceiling. He pulled it free.

Then, taking a huge gulp of air, he held his breath and swam through the van and out the open driver's-side window. Once clear of the watery tomb, he blew bubbles and slowed his ascent as much as possible to avoid the dreaded bends.

He surfaced seventy feet offshore, sucking in the humid night air, frantically searching for Paladin, looking for a splash, listening for the familiar bark.

Nothing.

He was drifting in the current at what he guessed was about seven knots, the lights of the riverbank sliding past like passing ships. Ahead, the Dorado pier loomed, the pier where Paladin had saved his life.

With his speargun in hand, Walker began swimming for shore.

CHAPTER FIFTY

"SEE ANYTHING?" GROMLEY asked, peering into the darkness, rain soaking him to the bone.

"No. That piece of junk sank fast as fuck," Dupuis replied.

"Don't you have any night vision in that truck of yours? You've spent enough on your arsenal in that thing."

"They are on my list for our next real payday."

The two police officers stood at the water's edge looking out over the Mississippi. Dupuis held a spotlight in his right hand, his Sons of Liberty AR was in his left. He had affixed a SureFire light and Aimpoint red dot optic and Vickers Blue Force Gear sling just like he had heard spec ops did on some podcast.

They turned toward a splash upriver.

"What was that?" Gromley asked.

Dupuis clicked a button on the handheld spotlight and turned it toward the noise.

"Just a fish."

Gromley hitched up his pants over his protruding belly.

"You stay here. Give it an hour."

"Come on, Hound, no one can hold their breath that long. He's gone."

"Yeah? Well, you damn well better make sure."

The older detective turned to leave.

"Where are you going?"

"I'm getting out of this weather. Hang out so we can tell Bates we observed the area for an hour. Just fucking do what I say."

"Yes, sir," Dupuis said, the sarcasm heavy.

———

Walker swam at a slight downstream angle. It meant he would have a longer patrol to his destination, but he would get to shore faster and would not waste energy fighting the current. Instead that current would be an asset.

He dragged himself ashore and turned to look at the night sky, catching his breath.

Paladin.

"Pal," he whispered. *"Heir."*

Nothing.

He pushed himself to his knees in the mud.

"Pal, here boy," he said louder.

Still nothing.

How far had he gone downriver?

A mile?

Two miles?

It was hard to tell.

Barefoot, in wet jeans and no shirt, it would take some time to make it back upriver. Whoever had attacked him might be long gone. But maybe not.

Walker inspected his speargun, ensuring it was in working order. Then he grabbed handfuls of mud and caked it across his chest, stomach, arms, and face.

It was time to go to war.

———

Sergeant Dupuis leaned against the brush guard of his Ford F-350 smoking his second Hooten Young cigar of the night. He had heard that Delta Force operators smoked them. His rifle was on the hood.

Every few minutes he would hear something and shine his spotlight in that direction.

He hit the light button on his Casio G-SHOCK, the same watch he had read that spec ops guys preferred. It had been forty-five minutes. Did he really need to wait fifteen more? Who would know?

He had grown tired of practicing his quick draw with his new Staccato C4X in the TXC waistband holster on his belt. He had a Vortex red dot on it. Only old-timers still used iron sights. A buddy who had stayed in the military had told him the most elite units were using these exact pistols, as were top tactical teams of federal law enforcement agencies so, of course, he had to add one to his collection. The four-inch compact compensated pistol even took his Glock mags. Now he was waiting and checking his watch every few minutes, thinking about the night vision and helmet he wanted to buy.

Maybe he should try out for SWAT. That had been his goal before Bates recruited him for COPE. Kicking doors, executing high-risk warrants, and rescuing hostages sounded more high-speed than rolling through the Ninth. But the extracurricular activities of COPE sure paid better. If he wanted to keep building his arsenal, he needed to stick with COPE. Besides, at this point he doubted that Bates would even let him leave.

He was dreaming about NODs and L3 Harris Next Generation Laser Aiming Devices when he heard a whimper.

He turned the spotlight downriver into the brush.

Then he heard it again.

What is that? A fucking animal?

Dupuis grabbed the rifle off the hood of his truck and made his way downriver toward the source of the noise, sweeping the path ahead with the spotlight, cigar clamped in his teeth.

The whimpers were getting weaker the closer he got.

He stepped over rotting logs and moved past cypress and oaks until he found the source of the noise.

A fucking dog?

Dupuis looked down, recognizing it as a Belgian Malinois.

The fucking thing escaped?

Bates would not be happy to hear that.

It looked dead but Dupuis could see a slight rise and fall of its ribs. He could also see where it had thrown up.

Should he just pop it in the head and toss it back in the river?

It might wash up somewhere, but who the fuck cared? Gators would probably get it anyway.

Dupuis adjusted his grip on the spotlight, sweeping the powerful beam on the river and through the trees and bushes around him.

Fucking creepy.

It's about time anyway. Pop this dog and get the fuck out of here.

The creature whimpered again. He would be putting it out of its misery.

He put the light on the dog and flipped the selector lever on his rifle to the fire position, moving his barrel to the side of the animal's head.

The sound startled him. At first, he thought his ribs had caught fire but that did not make any sense. The cigar dropped from his mouth and he looked down at his right side to see a stainless steel rod projecting from his rib cage. As he struggled to comprehend what was happening, he heard branches breaking. It sounded like he was being charged by a wounded animal, like a leopard or Cape buffalo that he had seen on the Outdoor Channel.

His brain still did not quite grasp the situation as a shirtless figure covered in mud sprinted from the undergrowth out of the darkness. The creature's right hand held a stone. Dupuis was still struggling to make sense of it when the rock connected with his head.

———

Belle answered his call on the first ring.

"Why are you picking up the phone from a number you don't know?"

"Chris, are you okay?"

"It's after three a.m., what are you doing up?"

"I could ask you the same. I'm working on the manifests. I think I found something. What number is this? Did you get a new burner?"

Walker looked at the tailgate of the yellow monster truck and slowly ran his fingers through the damp hair on Paladin's head. The dog was wrapped in an insulated poncho liner that Walker had found in the rear passenger area.

"I did."

He had opened both of Dupuis's phones using the dead officer's face. One was clearly a burner, which was the phone Walker had used to call Belle. Being an analog guy and having to memorize phone numbers sometimes had its advantages.

"Well, why are you calling me at three a.m.? Find something in the SSE?"

"Not exactly."

Paladin opened his eyes and looked up at his handler. He had swallowed a lot of water, and Walker assessed that he had a broken rib or two from the rollover. There was a danger that a rib had punctured an internal organ, but Walker did not think so. Still, he needed to get Paladin to a vet to be sure.

"Well?"

Walker moved his eyes to the bed of the truck, where he had placed Dupuis's rifle, pistol, Emerson folding knife, handcuffs, light, badge, wallet, and a stack of cash in a paper bag that must have totaled close to ten thousand dollars. One of Dupuis' boots was on it's side. It had been at least three sizes too small for Walker's foot.

After carrying Paladin to the tailgate and assessing him for injuries, he had wrapped him in the poncho liner. He had then retrieved his speargun from where he had dropped it, after sending the shaft into the dirty cop, and returned to where Dupuis lay face down in the mud. He extracted the shaft from the officer's body, threw on the dead man's rain jacket, and dragged him back to the truck, hoisting him into the passenger seat.

"I'll explain when I see you. Do you remember where you dropped me off?"

"Yes."

"Can you be there in twenty minutes?"

"Of course. Chris, you're scaring me."

"I'm okay. See you soon."

He disconnected the call and continued to rub Paladin behind the ears.

"It's okay, boy. You're going to be okay."

He then lifted Paladin from the tailgate and gently laid him on the ground next to the AR and bag of cash. Then he clipped Dupuis's folder to the right pocket of his own jeans, slid the Staccato into the holster, shoved it inside his waistband, and ensured the clips were in place over his belt just behind his right hip. The handcuffs went in Walker's back left pocket. The badge and wallet in his front left.

He then moved to the driver's door and opened it, looking across at the corpse slumped in the passenger seat. Walker slid into the driver's seat and started the vehicle, its heavy engine roaring to life in the darkness. He experimented with buttons and knobs until a light illuminated that indicated the car was in low four-wheel drive. He took an ASP baton he had found in the side door compartment and stepped from the vehicle, using the adjustable seat to wedge the baton against the gas pedal. He then reached across and put the truck in one low. It lurched forward slowly in its lowest gear setting, one made to pull it from mud, sand, or snow. Walker stood silent in the falling rain and watched it roll into and submerge beneath the waters of the Mississippi.

CHAPTER FIFTY-ONE

FROM THE TWELFTH floor of One River Place, Derek Matheson watched the Mississippi crawl past, a slow-moving leviathan.

The river was high this morning, swollen from spring runoff. The barges moved sluggishly through the current. Matheson liked the height of his perch. It gave him perspective. Distance. Safety. Even Cuchillo couldn't reach him up here.

The apartment was all glass and steel, minimalist and cold. A single espresso steamed on the marble counter. The news played on mute with footage of a teen who had OD'd, a high school football star with a bright future. A scrolling chyron warned of rising opioid deaths across the Southeast. Matheson frowned. The narrative was shifting again.

The door chime rang.

Matheson's security man set his protein shake on the glass table and went to the door.

He rounded the corner from the foyer a moment later and ushered in Irene Isaacson, followed closely by Walt Kimbel.

Icy was dressed in a tailored navy suit, her hair pinned back, her expression unreadable. She scanned the apartment, noting the changes since she had last been here. Matheson offered a smile that didn't reach his eyes, and Kimbel and Dale dropped into the other room to discuss an upcoming industry conference in the Napa Valley.

Icy took in the view and admired the kitchen, everything built into the walls, nothing on the counters, not even salt and pepper.

"You redid a few things," she said. "Looks nice."

"I'm teaching myself to cook."

"No more private chef? What was her name? Gina?"

"Who do you think is teaching me?"

Icy nodded and forced a strained smile.

"My team is waiting downstairs in the lobby. We have an event this afternoon."

Matheson led her to the low leather sectional in the main room. "May I offer you a drink?"

"I'm fine. I can only stay for a few minutes."

"Of course, you are a busy woman."

The media had responded favorably to the PR blitz after the earnings meeting in New York. But now three kids had died at a pill party outside Chattanooga. Tennessee law enforcement, accustomed to detecting fentanyl in tox screens, hadn't found it. That set up a media narrative now echoing through Louisiana with the death of the photogenic athlete. Matheson's carefully plotted PR strategy was losing steam.

"Let's get to it," she said, her piercing blue eyes moving from Matheson to the view of the river behind him.

Matheson remembered how she liked to gaze out over the Mississippi at night, glass of wine or champagne in hand, wearing only a thin silk robe. He gestured toward the window. "Five million dollars buys a hell of a view. And, I trust, a little goodwill."

"It buys a meeting to say thank you. It is not a quid pro quo. I want to be clear about that," she said.

Matheson nodded.

"Walt, please join us," he called to the next room.

Kimbel settled into the far corner of the sectional.

"We're not asking for much, Ms. Isaacson, just a little clarity in your messaging," Kimbel began. "The opioid crisis is getting worse, and we need to draw a line between what Genyra is doing and what everyone else is doing. You can help with that, rather than just, you know, bludgeoning Big Pharma to death."

"Xylaxyn," Matheson interjected, savoring the word. "It's not fentanyl. It's not addictive. We're starting to see local stories equating us to Purdue Pharma. Everyone associated with that company was an evil facilitator of the opioid crisis, from the CEO down to the lowest-level slimeball lobbyist. Xylaxyn is different. It wasn't that long ago that you helped me lobby the FDA."

Icy crossed her arms. "Is Xylaxyn so different? It's still a synthetic analgesic with limited clinical trials."

"And a cleaner safety profile than anything else on the market," Kimbel added. "We're not asking you to endorse it. Just to acknowledge the difference. Maybe even position Genyra as a company trying to change things."

Matheson leaned forward. "You're running for governor, Irene. You want to be the face of reform. This is your chance to back a solution instead of only prosecuting symptoms. It's a smart play."

Icy didn't blink. "Tell you what. I'll review the data. If it holds, I'll mention something in the right context, when and if appropriate."

There was a pause as Matheson evaluated the weakness of the offer, shaking his head.

Kimbel cleared his throat. "There's also the matter of escalating violence."

Icy's gaze flicked to him. "Such as?"

"Such as a drug murder in the Garden District. Wholesale violence out in the Ninth. Not a good look for the parish."

He neglected to mention the multiple homicides at Dorado Freight, as that was being dealt with quietly.

Irritated, she looked away from Kimbel to Matheson. "My office believes that's cartel spillover. What is this, Derek? Some kind of veiled threat? If I don't get in line with your messaging, then you flip the script? Get your PR girl to gin up a media campaign to hurt my run for governor? It won't work and you know it."

"Nobody's saying that. I'm your biggest donor, remember?"

She shook her head. "You think I need five million that badly? Your donation might just be the thing that taints my campaign and links me to one of the sources of the overall drug problem in this country. The very thing I'm trying to fix."

Kimbel leaned in. "Let's all relax here. We can both play offense if we want to, but that wouldn't serve anyone's interests. We all get what we want if we proceed with a bit of détente here, don't we? Ms. Isaacson, we want you to keep the five. There's more where that came from. All we want is a little softer, maybe even positive, messaging around Xylaxyn. Perhaps a better way to do it would be to talk up the Genyra wing at Tulane."

"Where Xylaxyn is relieving patients' suffering," Matheson added.

Icy stood up and slung her bag over a toned shoulder. "Thank you, gentlemen. I need to stay on schedule."

"What are you going to tell them?" Kimbel asked, laying it on the line.

"As you know, I can play it either way. Good day, gentlemen."

"Let me walk you out," Matheson said, getting to his feet.

"I remember the way," she said.

When he heard the door shut behind her, Matheson sat back down.

"Vargas would lose his mind if he heard that conversation," Kimbel said. "He expects us to get her under control."

"Unrealistic," Matheson replied. "I know her, and trust me, she'll throw us to the wolves if she thinks it'll help her campaign."

"I could leak some oppo research."

Matheson waved his hand in dismissal.

"What about our related issue?"

"Charlie Babineaux's dead. Vargas is sending some of his people in to take over the forwarding operation at the wharf. I'd normally tell you we should back off and lay low for a bit, but we just announced gangbuster numbers this quarter. We signaled to the Street that we'd beat our revenue target for quarter two by 20 percent."

"*We* didn't announce it, Walt. I did. What the fuck happened at Dorado anyway?"

"According to Bates, it was a guy and a dog. Single attacker. Killed Charlie, one of his foremen, and two of Vargas's enforcers."

"Jesus. Who is this guy?"

"You mean 'was.' That's the good news. The problem has been eliminated."

"They got him?"

"Bates confirmed it right before I walked in. It's not going to make the news, of course, but he's been taken out."

"Who the fuck was he?"

"I'm not sure. That's for Bates to worry about. Vargas will get Dorado back open, and we'll start moving product to hit our second-quarter numbers."

"I don't understand how nobody knows who this guy is, I mean *was*. Isn't there a body?"

"The hit was a little more creative than that."

"As long as we won't be hearing from him anymore."

"No chance."

CHAPTER FIFTY-TWO

THE DEA FIELD Office in New Orleans was a squat, windowless bunker tucked behind a chain-link fence off Tulane Avenue. It reminded Jarrett Stanton of the FBI's district headquarters on Lake Pontchartrain. It had the same brutalist architecture and the same institutional gray, but the vibe was different. The agents here looked like they had crawled out from under a bridge.

Stanton clocked one after another, each with a badge swinging from a lanyard and a wardrobe that suggested they shopped at thrift shops.

He followed Alvaro Mendez's administrative assistant down a narrow hallway lined with corkboards and wanted posters. Jennifer Jimenez was close behind, her heels clicking softly on the linoleum, a sound unusual enough in this building that several heads turned as she walked past.

They were led into a small conference room with a chipped laminate table and mismatched chairs. At the FBI, this kind of setup would have been replaced years ago.

Mendez was already waiting, cowboy boots crossed on a neighboring chair, a garish ceramic coffee mug in one hand and a cheap Naugahyde portfolio case closed on the desk before him. He didn't move until J.J. entered the room. Then he popped up like a jack-in-the-box, smile wide, hand extended.

Stanton suppressed a grin and took his seat.

"Can I get you guys coffee? Water?" Mendez offered.

"I'm good," Stanton said.

"J.J.?"

"I'm fine, thank you."

"You make any progress on your mystery man?" Mendez asked, settling back into his chair and taking a sip of coffee. "What did the witness call him? Cyclops?"

Stanton slid a folder from his bag and opened it to a grainy black-and-white still from a security camera. The image showed the back of a man's head as he exited the Federal Building.

"As a matter of fact, we did. Here he is at the Federal Building."

Mendez leaned forward, squinting. "Can't make out his face in these photos."

"We interviewed the U.S. marshal who interacted with him," J.J. replied. "The man refused to fill out the ID forms and bolted. The marshal remembered his vehicle, a VW van. A witness near the Staub home said the van was parked a block away. Another witness at the hit on the drug house in the Ninth gave us the sketch you saw."

"That still doesn't make him your Cyclops," Mendez said.

"No," Stanton replied. "For that, I had to make a trip up to D.C."

The DEA agent raised an eyebrow. "Oh yeah? Bureau database? Far as I can tell from this, your man is looking away. Not enough for facial recognition."

"I didn't tap the Bureau. I tapped the spooks."

Mendez sat up straighter, coffee mug forgotten. "What's this guy have to do with the Agency? And, for that matter, *this* agency?"

"His name is Chris Walker," Stanton said. "Twelve years as a Navy SEAL before transitioning to the Special Activities Center's Ground Branch. Served in Afghanistan. Picked up where he left off in the Teams."

"And the CIA just handed you that info?"

"I know a guy," Stanton said. "We worked counterterror together after the New Year's attack. I handled domestic leads. He handled international."

"The Agency isn't known for playing well with others," Mendez pointed out.

"We're not always arm-in-arm, but a lot of the pre-9/11 barriers have come down."

Mendez nodded slowly, lips pursed. "How can I help?"

Stanton glanced at J.J., who picked up the thread.

"Walker was at the Federal Building looking for a DEA contact. When presented with the standard forms to identify himself, he bolted. Now that we know more about his background, we looked up his known associates, specifically people he would have known in Afghanistan."

"One of them is John Staub, husband of the woman killed in the Garden District," Stanton said.

"Leigh Ann Staub was a charge nurse at Tulane. Her kid was found OD'd, heroin in the trunk," Mendez said, recalling his earlier conversation with Stanton. "What's that have to do with your *sicario*?"

"Chris Walker, our possible *sicario*, was tight with John Staub," Stanton said.

"You saying the son was mixed up in some shit and now rival dealers are using Walker to eliminate the competition?"

"It's a possibility," J.J. said.

She opened her folder and produced a page of names. "We cross-referenced associates in Afghanistan with federal agents who served with Walker and Staub. One was DEA, who also worked New Orleans. Javier Gonzalez. We'd like to talk to him."

Mendez swiveled in his chair, staring at the tabletop.

"We know Walker had a connection to Leigh Ann Staub through her husband," Stanton said. "We also know he had a connection to Javier Gonzalez. We suspect Walker is now working for the cartels as a contractor."

"You're going to buy the DA-NOPD narrative?"

"We are just following the evidence," J.J. countered.

"Other theories as to why Walker is in town?"

"Maybe a cartel hired him to hit Gonzalez next. Regardless, we need to talk to him," J.J. said.

"That's going to be tough."

"Why's that?" Stanton asked.

"Because Gonzo was killed yesterday afternoon in Mexico."

Stanton and J.J. shared a glance.

"When Jarrett told me your guy was looking for Gonzo, I made a few calls. I kept hitting brick walls, which told me he was undercover so I let it go. Our SAC called me in this morning and briefed me up. I had no idea Gonzo was even in Mexico. He was in deep. A farmer found him dead in a field, his throat slashed, tongue cut out. I'm going down tomorrow to escort his body home."

"I'm sorry," Stanton said.

Mendez retrieved three lukewarm water bottles from a stack on a side table. He offered one to each agent, then cracked his own and drank.

"What else can you share?" Stanton asked.

The DEA agent tapped his fingers on the portfolio.

"I don't know about your Cyclops guy, but I can tell you that Gonzo was chasing a lead in Mexico."

"What lead?"

"You've been following the recent uptick in opioid deaths around the country, I'm sure. After years of progress, we're seeing a reversal. Some of that's going on here in Louisiana."

"Yes," J.J. said. "We've analyzed the statistics. Recent trend is well above standard deviation. A lot of the Bureau intelligence is linking it back to Snowball."

"Well, if that's the case, then they're half-right. Some of it is Snowball," Mendez replied. "But it's the chemical agent inside Snowball that's doing the killing. We think it's getting cut into a ton of other pills: Adderall, Xanax, Valium. The stuff kids buy."

"Isn't that what happens with fentanyl?" J.J. asked.

"It is, but between DHS, DEA, and you guys, we've had material success degrading the fentanyl trade," Mendez said. "We worked upstream to Chinese labs, upped border detection, cracked down on the Mexican cartels. Then something took its place, a chemical compound known as nitazene. It's an opioid derivative and it's about five times as powerful as fentanyl. It's a killer."

"I don't get it," J.J. said. "Why would dealers use this stuff? Doesn't it just kill off their clients?"

"Portability," Mendez answered. "Because nitazene is so powerful, a little goes a long way and that makes smuggling easier. Dealers use it to juice up heroin or illegal prescriptions."

"What's the source?" Stanton asked.

"We don't know. It's an evolution of the drug trade. Ninety percent of users survive and buy another day, but you never know. The juiced-up versions mix with other drugs and body chemistry. That ten percent, their hearts just stop. We can't figure out where the hell it's coming from, other than the link to Snowball."

"Snowball is a nitazene?" Stanton asked. "Is that what you're saying?"

"It is, but it's diluted. The problem is that once Snowball is out there, dealers concentrate it. They boil it down and use acid to create a nitazene distillate. At least that's what we think."

"And Gonzalez was chasing this down?" J.J. asked. "Trying to get to the source?"

"That's what I learned from my boss this morning. Mexico may be the country of origin for nitazene-based product like Snowball."

"Can you trace it?" J.J. asked.

"Snowball just materialized all over the country, out of nowhere. We have yet to identify a single mule."

"And that lead?"

Mendez hesitated. "Remember when I said there's a CI in New Orleans who produces very good information who is way above my pay grade?"

"I remember," Stanton said.

"He's what we call a pearl."

"A *pearl*?"

"As in valuable but clammed up."

"I see."

"And in this case that pearl may be buried. This particular *pearl* is run through senior layers at headquarters to protect his identity."

"How do you know it's a he?" J.J. asked.

"Good point," Mendez acknowledged. "The pearl reported that Snowball was coming from the Jalisco cartel."

"And Gonzalez was working it?"

"I really don't know," Mendez said.

"We have a lot of connections here," Stanton said. "And they all seem to lead back to Chris Walker."

"All I know," Mendez replied, "is that the day your Cyclops showed up, a lot of people started dying." He tapped the surveillance photo. "We need to find this guy. Chris Walker, he's the key."

CHAPTER FIFTY-THREE

WALKER WOKE TO the sound of cicadas and the distant hum of a lawn mower. The guest room was dim, the curtains drawn against the sun. He sat up slowly, his body stiff, his head pounding. Paladin lay next to him, sleeping soundly under a down comforter.

Walker dressed in some of Alexandre's old clothes that Belle had laid out for him, khakis and a soft flannel shirt that fit surprisingly well. The shirt smelled faintly of cedar and pipe tobacco. He made his way to the kitchen.

Belle was already up, a binder spread out on the table.

"How's Paladin?" she asked.

"He's sleeping, dry and warm. Last night took a lot out of him, though. The bone broth and gumbo were just what both of us needed."

Belle's jeans and leather jacket of the previous night had been exchanged for a black Fleur du Mal flared corset dress. She still paired it with her scuffed Doc Martens.

"Why are you all dressed up?"

"Dressed up? It's hot. Found this thing at a thrift shop."

"Well, it looks, uh . . . it looks nice."

"A compliment? Thank you, kind sir," she said with a curtsy. "You hungry? It's almost lunch. How about Paladin, should we bring him something?"

"Let's let him sleep. He needs rest. Any more gumbo? That was delicious."

Belle pulled a Lodge cast-iron Dutch oven from the refrigerator and set it on the stove.

"Where's Gloria?"

"She went to the grocery store to get some dog food for Paladin and a few things for dinner. I get the feeling she likes having a man around the house. Be careful, I think she's writing up a 'honey do' list."

"I'm happy to help."

"She had me pull that old typewriter off a shelf in her closet," Belle said, motioning toward the dining room table just off the small living room. "She said she got it in 1966 from a salesman who told her that it was the same one Hemingway used."

Walker stepped into the dining room.

"Royal Quiet De Luxe," he said, reading the faded emblem. "Same as mine."

"She says the keys stick but that you are welcome to it if you can get it working."

Walker's eyes scanned the table. It contained the SSE binders from Dorado Freight and the security server he had yanked from the wall. It was attached to Belle's laptop.

Belle leaned against the archway between the kitchen and the dining room.

"I'll walk you through what I found after you eat," she said, her concern for him evident.

"Belle, I can't be here. It's not safe."

"We can talk about that after you eat. Come on," she said, gesturing with her head. "Gumbo's ready."

The gumbo was rich and smoky, ladled over a roasted quail. It was the kind of food that didn't just fill your stomach, it reminded you that you were alive. He ate slowly, methodically, lost in thought.

Belle picked at her food without really eating.

"Chris, the man who tried to kill you at the river. He was a cop. That makes three."

Walker finished his gumbo and pushed his plate to the side. He had given Belle the rundown last night on the drive to Gloria's.

"I know."

"They are going to find you."

"I know that too."

"That means they are going to find me. We are too connected now."

"I'm so sorry, Belle."

"We need to get this story out there with hard evidence that will blow this thing wide open. Get it to Greer, the reporter. If it's out there, then there is no need to silence us."

"There is another option," Walker said slowly.

"Why do I get a feeling I'm not going to like it?"

"This stopped being about Leigh Ann, Connor, or even John for me. Now it's about protecting you and Gloria."

"What do you mean?"

"I mean that after we map out this organization, everyone who's involved, I can do what I do best."

"What's that?"

"I can kill them all."

She bit her lower lip and slid her hand across the table, resting it on top of Walker's.

"Chris . . ."

"Like you said, I've already killed three cops. Dirty or not, they are not going to just let me walk, even if we expose this, and we don't really know what 'this' is yet. And if we do figure it out, the guilty might walk between the raindrops. People get off on technicalities all the time."

She squeezed Walker's hand.

"And all those books in your van on logic, reason, and meaning?"

"I'm using logic. I have reason. And meaning?" He paused. "You've given me that."

She brought Walker's hand to her lips, closed her eyes, lightly kissed it and then pressed it against her cheek, her tough exterior melting away.

"Belle, I . . ."

"Shhh . . . give me a second."

She held his hand to her face for another moment and then opened her eyes.

"Maybe one day you'll play a guitar for me," she said.

"Belle . . ."

"Come with me," she said, standing and walking into the dining room, her emotional armor back in place.

"I think I worked some of this out while you were swimming in the Mighty Miss."

"That's not funny."

"It's a little funny."

"Maybe a little."

"I've been working through these binders and cross-referencing them with Connor's decoded journal entries, searching for commonalities."

She leaned over the table and flipped open a binder; her dark nail polish–painted index fingernail stopped at a line and tapped. Then she opened another folder where she had highlighted a line on another page.

"See these? They are different. They aren't letters. They're numbers."

"Okay."

"You said you saw sacks of sugar at Dorado Freight."

"I saw sacks. The foreman I talked with told me it was refined sugar-cane, on its way to distributors."

"Right." She flipped a page. "If that's the main product at Dorado, you can see lots of activity; a bunch of repeating numbers in these notebooks. There was a railroad nearby, right?"

"Yes. Same line that runs along the river to the ports. Dorado is one of the port stops, probably dating back to the facility's Navy days."

"Well, if you look at most of the pass-through inventory flowing through Dorado, you can understand how they track it. See? The first four alphanumeric digits are coded the same. The next ones are five-digit numbers." She tapped the relevant entries with her black fingernail.

"I'm not following."

"I thought you were a genius. What do they teach you guys in the CIA?"

"Not whatever this is."

She opened her laptop and angled it in his direction. "I Googled the numbers. They're zip codes: Baltimore, Philly, New York. Within each of those zips is a food processing center. When I searched for information on them, I found that their customers are food service suppliers. They deliver food to restaurants."

"So?"

"So, if the bulk of the Dorado business is sugar, these were probably going off to those big consumer markets. That's legit freight. This set of numbers," she said, tapping one of her highlights, "is different. Only four digits. And it happens at irregular intervals. Every now and then, it's there with the probable sugar shipments. In this case, it's not."

Walker looked as she flipped through the various dates and coded outgoing shipments.

"I feel like I'm missing something."

"I told you I'm working on my master's in management information systems, right?"

"I still don't really know what that is."

"And I mentioned that I studied accounting at LSU?"

"You did."

"Well, this structure suggests that the first four digits are a different SKU and that the lack of a zip code means it was either a local shipment or set aside to be picked up at Dorado."

"Where are you going with this?"

"Here," she said, connecting her computer to the video surveillance server Walker had taken from the Dorado management office.

"How did you get this working?"

"It uses a standard USB-C power cable," she said. "I connected it via a regular HDMI cable into my laptop, downloaded the public software, and voilà."

"You didn't need a password?"

"This is a closed security system, not cloud-based, probably because they wanted to be able to destroy any video evidence rather than let it get subpoenaed. I was able to pull it right up."

"How do you know this again?"

"Management information systems, Chris. I kind of want a real job one day."

"How does this help us?" he asked.

"Simple. We cross-reference the dates from those shipments without zip codes with the dates captured on the video and see who is picking up what."

"Now that really is genius."

"I already did it. Check this out."

She tapped a date and then scrolled until she found a specific entry.

"Here's one of those frames."

Walker watched as a yellow F-350 pickup with a brush bar drove up to a container. A man stepped out of the passenger seat and stood talking with Babineaux while a forklift entered the container, backed up, swiveled, and deposited a loaded pallet in the back of the pickup.

"Can we figure out who that guy is talking to Babineaux?"

"Way ahead of you."

Belle paused the video.

"I went back and looked at the media reporting on the night of Leigh Ann's murder. One of the police officers they interviewed was a Lieutenant Cornelius Bates of the NOPD."

"Is that Bates talking with Babineaux?"

She moused to another browser tab.

"No. *This* is Bates talking to reporters." She paused the video. "See the guy just behind him? That's the same guy who stepped out of the yellow truck."

"And let me guess. You have a name."

She went to another tab that opened to the New Orleans Police Department COPE Unit.

"Meet Detective Howard Gormley. He's in a bunch of other video cuts, driving up alone in a Dodge Charger."

Walker's eyes narrowed, and for a moment he was back on the banks of the Mississippi River watching a yellow F-350 disappear into the current.

"It begs the question," Belle said, "why is a detective with the New Orleans Police Department picking up a pallet at Dorado Freight in the same truck that rammed you into the river last night?"

"There's one way to find out," Walker said.

"What's that?"

"We ask him."

CHAPTER FIFTY-FOUR

BUILT IN THE 1920s, the NOPD building on Royal Street had survived hurricanes, riots, and a thousand bad decisions. The walls were thick, the windows tall, and the floors were polished to a dull shine. It smelled faintly of dust and bureaucracy. The place had history. And Lieutenant Cornelius Bates liked history, especially when it made him look good.

He stood at the front of the basement briefing room, arms folded across his chest, the sleeves of his uniform rolled just enough to show off the forearms and biceps he had worked on that morning at the New Orleans Athletic Club. His shirt was crisp. His badge gleamed on his belt. His jaw was freshly shaved, and his head was shining.

The COPE squad sat in rows before him. Community Outreach through Police Engagement. He was proud of the acronym. He had come up with it after all. A dozen officers, handpicked, uniformed, sat before him. The room was cool, the air humming with the low buzz of fluorescent lights and the distant echo of Bourbon Street traffic. Even the AC was working.

Bates scanned the rows, his eyes sharp and calculating. He liked this part, the performance. The authority. He lived for it.

"It's been a long week," he said, voice smooth. "We've got heat in the Ninth. Gang activity's up. Got a few new faces pushing product. Some of it looks like heroin, some of it might be worse, based on the national trends we sent out in the reports. I trust you've read them?"

Respectful nods.

"Good. We're seeing movement near likely drug markets on Clouet. You know the drill. Stay frosty. I want particular attention here."

He clicked the remote. A map of the Ninth Ward appeared on the screen behind him, dotted with red pins.

"Same players," he continued. "Same turf. But there's chatter about a new supplier. We're hearing Mexican cartels but that's not confirmed. Keep your eyes open for cartel profiles—tattoos, accents, vehicles that don't belong. Sergeant Strickland, you'll take lead on the street where Rayne and Hendrick got hit."

"On it, Lieutenant."

"Hound, you back up leads any of these guys dig up related to the case." Bates raised his eyes to the rows behind Gormley. "Y'all catch that? If you hear anything about the hit on our people, you funnel it through Detective Gormley. Clear?"

A hand went up near the back.

Officer Tasha Campbell. Mid-thirties, sharp-eyed, earnest. One of the few in the room who still believed in the job. Bates had recruited her for optics, but she'd turned out to be competent.

Too competent.

"Yeah, Campbell."

She lowered her hand. "Sir, are we still looking for that blue VW van from the Garden murders? Any update on that?"

Bates cursed inwardly.

The van. That damn van had probably been swept like sewer shit five miles out into the Gulf. Good riddance. Fucking Campbell.

He kept his face neutral and defused the question.

"Keep an eye out for a vehicle matching that description, but more importantly stay alert for gangbangers—Bloods, 39ers, whatever's crawling out of the Ninth, and anybody fitting a cartel profile. Get all that to Detective Gormley."

Campbell nodded, but her eyes lingered on the map a second too long.

Bates moved on.

"I do have some darker news: Sergeant Dupuis did not check in today. His truck is not at his house and he is not answering any calls. With increased cartel activity in the Ninth and the recent murders of Officers Hendrick and Rayne, I want him found and I want him found today."

He looked around the room as heads nodded in agreement.

"Stay alert tonight," he said. "No heroics. No headlines. We're not here to make the news. We're here to keep it quiet."

That was a good line.

He dismissed them with a nod.

The officers filed out, murmuring among themselves. Campbell lingered momentarily and then followed her fellow officers into the hall. Bates watched her go, making a mental note to keep an eye on her.

Bates and Gormley were the last to leave. Bates led the way down the hall, past the bullpen and the evidence lockers, into a side room that had once been an armory. The walls were lined with steel cabinets and racks of riot gear. The lights were dim.

Gormley closed the door behind them while Bates confirmed they were alone.

"Give it to me," Bates said.

"I went back in the light this morning. No sign of Dupuis or the truck, but I found blood and followed it about seventy-five yards downriver. More blood on the rocks. Footprints, bare feet. And tire tracks."

"Slow down, Hound."

"Someone, probably Dupuis, was killed by a man in bare feet down by the water's edge and then dragged back to where I left him and the truck. Those bare feet then led out to the train tracks. And there were tire tracks in the mud, unmistakably from Dupuis's truck."

"Tire tracks?"

"They led right into the water. Fucking truck is gone and I think we have to assume Dupuis is gone with it."

"Damn it. Why did you leave him unattended? Neverfuckingmind. It's done."

"I saw the van go under. Nobody could have survived that. Goddamn it, who the fuck is this guy?"

"I ran the plate. Van was registered to someone named Chris Walker out of Oregon. No criminal record but I'm still digging."

"Corn, it's time to use the media. Get this guy's driver's license and plaster it all over the news. Give it to Greer. He can report that this Walker bastard is wanted for questioning in connection with the Garden murders or some shit."

Bates paused, put his hands on his hips, and drew in a deep breath.

"Not quite yet."

"What do you mean 'not quite yet'? He's killed three of us, seven Salvadorans, and our two most profitable dealers. You or I might be next."

"He couldn't possibly know who we are."

"We have underestimated this guy from the start."

"You let me worry about that. What's happening at Dorado?"

"Replacements from down south are coming up to replenish the losses along with a team of hitters to deal with our lone assassin."

"Just what we need in this city, more assassins. What about the bodies from Dorado?"

"I cleaned it up with some help from our friends. The Salvadorans went the way of the swamp. No one will miss them. Babineaux is with them, but as far as anyone knows he's lost at sea, out on his boat in the Gulf."

Gormley was a master at manipulating a crime scene. "How'd you pull that off?"

"He had an advanced nav system. After taking it downriver, I programmed a course all the way to Trinidad, though it won't make it that far."

"Coast Guard might pick it up."

"They might find the boat, but not Babineaux. Pirates, you know. Hell, that thing might be in Mexico by now."

"Okay," Bates said, exhaling. "Four fucking dead at Dorado. Shit, the press would have a field day with that, especially after the Garden and Ninth murders. You sure it's the same guy?"

"It has to be. He's getting closer, Corn. You should contact the Afghan."

"We don't talk about him within these walls."

"He's got fucking skills, you told me he does. I'll pay. I don't give a shit. Chris Walker needs to die."

"Hey, calm down. He's gotten as close as he's going to. And we still don't know for sure if Dupuis is dead."

"He's fucking dead, Corn. He didn't drive himself into the damn river. And there's something else." The sweat was beading up on Gromley's temples and upper lip.

"What?"

"Dupuis had that truck outfitted as a rolling arsenal. He showed me some tricked-out AR and a new pistol. Our mystery man has got to be in possession of them now."

"Shit. Just stay cool and keep your head on a swivel."

"You do the same, and promise me, the next time we find him we don't set up surveillance; no tails, no arrest. There is something about this guy that's not adding up. He's a fucking ghost or an avenging angel or some shit. He's not right."

Bates had never seen his lead detective so agitated.

"He's not a ghost, Hound. He's a man. He bleeds, you said so yourself. His vehicle is gone. He's just got the clothes on his back. The footprints indicate he doesn't even have fucking shoes. We'll find him, and when we do, he's a dead man."

CHAPTER FIFTY-FIVE

THE AMC EAGLE rumbled through the late-afternoon traffic on I-10, its engine a low growl beneath the hood. A canvas satchel filled with Alexandre's old tools was in the seat next to Walker. It held pliers, wire cutters, the soldering iron, and a roll of duct tape so old it had yellowed at the edges. He thought of his conversation with Gloria, out of earshot from Belle, when she had insisted that he take the car.

"I have not seen Belle this alive in a long time. I love her but I worry about her and now I worry about you too. I know that Connor and his mother were both killed and that she wants to know why. I wish she would stop but I know she won't. It's not our way. When you get as old as I am you can sense things, and I can tell you are hurt. So is Belle. You take care of each other."

"I won't let anything happen to her."

"I know."

Was that another promise he would not be able to keep?

Belle wanted to go with him, but he would not hear of it. It would have been safer for him if he had given her a shopping list, but some of the items he needed were extremely specific. He told her she could help by taking care of Paladin. The dog was not getting any worse, but now preferred to stay in the guest room. Walker asked Belle to take Paladin to the vet and had left her three thousand dollars from Dupuis's truck to cover the expense. He hated to leave Paladin behind, but the dog needed rest and Walker had a mission to complete.

The Home Depot parking lot was half-empty when he arrived. It was thirty minutes before closing. Inside, the aisles were quiet. A few last-minute shoppers wandered the rows, grabbing light bulbs and paint rollers. Walker moved with purpose, his ill-sized flip-flops slapping against the concrete floor. Alexandre had small feet and his shoes didn't fit. Walker would take care of that at his next stop.

He started in plumbing. PVC pipe, two-inch diameter. He selected three lengths, cut to size. Then end caps, threaded and smooth. A roll of Teflon tape.

Next, electrical, where he added wire, switches, zip ties, and a pair of battery-powered timers. He added a spool of copper wire and a pack of crimp connectors.

In hardware, he found nails, nuts, bolts, and a small pry bar.

In outdoor power equipment he picked up jerry cans.

In doors and windows he picked up the most inexpensive garage door openers he could find.

Then came the chemicals.

He moved to the garden section, where bags of fertilizer lined the shelves like sandbags. He scanned the labels, found what he was looking for, and added two fifty-pound bags to his cart. Then, from the paint aisle, he added a canister of aluminum powder, which was marketed as a metallic pigment. While in the paint section he picked up a roll of plastic meant to be used as a floor covering for interior house painting.

Finally, he turned into seasonal clearance. A bin of Christmas lights sat near the endcap, tangled and dusty. He picked out a jumbo string of two hundred bulbs, multicolored and deeply discounted.

He pushed his cart to the assisted self-checkout line, scanned his items, and then used the pay cash option, peeling off well-circulated twenties from Dupuis's stash and giving them to the plump young woman who monitored the self-checkout area to assist with transactions and provide change to anyone paying in cash. She was oblivious to the fact that everything in his cart was dual use, components to make a bomb.

Outside, the sun was low, casting long shadows across the parking lot. He loaded the supplies into the Eagle, scanning for any signs of surveillance.

His next stop was Cabela's.

It was ten miles north, just off the highway, its façade lit like a lodge, antlers and camouflage in every direction. Walker moved quickly. His first stop was the shoe department. They did not carry his favored Iron Rangers, but he found a pair of black Merrell Nova 3 boots that would do the trick. Next, he grabbed multiple layers of Cabela's branded camouflage and 5.11 Tactical clothing, nylon belt, and Benchmade Anonimus fixed-blade knife. Then it was camouflage netting, a sleeping bag and tent, headlamp, carabiners, webbing, freeze-dried food, cooler, dive mask, fins, snorkel, wet suit, dry bags, and a Nautica Navigator Seascooter. He paid cash again, declined the loyalty program, and packed up the Eagle.

He quickly ducked into a mini-mart across the street for a couple gallons of milk before hitting the road.

By the time he reached Chalmette, the sun had dipped below the horizon. The national battlefield memorial was quiet, the visitor center closed, and the last of the tourists had long gone. Sprawled along the east bank of the river, Chalmette was more than a hundred acres of preserved woods, fields, and eroded berms. It was here that Andrew Jackson had taken his Tennessee Volunteers to fight off the British in the War of 1812. Weeks after setting fire to the White House, the British had sailed south, intending to lay claim to the Mississippi and envelop the young United States, taking back the land Napoleon had sold to Jefferson. They hadn't counted on Old Hickory lying in wait.

Walker turned off the main road and followed a narrow gravel path that skirted the edge of the park. Beyond the visitor center, the manicured lawns gave way to a stand of oak, cypress, and willow thick enough to swallow sound and shadow. He eased the AMC into the woods, tires rolling softly over fallen leaves, and drove until he found a natural depression behind a thicket of oaks and parked beneath a canopy of moss-draped branches.

It was time to set up his combat outpost.

He draped the camo netting over the Eagle, anchoring the edges with tent stakes and lengths of rope. He adjusted the angles until the vehicle vanished into the terrain.

He set up the stove and boiled water, poured it into a pouch of freeze-dried chili, and sat on a log, watching steam curl into the night.

Nearby, a weathered sign caught his eye. It was half-hidden behind a vine-choked fence post, its lettering faded but legible in the twilight: *U.S. Government Property. No Trespassing. Violators Will Be Prosecuted.*

He had killed and bled for his country, buried friends under its flag. And now, here he was, trespassing on a battlefield, setting up a hide site and preparing for war.

The irony wasn't lost on him.

His council of inner philosophers had been silent most of the day, but now they started asking questions again. He thought of Heraclitus, who argued that no matter how much a man's circumstances might change, his nature would always draw him back to the same conflict. That idea led him to think about the eternal return and Nietzsche's ideas about the inevitability of repeated behavior as a cause of fate. Though his edition of *Twilight of the Idols* was now at the bottom of the Mississippi, one of its quotes and concepts was indelibly printed on his soul: *He who has a why to live can bear almost any how.*

CHAPTER FIFTY-SIX

SIX MILES UPRIVER from Walker's forward operating base, Walt Kimbel and Carloyn Boyle prepped Derek Matheson on the particulars of his upcoming speaking engagement at the BioFrontiers Summit in Dallas. With the heat on operations in New Orleans, Kimbel would stay behind on damage control while Matheson and his EVP of marketing handled the event in Texas.

"Remember," Carolyn said, "this is a victory lap. Everyone in that room wants to be you."

"There will be jealous parties," Kimbel interjected, "but that just means your success and that of Genyra Pharmaceuticals has eclipsed all competitors. Enjoy it. This is your time."

Kimbel's phone buzzed and he glanced at the caller ID.

Matheson noticed that it was his burner phone.

"Excuse me," Kimbel said. "I need to take this."

He moved into the next room while Matheson and Carolyn continued to go over the attendee list. When he returned, his face was lacking the color of moments earlier.

"Carolyn, I need to talk with the boss. Give us a moment?"

"I think we are about wrapped up," Matheson said. "We can go over any additional details on the flight. Thank you, Carolyn."

"Thank you, sir. See you tomorrow."

As she gathered her things, Matheson couldn't help but wonder what was under her black pantsuit. She was always so dammed professional. Maybe this trip to Dallas without Kimbel in tow would be the time.

Stay away from the help, especially your executive team.

Kimbel sat and tapped his phone against his knee, waiting until he was certain that Carolyn was gone.

"What is it?" Matheson asked.

"That news I gave you about our mystery killer not being a problem any longer seems to have been premature."

"Damn it, Walt! You told me the problem had been eliminated."

Matheson stood and walked to the window, his back to his chief commercial officer.

"I know, sir. That is what I was told."

"Incompetent assholes! The body. I specifically asked about the body." He turned back around.

"I know."

"Well, now fucking what?"

"It's, uh, worse than him just being alive."

"Of course it is."

"He may have killed another cop."

"Jesus."

"And . . ."

"And what?"

"And, it's possible he stole the officer's weapons, a rifle and pistol."

"So, not only is he still alive, but he killed another cop connected to us and has that cop's guns? Are we on his radar?"

"That's unlikely but unknown."

"I want you to brief Harris on all this, on the additional threat, part I mean."

"I will, sir."

"Now what?"

"Vargas is sending a team."

"Well, that's something."

"And we now have a name: Chris Walker."

"Who the fuck is Chris Walker?"

"They said he's a former SEAL."

"Like a Navy SEAL?"

"Yes, sir."

"Fucking terrific. Professional killers. I've seen the movies."

"There's more. He also worked for the CIA."

"What?" Matheson exploded.

"I know, sir, but they assure me he will be taken care of."

"They already assured us of that. Why don't they just put out an APB on this Walker guy and have every cop in the state looking for him?"

"I try to protect you from most of this, sir. There are some things you don't need to know."

"You just told me that some SEAL assassin CIA psycho with an arsenal who's killed three cops is coming after me. I need to know!"

"I didn't say that, sir. He probably doesn't know who you are."

"Probably, Christ! Listen to yourself."

"Let me put it this way: our contacts in NOPD don't want this guy talking. It's only a matter of time."

"Time is running out, as is my patience, to say nothing of Vargas. Jesus, Walt, they don't call him Cuchillo as a term of endearment."

"Vargas needs us and he needs his network of bought-and-paid-for law enforcement."

"Chris Walker. Jesus. I'm tempted to start drinking again."

"They'll find him, sir, either the cops or Vargas's crew. Let me put it this way: I wouldn't want to be Chris Walker right now."

"For all our sakes, let's pray they find him before he finds us."

CHAPTER FIFTY-SEVEN

IT HAD TAKEN three days of reconnaissance and preparation. Walker was ready.

He clung to a stanchion on the dockside crane at Dorado Freight in the darkness, observing. The Nautica Navigator Seascooter he had picked up at Cabela's had conserved his energy on his swim upriver. He was in a thin black wet suit with a nylon belt that held his fixed blade, pistol, and a short steel wrecking bar. Back camo paint was smeared on his face and in his hair, and Merrell Nova 3 boots were on his feet. A Sea to Summit Big River dry bag pack was stashed ashore. It was empty now, but just over an hour ago it had held his backup plan.

In his hide site at Chalmette, he had mixed the fertilizer and aluminum powder in jugs and built detonators from rifle cartridges, combining hydrogen peroxide, acid, and acetone into a white powder after being filtered and dried. He had learned how to build the devices from the EOD techs in his SEAL platoons and Development Group squadrons. He had also excelled at the HME—Homemade Explosives—course at Dugway Proving Ground in Utah and gone even deeper studying the IEDs of the enemy in both Iraq and Afghanistan. He built upon that foundation in the CIA through advanced courses at Harvey Point, North Carolina, where he had perfected the darkest of arts. Now he was going to use that expertise on U.S. soil.

He was ready. All that remained was to wait for Gormley.

On his first day of reconnaissance, he was surprised that the area where he dispatched Babineaux and the three henchmen was not a crime scene. Had they simply cleaned it up and continued with business as usual? *Who can make four bodies disappear?*

Belle's video analysis indicated that Detective Howard Gormley met someone at Dorado Freight on Mondays, Wednesdays, and Fridays at midnight. Walker had confirmed it on Monday. He met with a man who

Walker guessed to be Babineaux's replacement. If the pattern from the hard drive Walker had liberated from the office held true, the detective would be there in an hour. Walker would be ready.

The river lapped softly against the pilings. A barge sloshed in the distance.

Walker adjusted his position and scanned the road. Headlights. A Dodge Charger. Same make and model as in the video. Why was Gormley early? Why had he broken the pattern?

Should he wait until Friday to make his move?

That would give the authorities two more days to tighten the noose. Walker needed answers tonight. The longer this played out, the greater the odds that the violence that found Connor and Leigh Ann would also find Belle and Gloria.

Walker climbed down from his perch on the crane, rubber soles silent on steel rungs. He moved quickly to the back side of a dumpster.

Walker had thirty seconds before Gormley's vehicle would emerge from the other side of a row of containers. He slipped the Dewalt twenty-four-inch wrecking bar from his belt, sprinted low across the dock, and took up his position behind a stack of pallets. Heart steady. Breath slow.

The cruiser rolled to a stop. The door opened. Gormley stepped out. Walker watched as he pulled up his pants, burped, and looked around. He reached back into his vehicle and extracted a long flashlight. He turned it on and shined it into the darkness.

Don't move.

Walker remained perfectly still. Movement would draw the eye.

Gormley had never done that before. Maybe with Dupuis gone he was being more cautious.

The light passed over him once and then returned.

Stay still but be ready.

Gormley turned off the light and threw it back into his vehicle.

The detective grunted and approached the trailer.

As he fumbled with his keys, Walker made his move, sprinting toward his target.

The short crowbar connected with the base of Gormley's skull with a sickening crack that reminded Walker of a gunshot.

The detective fell forward against the door and then back onto the concrete.

For a moment Walker worried that he'd killed him.

He quickly checked for breathing and a pulse.

Still alive.

Walker slid the crowbar into his belt and frisked the downed officer, relieving him of his duty pistol and extra mag, his backup ankle gun, badge, wallet, and his car keys. Setting them aside, he removed Gormley's handcuffs and secured them around the man's meaty wrists, locking them behind his back.

Then he grabbed him by the cuffs and dragged him toward his Charger, feeling and hearing both shoulders pop from their sockets. It was a struggle but he managed to work the larger man into the cage in the back of the police cruiser, locking him behind the partition that usually separated the good guys from the bad.

He retrieved Gormley's personal items from where he had fallen and deposited those in the passenger seat. Then he started the car and slowly drove down the pier, stopping about ten yards from the end. He cut the engine.

As he waited for Gormley to come to, he inspected the interior of the unmarked cruiser. No shotgun or rifle. He popped the trunk and found a medical kit and Remington 870. It's tubular magazine was fully loaded but the chamber was empty. He put both in the passenger seat and slid behind the wheel.

Hearing movement in the back seat from behind the protective partition, he twisted in his seat.

Gormley blinked, dazed, then attempted to push himself up, screaming in pain at the effort.

"I heard your shoulders pop out of their sockets, Gormley. Probably rotator cuff tears. Painful. A good surgeon could fix you right up, but after tonight you won't need a doctor, you'll need a mortician."

"Who . . . who the fuck are you?"

Walker saw the recognition dawn across the detective's face, a recognition quickly replaced by terror.

"Please," Gormley gasped. "Please, I'm not the guy you want."

"Who do I want?"

"Fuck." Gormley strained and fought through the agony, positioning himself upright in the back seat. He was sweating profusely and breathing like he had just finished a marathon.

"It's time for a little talk, Detective. I took out Rayne, Hendrick, and Dupuis. I'm working my way up the chain. Tonight, you are going to tell me who else is involved in your little operation. If you are truthful with me, I might let you live. If you are not, well . . ." Walker started the Charger. "We are going to see if your car here floats."

"Jesus, come on. Don't do this. What do you want? Who hired you? The cartel?"

Cartel?

"That's not how this works. You don't ask the questions. You're in the back seat tonight."

"Okay, okay," Gormley said, straining to catch his breath.

"What are you moving through Dorado?"

"Sugar."

"Not the legal product. The stuff you *personally* move. In your partner's yellow truck, the same one I sent into the river."

"Pills."

"What kind?"

"Jesus, man, they'll kill me."

"I'll kill you just as dead."

"Fuck! Snowball."

"How does it get here?"

"On ships from down south. With sugar."

"Whose sugar?"

"Nectar. It's a refinery downriver, not far from here, just down the tracks. Big company. I just do what I'm told, buddy, that's it."

Walker's eyes narrowed. "But you get a cut, don't you? I've seen you pick up product in that F-350. What do you do with it?"

"We sell it."

"Like in the Ninth? Through dealers under NOPD control, officers like Rayne and Hendrick?"

Gormley nodded slowly, still catching his breath. "Yes."

"I've seen the video here at Dorado. I've watched you pick up pallets, probably six or eight hundred pounds' worth. If that's all pills, you're not unloading it all in the Ninth. It'd be everywhere in this city."

When Gormley didn't answer, Walker revved the engine and rolled down the driver's- and passenger-side windows.

"Okay, okay," Gormley screamed.

"Where does that Snowball go?"

"We sell it to a company. A pharma company. We just get a slice."

"What company?"

"Genyra. That's all I know."

"Genyra?"

"A drug company."

Walker thought of Connor's theories, a corporate conspiracy.

"How do you get it to this . . . Genyra . . . the drug company?"

"I drive it."

"When you load up here with a truck, where do you go?"

"I deliver it to their depot in Metairie. A distribution center."

"Who picks it up there?"

Gormley's eyes shifted. "I don't know. I leave it at the edge of the warehouse."

Walker shifted the cruiser into gear and edged closer to the end of the pier.

"I need a name."

He inched forward farther.

"Oh, come on, man."

"Name."

He gunned the engine again.

"Walt Kimbel," Gormley blurted.

"Who's he?"

"Senior exec at Genyra. Oversees deliveries. We code pallets for him. That's all I know."

"Does he work for the DA?"

"The DA? Isaacson?"

"Yeah."

"I don't fucking know, man! I'm just a low-level cop trying to get by. I swear!"

"What about Connor Staub?"

"Who?"

"You know who I'm talking about. You kill him?"

"No."

"Did NOPD kill him?"

Walker floored the accelerator, ate up a few more feet, and then slammed on the brake, sending Gormley careening into the partition.

"Stop! Stop!" he screamed. "Rayne and Hendrick found out he was snooping around, asking questions, putting together a story. Dumbass kid. He wasn't even a reporter. They tried to warn him off, but he kept investigating. Started getting close."

"So, you killed him?"

Walker inched the car forward.

"The end of the pier is getting close, Gormley. Who killed Connor Staub?"

"Oh fuck. We outsourced it. I don't know how, exactly. My boss handled it."

"Bates?"

"Oh shit, yeah, Bates," he said, through the snot and tears that were now falling down his face.

"Who did he hire?"

"He won't tell me. He calls him the Afghan."

For a moment, Walker was back on the Afghanistan-Pakistan border, leaving his dead friend behind.

"The Afghan?"

"Some refugee that Bates met in the 2025 New Year's attack investigation. The guy had nothing to do with it, but Bates got to know him. He worked for the U.S. in Afghanistan. Came to New Orleans in 2021 after the withdrawal. I've never met him, but Bates swears he's solid."

"What's his name?"

"I don't know his fucking name. I just told you. We just call him the Afghan. We use him when we need to keep some distance."

"You son of a bitch. And Leigh Ann Staub?"

"That was you fucking guys!" Gormley hollered.

"What do you mean?"

"Cartel!"

"What do you do here at night?"

"I pick up cash from a safe in the office."

"Why were you early tonight?"

"Early? I just came for money. My cut."

"Why early?"

Headlights from two vehicles illuminated the trailer.

Gormley twisted his head and saw them too.

He laughed.

"That's what I was doing here early, you dumb motherfucker."

The headlights shifted toward the pier.

"Who are they?"

"They're here for you. Hitters from down south. Six, maybe more. Now let's make a deal. You let me go and I keep them from killing you tonight. That's the best offer you are going to get."

Walker watched as the two cars sped toward him.

"Wait here."

Walker grabbed the shotgun, exited the vehicle, and unzipped his Orvis waterproof sling, extracting a garage door opener.

As the cars got closer, he recognized them as a minivan and a full-sized truck.

He waited until they were mid-pier and then he pressed the button.

The garage door opener sent a radio frequency to its receiver that completed a circuit and delivered a small electrical charge to the Christmas light bulbs buried in the milk jugs that Walker had set next to the concrete pier pilings hours earlier. Instead of illuminating a festive light, the electric spark ignited the peroxide powder, which in turn detonated the ammonium nitrate and aluminum mixture packed into milk jugs wrapped in nails, nuts, and bolts.

The four simultaneous explosions lit up the night and sent the shrapnel flying through the thin metal doors of the approaching vehicles, the blast directed inward due to the IEDs' placement against the pilings.

The lead vehicle swerved to the right and smashed into one of the supports. The truck continued, rolling past the disabled minivan and slowed to a stop.

Walker racked the shotgun and moved forward.

The driver of the truck kicked open the door and fell to the pier. Walker's double aught took him in the chest. Walker racked the shotgun and fired into the man's head. He then set the weapon's stock on top of his right shoulder and twisted it to the outside. He grabbed the most forward shell on the side saddle with his index finger and the next shell in line with his pinky. He moved his thumb behind the second shell and slid both into the loading port on the underside of the shotgun to top himself off. He then approached the open driver's-side door and looked across to see a man in the passenger seat struggling to breathe. Walker aligned his sights on his face and pressed the trigger, immediately racking the shotgun again to chamber another cartridge.

He stepped to the rear passenger door on the driver's side and unloaded two more barrages through the closed window before he opened it to find a man sprawled in the back seat. Walker leveled the barrel at the top of the man's head and fired again.

He topped off the shotgun with the remaining four shells in his side saddle and moved to the minivan. As he came around the back corner of the pickup, he saw a man in khakis and a tank top holding a stainless revolver wiping blood from his face. Walker shot him once in the chest and again in the face as he dropped to his knees. Gunfire erupted through the windows of the minivan, in his general direction, but it was wild and ineffective.

Four rounds left.

He continued his approach, sending his final four rounds into the source of the shots. As his weapon went dry, he dropped it to the ground and drew the Staccato from his belt. He fired as he walked to the open sliding door of the vehicle, adjusting aim as bodies came into view: driver, passenger, and another man in the back seat. Walker put rounds into each of their heads before walking back to the Charger.

He was now on the clock.

"Jesus," Gormley stammered. "You killed them all."

"And you tried stalling, talking to me, knowing you had men on the way."

"I'm sorry. Please, let me live and I'll tell you anything you want to know."

"Unfortunately for you, those explosions mean that cops will be here any minute. If it's any consolation, your buddy Bates will be joining you soon."

"No, please," he pleaded.

Walker revved the engine.

"Christ, man, who the fuck are you?" he asked, eyes wide in horror.

"You know who I am."

Walker put the car in drive, and then stepped from the vehicle, letting it roll forward and plunge into the Mississippi.

Gormley screamed the whole way down.

CHAPTER FIFTY-EIGHT

NEW ORLEANS FIRE Department trucks, ambulances, marked and unmarked police cars, and vehicles from a slew of federal agencies had descended upon Dorado Freight. Mobile command centers and tents had gone up to process what was already being called an act of terrorism by the media.

The scene had been cordoned off until the NOPD bomb squad finished a thorough clearance of the entire facility to ensure there were no additional IEDs. The morning rain mixed with the remnants of the four explosive devices and gave the air around the pier an edge of acrid metallic notes as if to remind those standing among the bodies and wreckage of their own mortality.

But by the Grace of God . . .

The press was being held outside the front gates for safety reasons and to preserve an active crime scene. Local media had arrived before sunup, with national news networks steadily increasing their presence in the intervening hours. All of them were scrambling for sound bites and video. Helicopters were grounded due to weather but would be up as soon as they had clearance.

Stanton stood by what was left of the truck as a team of CSI technicians continued to take photos and bag evidence. His FBI windbreaker was soaked, collar turned up against the downpour. Water dripped from the brim of his Bureau-issued cap. Beside him, J.J. squinted through the rain taking notes on a small pad streaked with ink. They had been on the scene since before dawn, waiting for the go-ahead from the bomb squad.

The blasts had done minimal damage to the pier but maximum damage to the two vehicles. The seven dead bodies were covered in gang-affiliated tattoos. None of the victims carried driver's licenses or passports. Audie Lloyd had been getting twitchy. Icy was breathing down his neck, pushing the Mexican *sicario* angle. Lloyd wanted results and he wanted them fast.

"Are we sure there is no video surveillance system?" Stanton asked. "Seems strange that this place wouldn't have security."

J.J. shook her head. "There are cameras, but someone ripped out the server. Wires are torn and twisted where it was set up in the office."

"Ripped out before the blast?"

"Hard to say."

Stanton scanned the two-vehicle wreckage and seven bodies.

"This was Chris Walker. No doubt in my mind."

"You share that with Bates yet?"

"I called him on the way here and filled him in. It was time."

"IEDs, more dead bangers, and a missing cop. We have a pattern," J.J. said quietly.

They moved closer to the minivan.

"Look at these head wounds," Stanton said. "He took out the guys in the truck with a shotgun, goes dry when approaching the minivan, and transitions to a pistol. Confirms they are all dead with security rounds. And that smell; these were fertilizer-based IEDs."

"Why would Walker be meeting foreign nationals on the pier of Dorado Freight? And why was a detective from NOPD here? The GPS on his vehicle puts him on this pier about the time of the incident and then he just disappears?"

Stanton looked to the end of the pier where the NOPD dive team was surveying the conditions.

"He didn't just disappear," Stanton said.

"You think Walker put him in the drink?"

"We'll know soon enough."

J.J. flipped through her notes. "NOPD says the GPS in Gormley's cruiser pinged by the office. Last location was the end of the pier."

Stanton looked back over the destruction.

"Are we sure one guy did all this?" J.J. asked. "It would take serious skills to pull this off."

"The kind of skills they teach in the SEAL Teams and in the CIA," Stanton said.

She glanced at her damp notebook. "According to what I've been able to put together, Walker was a philosophy major at NYU, working on a doctorate. This doesn't seem like the work of a philosopher."

"My CIA contact said he was unstable. Manic depressive. Possibly schizophrenic, maybe on the spectrum. He was drummed out of the CIA for reasons that remain classified."

"That's a big piece of this puzzle."

"It is."

"A theory," she said. "Walker was working for the cartel. They somehow burned him or failed to pay him, so he ambushes them with these IEDs and takes off with the dough?"

"How does Detective Gormley fit in? Dirty cop? There's more to it."

They turned to see Lieutenant Cornelius Bates making his way down the pier, umbrella in hand, his stretch-fabric shirt immaculate despite the weather. Four uniformed officers followed, boots splashing through puddles.

"What a fucking mess," he said as he shook both agents' hands. "Let me ask you, respectfully, to stay out of our way on this one."

"We've got IEDs and possible transnational narco-terrorists, Bates. This is federal," Stanton said firmly.

"I've got two dead cops and two missing cops. We've got a serial killer targeting my unit."

"Why would someone do that?" Stanton asked.

"Who fucking knows? You share that you have a person of interest in the cases and that he just so happens to be a Navy SEAL. Now we have bombs going off and bodies stacking up in New Orleans. I'd say we've found our guy."

"The question is why. Why is he doing this? We answer that, we find him."

"He's obviously a crackpot who's working for the cartels."

"Then why is he killing them?"

"He's killing *rival* cartels. This guy is a merc who is selling his skills to the highest bidder."

"And Detective Gormley?"

"There were multiple 9-1-1 calls reporting an explosion. Gormley responded. This psycho kills him and probably shoved his car into the river.

This is a city homicide. Fuck, it's a mass shooting, Jarrett, and an attack on a local business."

"Gormley just happened to be in the area?" Stanton asked, pushing.

"Yeah, it's all hands on deck these days. Everyone's putting in extra hours."

"I am sorry for your losses," Stanton said, softening his tone. "You have the Bureau's complete support. We'll find Chris Walker and then we'll unravel this thing. Until then, never hesitate to reach out if there is anything we can do."

Bates's face was calm and controlled.

"Thank you, Jarrett. I'll be in touch."

As Bates walked off to the end of the pier with his entourage to get an update from the dive team, Stanton noticed a female uniformed officer watching their exchange. When she caught his eye, she turned away.

"You buying that bullshit?" J.J. asked her boss.

"Not for a second. Let's get out of the rain."

They turned and walked back to Stanton's Tahoe.

"We need to dig deeper," he said.

"You worried about what, or who, we might find?"

"I'm just after the truth."

———

Half a football field away, Walker lay flat inside a rusted boxcar that smelled of oil and iron, its floor lined with burlap sacks. Rain hammered the leaking roof above him.

He ignored it.

Through the open hatch, he had a clear line of sight to the dock. He moved the camera lever with his thumb like a sniper pressing the trigger.

Gloria's Nikon F2 was fitted with a 300mm telephoto lens, long and heavy. Wildlife. War zones. Today, it was the latter.

Walker adjusted the lens and focused on the FBI agents.

Then he aimed at the broad-shouldered man in the tight shirt with the umbrella, recognizing Bates from the news footage Belle had pulled up on her computer. Bates ran the COPE unit, the same unit staffed by the late Rayne, Hendrick, Dupuis, and Gormley. They were all tied to the Garden District Staub investigation even though they patrolled the Ninth.

Who were the two FBI agents talking with him? Were they all involved?

As the FBI agents walked off, Walker turned his attention back to Bates, who was talking with the dive team.

Who was Walt Kimbel, and who was the Afghan?

He zoomed in on Bates and snapped another photo.

He wasn't sure who else was involved, but he did know one thing.

He was looking at a future target.

CHAPTER FIFTY-NINE

WALT KIMBEL STEPPED out of the elevator, the polished soles of his Ferragamos clicking against the marble. Much of his job was simply acting, and right now he had to act like he was not concerned about four dead cops, two dead dealers, a stack of Cuchillo's Salvadoran hit men, and a terrorist attack at Dorado Freight, all of which had connections to Genyra Pharmaceuticals.

He adjusted the cuff on his tailored shirt sleeve, letting the gold Cartier peek out just enough to catch the light. He liked the heft of it. He liked the heft of everything these days: his watch, his car, his title. He wore them well.

He nodded once at the cluster of employees he passed—research scientists, marketing staff, the VP of sales—acknowledging them without slowing. His expression was calibrated: confident, detached, just enough warmth to suggest leadership, not enough to invite conversation. He wasn't the CEO, but he moved like one.

Genyra Pharmaceuticals was surging. The messaging was back on track, thanks to Carolyn Boyle's human-interest piece in *The Times* on life expectancy gains in Genyra's Tulane wing. Matheson was pleased enough to stop micromanaging for a few days. The stock was up. The board was quiet. Kimbel had delivered.

He had kept the logistics humming, the DEA distracted, and the cartel's product flowing through Dorado and Nectar like clockwork. The NOPD was taking hits, but Icy was managing the optics. That five mil was paying off.

And what of the killings? The attention was bad for business. Too many unknowns; second- and third-order effects that were impossible to predict. And the dead cops? That was regrettable, but in the end they were disposable. Much like busboys in a Michelin-starred restaurant, they were necessary but forgettable. Bates would replace them.

He walked through the revolving door at the main building on the Genyra campus in Metairie, the building's glass façade reflecting the late-afternoon sun. The executive section of the parking lot was nearly empty. Kimbel slid into the driver's seat of his Mercedes AMG GT Coupe and tapped the infotainment screen to get Spotify blasting. The smooth jazz of Chuck Mangione seemed appropriate this evening.

The drive was familiar. Eastbound on I-10, then north toward the exclusive acreage outside New Orleans. Horse country. Old money. The kind of place where neighbors kept to themselves. His home sat on twelve acres, tucked behind an iron gate and a line of cypress trees, ringed with security cameras and guarded by a neighborhood patrol force that carried serious firepower.

He passed the exit for Kenner, and eventually Lake Pontchartrain shimmered to his left. The Mercedes glided over the asphalt, the suspension absorbing every bump. He turned up the volume and let David Sanborn's sax, mellow and smooth, fill the cabin.

His exit came up fast. He signaled out of habit and veered off the freeway onto a two-lane country road. The trees thickened. The houses grew farther apart. He passed a white-fenced pasture where a pair of chestnut horses grazed lazily.

He liked the quiet of this world.

He glanced in the rearview mirror and noticed an old-model station wagon with large tires behind him. It looked like a giant had stepped on an old Wagoneer. Vintage American. Maybe the beefed-up station wagon was a rare classic.

He turned onto a narrower road that dipped toward a culvert where the drainage ditch ran beneath the asphalt. The unfamiliar vehicle followed. He hadn't seen it before. Probably belonged to a spoiled kid whose parents owned property out here.

The road narrowed over the culvert into a single lane.

But suddenly, there was no culvert. There was no road. There was only smoke, flying grit, and asphalt slamming into his windshield. Fumes filled the cabin and he felt his body surge against his seat belt as the airbags deployed with a brutal hiss, exploding into Kimbel's chest and face.

A bout of nausea overwhelmed him and he vomited down the front of his suit and deflating airbag, confused by the realization that his Mercedes was half-submerged in a smoking crater. Reality had yet to seep in. David Sanborn was still playing his sax.

Before Kimbel could realize that his vehicle had been hit by an IED, a man was at the window pulling him out. Kimbel's wrists were zip-tied, then his ankles. Moments later, he was thrown into the sturdy station wagon. He was vaguely aware that someone had pressed what felt like an adhesive bandage to his neck.

———

The AMC Eagle's tires crunched over gravel and pine needles as Walker turned off the county road and onto a narrow dirt track that wound through the woods. The sun was low, bleeding orange through the canopy, casting long shadows across the windshield. Behind him, Walt Kimbel slumped in the rear seat. Walker wondered if the fentanyl patch would kill him.

The former SEAL drove deeper into the trees, past a rusted gate and a collapsed hunting blind, until the road ended in a clearing surrounded by cypress and oak. He killed the engine and stepped out. The air smelled of moss and spring rain.

He opened the rear passenger door and yanked Kimbel onto the dirt.

Kimbel blinked at him, face pale, lips cracked. "You're making a mistake," he croaked.

Walker dragged him to his feet and zip-tied his hands to the rack on top of the Eagle.

"Who the hell are you?" Kimbel asked, his speech slurred from the patch.

"I think you know," Walker said.

Kimbel nodded slowly. "You're the one they said was dead."

"And you're the chief commercial officer for Genyra Pharmaceuticals. You oversee all business operations, including logistics, including certain pallets that arrive at your facility through Dorado, coming in with sugar and Snowball. The cops get a cut to not just look the other way but to help transport and distribute. How am I doing so far?"

"I'm a businessman," Kimbel said. "I don't move anything. I manage distribution."

Walker's voice was low. "You move poison."

Kimbel looked away. "You don't understand how this works."

Walker paced, scanning the woods. He turned back. "Then tell me how it works and you might just survive the day. I want names, places, process, all of it. You may even be able to work a plea deal or turn state's evidence and avoid prison time, if you have something of value to trade."

"What do you want to know?"

"Let's talk about Nectar," Walker said. "The sugar company."

Kimbel hesitated.

"You'll let me live?"

"Depends on your answers."

"Did you give Dupuis and Gormley the same option?"

Walker remained silent, unholstering his Staccato.

"You can take solace in the fact that you really don't have a choice."

"Fuck! Okay, okay, just don't fucking kill me. Nectar's a partner. A sugar company. We combine certain pharma shipments coming up from Central America."

Walker stepped closer, boots crunching on damp leaves. "I saw the pallets. I saw the codes and have the manifests. Don't lie to me."

"There's more to it."

Walker stepped in so that his face was just inches from Kimbel's. "Tell me. Or you'll die right here."

Kimbel hesitated. "We have a deal, right? I tell you, and I live. Like a protected witness."

"Just like that."

"I can help you take these people down. I'm only a manager. You want the higher-ups, not me."

"Let's hear it."

Kimbel cleared his throat. "I'm dying here. Can I get some water?"

"No."

The executive swallowed and went on. "Nectar's been around forever. It's owned by a man named Fulgencio Vargas, but people call him Cuchillo. It's a legit company with a major sugar refinery downriver."

"What about them?"

"They bring product in via ship. It offloads at Dorado. They offload our product, separate it from the sugar."

"By product you mean Snowball?"

A nod. "Pills from his factories down south."

"Who moves it at Dorado?"

"Cops."

"Their names?"

"Detective Gormley heads up that part of the operation."

"Not anymore."

"Fuck."

"What about Bates?"

"Bates, I never should have listened to that guy."

"Why?"

"He said he could handle it and now look at me."

"I want to know about Genyra."

"I make sure the pallets end up in our warehouse in Metairie and are coded into the system for distribution."

"To where?"

"To pharmacies run by Vargas."

"Real pharmacies?"

"Yes, but they are set aside and picked up by Vargas's associates. He has people all over the country. That's the genius; using a legitimate distribution network to transport illicit product."

"And then, those Snowball pills go to dealers?"

"I don't know. I lose sight of it at that point."

"But you get paid for your distribution."

"That's the part where I can help you. As a protected informant."

Walker stood, pacing again. "You're responsible for the death of my friend's son."

"That's what this is about? That Staub kid?"

"It's about more than that now."

"Listen, I'm responsible for keeping Genyra profitable. That's my job. I do what Derek Matheson, our CEO, tells me to do. He partnered up with Vargas. My job is to pad the books. I can be a hell of a witness for you when you take this to law enforcement."

"In case you hadn't noticed, law enforcement isn't a lot of help around here."

"The feds, then. The FBI."

"Are they in on it too?"

"What? No! Fuck, they are just a pain in the ass."

Walker stopped.

"What about the Afghan?"

"The who? What are you talking about?"

"Before I sent your buddy Gormley over the edge of the pier, he told me about a man they hire when they want more separation between law enforcement and someone they need removed from the board."

"I don't know shit about that, man. I swear."

"But you knew about Connor Staub."

"Oh shit, I didn't know they were going to kill him. There were supposed to just scare him off."

"They went for a more permanent solution."

"That fuckin' kid has caused us so many problems. Hey, I've told you everything I know. Let me live and I'll go with you to the DA."

"Isaacson? She's in on it too, isn't she?"

Kimbel paused and gathered his thoughts.

"I really don't know. That's between her and Matheson. They had an affair. Ruined both their marriages. I stay out of that part."

"I think I've got what I need from you."

Walker held up a plastic bag and stood over Kimbel. He removed a handful of plastic-wrapped drugs. "I got these from that trap house in the Ninth."

"Where you killed Rayne and Hendrick?"

"The white ones in the plastic wrap are Snowball."

Kimbel looked away.

"That trap house had boxes of drugs. I grabbed these fentanyl patches when I was in there. I didn't know at the time that I'd actually use them."

"I can give you more."

"Yeah?"

"They know who you are."

"Who does?"

"The cops, the FBI, Matheson."

"Who am I?"

"Some kind of commando or CIA or whatever. Some kind of mercenary. That's what the cops think."

"If I'm a mercenary, then who hired me?"

"They think it was the cartels. That's from the DA. They think this is some rival cartel beef with you taking out the competition."

Walker opened the fentanyl derma pack.

"What did you call Connor again?"

"What?"

"You called him 'that fuckin' kid.' That's just what he was, a kid. Just like thousands of other kids who die because of what you call a 'product.' I want you to experience that same sort of high."

Walker ripped Kimbel's shirt open and slapped the fentanyl derma pack over his heart.

"Wait, goddamn you!" he yelled. He thrashed against the side of the Eagle in a vain attempt to knock the patch off.

Walker stuck another one on his stomach.

Kimbel screamed, but the scream quickly turned to a whimper, his voice slurring in a way that made it hard to decipher. "They don't get it ... the cops. But, I do. You aren't a mercenary. But you are a killer."

Kimbel stopped thrashing. His legs had given out, and he hung against the side of the vehicle, hands stretched over his head to where they were connected to the roof rack.

Walker put another fentanyl patch under Kimbel's left armpit, then his right. He began to convulse and foam from the mouth.

"How's the customer experience?" Walker asked.

Kimbel gagged on the fluid bubbling up from his lungs and attempted to mumble something.

"What?"

"Have you no honor?" the dying man asked.

"I left honor behind a long time ago, friend."

"You ..."

"I what?"

"You have no idea what you're up against."

Kimbel's head slumped forward.

Walker felt for a pulse and looked for signs of breathing.

He let Kimbel hang from the rack for a few minutes as he went over all of what he had just learned.

Then he cut the Genyra executive from the rack and let him fall to the ground.

"One step closer."

Walker shut the rear passenger door and got back behind the wheel, leaving Walt Kimbel to rot on the forest floor.

I left honor behind a long time ago.

CHAPTER SIXTY

AUGIE LLOYD HAD claimed one of the corner offices on the third floor of the FBI's New Orleans Field Office, overlooking Lake Pontchartrain. The building's upper floors were secured by keycard access and biometric scanners, but Lloyd's office felt more like a private club than a federal workspace.

He sat behind a polished mahogany desk, eyes sharp behind rimless glasses that caught the morning light. Floor-to-ceiling windows framed a sweeping view of the lake, shimmering in the afternoon heat. Lloyd's walls were curated with precision: framed commendations, photos of him shaking hands with senators and cabinet secretaries, and a shadow box displaying his Bureau badge alongside a pair of brass handcuffs engraved with the FBI seal.

Stanton stood with arms folded, his posture rigid. J.J. stood just behind him, silent.

Lloyd didn't bother to rise. He had summoned them to his desk like a principal calling in a pair of underperforming students. He tapped the printed police report on the Dorado Freight attack, the bolded line referencing the suspected death of a law enforcement officer.

"The DA sent this over," Lloyd began. "Wanted to make sure I saw it personally."

Stanton gave a curt nod.

"This *sicario*, this mercenary, the man you identified as Chris Walker, is starting to look more like a domestic terrorist," Lloyd said, voice low and deliberate. "At minimum, he's a serial killer. And that's not a good look for the Bureau."

You mean for Icy, Stanton thought, noting his boss's tired eyes.

"Please give me some good news."

"We just came from Dorado," Stanton said. "Scene's a bombed-out mess. No video. No prints. But the blast was surgical. It only took out two vehicles of foreign nationals of unknown origin. Whoever did it knew exactly what they were doing."

Lloyd didn't blink. "Where are we with it?"

"We are following the evidence," Stanton said evenly. "Not the optics."

"Your job is to produce results."

"And to get it right," Stanton retorted. "The facts point to Dorado's involvement in something bigger. The absence of evidence is just as telling as the blast itself."

"What do you mean?"

"Dorado looks less like a warehouse and more like a pipeline. Sugar for sure. But something else as well. I'd like to loop in the Coast Guard to help locate the company owner, Charlie Babineaux. With your approval."

Lloyd leaned back, his chair creaking beneath him. "Your job, Agent Stanton, is to find the *sicario*, or contract killer, mercenary, or whatever the hell he is."

Stanton's jaw tightened. "We're trying to understand the whole picture. Casting the net as wide as we need to."

"No." Lloyd's voice was calm but edged with finality. "You're chasing a killer. That's your priority. Not corporate logistics. Not sugar manifests. Not cartel economics. And certainly not maritime manhunts for a guy who's out on his boat fishing."

He paused, letting the silence stretch.

"A man is killing cops in this city," Lloyd continued. "That's what matters. Stop the bleeding. Then worry about what caused it. I want to know what you're doing, now, to nail this guy."

Stanton held his ground. "We're building the case. If we move too fast, we miss what's underneath."

Lloyd's eyes narrowed, just slightly. "You've always been thorough, Jarrett, but the Bureau doesn't get credit for patience. It gets credit for arrests. I want one."

J.J. glanced at Stanton for the briefest moment.

"We're building a profile based on the information Agent Stanton was able to cull from the Office of Personnel Management and what he could extract from the CIA."

Lloyd's eyes shifted between his two agents, landing back on Stanton. "Your contact at the Agency. Fisk?"

Stanton gave a single nod.

J.J. flipped a page in her notebook and continued, her voice steady. "Chris Walker is a former SEAL Team Six operator recruited into the CIA's Ground Branch. Medically retired. Multiple deployments to Afghanistan with both the Navy and CIA. His last mission in 2021 seems to be the reason he parted ways with the Agency."

"And the CIA won't give us details, is that right?" Lloyd asked, his tone clipped.

"This was Special Access Program level. Fisk wasn't willing to fill in the blanks," Stanton said.

J.J. pressed on. "It took some digging through the Portland Field Office, but they were able to find early childhood records. He's adopted. The adoptive father split early on. Adoptive mom passed away from cancer when Walker was in his teens. Oregon State testing indicates he has a Mensa-level IQ and OPM records confirm him as exceptionally intelligent based on all his military aptitude tests. He completed his degree right after leaving the Navy, then pursued a doctorate in philosophy at NYU. I spoke to one of his former professors."

Lloyd raised an eyebrow. "And?"

"He said Walker was a brilliant thinker, obsessed with moral philosophy. As if he had seen too much war, too much death, and could not quite put it behind him."

"Well, his morality seems to have found a home with the cartels."

"Possibly," J.J. said. "But he's not sloppy. He's tactical. He's choosing his targets. Our interest in Dorado is to understand the motive behind those choices. That part's still unclear."

Lloyd stood abruptly, the chair snapping upright. He walked to the window, hands clasped behind his back, staring out at the lake. His reflection hovered faintly in the glass.

"You need to find him," he said. "Leave Dorado to the DEA. You focus on Chris Walker. Bring this killing to an end."

"Understood," Stanton said.

"I've reached out to contacts at CIA and DEA as well. If they can shed any additional light you'll know as soon as I do," Lloyd said. "For now, I want you two bloodhounds to track down Chris Walker. He is our number one priority. That's your job. Clear?"

"It's clear, sir," Stanton replied.

"Give me a minute with Jarrett, would you," Lloyd said to J.J.

She closed her notebook with a soft *snap*. "Yes, sir."

When Stanton and Lloyd were alone, the SAC turned from the window, his expression unreadable against the bright sky.

"I know you've got your eye on this seat when I retire next year, Jarrett. You've more than earned it. But let me give you a little piece of advice. A parable, if you will."

He stepped closer to his desk, voice dropping.

"You know," he said, "a man can build a thousand bridges, but then he sucks one cock and he's forever a cocksucker. Don't make a mistake here, Jarrett. You fuck this up and that's all anyone will remember. If Walker keeps killing, you can kiss this office goodbye."

His eyes bored into his subordinate.

"Find him before he kills again."

The phone on Lloyd's desk rang. Annoyed, he gestured for Stanton to stay and picked up the receiver.

"I thought I said no calls . . . I see . . . Put him through . . . Hey . . . You've got to be kidding me . . . Keep me posted."

He hung up the phone and sank into his chair.

"That was the superintendent. The divers found the car. Detective Gormley's dead. Drowned. Locked in the back of his Charger."

"I was afraid of that."

"There's something else."

"Oh?"

"Another bomb went off."

"Where?"

"Horse country."

"What?"

"A car belonging to Walt Kimbel of Genyra Pharmaceuticals. Seems someone made off with the body."

"I'll get out there right away."

"Jarrett, you and J.J. watch your backs. We've lost enough of the good guys. Walker's a trained killer. If there's any doubt, put him down."

CHAPTER SIXTY-ONE

THE MISSISSIPPI RIVER was quiet, calm after the earlier storm.

Walker crouched beneath the camo netting draped over the Eagle, the tailgate lowered to form a makeshift workbench. Spread across it were supplies from Home Depot and Cabela's. Under the muted glow of his headlamp, the workspace looked improvised but surgical.

Tonight's charges would be heavier, made with more ammonium nitrate and additional powdered aluminum, mixed into three green Scepter MFC jerry cans.

He had used garage door openers at Dorado and to trigger the Kimbel ambush. But this was different. These charges were bigger and he would need to be farther away when they blew.

He remembered the lessons from his sensitive site exploitation courses at Harvey Point. Tonight, he would put them to use. This mission was aimed at destroying the enemy's infrastructure; multiple charges, placed with precision and synchronized to detonate in sequence.

Walker checked the wiring one last time. Each jerry can was fitted with a mechanical kitchen timer wired to a nine-volt battery and an Estes-model rocket igniter. When the timer expired, the circuit would complete, igniting a match head embedded in steel wool, a homemade fuse that would light the improvised detonator and provide the molecular shock to set off the main charge. Crude, but reliable.

He packed the timers into waterproof Rubbermaid sandwich containers, sealed them with duct tape, and tucked them into the jerry cans. Then he placed all three into a dark green cooler, strapping it shut with paracord.

The Agency playbook was etched sixto his mind. First, find a source. The source would give up a name. The name would lead to surveillance of a broader network. Watch. Learn. Understand their tactics and note their resources. Take off the leaders' heads, then strangle the supply lines in one coordinated strike. After that, turn on the lights and stomp cockroaches.

He slipped into his wet suit and smeared black camo paint over his exposed skin and hair. His belt held his fixed-blade knife and Staccato pistol.

He secured the jerry cans with paracord and clipped the cooler to the last can. Then he switched off the headlamp and scanned the quiet battlefield of Chalmette. Crickets chirped. A quarter moon hung low, partially veiled by clouds. Light winds. He would have preferred worse weather for a night amphibious interdiction op, but he was on the clock.

The waterproof bags were now flotation devices. He tested the water scooter and then ferried his arsenal to the water's edge.

He muscled into his fins and pushed his gear into the river. The current caught him immediately, the river pulling at him like a living thing.

He used his fins and the angle of the water scooter to navigate. It took a while to adjust course considering the bulk of his equipment, but he would be coming back lighter. Walker kicked steadily so the scooter would not have to do all the work, his fins pulsing through the dark water. The jerry cans and cooler drifted with him, deadly flotsam drifting on the Mississippi. Tonight would put a serious dent in his enemy's operation.

As he got closer to his target, Kimbel's dying words echoed in his head: *You have no idea what you're up against.*

Neither do they.

Ahead, close to the steep shore, he spotted the first set of pilings beneath the pier. He cut the propulsion device and kicked against the current to remain stationary while reconning the target.

The hulking silhouette of the Nectar Sugar Refinery loomed just up from the dock. The rust-streaked silos, skeletal catwalks, and the massive conveyor towers that fed raw cane into the processing lines were prominent against the night sky. Sodium vapor lights cast a jaundiced glow over the dock, where a bulk cargo ship sat moored, its hull towering like a fortress wall. A hummingbird logo was stenciled below the bridge windows.

The factory was feeding America's addiction to sugar, and something else: opioids.

Walker had the Dorado manifests and had seen the pallets. He had read stories in Connor's journals of kids twitching and dying on ER gurneys. Connor had been documenting all of it. He was trying to stop Snowball before it became the next fentanyl.

Stay focused on the enemy's resources within tactical reach.

There it was, right in front of him.

He maneuvered beneath the dock pilings and waited. No movement. No sentries. Just the low hum of machinery and the distant clank of metal.

Walker removed his fins and clipped them along with the Seascooter to the piling with one-inch webbing. The gear bobbed gently in the eddy, ready for exfil.

He reached for the ladder bolted to the dock's underside and climbed with practiced efficiency. At the top, he crouched low, eyes sweeping the refinery grounds. The air smelled of molasses and rust. At this hour, the plant was shut down. A conveyor belt stretched overhead, designed to feed cane into the processing tower. Even now, at 0200, steam hissed from a nearby vent. He pulled on the paracord, bringing the jerry cans up to the dock.

From there, he moved quickly, low and deliberate, hugging the shadows between the silos.

First target: the centrifuge building, where refined sugar was separated and dried. He placed jerry-one behind a steel support column, wedging it into a recess near the electrical conduit. From the cooler, he retrieved the timer and armed it, setting it to detonate in ten minutes.

Second target: the boiler house, a squat brick structure with aging pressure tanks and exposed piping. Walker ducked beneath a catwalk, climbed a short ladder, and placed jerry-two behind a rusted valve cluster. He set its timer for twelve minutes.

Final target: the loading dock, where pallets of bagged sugar were staged for shipment. He crept past a forklift, parked and silent, and tucked jerry-three beneath the dock ramp, behind a stack of pallets. Fourteen minutes.

Each placement was surgical. Each timer staggered. The sequence would cripple Nectar's core operations, their refining, power, and distribution.

Walker retraced his steps, slipped back to the dock's edge, and climbed down the ladder. He reattached his fins and connected the cooler to the dry bags. He then activated the Seascooter and kicked back into the current, moving into deeper water.

He rolled onto his back. The refinery loomed behind him, a rusting beast of industry. He swam to a buoy, clung to the cable to steady himself against the current, and watched.

The first fireball erupted from the centrifuge building with an orange bloom that lit the riverbank like a sunrise.

Minutes later, a deeper explosion tore through the boiler house, sending a plume of steam and debris skyward.

The final blast ripped through the loading dock, scattering pallets and igniting a brief inferno. Metal groaned. An elevator tore loose as a silo toppled, knocking another over like a set of flaming dominoes.

Walker floated in silence, watching Nectar burn.

CHAPTER SIXTY-TWO

DEREK MATHESON SAT before his laptop in a sleek suite at Hôtel Swexan, high above the Dallas Arts District. Windows beyond his screen framed the city's skyline, bathed in golden haze. Reunion Tower blinked in the distance. The glass spires of downtown mirrored the sky.

The annual BioFrontiers Summit conference was in full swing downstairs, but Matheson had retreated to his suite, preferring solitude to schmoozing. He had left her downstairs to deal with the media. Though he had never been shy in front of a camera, the news that Walt Kimbel had been murdered had sent shock waves through the industry. The only good news was that the Metairie Police Department had kept the death-by-fentanyl details quiet. Matheson had learned of it from Icy.

He wore a tailored gray Ermenegildo Zegna suit, looking every inch the man of the hour, but his posture betrayed him; shoulders hunched, fingers twitching at the edge of his desk.

Vargas glared at him from the screen. Behind the drug lord, the Pacific glittered under the mid-afternoon sun as waves crashed against the cliffs below in rhythmic bursts that echoed through the airy villa perched high above the Salvadoran coast. The studio-grade webcam, rigged to track movement, followed him as he paced, shirt open, cigar unlit. His home office walls were lined with polished rosewood, gold-framed oil paintings.

"You've lost control of your DA girlfriend," Vargas snapped, voice sharp with contempt. Despite the satellite bounce and the heavy encryption software running on both ends of the connection, Vargas's image was in high fidelity, which only made things worse. "Why hasn't this assassin been caught?"

Matheson cleared his throat. "I assure you, no stone is being left unturned in the search for Chris Walker."

Vargas stopped pacing and glared into the camera.

"I don't want stones turned over, I want him dead!"

Matheson continued carefully. "Ever since Irene pushed the cartel narrative, she's been at arm's length from the FBI, but they've assured her they're working on it. Killing an industry executive like this is beyond the pale. They will find him."

Vargas turned, the camera tracking his movement.

"You lost your ace deputy. I lost an entire factory!"

Before Matheson could respond, a shriek pierced Vargas's home office. Matheson watched the scene unfolding fifteen hundred miles to the south as Vargas's daughter, no older than four, burst into the room, mid-tantrum. His wife, twenty years younger, stunning in a silk robe, snapped something in rapid Spanish. A nanny followed. It took Vargas thirty seconds to corral all three of them and send them out of his office.

"*¡Ya basta!*" he barked as he shut the door with a sharp snap.

As the tantrum behind him fell into muffled silence, Vargas returned to the camera, smoothing his shirt and compartmentalizing the domestic chaos. His face was taut, eyes glowing with restrained fury.

"How the hell are you going to get control of this?"

Matheson hesitated. "I'll talk to Irene again. But it might not work. She's under pressure. It might be better to—"

Vargas's voice cut through Matheson's like a machete. "To what? Give that bitch more money? She's taken in five million already. She's running for governor, not president. At least for now."

Matheson swallowed. "I wasn't talking about money. We could build a narrative around competitors coming after me because they hate the fact that Xylaxyn will eliminate the need for fentanyl-based products."

Vargas stared at him, then shook his head slowly.

"You aren't only a pharma CEO, Derek. You're a drug dealer. You don't invite wolves to investigate your sheep."

Matheson blinked, rattled.

"You don't have Kimbel to hide behind anymore. That means you have to deal with all these nasty little bits of your business that deliver profits. Your job is Icy."

Vargas reached for the remote, his hand steady.

"Make that bitch earn her money!"

The screen went black.

CHAPTER SIXTY-THREE

New Orleans

THE MOON HUNG low over the Quarter, casting long shadows across Gloria's backyard. Upstairs, above the garage, blackout curtains hung from a clothesline, enclosing the makeshift darkroom in a soft, red glow. The air smelled faintly of vinegar and chemical fixing agent.

Belle moved with quiet precision, her hands gloved, her voice steady.

"Gloria taught me this years ago," she said, gently agitating the tray. "You know, before music and fine-line tattoo artistry, I had a photography phase. Didn't last long. But I remember the steps."

Walker stood just inside the curtain, arms folded, watching the image emerge in the developer tray, an image he had taken with Gloria's old Nikon F2 from the boxcar overlooking Dorado Freight. The black-and-white photo sharpened slowly, revealing three figures in the foreground: a male and female in FBI windbreakers and another man in a tight suit, hands on his hips, jacket open to reveal the badge on his belt. Behind all three, out of focus, lay the twisted wreckage of a truck and minivan. Bodies littered the ground.

"That's Bates all right," Belle said, lifting the print with tongs and sliding it into the stop bath. "The other photo is him getting out of an unmarked."

Walker memorized the license plate.

"He's the one I showed you from the Garden District press conference," she said.

Walker leaned closer, eyes narrowing. "I remember. And the FBI people?"

Belle peeled off her gloves, dried her hands, and picked up her phone. She snapped a photo of the print and opened Google Images. A few keystrokes later, the screen lit up.

"Reverse image search," she explained. "Let's see what we get."

Walker stepped beside her, watching over her shoulder. She was dressed in a black ribbed flared skirt and matching tight ribbed colored shirt buttoned to the neck. Belle had made Walker take a shower after his arrival while she prepared the makeshift darkroom, after which he had changed into more of Alexandre's old clothes, jeans and a musty work shirt.

The results populated quickly. Photos from a gala at the Four Seasons, a fundraiser for a youth development charity called New Leaf, filled Belle's screen.

"There," Walker said, pointing. "That's Jarrett Stanton."

Belle paged through the gallery. "Stanton. Walt Kimbel. Derek Matheson. Bates. And there's the DA, Irene Isaacson. She gave the keynote. Everybody was there."

Walker turned toward the desk, where Connor's Moleskine journal lay open beside Gloria's Royal De Luxe typewriter. Notes and clippings were scattered across the notebook, marked up in red and blue ink. Walker had added additional pages to his own research, typing out fragments of intel and cross-referencing names, dates, and locations.

"Go back to that gala site," he said.

She paged through the gallery. "Here you go; the rogues' gallery." She turned the screen toward Walker. "Isaacson and Matheson are ten feet apart. Looks like she's staring daggers at him."

Walker's jaw tightened. "What do we know about Matheson's relationship with her?"

"Let me do this on my laptop," Belle said, moving to sit cross-legged on the bed. Her fingers flew across the keys. "According to this New Orleans gossip blog, she and Matheson had an affair. Both divorced over it. The flame went out after that."

She clicked again, her brow furrowing. She typed additional key words into the search bar. "There's something else. This LSU political science site lists major political contributions. Genyra Pharmaceuticals donated five million dollars to Isaacson's Super PAC called T-JAW. Truth, Justice, and the American Way. Legal, it says, because it was a Super PAC, not an official campaign."

She flipped another page. "Connor thought he was working his way up to one company, Genyra. Of course, we know now that it was three firms in partnership: Nectar, Dorado, and *then* Genyra."

"I think it's time for me to pay Matheson a visit," he said quietly. "If the DA's involved, he'll give her up."

Belle's finger tabbed to another site. "Well, you can't do it today. He's in Dallas, giving a speech at a biotech conference."

Walker raised an eyebrow. "Amazing what you can learn with that thing."

"The internet?" she smirked. "Yeah, Chris. It's kind of useful."

He scooted closer, studying the screen. "Can it tell us where Isaacson is?"

Belle typed again, scanning. "Not right now, no. But I can tell you she'll be in Baton Rouge tomorrow night, giving a speech at the Shaw Center for the Arts. Five-thousand-dollar-a-plate dinner."

Walker nodded slowly as they scrolled through the center's website.

"How far is that place?" he asked.

"About eighty miles from here."

"I wonder if Bates will be there. Maybe Stanton? They were all in the New Leaf fundraiser photos."

"I don't know. It's possible. What are you thinking?"

"I need to get out of the city. Every moment I'm with you I'm putting you in danger."

"We are just steps away from being able to implicate everyone involved in this thing. We are so close to finishing what Connor started."

"I need to think through next steps, but I need to do it away from you and Gloria."

"Let me help you. We are almost there."

"I know, but I've put you at too much risk already. I'll finish writing up Connor's exposé and then you can help by arranging a meeting for me with that newspaper reporter, what was his name? Greer?"

"That's right."

"We might have enough to hand this off to him, get it out in the open."

"And then what?"

"What do you mean?"

"They are not going to let you go."

"Let me worry about that. How far is your family cabin from Baton Rouge?"

"Not far, about an hour drive from here, in the middle of the Jean

Lafitte Nature Preserve. I'll write out directions. I haven't been out there in years, but I remember cell service sucks."

"What's that name mean? Who is Jean Lafitte?" Walker asked.

"He was a famous pirate."

"Perfect."

CHAPTER SIXTY-FOUR

THE CAROUSEL BAR creaked beneath him, gradually revolving. Every fifteen minutes, the circular bar made a full rotation, its polished brass rail and painted horses gliding past velvet drapes and mirrored walls. The ceiling above was a swirl of gold leaf and carnival blue, and the bar itself was an antique merry-go-round, lit like a stage.

Cornelius Bates sat alone, bourbon in hand, watching the world orbit around him. The Hotel Monteleone was his haunt, classy with craft cocktails and eccentric enough to make him look like a solid rock of masculinity. It was a few minutes past eight. He had walked over from the office, needing a drink and a distraction after the news that Fulgencio Vargas's refinery had gone up in smoke. It had to be Chris Walker. He was destroying everything they had worked so hard to build.

Across the room, seated at a window table overlooking Royal Street, a pair of women caught his eye. The older one wore pearls and a linen blouse, her posture regal, a glass of wine in hand. The younger, dark-eyed, early thirties, legs crossed, sipping a French 75, was something else entirely. The younger one hadn't looked his way yet, but she would.

His phone buzzed. He frowned and pulled it from his coat pocket.

"Bates," he answered curtly.

"Sorry to bother you, sir," came Sergeant Strickland's voice on the other end.

"What is it?"

"Traffic cam in Metairie picked up an AMC Eagle following Walt Kimbel's Mercedes just before the murder. Male driver. Ball cap. Alone."

"What the fuck is an AMC Eagle?"

"I had to look it up. It looks like an old station wagon with wood paneling except with a lift and bigger tires. Some piece of shit from the eighties."

"You get a plate?"

"Yeah. Registered to a woman near the Quarter. Gloria Travois. Old lady. A widow, lives alone."

"An old woman is helping him?"

"Maybe."

"Or he stole her car."

"Also, more good news," Strickland continued. "State Police just responded to the Metairie PD's alert. Vehicle with that plate passed over the Huey Long Bridge about twenty minutes ago. Headed northwest."

Bates felt the bourbon sour in his gut.

He did not want other departments involved. This was his mess to clean up, his case. He stepped off the slowly rotating platform and into the hotel lobby.

"He's leaving town."

"Appears that way, sir."

"Call my contact at LSP," Bates said. "Captain Hagerty. Tell him this is an undercover op and part of an ongoing interagency investigation. Location alerts go to me only."

We need to eliminate this problem before he gets picked up by another department.

"Understood," Strickland said. "You want to talk to this Mrs. Travois tonight?"

"I am going to do a little background first. Let LSP know we want all locational data on that Eagle."

"Yes, sir."

"And Strickland."

"Yes, sir."

"Keep it tight."

Bates disconnected his call and looked around. No one seemed to be paying extra attention to him.

He slid his phone into his pocket and extracted his burner. It was time to call the Afghan.

He dialed a memorized number. On the fifth ring a man answered.

"Salaam." Hello.

"It's me."

"I know who it is." The Pashto accent was heavy and guttural.

"That job I mentioned earlier, are you ready?"

"Yes."

"I'm getting a location. It might be a ways outside of town. Stay by the phone."

"*Khoda Hafez.*" God protect you.

Bates disconnected the phone and stared at the burner.

Zarak Fazli. Bates had questioned him in the aftermath of the 2025 New Orleans terrorist attack. He and a group of Afghans who were resettled in New Orleans and Baton Rouge after the withdrawal from Afghanistan in 2021 were approached by law enforcement in the wake of the Bourbon Street event. Fazli was different. Bates had recognized a weakness and seen an opportunity. Fazli was having trouble with his special immigrant visa, even all these years later, due to the sensitive nature of his work for the U.S. government. Finding new work in this country was difficult. Bates had pressed and promised to help. Eventually Fazli had confided to the lieutenant that he had been part of a Zero Unit. When Bates pressed further, he discovered that the Zero Units worked for the CIA. Fazli had skills, skills useful to a man like Bates.

He dropped the burner phone back into his pocket and debated returning to the bar to work his magic on the two women he had spotted earlier, but his mind was not in that game, it was in another. He briefly wondered if Fazli and Walker may have known each other, and if so, would that make it easier or harder for Fazli to kill him?

CHAPTER SIXTY-FIVE

WALKER'S DRIVE OUT of the city had felt like slipping through layers of time, leaving behind the neon pulse of the French Quarter for the shadowed stillness of the bayou. He kept one eye on the rearview mirror the entire way, watching for tails, police helicopters, and drones.

The Travois cabin sat at the end of a gravel lane in a quiet bend of Bayou des Familles, surrounded by cypress and live oaks that leaned over the water like sentinels. The inlet was narrow, the water black and still, broken only by the occasional ripple of a frog or the distant slap of a fish. Technically, it was part of a neighborhood of vacation homes, but the trees and water had long since isolated each property into its own world.

The cabin itself was rustic, built in the 1950s by Alexandre as a retreat from the city. Weathered wood shingles, a screened porch, and a boat shed with a sloped tin roof turned to rust. Inside, the walls were lined with yellowed maps, faded photographs, and shelves of field guides. An old hand-crank telephone from the turn of the previous century was attached to a wall. Under the mattress he found a Browning Auto-5 shotgun that was probably over a hundred years old. The five rounds of double aught made Walker think that Alexandre kept it handy for more than just birds. He found Alexandre's tools in the shed, rusted but serviceable. He would need them if he had any hope of repairing the old swamp boat that sat on a trailer covered in tarps.

He spent the night on a creaky hospital bed in the back room, the windows open for airflow and so that Walker could hear the noise of an approaching vehicle. The frogs croaked in the inlet beyond the screens, and the air smelled of damp earth and dusty linens. He woke at every rustle.

By morning, he was sitting in front of Gloria's Royal De Luxe typewriter. The pieces were there but parts were still missing. Derek Matheson and Genyra Pharmaceuticals, Fulgencio Vargas, Dorado Freight,

Nectar Corporation, Cornelius Bates's COPE Unit, and Irene Isaacson. This was big business.

Would Matheson and Bates be at Isaacson's event at the Shaw Center for the Arts in Baton Rouge?

Are you judge, jury, and executioner?

There had been a change in his tactics, one he had been ignoring, but in the solitude of the swamp he had to confront it. He had no choice at the Staubs' home or at the trap house in the Ninth, his first visit to Dorado Freight or with Dupuis. Those kills had been righteous. What about Gormley and Kimbel?

Did you have to kill them?

It was justice.

Was it? Not according to Plato or Aristotle.

I told myself I was doing it for justice, for Connor and Leigh Ann. For John.

You told yourself . . . What about honesty?

Honesty?

What would all your philosopher friends say about honesty? Kant, Hume, Nietzsche, Wittgenstein, how would you justify your actions to them?

I thought I was doing it for justice, but when I killed Gormley and Kimbel, was it for justice or for me?

Then turn what you have over to Greer and finish what you started in Washington State; put the gun to your head and pull the trigger.

Not yet.

You've done enough damage.

He tried to put the debate in his head to rest by walking the perimeter of the property, noting the terrain: a narrow dock, a shallow inlet perfect for boat access, and a thicket of palmetto and cypress. It was peaceful. He imagined Gloria and Alexandre sipping sweet tea on their porch. By late afternoon, as the sun filtered through the moss like golden smoke, he was back at the typewriter.

Finish this, attach what evidence you have, turn it over to both Greer and someone you trust at the federal level, and then put that pistol in your mouth. Or you could kill Bates, Matheson, Isaacson, and Vargas.

Philosophers have debated the merits of justice for centuries.

While you continue to debate, get that swamp boat running, and build more bombs.

CHAPTER SIXTY-SIX

New Orleans

JARRETT STANTON STEPPED out of his house, coffee in one hand, keys in the other. His girls were on the balcony, giggling at something on their tablets. Alma leaned against the doorframe, arms crossed, smiling.

"Don't forget the recital tonight," she called.

"I wouldn't dare," Stanton replied, flashing a grin.

His watch let him know he was at 1,842 steps. He made a mental note: ten thousand before bed. No excuses.

At the rear of the Tahoe, he opened the hatch and laid his suit coat neatly across the flat top carpeting of the TruckVault next to his FBI windbreaker, then climbed into the driver's seat and started the engine. He adjusted the AC vents with the same methodical care he applied to casework.

He had just maneuvered out of the parallel spot when his phone buzzed.

J.J.

He answered on speaker. "Morning."

"*Don't bother driving out to the office,*" she said.

Stanton frowned. "Why? Please don't tell me that something else blew up."

"*Two days ago, the Metairie police put out a BOLO for a suspect vehicle in the Walt Kimbel murder. Then they abruptly pulled it.*"

"Why'd they pull it?"

"*According to the detective I interviewed, it was at the request of the NOPD, specifically Lieutenant Cornelius Bates, who said it was related to an undercover case.*"

Stanton's grip tightened on the wheel. "Is that so. You talk to Bates?"

"*I thought I should speak with you first.*"

"And the BOLO?"

"It was for an older vehicle. An AMC Eagle, manufactured back in the eighties. Plates trace back to a house in the Quarter, about a mile from your house, which is why I called. It's registered to an elderly woman named Gloria Travois. The Metairie detective said the suspect vehicle had been following Kimbel's Mercedes just before the IED detonation."

Stanton pulled out his notebook, steering with his knee. "Give me the address for Ms. Travois."

J.J. rattled it off.

"There's something else."

"What?"

"I reviewed Detective Gormley's investigative case files in Connor Staub's death. One of the people he interviewed was a young woman named Mirabelle Travois, a college associate, listed as a possible romantic partner."

"Daughter? Granddaughter?"

"Looks like a granddaughter. I'll confirm."

"Let's keep that part between us for now. Meet me there," he said, accelerating down the street.

———

The house was tucked behind a fence overgrown with laurel, shaded by crepe myrtles and live oaks. Stanton parked across the street and spotted J.J. already waiting in her unmarked sedan.

They walked up the drive together, keeping their voices low. No AMC Eagle in sight.

"Bates countermanding that BOLO means he either found the car or didn't want anyone else to," J.J. said.

"Or someone told him to back off," Stanton muttered. He paused to survey the front porch. "This look like the safe house of a CIA assassin turned cartel contract killer?" J.J. asked."

"Looks can be deceiving."

Stanton reached the door, hand resting on the grip of the pistol under his jacket. He turned an ear toward the door and listened, hearing an older woman's voice muffled by the walls. The place reminded him of a Hallmark card version of Grandma's house. He knocked.

A silver-haired woman answered the door. "Yes?" She stood in the entryway, dressed in a crisp blouse and slacks. Her eyes were sharp, her smile warm.

Stanton flashed his badge. "Ma'am, I'm Special Agent Stanton with the FBI." He gestured toward J.J., who had appeared beside him. "This is Special Agent Jimenez. Are you Ms. Gloria Travois?"

"Last I checked."

"We have a few questions for you regarding your car."

"Of course," Gloria said. "But the police are already here."

"Police?"

"An Officer Bates arrived just five minutes ago."

CHAPTER SIXTY-SEVEN

STANTON AND JIMENEZ followed the old woman into the house and down a short hallway. The kitchen smelled of French roast and lemon polish.

"Coffee, Special Agent Stanton? You, Ms. Jimenez?"

Stanton's jaw tightened. "Yes, ma'am. That'd be nice."

Bates sat at the table, sipping from a porcelain cup. His suit coat hung over the back of a neighboring chair.

Gloria moved with quiet grace, pouring coffee for the newcomers.

"I was just telling Lieutenant Bates that I haven't driven that old Eagle in over a year," she said. "It's been parked out back. I suppose someone must've stolen it."

Stanton and J.J. remained standing, their eyes scanning the room. J.J. raised an eyebrow. "You didn't notice it was gone, ma'am? Didn't report it?"

"I don't go out much these days," Gloria replied smoothly, setting the coffeepot down. "My knees aren't what they used to be."

"Anyone else have the keys?" Bates asked.

"Oh, no," Gloria said, shaking her head. "Just me."

"Could we see them?" he pressed.

"I don't know where I put them. At this age things get, well, grayer."

Stanton's gaze drifted to the walls decorated with wildlife photos, framed magazine covers, a signed letter from *National Geographic*. The furniture was elegant, Empire-style, with silk cushions and polished wood. He turned back to Gloria.

"Do you live alone, ma'am?"

She hesitated, just a beat, but enough for Stanton to notice. "Yes, I do."

"Just you and your dog?"

"Excuse me?"

"Your dog," he said, pointing to the water and food bowls in the corner.

"Oh, those are for my granddaughter's dog when she stays with me. I just leave them there now."

"What kind of dog?" J.J. asked.

"Oh dear, I believe it's more of a mutt."

"Do you mind if we take a look around?" Bates interjected.

"I don't see why, but be my guest," Gloria replied, her voice light. "Might take a minute. I'm not as spry as I used to be."

She led them through the hallway, pointing out framed photos of her travels: elephants in Botswana, glaciers in Patagonia, a faded snapshot of her late husband beside a fishing boat at a dock. Her stories flowed easily, a practiced rhythm of names and dates.

In the guest room, Stanton paused. The space was tidy but unmistakably lived in. He noted Bates's careful reaction to the scene too, taking it all in. A denim jacket hung on the back of the chair. A stack of used textbooks on accounting and business management were stacked on a nightstand. A pair of headphones peeked out from under the pillow. The window was cracked; lace curtains moved in the breeze.

"My granddaughter stays with me sometimes," Gloria said, her voice soft.

J.J. exchanged a glance with Stanton, but neither pressed.

"Why don't we have some scones?" Gloria asked, turning back toward the kitchen. "Fresh out of the oven. Lemon poppyseed."

Back at the table, the police officer and FBI agents accepted out of courtesy. Bates asked a few more questions about the Eagle. Gloria answered with the same calm cadence.

Bates's phone buzzed and he looked at it, his eyes fixed. He stood, brushing crumbs from his slacks. "All right, folks. Best I get on with my day. I'll make sure we get the auto theft filed. I may have to come back for some details, or it might be another officer from my unit."

"Thank you, Officer Bates. I should have sold that old thing years ago."

The front door creaked open and a female voice called from the foyer, "Forgot something for work!"

Stanton raised an eyebrow and looked at Gloria.

"My granddaughter," the old woman said.

"She's staying with you now?" Stanton asked.

"We're both somewhat forgetful," Gloria said. "Her because she's young; me because I'm old."

She followed the comment with a gracious smile as Belle stepped into the kitchen, leather jacket slung over her tattooed arm, skirt brushing her thighs, and Doc Martens thudding softly against the tile.

She froze mid-step, eyes widening at the sight of the three visitors.

"Oh," she said abruptly. "Didn't realize we had company."

Bates stood and nodded. "Hello, ma'am." Stanton and J.J. followed suit. They went through the introductions and mentioned the purpose of the visit as related to the missing Eagle. "When was the last time you saw it?" Bates asked.

"It's stolen. I haven't seen it in months."

Stanton looked outside at the faded green vintage BMW.

Belle tracked his gaze.

"I let Belle park in the garage when she's with me," Gloria said. "Safer that way. I never bothered to put my car back."

"Where's your dog today?" Stanton asked.

"My dog?"

"Yes," Stanton said, motioning to the dog bowls.

"Oh, my dog. He's at the vet. Not really sure what's wrong with him."

"I'm sorry to hear that," Stanton said.

"What kind of dog is it again?"

"It's a—"

"I told them it's a mutt, dear," Gloria interrupted. "Am I right about that? I do get confused sometimes."

"Yes, that's right. A mutt. A rescue."

"That's nice. We are thinking of getting a rescue for our family," Stanton said. "What's the dog's name?"

"Name?"

"Nikon," Gloria said.

"Nikon?"

"Yes, Belle named him after my favorite camera," she said, indicating the photos on the walls.

"Well, that is nice," Stanton said.

Bates's phone buzzed again. He glanced at it, his expression sharpening.

"Excuse me, ma'am," he said, standing. "Like I said, we'll get going on the official report. It was nice meeting you both. Jarrett, J.J.," he said, nodding as he threw on his coat and let himself out.

Stanton's phone buzzed next. He looked at it and then at J.J.

"Thank you for your time," Stanton said. "If you think of anything that might help with the vehicle, please reach out."

They each gave Gloria and Belle their cards and said their goodbyes.

Outside, the two FBI agents watched Bates drive off in his unmarked NOPD Dodge Charger. Stanton paused on the cracked sidewalk just outside the laurel arch and looked at J.J.

"Thoughts?" he asked.

"A lot of them."

"Such as?"

"For starters, Bates investigating this personally, not telling us about the BOLO."

"And the dog. That's not the granddaughter's."

"Yeah, Nikon? Really?"

"Chris Walker was here, and he has that Eagle. They're protecting him."

"Also, there's more on Bates."

"You mean acting like he didn't know who Belle was. He would have read his subordinate's report on the Connor Staub investigation last month."

J.J. folded her arms. "Bates has the case file on Connor Staub right now. According to the NOPD records custodian, he signed it out last week."

They walked together to Stanton's Tahoe. He turned to her. "Keep digging into Ms. Mirabelle Travois. Run the plates on that Beamer."

"Will do," J.J. replied.

"Something else has been nagging me," Jarrett said. "The incident report on Dorado. Did it mention anything about Charlie Babineaux's boat?"

"Nothing in the report. I didn't get the title registry until a few hours later."

"Forty-six-foot Viking sport fisher, right?"

"Yes."

"And it hasn't been found?"

"Not yet. I have alerts out for it now."

Stanton exhaled sharply.

"Keep me posted."

"Sure will. What now?" J.J. asked.

"That call I got was the DA's office. Icy's requested a meeting."

From the kitchen window, Belle and Gloria watched the agents hover near the Tahoe that was parallel parked across the street.

"They know we were lying," Belle said, her face pale, all the more emphasized by her dark mascara.

"Yes, I believe so. What did the vet say about Paladin?"

"She used the term 'lethargy' and is going to run a series of tests. They are going to call me later today when I can pick him up."

Gloria collected the dishes from the table and swept scone crumbs into her cupped hand. "Well. Maybe you should talk to the FBI about Chris? We have their cards."

"Not a chance. If there's one thing we've learned, it's that you can't trust any law enforcement in this town."

The tap hissed as Gloria rinsed a plate. "That might not be fair," she started, but then paused when she realized Belle was no longer in the kitchen.

She killed the tap and followed the footsteps into the hallway. She found Belle in her room, throwing clothes into a bag.

"Where are you going?"

"Chris is staying out at the cabin," she said. "I haven't heard from him since he left. If I don't hear from him soon, I'm going out there."

"Did you call him?"

"I tried. Coverage is terrible out there."

"Well, if you're worried about the police finding Chris," Gloria said, "it didn't seem like they knew where he was."

"They found us. They know we were lying. They will find the cabin next. I don't trust any of these cops. If they come back, clam up. Don't let them in. Make them get a warrant." She hoisted her stuffed backpack over her shoulder. "I'm sorry, Grandma."

"Don't apologize, dear girl. There is something about you and that boy." Belle rolled her eyes.

"Oh, come on, Grandma."

"And besides, this is the most excitement I've had in years."

CHAPTER SIXTY-EIGHT

STANTON TURNED OFF Dauphine and headed toward Rampart, the morning traffic thinning as he crossed into the civic corridor, his Tahoe rumbling over wet, uneven cobblestones.

The French Quarter was wide awake and sizzling; delivery trucks were idling at curbs, café tables were being wiped down, the scent of lemon wash from the pumper trucks was hanging in the air.

The Orleans Parish Courthouse soon loomed ahead, its neoclassical façade weathered by time and the on-off-push-pull maintenance of local politics. Stanton veered into the secured lot, flashed his badge at the gate, and parked in a shaded corner near the rear entrance. He removed his suit coat from the top of the TruckVault, donned it, and checked his appearance in the truck's window reflection to make sure his tie was straight. He locked the vehicle and headed inside.

The lobby was cool, attorneys and clerks shuffling through the dim light. It smelled of floor wax.

He nodded to the bailiffs at the security desk, held up his badge, and stepped through the metal detectors without breaking stride.

Knowing the way, he jogged up the wide staircase, two steps at a time, passing portraits of retired judges and plaques commemorating long forgotten civic milestones. The second floor was quieter, with less foot traffic, more closed doors. He glanced at his watch: 2,300 steps, still a long way to go. He turned down a hallway lined with frosted glass offices and paused outside the one marked *Irene Isaacson, District Attorney, Orleans Parish*.

He knocked once, then stepped inside.

Isaacson was seated behind an oiled oak desk that looked like it had been there since Prohibition, sunlight catching the edge of her gold earrings. She wore a tailored charcoal suit, and her hair was swept back. A laptop was open beside a stack of legal briefs. She looked up and offered a composed smile.

"Special Agent Stanton," she said. "Thank you for meeting me here on such short notice."

"I imagine your campaign schedule is quite hectic."

She nodded, gesturing to the chair across from her. "Constant speeches and fundraisers. Shaking hands and kissing babies, all while ensuring nothing gets dropped here in the DA's office. Last night's event went particularly long. I then had to prep for a court appearance this morning; motion to suppress in a narcotics case. One of our more slippery defense attorneys. People don't tell you that your day job continues while you're running for office at night."

Stanton sat, adjusting his cuffs. "For what it's worth, you appear equal to the full docket."

"Thank you," she said. "I heard you live in the Quarter. I hope I caught you before you drove all the way out to Lake Pontchartrain?"

"You did, thank you." Stanton retrieved his notebook and pen. Icy noted the shift.

"If you don't mind, I'd like to start with a few questions for you," she said.

"Of course," Stanton replied.

She folded her hands on her desk. "A high-profile murder in the Garden. Foreign nationals gunned down at two sites. Three cops dead, another missing. Bombings at two industrial sites on the river. A senior business executive murdered. We have a major terror campaign on our hands. I was impressed with how you handled the New Year's incident in the Quarter. I was hoping you might give me a personal briefing on this one."

Stanton studied her. Ambitious. Her record was solid and her courtroom reputation formidable. He had sat in that meeting where she had steered the narrative toward a *sicario*, the Staub drug ring, and cartel connections. Bates and Augie Lloyd had followed her lead.

He could still hear Alma's voice in his head: *Learn to play the game, Jarrett.*

With bodies stacking up, bombings dominating the headlines, and fresh from the encounter with Bates at the Travois house, Stanton wasn't in the mood to play the game.

"We have identified a person of interest," he said.

"Yes. I've been kept up to speed. Chris Walker."

"We are close to naming him as a suspect and bringing the media in."

"What are you waiting on?"

"We don't have anything that would hold up in court yet."

"What do you have?"

"Background and circumstantial evidence. As you know, Walker is former CIA and military. U.S. citizen, Oregon resident."

She raised her finely sculpted eyebrows.

"I also visited a CIA contact, the same guy I worked with on the New Year's shooting. Turns out that Walker was a friend of the Staub family. Served with the husband, John Staub, in both the SEAL Teams and, later, at the CIA."

"So, we have a trained killer who just happens to have a personal connection to a local family, running around New Orleans killing cops and blowing things up? What about the theory pointing to the Staubs as part of a drug ring?"

Careful, Stanton reminded himself. Alma's warnings echoed again. *Choose your enemies carefully, darling.*

"I don't have the facts to support that, not yet anyway. But there are certain oddities around the Staub woman's death."

"Such as?"

"First, the death of the son, Connor Staub. The investigation moved fast, handled by the COPE unit. No indicators that Connor was a drug user before he was found dead from an OD."

The revelation didn't seem to surprise her. "That's not unusual. A lot of first-time users are dying from fentanyl-laced drugs."

"Connor's mother is murdered six weeks later," Stanton continued. "His room was ransacked, and Ms. Staub was viciously tortured. It was like the kid knew something and was killed for it. And that Ms. Staub knew something too or guarded whatever her son told her."

"And your person of interest?"

"We are getting closer," Stanton said, deciding to keep the information about the suspected Travois involvement to himself for now. "Here's the rub: this cop killer is targeting the very officers assigned to look into the murders of Connor and Leigh Ann Staub."

"Because he was close with the husband and father, John Staub. But why target the officers trying to bring Leigh Ann's killers to justice, unless he was part of their drug ring?"

"He may think they are connected. It would not be the first time law enforcement was involved in kickbacks and protection with ties to the drug trade."

Stanton noted a trace of concern cross her face that was not evident when he entered the room. Was it guilt?

"And the other murders? The house in the Ninth? Dorado? Nectar? Walt Kimbel?" she asked.

"We're still working on all of that," Stanton said.

"How much more do you need, Agent Stanton? Walker sounds like he's part of the drug scene. After taking out a rival gang at the Staubs', for whatever reason, he went on to shoot up that house in the Ninth, took whatever drugs there were, and is killing the cops closing in on him as a suspect."

"Then why the bombings at Dorado and Nectar?"

"Find him and ask him. I assume you've put a request into the DEA to look into those establishments?"

"Augie Lloyd is working the DEA angle. I've been directed to focus on catching Walker."

Icy nodded, her expression tightening. Her eyes drifted for a moment, as if pondering something just beyond reach. Stanton interpreted her expression as genuine confusion rather than the cold calculation he had expected.

"There's something else," he ventured, his long experience with suspects telling him he was at the proper moment. "And I'm afraid this may be uncomfortable for you."

"I appreciate your candor, Agent Stanton."

"We learned in the course of our investigation that you met Leigh Ann Staub shortly before her death."

"I did, briefly, yes."

"Why?"

"My campaign advisor thought it would be good for me to visit the ER, to show that I'm concerned about crimes in this city 'all the way through the line,' as he put it. The ER was a mess that day. The nurse in charge, who I now know as Leigh Ann Staub, met with me along with a group of nurses."

"Were you alone with her?"

"No. But something odd happened as I was leaving. I thought you were aware of it."

"Enlighten me."

"She passed me a note."

"A note?"

"I thought it odd, but you get used to these things as a public figure."

Stanton spoke carefully. "What did it say?"

"It said she had proof that the NOPD was complicit in her son's murder, that he was an amateur reporter hoping to break a big story before going to Columbia Journalism School and had compiled hard copy notes linking law enforcement to a drug cartel. Specifically, it said that dirty cops had murdered her son."

Stanton exhaled slowly. Alma's voice rose in his head. He pushed it aside. Playing the game didn't trump justice.

"Ms. Isaacson," Stanton said slowly, "it feels like you've been hiding this information."

"It was very sensitive, Agent Stanton. I am sure you can appreciate that. If true, it could undermine all credibility in the NOPD."

And undermine your campaign, Stanton thought.

"It could also have been the rantings of a madwoman," she said.

"Why didn't you inform the FBI?"

A genuine look of confusion crossed her face.

"That's exactly what I did. Given its sensitive nature, I immediately informed your SAC, Augie Lloyd. I gave him the note and told him all about this."

CHAPTER SIXTY-NINE

THE CABIN LOOKED like a bomb factory.

Walker had made his decision. He had put the debate on justice to rest in his head. He had come to terms with the fact that he had become the monster Nietzsche had warned against. It was now about protecting Belle and Gloria, and that meant removing certain players from the battlefield, namely Bates, Matheson, and Isaacson. When that was done, if he was still alive, he would hunt down Vargas. Then he would turn the weapon on himself.

He had spent the better part of two days building charges and working on the airboat in the shed. It was always important to have a secondary extract and a new means of insertion and extraction for upcoming missions. Now that he had it up and running, he would get it out on the swamp in the evening to make sure he could operate it effectively.

With the bombs built and the airboat operational, he was ready.

As he stepped into the cabin wiping his greasy, sweaty hands on his jeans, the first indication that something was off was the burning sensation that followed the impact of the two sharp barbs from the Taser cutting through his T-shirt and burying themselves in his skin. Excruciating pain trailed the electrical charge that ran down the attached wires, the voltage overriding his central nervous system, resulting in complete incapacitation. He was briefly aware of his muscles seizing as he fell to the floor.

———

New Orleans

Even at midday, shadows dappled the cobblestones of the French Market just downriver from Jackson Square. The humid air swirled with the scent of grilled shrimp, popcorn, and freshly baked baguettes. Stanton moved slowly past the vendors, his eyes scanning the crowd.

Stanton's investigation had gone into overdrive following his meeting with Isaacson the previous afternoon. It was time to read his partner in on the latest development. He spotted J.J. near a stall that was selling hand-carved cypress bowls. She wore jeans and a loose blouse that hid her Glock. He gestured for her to join him.

"I was just about to call you with a big update," she said by way of greeting.

"Let me go first," Stanton said as they walked. "I didn't want to meet at the office."

"What's up?" J.J. asked, the concern evident in her tone.

"Remember when I asked you about how you might have reported Babineaux's fishing boat?"

"Sure."

"Well, that day Lloyd had us in his office, he said something like 'Maybe Babineaux is just off on his fishing boat.' Remember?"

J.J. stopped in her tracks.

"I never told Lloyd about the boat," he said.

"Fuck. I should have caught that."

"You didn't, because you trusted him. You figured that maybe I told him about it. I would have thought the same thing had our positions been reversed."

"Maybe."

They continued walking and stopped at a T-shirt vendor. Stanton looked over a few before proceeding.

"There is no easy way to say this: Augie Lloyd is compromised. I think he's bought and paid for by an El Salvador–based cartel run by a man named Fulgencio Vargas."

"What?"

"Irene Isaacson gave him information passed to her by Leigh Ann Staub before her murder, information on cops possibly involved in the drug trade here in New Orleans, information he never shared with us."

"There has got to be another explanation. You've met with the DA before. Why didn't she mention it then?"

"Because Bates was there too. Augie was stringing her along. She trusted him. Just like us."

They stopped at a wrought-iron bench along the river. Stanton pulled a folded printout from his jacket pocket and handed it to her.

"Isaacson got us a warrant," he said. "She moved fast and called in a favor with a judge."

J.J. looked through the tightly spaced records. "All of the prominent wireless carriers."

"I used the warrant to pull cell signal identifiers—tower pings—from Lloyd's home, his commute, and his office. Then I looked for commonalities."

J.J. flipped a page. "You suspected he has a burner."

"We can't trace it directly to him, not yet anyway, but I found a number that shows up consistently in those locations, the same locations and times as Lloyd's FBI phone. That number has been transmitting scrambled data, not regular texts or calls, just encrypted bursts."

"Using an app?"

"Military-grade encryption. But with that warrant and with Alvaro Mendez's help, I was able to trace the endpoints. One terminated at a residence in El Salvador belonging to Vargas. Another at the Nectar Sugar facility. And one more at the Four Seasons Hotel on the river."

J.J. looked up. "Who was staying there?"

"Same guy. Fulgencio Vargas. He's the CEO of Nectar Sugar. Mendez had ICE confirm that Vargas's private jet often lands at Lakefront Airport. He stays at the Four Seasons when he's in town."

J.J. exhaled. "So, Augie Lloyd has been speaking with Fulgencio Vargas on an encrypted burner phone?"

"Yes."

"What do we know about Vargas? Is he allied with the cartels?"

"The Bureau doesn't have a record on him. Google says Vargas officially took control of Nectar a few years ago. His mother had been running it before him, having inherited it from her husband. The mother is in hospice. Guess where?"

"Tulane Medical Center," she said.

"Exactly."

"Okay, playing devil's advocate, maybe he just wanted his mother to have really good care."

"She's also in clinical trials for Xylaxyn made by Genyra Pharmaceuticals."

They walked a few steps in silence, the crowd thinning as the sun dipped below the horizon at the market's edge.

"You notify the DEA yet?" she asked.

"Not officially. Then Augie will know we are onto him. Maybe he bolts. I asked Mendez to start digging and to keep it quiet. When I suggested that Lloyd might be coordinating something with a Salvadoran sugar czar with potential ties to drug trafficking, Alvaro reminded me that the DEA's untouchable pearl, their classified CI, is reporting information that supports the Mexican theory. He also reminded me that John Staub's old acquaintance in the DEA, Gonzalez, was working in Mexico when he was killed, right after Walker asked about him in the Federal Building."

"The Mexican cartel angle is the same one Lloyd keeps pushing on us," J.J. said.

"It is. I think Lloyd is protecting Vargas, shielding him from DEA scrutiny."

"That's a hell of a betrayal."

"I know," Stanton said. He turned toward the river, watching the last light fade over a paddle wheel steamer, a tourist boat that went down to the Chalmette battlefield.

"And Leigh Ann Staub?" J.J. asked. "Why was she killed?"

"I've been thinking about that. Maybe she called Chris Walker to New Orleans out of desperation. Maybe she needed him to do exactly what he ended up doing—killing off the people she thought murdered her son."

"Or maybe she just needed protection," J.J. added.

"She could have known she was a dead woman for some reason. Something to do with Connor; information he had on their network or operation. Those bangers were looking for something in that house. They had a reason to torture her."

"But by then, she'd already unleashed the dogs of war."

"The truth is in there."

"Somewhere," J.J. said.

"What did you find out about Gloria Travois and her granddaughter?"

"That's why I was about to call you. They each own one car, the Eagle and that old BMW. House was paid off before I was born. No warrants or outstanding traffic tickets. No IRS back taxes."

"Clean."

"Yes, but just before I left to meet you, I looked into deeds."

"Property?"

"There was a property deed transferring the home near the Quarter to Gloria Travois from Alexandre Travois after his passing, along with a second deed."

"A second deed?"

"A family cabin in the Bayou, near Jean Lafitte."

Stanton stopped in his tracks.

"Who else knows?" he asked.

"Just us. Let's go find Chris Walker."

CHAPTER SEVENTY

Jean Lafitte Nature Preserve, Louisiana

CICADAS. AN ENDLESS, electric hum that seemed to rise from the earth itself. Then came the smell: brackish water mixed with humidity and the faint copper tang of blood.

Walker opened his eyes, confused, his vision blurry.

He tried to bring his arms to his head, but they wouldn't move.

Then he became aware of the intense pressure in his shoulders and something cutting into his hands.

Late-afternoon light filtered through the windows.

He blinked his eyes and his bare feet came into focus, dangling just inches above the wooden floorboards. They were secured with twine. He lifted his head slowly and saw that his arms were secured to a chain that had been looped over the cabin's central beam. He was suspended, lightly swaying. He shook his head to clear the cobwebs and looked back down at his body, realizing that he was naked.

"You are heavier than you look."

The voice was deep. The accent was one he recognized from another life.

A man stepped forward from the shadows. He was about Walker's height and build. Features dark. His black hair was cut short and the stubble on his face was only a day or two old. He wore leather sandals, light beige pants, and a thin gray T-shirt.

"*Salaam Alaikum*, Mr. Walker." Peace be upon you. "*Sanga yaast?*" How are you?

"Been better."

"I see you remember our language."

"I remember. Who are you?"

"That's hardly important."

"Seems relevant at the moment."

"We don't know each other if that's what you are asking, though we once worked for the same intelligence service."

"And now you are a gun for hire who kills kids like Connor Staub?"

The man grabbed Walker's hair and yanked it back.

"And where would you have heard something like that?"

"A dead man told me."

He let go of Walker's hair and stepped back.

"I do a job just like you trained me."

"I didn't train you."

"Your CIA did. Men just like you. The man who hired me will be here soon. He has some questions for you. While we wait, my job is to soften you up. You remember, don't you, what we used to do to prisoners in the Salt Pit?"

"I didn't catch your name."

"No, you didn't. My boss calls me the Afghan. Not very original. I worked out of Kandahar with Zero Three. I understand you were farther north."

"Why don't you cut me down so we can reminisce about old times? Maybe let me put some pants on."

"I always respected that about you Americans."

"What?"

"Your sense of humor, even in the most dire of conditions."

"It's a gift."

"Because you are wondering and because you are not long for this world, I will tell you."

"Tell me what?"

"Why I am standing in front of you, about to visit upon you more pain than you thought imaginable."

"Anything that delays the inevitable."

"We fought for you, for your country, and you abandoned the cause."

"You deserved better."

"You promised us you would get us out."

"Of Afghanistan? You're in America, slick."

"I was supposed to meet my family and get to the planes at the airport in Kabul. By the time I got home, my wife and two children were dead.

My wife was raped, tortured, and killed by the Taliban. I don't know if they made my children watch before they were killed as well. Do you know why they were killed, Mr. Walker?"

"Because of your work for us."

"Yes. Unlike my family, I made it out. I was relocated to Baton Rouge. I looked for work; a car wash, a 7-Eleven. I see my wife and children in my dreams. We live together, me and others waiting on special immigrant visas. The CIA has forgotten us."

"I'm sorry. It's not right."

"I used to play Afghan chess with my son. Do you remember this game?"

"I do."

"Then you recall what makes it an Afghan game."

"No checkmate."

"Bravo, Mr. Walker. I still play with some of the men in my flat, but it is not the same. It reminds me of my son and of the country I had to leave behind. The country we lost. Without a checkmate, one player must take all his opponent's pieces to win. America should have studied this game before sending its sons and daughters to die."

"What do you mean?"

"Attrition, Mr. Walker. The Brits, the Soviets, and now the Americans have learned that there is no checkmate in Afghanistan, there is only attrition, and when you lose enough pieces you will go home."

"Sounds like you should have studied the game before you joined the Zero Units."

The uppercut to Walker's stomach almost caused him to vomit.

"Perhaps you are right. Now I work for a man who pays well. I can use what I learned from you."

"It's not the way, brother."

"I am not your brother. I am trash, thrown away by your CIA."

"I think we have more in common than you might think."

"We might, but that is not my concern."

Walker looked down at the big toe of his left foot and noted the wire tied to it. His eyes traveled up to his groin, to another wire constricting his genitals. Both wires led to the old hand crank telephone, which had been removed from the wall and was sitting on a small end table.

"You remember how this works?" the man asked.

"I do."

"Tell me."

"You rotate the crank, which spins the coils around the magnets, creating a high-voltage surge of electricity."

"That's it. I don't even need to douse you with salt water like we used to do to our prisoners back home for these kinds of treatments. Your sweat will act as a perfect conductor."

"What do you want to know?"

"Oh, Mr. Walker. You misunderstand. I am just here to turn the handle. My employer will be the one to ask you the questions."

"Who is your employer?"

"He told me you were smart, but all I see is a schoolboy, using schoolboy tricks. They will not work. You have reached the end of the line."

"Good. I was getting tired of this life anyway."

"Then let me get you ready for the next."

The man walked to the small side table with the old phone that he had moved closer to his victim.

"I'll have you know, I get no pleasure from this," he said.

"Me neither," Walker responded, bracing himself for what was to come.

The Afghan was about to turn the handle when headlights illuminated the window.

"My boss has arrived."

Walker lifted his head and squinted his eyes as a car came to a stop in the dirt. The driver extinguished the lights. It was a car Walker recognized.

"*Za na poheegum,*" the Afghan said as he glared out the window. I don't understand.

The door to the vintage green BMW opened, and Belle Travois walked toward the cabin.

Before Walker could shout a warning, his tormentor cranked the handle and ran for the door.

CHAPTER SEVENTY-ONE

THE AFGHAN HURRIED down the steps and rushed toward the young woman.

"Who the fuck are you?" she barked, marching forward.

The stranger put a smile on his face that shifted to loathing as he got within striking distance, his open palm slapping her across her cheek and jaw with a force that dropped her to her knees. He yanked back on her black hair and grabbed her around the throat.

"Who the fuck am I? Who the fuck are you?" he spat.

Before she could respond, the Afghan threw her forward into the dirt and placed his knee against the base of her spine, pressing his hand into the side of her face, pinning it to the ground. His free hand frisked her from her Doc Martens up her bare leg beneath the fabric of the long black silhouette, along her waistband, and up the spaghetti straps that held the gray-and-black bodice to her upper body. He roughly turned her over, sliding his knee between her legs and slapping her across the face once more. He then exerted downward pressure against her neck with a grip of iron while he frisked her front.

Satisfied she was unarmed, he wrenched her to her feet, forced her up the steps of the cabin, and threw her to the floor just inches from Walker's suspended naked body.

Walker opened his eyes, regaining consciousness from the electrical current that had shocked his system.

He struggled to speak. "Belle . . ."

"Chris!" she cried.

The Afghan cranked the telephone again, sending the incapacitating current through Walker's body, the air heavy with the smell of burnt flesh from his toe and genitals. As his eyes rolled back in his head and his body spasmed, the Afghan turned and kicked Belle in the ribs, doubling her over from the pain.

He rummaged through a small bag in the corner and removed two short lengths of rope, before dragging Belle by the hair to a post that supported the roof. He knelt down and wrenched her hands behind her back, securing them around the wood pillar. He slapped her hard across the face to get her to stop thrashing, which allowed him to tie her feet together with the twine.

Standing up, he wiped his sweaty hands on his pants and walked back to his bag, pulling out a long Choora knife. He drew it from its wooden sheath and placed the tip of the eleven-inch blade under his prisoner's chin, pressing it up. It cut through the skin on the underside of Walker's jaw, driving his head up from his chest.

When the Afghan spoke, he was not talking to his debilitated captive, he was talking to the girl.

"Who are you?"

Belle drew her knees to her chest and glared at the monster before her.

"Who?" he said, driving the knife farther up, blood starting to flow down the blade and onto his hand.

"Mirabelle Travois."

"What are you doing here?"

"This is my cabin."

The Afghan removed the knife from under Walker's chin, wiping his bloody hands on the leg of his pants.

"You picked a bad time to visit."

"Are you going to kill him?"

He found it interesting that the girl asked about Walker before herself.

"That is probable, but it's not up to me."

"You waiting for orders from Bates?"

The Afghan stepped to the frightened girl, knelt, and put the knife against her throat.

"How do you know that name?"

"I know you are going to kill me too, so it doesn't matter. Fuck you!"

The man stood and backhanded her across the face with his empty hand.

Her nose began to bleed, the blood dripping into her mouth.

"You American women need to know your place. You talk to me like that again and your death will be more painful than his," he said, jerking his head toward the unconscious man dangling from the rafter. "You dress like a whore and talk like a whore, and you will be treated like one, do you understand me?"

Belle spat at her tormenter.

He reared back again, only to pause when a new set of headlights sliced through the darkness.

CHAPTER SEVENTY-TWO

LOWERING HIS HAND, the Afghan walked to the telephone and spun the dial again, sending another shock wave through his captive's unconscious body. Then he opened the door for Cornelius Bates.

"Smells like shit in here," the lieutenant said.

"Burning flesh," the Afghan said. "You get used to it."

"Is he dead?" Bates asked.

The Afghan yanked back the former SEAL's head and pried open his left eye.

"No, but there's not much resistance left in him."

"Wake him up," Bates ordered, turning his attention to Belle. "And who have we here? Mirabelle Travois. You should have left well enough alone and you might have survived all this."

"Fuck you."

Bates crossed his arms against his chiseled chest.

"That's no way to talk to law enforcement."

"Excuse me," she said. "Fuck you, cocksucker!"

Bates laughed. "This will all be over soon. You might have a bigger role in this than you imagined."

Bates turned back to the Afghan and the naked man hanging from the rafter.

He slapped Walker across the face.

"Wake up, hero," Bates said.

Walker's eyes slowly opened.

"Ah, you've come back to us," the police lieutenant said. "Can you hear me?"

"I hear you."

He nodded at the Afghan, who twisted the crank on the old phone, shooting another jolt of current through Walker's body, sending it into convulsions. He slapped Walker across the face again.

"What made you want to complicate my life?"

Walker stared into Bates's eyes.

"Hit him again!"

The Afghan spun the crank.

Walker's eyes rolled into the back of his head as his body spasmed.

"Again!"

The Afghan spun the dial once more.

Walker's screams were arrested by the current, resulting in a gargled, fragmented howl.

"Why are you here, cowboy? You kill Sergeant Dupuis? How about Walt Kimbel? You blow up Nectar? We know you killed Gormley. Gormley was a friend of mine. Why did you do it? More importantly, who did you tell?"

Walker's body rocked back and forth above the floor. He remained silent.

"Hit him again. And keep cranking that thing."

Walker's body thrashed in violent spasms as the Afghan continued to turn the crank. More electricity flowed through his body, the smell of sweat and burnt flesh permeating the small room.

"Enough!" Belle screamed.

Walker fought to catch his breath.

"I brought something with me," Bates said, reaching into his pocket. "I thought you'd want to see it."

He produced a vintage Tudor dive watch.

"I believe you know it," Bates said as he strapped it onto his wrist. "When I took it off Leigh Ann, I thought it was sized a bit large for her. John Staub's if I'm not mistaken. Just wanted you to know how badly you lost."

"Fuck you, Bates."

The lieutenant delivered a devastating hook to Walker's ribs and another to his jaw.

"I felt some ribs break on that one," Bates said. "Bet that hurts."

Walker struggled to catch his breath.

"I didn't notice," he managed.

Bates studied the man hanging before him.

"Badass soldier, huh? You're nothing. And look who's in the corner. Sweet little foul-mouthed Belle. She's made this much easier on all of us.

You look like you are almost dead as it is. Instead of torturing you, I'll have one of my associates carve up Belle in front of you. Maybe do worse. These boys are not long out of prison. They'll probably run a train on her right here for you to see. You'll watch, knowing you put her in this hell. You are both going to die tonight. The 'how' is up to you."

"Your 'associates'?" Walker asked, his breathing labored.

"You don't think I came out here without backup, do you?"

"Shitbirds like you need backup. Just so you know, your men that I killed, they didn't die well."

Bates stepped toward the prisoner and slammed his head into Walker's nose. It broke with a crack. Blood started to flow. Bates delivered four uppercuts to the suspended man's abdomen and then continued his assault on Walker's face with jabs, crosses, and hooks, using the defenseless man as a human punching bag. He then brushed past the Afghan and wound the hand crank, watching Walker spasm on the chain, smoke rising from his feet and groin, his naked body absorbing the deadly current.

"You want to kill him?" the Afghan said by way of warning.

Bates continued to crank the handle and only stopped when the sound of another vehicle echoed through the swamp.

CHAPTER SEVENTY-THREE

STANTON DROVE THE Tahoe while J.J. navigated from the passenger seat.

"We're getting close," she said.

They maneuvered around the ruts and holes in the gravel and dirt road that led out to the Travois cabin, the headlights illuminating the Spanish moss hanging from the cypress and oak trees that lined the approach.

"This place gives me the creeps," J.J. said.

They had lost cell service where the main road branched deeper into the marsh.

"Yeah," Stanton agreed. "Make sure we are on the right path. I have a feeling that folks out here don't care much for unannounced visitors arriving in the middle of the night."

J.J. looked at the screenshot she had taken earlier.

"I think it's right around a few more bends," she said.

Stanton kept it slow, the trees and moss seemingly constricting around them as they ventured deeper into the swamp.

They turned a corner, the high beams tracking across three vehicles that were familiar to them.

"There's the Eagle," J.J. said.

"And Belle's car," Stanton noted.

The cone of light from the SUV illuminated a third vehicle.

"Bates," Stanton said.

"What is he doing here?"

Stanton found himself wishing they had called in SWAT, or at least worn their body armor. He contemplated backing out, but the cabin door opened and Bates walked down the steps. He waved, a smile on his face.

"Stay sharp," Stanton said as he put the car in park and turned off the engine.

He opened the door, ensuring his suit jacket was unbuttoned and that he had unencumbered access to his pistol.

"Special Agent Stanton," Bates said from the base of the stairs. "J.J."

"What are you doing here, Bates?" Stanton said as he walked toward the lieutenant.

"I could ask you the same thing. So much for sharing information."

"Just checking out a lead," Stanton said. "I see you are doing the same."

"Not quite," Bates said.

Four men appeared out of the darkness. They were of various heights and builds, of Latin origin and covered in tattoos. They had one other thing in common—they each held an AKM rifle and leveled it at the federal agents.

"Bates, what the fuck are you doing?"

"Don't give me that shit, Jarrett. You had your suspicions. Raise your hands. If you go for your pistols, you are both dead."

J.J. looked to her boss.

Stanton shook his head in response, slowly raising his hands.

"Don't be stupid, Bates. We have FBI SWAT inbound. It's over."

"You forget who you are dealing with, Jarrett. I know you and J.J. are investigating this off the books because you don't know who you can trust. That was the right move. The wrong move was pushing it when you suspected what you were up against."

"Give it up, Bates. We can work a deal."

"A deal?" He shook his head. "I'm afraid it's too late for that."

"It's not. We can work this out."

"Search them and bring them inside," Bates said to the largest of the four bangers.

One kept his weapon on Stanton while another approached and disarmed him of his pistol, frisking his ankles up to his groan and waistline and the inside of his jacket.

"Clean."

The other two moved toward J.J. While one kept his AK on her, the other took her Glock and frisked her in much the same way as the other had searched Stanton, except his hands lingered on her breasts.

"Hey!" J.J. yelled, whipping around and bringing a hammer fist down that connected with her accoster's temple. Her other hand followed.

Stanton stepped toward her but was thrown to the ground by the man who had just frisked him. He looked up in time to see J.J. catch a blow from the butt of an AK to her head. Stunned, she stumbled back.

Her tormentor hit her twice more in the face with the AK and she fell to the dirt.

"No!" Stanton yelled.

The man standing over her looked back at the downed FBI man and smiled. He then delivered two more strikes to the woman's head, the last of which split the night with a sickening crack.

"You motherfuckers!" Stanton shouted.

"*Alto!*" Bates's voice boomed from the base of the steps.

J.J.'s attacker looked at Bates and then kicked her once more.

"*Puta!*" he said, spitting on her face from above.

"Bring Agent Stanton inside," Bates said to the two men towering over the FBI man.

"Bates, don't do this," Stanton said as they hauled him to his feet.

"It's already done, Jarrett." He turned to the two men with J.J. "Stay on guard out here and make sure she doesn't go anywhere."

"*Sí,*" the taller of the two replied.

"Jarrett," Bates said as the FBI agent was dragged past him into the cabin. "I am glad you are here. We have much to discuss."

CHAPTER SEVENTY-FOUR

STANTON'S EYES OPENED wide in horror as he glimpsed Walker's naked body suspended from a chain in the room's center. The blood from a cut under his jaw had bled down his chest, stomach, genitals, and legs, finally running out of steam halfway down his thighs.

Stanton noted the thin olive-skinned man holding a long knife and standing next to an old turn-of-the-century telephone that had wires attached to the former SEAL he had been hunting.

The Tucker Telephone, he thought, remembering his legal classes in school and at Quantico on the torture device used at Tucker State Prison Farm in the 1960s.

His eyes then went to the girl on the cabin's floor, blood drying around her nose and mouth.

The FBI special agent was grabbed by the neck and manhandled into place next to Belle. Bates tossed the two gangbangers plastic flex cuffs, which they used to restrain Stanton against the support column. They wrestled him into submission and applied a second set of cuffs to his feet.

"Bates, have you lost your goddamned mind?"

"Special Agent Stanton, you are about to become a hero. Posthumously, of course."

"Whatever you are thinking, don't do this."

"And what is 'this'? What do you think I'm doing?"

"Runing a criminal enterprise."

"You give me too much credit, Stanton. I work for one. I don't run it."

"And your friends here? Vargas's guys?"

"Well, well, well, look at the big brain on you, Jarrett. What else have you figured out?"

"It's all in files on the DA's desk and with the task force."

Bates's laugh filled the cabin.

"Don't bullshit me, Jarrett. If that were the case, SWAT would have taken me down already. As you correctly ascertained, there is someone higher up the food chain who will make sure the correct story is told."

"What about the DA?"

"What about her?"

"She knows what I know."

"I doubt that, Jarrett. Not that it matters. When these boys are finished with you, J.J., Walker, and little Belle here, they intend to pay Icy a visit. Cuchillo needs someone he can control in that chair."

"You just going to kill your way through everyone who knows about your arrangement?"

"That's how most of the world works, Jarrett. Don't be naive. Walker knows it. He was doing a pretty good job of going through my men. Really put a dent in the business, which is why he's hanging from a rafter with wires attached to his nuts."

"Who's your friend?" Stanton asked, looking at the man with the blade.

"Not that it matters to you, but I just call him the Afghan. He does some work for me from time to time. Turns out the CIA trained him and then abandoned him. He's pissed. Cuchillo, through me, pays well. It's certainly better than welfare. Tonight, his job was to extract information from Walker, specifically to find out who else might be a threat to us, but all those people are now on-site."

"You've got a mess on your hands, Bates."

"You are seeing it all from the wrong perspective. You coming here has done me a favor."

"Yeah?"

"It wraps up neatly, Jarrett. Walker and Belle are part of a drug ring that included Connor Staub. They got in over their heads, in the middle of a drug war in New Orleans, and were hit here at the Travois cabin by the cartel. It plays right into the official reports and the media narrative. You and J.J. discovered the connection as part of your investigation. You are under orders to find Walker, aren't you? Well, you found him and his accomplice, Mirabelle Travois. Unfortunately for you and J.J., you found him at the same time as the cartel, and you were both killed in the ensuing gun battle. The cartel tortured and killed Walker and Belle and then disappeared. It's all very convenient. We get shipments going into Dorado again and rebuild Nectar. We get back to business as usual, minus two FBI agents."

"And you? How will you explain what you are doing here?"

"I won't be here, Jarrett. I'm going back to New Orleans. I'll go to a bar where a lot of people will see me. I'll have a rock-solid alibi, not that anyone will look into it. It's just a safety net. I'm going to tell my friends here to keep you alive for a good four hours so the times of death coincide with my third bourbon."

"You are sick."

"At some point someone at the FBI or your wife will notice you have gone missing, and they will track your vehicle to its last known location. Then I'll get a call and drive out to assist in this homicide investigation since it ties into mine in the Ninth and in the Garden. I'll be certain to write it up in a way that makes whatever medals the FBI gives for valor a sure thing, though they will be awarding it to your wife. Speaking of your wife, did you happen to tell her any of this?"

"Fuck you, Bates!"

"No matter, these cartel boys will pay her a visit and find out."

"Boss," the Afghan said, speaking for the first time in front of Stanton.

"Yeah?"

"What do you want me to do with him?" he said, nodding toward Walker.

"Is he dead?"

"Close. Nobody can take that."

"As you know, he was CIA, so take out your frustrations on him. Keep shocking him until his heart stops or gut him. I don't give a fuck. Just make sure he doesn't die until I'm back in New Orleans. Did he have weapons?"

"Over there," the Afghan said, pointing to an AR and a pistol.

"Dupuis's guns. I'll stash them in his car. Being found with the personal weapons of a dead cop will assist me in my future investigation."

"And the girl?"

Bates looked at Belle. Her legs were still drawn up to her chest, her face buried in her knees. He turned to the leader of the Salvadorans. "She's your reward, and the one outside if she's still alive. Do what you want with them."

"You son of a bitch!" Stanton hissed under his breath.

"What was that? I couldn't hear you."

"You are going down for this."

"Give me a break, Jarrett. There are no more heroes left in the world."

CHAPTER SEVENTY-FIVE

WALKER WATCHED THE exchange between Bates and Stanton through the slit of his swollen left eye.

Hold.

All warfare is based on deception. When strong, appear weak.

You are going to have one shot at this.

He watched Bates leave the cabin and heard his footsteps descend the stairs.

He saw one of the gangbangers kneel to Belle's side and remove a straight razor from his pocket. He whispered something in her ear, held the blade to her throat, and then slowly moved it along her skin to the spaghetti strap of her dress. He slipped it underneath and sliced up. The material fell away, revealing her left breast.

He could see Stanton struggling in a futile attempt to free himself, shouting at the men who now controlled the room. Walker blocked it out and focused on what he needed to do.

Belle slowly turned her head toward the man with the knife and spat in his face. The gesture was returned. He grabbed her hair and slammed her skull against the wood support. He moved the blade to her wrists and sliced through the plastic restraints. She lashed out, but with her feet still restrained she fell forward onto the floor.

The Latin men laughed.

The Afghan said something Walker couldn't understand over the commotion, but Cuchillo's men immediately grabbed Belle by the hair and under her arms and dragged her screaming from the cabin.

The door shut behind them, and Walker heard Belle's feet bang off the steps. From the direction of her cries he knew they had taken her to the shed.

You have four hours. Bates ordered him to keep us alive for four hours.

Belle doesn't have that much time.

Belle has minutes.

Walker heard Stanton try to reason with the Afghan, first appealing to his sense of justice, humanity, and moral decency, then a direct plea with a promise of preferable treatment, and then finally immunity.

"Don't you have a family? You are going to let them rape that girl?"

"I had a family. Men like this one," he said, motioning to Walker. "Men like him killed them as surely as if he had raped and killed them himself."

"We can work this out," Stanton said.

The Afghan stepped closer to Walker.

"That's what the CIA promised. They said they would take care of us and get our families out of the country. They lied. You work for the same government that made those promises."

"I'm not CIA."

"You are the domestic version," the Afghan said. "You and this man are the same."

"I have an agent down outside. Let me help her."

"She's as good as dead, just like you."

"There is still time. You can assist me, I can help you on the other side of this. Trust me, if you don't, this will not end well for you."

Almost. Just a little closer.

"You have a few hours, but your end is inevitable," the Afghan said.

He moved within arm's reach of Walker and pulled back on his hair.

"I don't know if I can keep this one alive much longer."

Just turn slightly to either side.

"If he dies too early, I'll feed him to the crocs."

"They're alligators," Stanton said.

The Afghan angled his body as if he was contemplating a move toward the FBI man.

Go.

Walker exploded, bringing his knees up and cracking the Afghan under the chin. At the same time, he wrapped his hands around the chain and heaved himself up, grabbing the higher links as he propelled himself upward, which allowed him to wrap the Afghan's neck between his legs in a modified triangle choke. He twisted on the chain, exerting more pressure, constricting the carotid artery's blood flow to the Afghan's brain.

The Afghan's hands went to Walker's legs, frantically trying to pry them apart, slipping on the sweat and blood that covered the exposed skin.

Walker applied more pressure, staring into the man's dread-filled eyes as his frenzied grasps failed to find purchase on Walker's bare thighs.

The man's hands went behind his back and produced the Choora knife, which he unsheathed and slashed at Walker's legs, slicing through the outside of his quad.

Walker roared and twisted tighter.

The Afghan's eyes rolled back into his head as the loss of blood flow to his brain resulted in unconsciousness. The knife that had originally been designed to penetrate the armor of invaders when wielded by Pashtun tribes in the Khyber Pass dropped to the floor.

Walker felt the body go limp between his legs but held him in place for another minute to be sure. He then kicked him away.

Walker pulled himself up the chain inch by inch until he was at the support beam. He threw his legs over it to relieve the pressure on his hands and unhooked the chain from the spike that had held it in place. He dropped to the floor and used the Choora knife to cut through his leg and hand restraints. He carefully uncoiled the wire from his big toe and even more carefully unwound it from his genitals. He then took a knee next to his enemy and drove the traditional Afghan blade into his throat.

CHAPTER SEVENTY-SIX

WALKER STOOD, NAKED, sweaty, and caked with blood from his jaw to his thighs, the new wound in his right leg seeping, his chest heaving, looking down at the dead Afghan at his feet.

He turned and walked toward the FBI agent, the long, bloody blade in his hand.

He knelt and sliced through the restraints around Stanton's hands and feet.

"Jarrett Stanton, I'm Chris Walker. I believe you've been looking for me."

The FBI man's eyes shifted between the naked warrior before him and the dead man whose blood was pooling on the floor.

"Hold this," Walker said, handing Stanton the blade. "Stand by the door, and if anyone comes in, stab them in the heart."

The former CIA operative darted into the attached bedroom and returned moments later with a Browning A-5 shotgun in his hands and a ripped bedsheet tied around the deep gash on his leg.

He quickly peered through one of the small windows and leaned the shotgun against the wall.

"Hard to see out there," he said, pulling on his jeans and T-shirt that the Afghan had thrown into the corner. He then knelt to put on his socks and boots.

"This is a Browing Automatic 5 shotgun," he said, picking it back up. "It's only got five shells, hence the Auto-5."

Stanton still had not said a word.

"I checked and it's loaded with double aught. Belle's grandfather had it here for home defense. Stanton, are you getting this?"

"Yeah," Stanton stammered.

"Okay, five shells. How many bad guys did your buddy Bates leave outside?"

"What? Ah, two. Two guards armed with AKs."

"Where did your partner go down?"

"Just in front of the Tahoe."

"Do you have more firepower in there?"

"My M4."

"Good. This is our plan. We are going to walk, not run, out of here. For a split second they might think it's the Afghan. They believe the noises they heard in here were torture. As soon as I see one of the guards, I am taking him down. Then I'm finding his friend. If we only see one guard, the other might have gone with the two who have Belle in the shed."

"How do you know she's in the shed?"

"I heard her scream as they dragged her in but she's not screaming now, so we have to move. You with me, Stanton?"

"Yeah."

"You hold on to that blade. Once I take down the guards, I want you to get to the Tahoe and retrieve your M4 from the truck. I won't have time to see if Bates really put my weapons back in my car so I'm going with the shotgun. When you get your rifle, come help me in the shed. Don't go to your partner until all of them are dead. As hard as it is, we need to win this fight first. You have a trauma kit in the car?"

"Yes."

"All right, then it's win the fight first and then render aid."

"Who are you?" Stanton asked.

"Just a guy with five rounds in a shotgun. You ready?"

"Ready."

"Good. Now let's go save the fucking day."

Walker tucked the shotgun under his arm and opened the door. He walked across the narrow porch and was halfway down the steps when an overly muscled man covered in tattoos standing over a woman on the ground turned toward him.

Before he could raise his AK, Walker seated the Browning firmly in the pocket of his shoulder and pressed the trigger. The double-aught pellets ripped through the night and tore into the upper chest, neck, and head of the Kalashnikov-wielding guard. He was dead before he hit the dirt.

Walker scanned the front drive, but there was no sign of the second guard.

He turned, ran for the shed, and was halfway to it when a man in khakis and a white T-shirt threw open the door with an AKM at waist level, finger on the trigger.

Most of Walker's 0.33-inch-diameter lead balls impacted his head. Gravity took him straight down, his body wedging the door open.

The recoil-operated semiautomatic shotgun fed its third shell as Walker charged through the entry.

The inside was lit with an old lantern that cast a light orange glow across the swamp boat, workbench, and tools.

Walker clocked three bodies. One man at the back of the shed was struggling with Belle. He had an arm around her neck from behind. His other hand was fighting to maintain his grasp on the pistol grip of his AK as Belle thrashed, attempting to break free. Another man closer to Walker was fumbling to pull up his pants.

The SEAL adjusted his aim and sent his next barrage into the man's naked pelvis. The lead pellets shredded his penis and testicles, breaking his pelvic bone, which caused him to stumble forward and crash to the ground. Walker put another volley of lead into his head from inches away as he passed.

He pressed forward toward the man struggling with Belle. The banger's left arm was still hooked around her neck, using her as a human shield. His back was to the far wall. He saw Walker advancing, shotgun in hand, and attempted to turn the AK in line with the demon coming for him. Belle spun around in a violent rage; the roar emanating from her lungs echoed in the confines of the small space. Her thumbs went into her assailant's eyes. He threw her to the side just as Walker shoved the barrel of the shotgun into the jugular notch between where his two clavicle bones met at the top of the sternum. Pinned to the back wall of the shed, the man's eyes were shades of horror and disbelief.

"*¿Quién eres? ¿Qué eres?*" Who are you? What are you?

Walker pulled the trigger.

CHAPTER SEVENTY-SEVEN

STANTON APPEARED AT the door with his M4 as Walker took off his T-shirt and slid it over Belle's head. The lower part of her dress remained around her waist, and her Doc Martens were still on her feet.

"It's clear," Walker called to Stanton.

"Mirabelle?"

"I've got her," Walker said back.

Stanton pivoted and ran back toward his vehicle.

Belle buried her face against Walker's chest, her rage turning to sobs.

"I've got you," Walker whispered.

"They didn't . . . I mean, I fought them and you got here in time," she said.

Thank God.

"Come with me," he said. "We've got to help Stanton's partner."

With his arm supporting Belle, they made their way outside, stepping over the body in the doorway and moving to the front of Stanton's FBI Tahoe, where he knelt cradling his partner's head. His M4, trauma kit, and a Streamlight were next to him.

"She's breathing and has a pulse, both are weak," Stanton said as Walker knelt. "Come on, J.J."

"Hold this light, Belle," Walker said, handing her the black flashlight.

Walker started at J.J.'s feet and conducted a visual inspection while feeling for blood and broken bones.

"Did you see her go down?" he asked.

"I did. They beat her in the head with a rifle."

"She needs to get to a hospital. Help me get her to your truck."

They carried J.J. to the left rear passenger door of Stanton's vehicle and laid her across the seats.

"Was Bates driving his Charger?" Walker asked.

"Yes," Stanton responded.

"Belle, go with Agent Stanton. Ride back here with J.J. Hold her head and neck."

"You need to get to the hospital too," Stanton said.

"I'm going after Bates."

"Not like that you're not."

"Don't try and stop me, Stanton."

"On the contrary," Stanton said. He reached into the back cargo area and threw Walker a navy-blue windbreaker emblazoned with gold letters that read "FBI."

CHAPTER SEVENTY-EIGHT

WALKER PUSHED THE old AMC Eagle to the limit, its four-wheel drive grinding through the gravel around the back-road turns. He checked the Sons of Liberty AR and Staccato pistol he had taken from Dupuis, the weapons that Bates had stashed back in the Eagle. They were ready to go to work.

A subtropical thunderstorm that had worked its way up from the Gulf began its attack as Walker hit the freeway and turned south. He wondered what he would do if he was pulled over by a Louisiana state trooper.

His body felt cold despite the humidity and sweat, drained of energy, permeated by a numbness accentuated by a painful tingling, like it had been cooked from the inside.

You're dying.

That's what you wanted, isn't it?

The car's heavy V-8 engine groaned in protest as Walker accelerated to a max speed of just under ninety miles an hour.

How far could Bates have gotten?

"Come on!" Walker shouted, urging the car to go faster.

A few cars drove through the downpour in the opposite direction on the other side of the grass median, leaving New Orleans in their rearview mirrors. Walker weaved around a Ram truck, a Jeep Cherokee, and a Mini Cooper as he ate up the distance between him and his prey.

He concentrated on the hunt to keep his mind off the burnt flesh on his feet and between his legs. He could feel the knife wound on his thigh bleeding through his makeshift bandage.

There, taillights ahead. Was it the Charger?

Walker killed his headlights.

Don't PIT the wrong car.

He kept the hammer down.

Black Dodge Charger.

But was it Bates?

Walker got closer and read the plate number he and Belle had identified in photos from Dorado Freight.

Bates.

The Charger was in the fast lane.

You got this.

Go!

When the front of the Eagle was parallel with the back right quarter panel of the Charger, he edged his vehicle to the left and made contact.

The PIT maneuver was one he had practiced countless times in courses with the SEAL Teams and CIA at BSR in West Virginia, the Farm in Virginia, and the Constellis Training Center in Moyock, North Carolina. At lower speeds it was a relatively safe way to end a pursuit by putting the target vehicle into a predictable spin. At the speeds of the Eagle and Charger, the result was an uncontrollable rotation. As the newer car's electronic stability control system attempted to correct the sudden turn, the front left tire caught a rut just off the right shoulder, interrupting its forward motion. The friction at such a high rate of speed, combined with the car's momentum and center of gravity, caused the Charger to rotate and flip off the road.

Walker slammed on his brakes and the Eagle skidded to a stop. He threw the car in reverse and maneuvered it off the road onto the shoulder. He then exited the vehicle, sticking the Staccato into the holster that was still on his jeans, and grabbing the AR. He activated the weapon-mounted light as he limped down the slope toward Bates's car.

Walker's beam found the vehicle upside down. The hood and front tires were submerged in the swamp. Steam rose from the undercarriage as the downpour made contact with the hot exhaust manifold, pipes, and chassis. The slope of the embankment had provided ideal conditions for a violent rollover.

As he got closer, he saw that the airbags had deployed.

Movement.

Bates was struggling to get out of the car.

The numbness in Walker's left leg became more pronounced as he stumbled forward. The rest of his body felt like an overused pincushion, an aftereffect of the electricity. He shook his head to clear his blurry vision.

Just hold it together for a few more minutes.

He got to the car, tucked the butt of the rifle under his right arm, and grabbed Bates by the back of the shirt, pulling him through the broken window.

He then stepped back and trained his rifle on the dirty cop.

"Tell me about the Afghan."

Bates coughed and pushed himself to his hands and knees. He stood and fell back against the closed door of the overturned Charger, looking at Walker in disbelief. His nose was clearly broken.

"Keep your hands where I can see them," Walker said.

"You look like death," Bates said. "Nice FBI jacket."

Walker was dizzy and off-balance. Even though he had only walked fifty yards down an embankment, it felt like he had just sprinted to the end of the BUD/S obstacle course. Sharp, stabbing pains radiated from his broken ribs.

"Where's Stanton? Dead?" Bates asked.

"I want to know about the Afghan."

"I bet you do. Did you kill him?"

"Tell me."

"You can hardly stand up. You were half-dead when I left. The Afghan said that nobody could take what he did to you."

"He was wrong."

"Funny how you are no longer interested in Snowball, cartels, and Big Pharma conspiracies. On your deathbed you want to know about an Afghan refugee."

"Your cop cartel is finished. Stanton's alive. All of you are going down."

"You don't quite have it all figured out."

"I figured out enough."

"You missed your calling, Walker. You should have been a cop. Well, your little girlfriend helped."

"The law part trips me up."

"She used you, Walker."

"Who?"

"Leigh Ann Staub. When we killed Connor for getting too close, she called you to clean up her mess."

I owed her husband.

"Think about it. You're just a tool, Walker. First your country used you in two lost wars and then Leigh Ann Staub used you to kill off everyone responsible for her son's death."

Walker felt a sudden tightness in his chest, coupled with a pain that seemed to pulse in rhythm with his slowing heartbeats.

Rhythm.

Death.

His organs protested the agonizing onslaught of otherworldly searing torment. He struggled to breathe as a wave of dizziness sent him to his knees.

Bates went for his gun.

Don't you die on your knees in this fucking mud!

What did Epicurus say about death?

"It is nothing to us."

You will not die out of rhythm.

It is nothing to me.

With his AR barrel in the dirt, Walker shot his left hand out, catching the Glock palm up before Bates could get it online. His right hand grabbed Bates's right wrist as he twisted the pistol away from the police officer's body. He felt Bates's trigger finger break and heard the big man grunt.

Only one of us walks away.

Walker shot to his feet, delivering a palm strike to the underside of Bates's chin, following it with a left hook to the side of the larger man's head with the hand that still held the Glock by its slide. He immediately dipped his hips and threw a right uppercut into the lieutenant's midsection.

Walker felt a rib break as the lieutenant was driven back against the overturned vehicle. With the slung rifle caught between them, Walker's right hand grabbed Bates by the back of the neck and pulled the taller man down as he propelled his body upward, smashing the top of his head into the officer's already broken nose.

With Bates on the defensive, Walker reached for the Staccato in his waistband with his right hand. His draw was impeded by the AR, which allowed Bates to slam his left hand down, knocking the pistol to the ground.

Walker stepped to the inside, catching a glancing blow, but countered with a left elbow, which caught Bates in the jaw. The SEAL immediately shifted his hips to deliver another uppercut with his right, followed by two left hooks with the Glock and a devastating right cross. Walker focused his rage on the larger man before him, continuing his assault with elbows, knees, and fists.

You are running on reserves. Get on the gun before you die.

As Walker moved the Glock 22 into his right hand, Bates used his leg to propel himself off the overturned vehicle at his back, knocking the pistol into the mud.

Walker adjusted to the charge and wrapped his right arm around Bates's bald head in a front headlock. As Bates pressed the attack, Walker fell to the ground on his back, kicked his right leg up, and used the larger man's momentum to flip Bates behind him into the wet soil.

Get your AR back in the fight before Bates finds that Glock.

Walker reached for the rifle that dangled from its sling but was close enough to see Bates grabbing for his pistol in the mud. As both men scrambled to their feet in the rain, Bates punched the Glock toward Walker, who stepped toward the weapon and pivoted to the outside. With the cop's arm now trapped to his chest, Walker spun and threw Bates against the Charger, pinning him to the rear passenger door. He turned his left hip and used it as a fulcrum, yanking back and breaking Bates's arm above the elbow. The Glock dropped to the ground as Bates howled in pain.

Walker continued his spin and elbowed Bates in the back of the head, hooking his arm around the cop's throat. He then reversed directions and threw Bates over his right hip.

The cop landed on his pistol, rotated to the side, and snatched it with his offhand. Walker dropped his right knee into Bates's stomach, catching the hand that held the weapon, but slipping off as Bates frantically tried to regain control.

As the two alpha males struggled in the mud for control of the pistol, Bates began to turn it toward the smaller SEAL.

Even with a broken arm and finger, he's still bigger and stronger than you are.

But he's not smarter.

Walker's left hand wrapped around the police lieutenant's neck, pulling it toward him while his right maintained contact with the pistol.

What would Paladin do?

Walker sank his teeth into the big man's neck, which ignited a primal scream that reverberated through the rain. The hysteria that sets in when a primeval animal tears into one's neck in the dark of night allowed Walker to slide away in the slick mud and then claw his way back on top of his opponent. Instead of pushing the pistol away, he pulled it toward his face and thrust his neck forward. He opened his mouth and sank his teeth into the soft flesh of Bates's wrist. As Bates screamed and his body thrashed, Walker bit into the man's thumb and yanked the weapon from his grasp.

Bates rolled away, his retreat halted by the Charger.

Walker stood, weapon in hand. It was one he knew well. He tapped the magazine with the heel of his left hand to ensure it was still in place. Then he stepped back and performed a press check to ensure the round was chambered, then hit the back of the slide to make sure it was in battery.

He put the Glock into his waistband at the small of his back and brought the AR back into his shoulder.

"Why can't you just die like everyone else?" Bates roared, holding his immobilized arm to his body.

"You have something on your wrist that doesn't belong to you," Walker said, his breathing labored, his voice raspy.

"You bit me, you fucking savage," Bates howled.

"The watch."

"The fucking watch? You want the fucking watch? Here, take it," Bates said, rolling to his knees. He removed the Tudor from his wrist with his good hand and threw it at the SEAL.

Walker caught it and slid it into his pocket.

"You lose, Bates," Walker said.

The lieutenant glanced over Walker's shoulder, a smile coming to his lips.

"I wouldn't be so sure."

Walker heard footsteps behind him and spun, rifle up, ready to engage.

"It's me," boomed Stanton's voice through the wind and rain.

The FBI man was moving toward him, M4 in hand.

"What are you doing here? I thought you were going to the hospital."

"I was. J.J. didn't make it. She was dead before we hit the pavement."

"Jarrett," Bates said, "you going to arrest the most wanted man in Louisiana? You've got your man."

"Don't move, Bates," Stanton shouted back.

Walker pivoted back to the lieutenant, his thumb moving his rifle's selector to fire.

"You going to murder me in front of an FBI agent?"

Stanton moved down the hill and stopped next to Walker.

"Belle?" the SEAL asked.

"She's in the car."

"Jarrett, listen," Bates said. "I'll deal you in, call off the Salvadorans that are going to spend some time with your wife and daughters. Only I can do that. That's how this works. You can be a live hero instead of a dead one. Kill Walker. He's got a rifle so it's a justified shooting. Kill him and be a hero, get the SAC job you want, save your family. Wrap up the investigation; Connor Staub, Mexican cartel, and Walker are all guilty. That's your move."

Bates slowly got to his unsteady feet and lurched back against the overturned car, his right arm hanging limp at his side.

"If you won't do it for justice, do it to save your wife and kids."

Sirens blared in the distance.

"Not much time," Bates observed. "State Police will be here soon. Kill that son of a bitch and make this right. Think of your family. Think of that pretty wife of yours."

Stanton kept his eyes trained on Bates, who shifted his attention nervously between the two men with rifles.

"There is something you missed. The 'why,'" he said, stalling for time.

"The why doesn't matter as much after tonight," Stanton responded.

"All right, you want to arrest me? Then fucking arrest me."

"I'm not a cop," Walker said.

"And I," Stanton said, "I'm not here to arrest you."

"You are a sworn federal law enforcement officer, Jarrett! I know you. Law and order every time. Justice. The system. Due process. You wouldn't shoot an unarmed man."

Vehicles came to a stop at the top of the embankment, their sirens changing pitch, their red-and-blue lights cascading over the swamp.

Walker reached behind his back and tossed Bates's pistol into the mud at the lieutenant's feet. He turned his head, his eyes meeting those of the FBI man.

They looked back to Bates, raised their rifles, and fired.

EPILOGUE

"For the world is Hell, and men are on the one hand the
tormented souls and on the other the devils in it."
—Arthur Schopenhauer

New Orleans
Three Months Later

THE TWO MEN sat in chairs on Stanton's deck, sipping sweet tea, watching the world go by, and listening to jazz that floated up from the French Quarter.

"You boys need a refill?" Alma asked, cracking the screen door.

"I'm okay, ma'am," Walker replied. "Thank you."

"And you, dear?" she asked her husband.

"I'm good, sweetie."

An argument erupted behind Alma over which daughter had custody of a certain doll.

"Duty calls," she said, disappearing back into the house.

"Did you see Greer's latest article?" Stanton asked, handing Walker *The Times-Picayune/The New Orleans Advocate*. The headline on the front page read: *Sweeping Arrests Shock Crescent City*.

Walker had collapsed in the mud after Bates went down. He was transported to Tulane Medical Center while Stanton dealt with the immediate aftermath of the incident on-site. Walker arrived unconscious and in critical condition from a combination of burns, nerve damage, heart arrythmia, broken ribs, lacerations, and severe internal organ damage brought about by direct-contact electrocution.

A week later, when he was downgraded to serious condition, he was visited by a prominent New Orleans defense attorney, former FBI agent, and federal prosecutor, Jon Weis, who advised him to make no statements to law enforcement without an attorney present, as was his constitutional right. He later spent untold hours answering questions from federal investigators after Weis worked out a deal.

When he was not being questioned by federal agents with the most feared and respected defense attorney in the state by his side, he was visited by a young woman dressed in black accompanied by a service dog named Paladin. She always arrived with a philosophy book under her arm, unearthed from one of New Orleans's many secondhand bookstores. She had made it her mission to replace his collection lost to the waters of the Mississippi and had become a well-known and welcome fixture in Beckham's Bookshop, Blue Cyprus Books, Faulkner House Books, Crescent City Books, Arcadian Books & Prints, and Dauphine Street Books. Paladin was especially fond of "Dog Days" events at the Garden District Book Shop. He had been inseparable from Belle as she recovered from the traumatic events at the cabin. Dogs and humans had a way of knowing when they needed each other for healing, support, and companionship.

Walker found a channel on his hospital television playing old Westerns. When he needed a break from the philosophers, he watched reruns of the black-and-white TV show from the late 1950s and early 1960s called *Have Gun—Will Travel*. He became quite fond of it.

After improving to fair and finally good condition, with the burns between his legs and around his toe healed and the stitches on his leg and the underside of his jaw removed, Walker was discharged and referred to the New Orleans VA Medical Center for rehabilitation appointments, which he missed regularly.

Derek Matheson was put under surveillance following the revelations at the Travois cabin and what was pieced together from evidence collected by Walker and Belle as federal prosecutors built their case.

Matheson and his longtime bodyguard were arrested in a coordinated sting operation coinciding with the arrest of Salvadoran sugar magnate Fulgencio Vargas when his jet touched down at the New Orleans Lakefront Airport to transport his mother's body to El Salvador for Catholic services at Catedral Metropolitana de San Salvador following her passing at Tulane Medical Center. Instead of a luxury car service, Vargas was met by FBI SWAT and taken into custody. A grand jury had found probable cause of criminal activity and issued a sealed indictment to protect the integrity of the investigation.

Genyra executive Carolyn Boyle met with and was questioned by authorities in the New Orleans Federal Building. They determined that she was not a conspirator in the case against Derek Matheson and Genyra Pharmaceuticals. She became a cooperating witness for federal investigators and was currently under the protection of the U.S. Marshals Service for the remainder of the investigation and follow-on court proceedings.

Also charged was bodyguard Dale Harris, who immediately agreed to turn state's evidence in exchange for leniency.

Most shocking of all was the arrest of FBI Special Agent in Charge of the New Orleans Field Office August Lloyd. He remained in custody after a federal judge ruled in favor of pretrial confinement. The article noted that Jarrett Stanton had been promoted to acting special agent in charge following Lloyd's arrest.

Special Agent Jennifer Jimenez was posthumously recognized with the FBI Medal of Valor for her actions. It was presented to her parents along with the FBI Memorial Star by the director of the Federal Bureau of Investigation. Her official photograph was added to the FBI's Wall of Honor at headquarters and Field Offices next to those of agents killed in the line of duty.

Reporter Evan Greer broke the story in an article that credited aspiring journalist Connor Staub with uncovering a web of corruption whose tentacles touched local law enforcement, federal law enforcement, the pharmaceutical industry, and an international drug lord in El Salvador, an investigation that led to Connor's death at the hands of a corrupt ring of dirty cops led by Lieutenant Cornelius Bates.

Not yet mentioned in any articles to date was former Navy SEAL and CIA clandestine services officer Chris Walker. He was offered immunity from local, state, and federal crimes thanks to the legal prowess of Jon Weis and the intervention of FBI Special Agent Jarrett Stanton and District Attorney Irene Isaacson. Icy was none too pleased to discover that Lieutenant Cornelius Bates and Fulgencio Vargas had targeted her for assassination for the information she passed to Augie Lloyd and for her failure to play ball even after a significant contribution to her Super PAC. She used the revelation to bolster her "tough on crime and corruption" platform in her campaign for governor. Weighing heavily in Walker's favor with prosecutors were his service to the country and his actions that saved the lives of Jarrett Stanton and Tulane student and

Louisiana native Maribelle Travois. Though he was not mentioned by name, a sub-headline read: *Mystery Informant Brings Down International Drug Cartel.*

It stated that very little was known about an undercover informant with ties to the military and intelligence services who was instrumental in taking down the drug ring. His identity remained sealed for purposes of national security.

"It is good tea," Walker admitted, setting the paper to the side.

Since his release from the hospital, he had been spending time with Belle and Gloria, staying in the room above the garage. On nights that Belle worked, he joined Jarrett Stanton and his family. The Stanton kids had taken a liking to the former SEAL who saved their father's life.

"Your name will come out eventually," Stanton said.

"I know."

"Weis owed me a favor," Stanton said, referring to the attorney who had negotiated Walker's immunity deal.

"Favors," Walker whispered.

"What was that?"

"Nothing. What do you think Bates meant when he said we were missing the 'why'?"

"We might never know for certain but we found out that Nectar had been in the Vargas family for three generations and that for a time he went to school here, same high school as Bates, though Vargas was a year older. They both worked at Nectar in their teens. That could be where the partnership started."

"That, or he was just stalling for time, hoping the State Police would get there in time to save him. He knew he was dead as soon as you said that J.J. didn't make it."

"We might never know."

"Life is full of unknowns. It's an undeniable aspect of the human condition."

"Which philosopher said that?"

"Pretty much all of them, though they frame it as certainty versus doubt, and include the nature of justification in their theories."

"Justification." Stanton let the word linger. "And Leigh Ann?"

"What about her?"

"Why did she do it?"

Over the past three months the two men had spent many evenings together discussing the case, and Walker had told Stanton about Bates's assertion that Leigh Ann had used him to kill those connected to her son's murder.

"Why does anyone do anything?"

"Philosophy again?"

"Aristotle had *telos*, an ultimate goal or endgame. Blondel studied the essence of human action. And then there was Nagel, who thought that trying to discern any of that in your fellow man was an absurdity unto itself. I think Nagel had it right."

"Do you resent her?"

Walker swirled the ice in his glass.

"Resent her?"

"For pulling you into this."

"No. I came back and her husband didn't, yet she forgave me. Least I can do is the same. Plus, I owed her."

"Owed her?"

"Well, I owed her husband a favor."

"Alma tells me that favors are how the game is played."

"She's a wise woman. What about Icy?"

"She's on the warpath. Leigh Ann gave her the information about corrupt cops. She trusted it to Lloyd, who told Vargas, who sent in the hitters."

"Think she'll be the next governor?"

"I don't think anyone can stop her."

"And Genyra?"

"The board is scrambling to save the company, but their stock is in the tank so they have applied for Chapter 11 bankruptcy protection."

"I can't believe they got away with it as long as they did—using a legitimate pharmaceutical distribution network to move illicit product around the country."

"Hiding in plain sight," Stanton said. "They would still be getting away with it had you not ventured on the scene."

"I brought you a gift," Walker said, changing the subject. He reached into his bag and handed Stanton a box.

"A gift? With all the free dinners you have enjoyed under my roof this month, it's about time," he joked.

"Just open it."

Stanton tore open the package, poorly wrapped in New Orleans Saints gift paper.

Inside was a wooden box.

"This isn't going to explode, is it?"

"Not this one."

Stanton lifted the lid to reveal what looked like an antique 1911 pistol pressed into the soft green satin lining. He looked at Walker, puzzled.

"Mine was lost in the van when it went in the drink. That one you have there was probably made before World War One."

"Thank you, I guess?"

"I got it to replace the one I lost recently, but as I've been reading and reflecting, I realized I don't need it anymore."

"I'm not sure I understand."

"Just accept it. It's more for me than for you. Represents a new lease on life."

"Did you have an epiphany or something?"

"Of sorts."

"Saint Paul on the road to Damascus–type thing?"

"You could say that."

"Well, thank you. How about I hold on to it for you?"

"Good enough. Did you find anything else out about the Afghan?"

"Just that his name was Zarak Fazli and that he came here alone, no accompanying family members, in 2021 after the Afghanistan withdrawal. Like so many others, he was still waiting on his special immigrant visa."

"Just like he said."

"I reached out to Fisk at CIA. He didn't give up much, just that he was not free to discuss what the Agency did or did not do to help Afghans settle in the United States who worked for them directly or indirectly during the war. He did not acknowledge the existence of Zero Units."

"Typical. Fazli said we were in Afghanistan with the Zero Units at the same time, but I didn't know him. It's possible we crossed paths."

"Are there more like him?" Stanton asked.

"Like Fisk?"

"The Afghan."

"There must be. The betrayal, intentional or not, is real. He died with all the secrets."

"You know," Stanton said, taking another sip of iced tea. "Fisk never told me why you left the Agency."

"He wouldn't," Walker responded. "They slapped it with a SAP classification." He paused to gather his thoughts before continuing. "It has to do with a man and his family, a man who helped us, who was being left behind. John Staub and I arranged to get him into Pakistan, to the U.S. Embassy in Islamabad where he could claim political asylum. Agency wanted him to remain in Afghanistan as a stay behind asset to keep feeding them information."

"By 'Agency' you mean Fisk."

"Yes, but the problem is bigger than just him. He's more of a symptom."

"What happened?"

"We got them into Pakistan, well, really into the FATA, the Federally Administered Tribal Areas. Before we could meet up with the element that had guaranteed their safe passage to Islamabad, we were ambushed. Staub and our asset were killed, as was our asset's wife and daughter."

Walker paused and looked out onto the street. The smell of rain was in the air.

"His other daughter was wounded. We escaped and I carried her farther into Pakistan. Held her for sixteen days."

"Dear God."

"We were eventually picked up by a tribe. I was in a delirium, dehydrated, probably on the verge of death. They pried the little girl from my arms."

"Did she make it?"

"She'd been dead since I picked her up at the ambush site. I'd been carrying a dead child for over two weeks. My brain refused to accept that she was gone. Psychologically, my mind had made her the incarnate of John Staub, at least that's what the doctors said who examined my head at Langley."

"And they kicked you out for that?"

"For my head not being right and for what they said amounted to violating a ceasefire and invading a foreign country. They tend not to look kindly on those sorts of things."

"I suspect not."

"The official investigation found me responsible for John's death. I was on the wrong side of a border, so it remains classified. They are right about all of it."

Walker looked at the vintage Tudor Sub on his wrist and finished the last of his iced tea.

"I better get going. Thanks for the tea, and for my present."

"You gave me the present, remember?" Stanton said, tapping the box that held the 1911. "And you saved my life. Thank you, Chris."

The two men stood.

"You leaving town?"

"It's time. I feel like I need to get moving."

"How will you live? What are you going to do? You going to finish your doctorate?"

"That's a lot of questions."

"I am an FBI agent."

"I have a medical retirement. It's enough for gas money. And I'm in no rush on the doctorate."

"I thought your car was at the bottom of the river?"

"I found a 1976 VW pop-top camper in need of a lot of work. I got a great deal on it. I'll make upgrades and repairs as I go; a rolling restoration project, not unlike me."

"Too much technology in those eighties vans?"

"Something like that."

"How's Paladin?"

"He's doing better. Vet says nothing physical is wrong with him."

"He's dealing with trauma," Stanton said.

"Aren't we all?"

"What's your first stop?"

"You want to warn the local field office?"

"Maybe."

"I'm not really sure. Going to explore the country. My mom took me on a long road trip when I was a kid. I think I'm going to retrace the route, maybe get in touch with a few memories."

"You take care of yourself, Chris."

"You too, Jarrett," Chris said, extending his hand. "And remember, if the wheels of justice start to move in reverse on Vargas, Matheson, or

Lloyd, you know where to find me." He held up a burner phone that he and Stanton had agreed would be their means of communication.

"Leaving today?"

"I have a stop to make first."

"Not one that will require CSI in your wake, I trust."

Walker shook his head.

"It's not that kind of stop."

———

The old seventies-era camper sputtered along the streets of New Orleans, passing the vibrant shops, cafés, restaurants, bars, art galleries, and homes with distinctive Spanish/French architecture unique to the Big Easy. Over the past fifty years the vehicle's original red had faded to a rust-colored orange that reminded Walker of fall, of cinnamon or clay. He kept the windows down since the air-conditioning didn't work.

He turned onto Kerlerec Street and pulled to a stop outside the weather-beaten Creole cottage he had started to think of as home. He turned off the vehicle, put it in first gear, and drew back on the parking brake.

He was going to miss it here.

He moved to the interior living space and removed a vintage 1954 Martin guitar from its case. He had picked it up at Todd's Music Express in Metairie earlier that day and tuned it by ear in the back of his bus.

As he pulled back on the handle of the sliding door, he heard a familiar bark coming from just inside the home's front door.

The door opened and Paladin ran down the steps. He sprinted toward the old Volkswagen and leaped into the van. Walker took a knee and let the dog lick him before stepping to the sidewalk, vintage guitar in hand.

"Come on, boy," he said.

Paladin jumped to the curb and ran back up the driveway toward Belle, who stood in the doorway.

Walker smiled, shut the door to the van, and followed.

He had a song to play.

ACKNOWLEDGMENTS

First, a heartfelt and sincere thank-you to M.P. Woodward for all his incredible work on this project. Without him, Chris Walker, Jarrett Stanton, and Paladin would still be confined to the inner sanctum of my mind and trapped in a Word document executive summary and PowerPoint treatment on one of my old computers.

Another special thank-you to Mr. Phillip Kile who was the top bidder in a Special Forces Trust auction and won the inclusion of his name as a character in this novel—hence Detective Phillip Kile. The Special Forces Trust is an organization that provides timely, innovative, and comprehensive programs and services designed to enhance the well-being and health of Special Forces soldiers and their families. Find out more at sftrust.org.

To Emily Bestler, my publisher, editor, and friend, thank you for continuing to take risks with me. From publishing a complete unknown with *The Terminal List*, to supporting the inclusion of the first third of *True Believer* when I believe most editors and publishers would have cut that section away in a move I think would have been disingenuous to readers and to the story, to saying yes to my first project in the nonfiction space with the *Targeted* series, and to taking yet another risk on my first co-written thriller series with Chris Walker and *The Fourth Option*, thank you from the bottom of my heart.

To Lara Jones, for being so kind while doing everything humanly possible to make sure the trains run on time.

To David Brown, the best publicist in the business! How do I know? Because everywhere I go, people tell me.

To Libby McGuire, for your patience and support. You are a champion!

To Jon Karp, thank you for your leadership as CEO of Simon & Schuster. Best wishes on your next chapter with Simon Six! I can't wait to read the books you put on shelves.

To the rock stars at Simon & Schuster, Atria, and Emily Bestler Books, a humble and sincere thank-you for all you do to make books like this possible: James Iacobelli, Dana Trocker, Suzanne Donahue, Paige Lytle, Shelby Pumphrey, Sofia Echeverry, Karlyn Hixon, Morgan Pager, Davina Mock, Katie Rizzo, Alysha Bullock, Jane Herman, Fausto Bozza, Chrissy Festa, Teresa Brumm, Kim Shannon, Heather Musika, Wren Watkins, Hydia Scott-Riley, and Lexi Mangano.

To the team at S&S audio: Sarah Lieberman, Gabrielle Audet, Chris Lynch, and Tom Spain, thank you! I hear from listeners every single day applauding your efforts.

To Ray Porter, whose voice gives life to these characters. Nobody does it better.

To my agent, Alexandra Machinist, for juggling all my ideas—there are more where this came from—and to the entire CAA team: Josie Freedman, Howie Tannenbaum, Courtney Catzel, Yuni Sher, and Billy Hallock, thank you.

To David Lehman, Dan Gelston, Caleb Daniels, Brad Haynes, and James Rupley, thank you for taking the time to review a rough draft of this manuscript. Your input was invaluable and sincerely appreciated.

Thank you to former Chicago prosecutor and FBI Special Agent Jon Dubin for going through the FBI chapters; Jeff Rotherham and Justin Mayo for looking over the IED-centric chapters; John Devine for all the assistance on the dog-handling scenarios; Watches of Espionage for taking a look at the CIA and watch sections; Brendan O'Malley for answering my spearfishing questions; Dylan Murphy for your ideas on book violence; and Dr. Robert Bray for looking over the medical pieces. All mistakes are mine and mine alone.

To all the authors whose work is so integrally intertwined with my life and who guided me along my path without even knowing: David Morrell, Nelson DeMille, Ian Fleming, John le Carré, Richard Connell, Graham Greene, Charles McCarry, Tom Clancy, James Grady, A. J. Quinnell, J. C. Pollock, Marc Olden, Eric Ambler, Robert Littell, Jack Higgins, Alistair MacLean, Clive Cussler, Wilber Smith, Adam Hall, Vince Flynn, Daniel Silva, Thomas Harris, Michael Connelly, Steven Pressfield, John D. MacDonald, Robert Louis Stevenson, Robert Ludlum, Helen MacInnes, Frederick Forsyth, Rudyard Kipling, Stephen Hunter, Michael Crichton, David Baldacci, Dan Brown, John

Grisham, Lee Child, Geoffrey Household, Ken Follett, John Edmund Gardner, Agatha Christie, Louis L'Amour, Eric Van Lustbader, Don Pendleton, Gérard de Villiers, H. Rider Haggard, Jack London, and Len Deighton. Without the foundation you built, this book would not exist.

To Kevin O'Malley, always the first person to get back to me when I send out rough drafts and always with the same feedback: "I loved it." You are in my prayers each and every day. And to Kevin's amazing wife, Allison O'Malley—you are an inspiration for us all.

To Andrew Kline, Frank Lecrone, and Jimmy Klein for all you are doing for our friend Kevin.

To David DiGilio, Max Adams, Jared Shaw, Chris Pratt, Taylor Kitsch, Kat Samick, Antoine Fuqua, and Gareth Kantner, for all your encouragement and for the work and dedication you put into the *Terminal List* universe as I am locked away writing in the mountains while you are on set bringing the stories to life. And thank you to the cast and crew of the shows—your enthusiasm and professionalism are unmatched. To MRC Studios and Amazon MGM Studios, for taking this risk with us and trusting us to deliver, thank you.

To Russ Bucholtz in L.A. and to the team at Bright North Studios for the incredible work on the upcoming documentary for Fox Nation, *Jack Carr Investigates: Carlos the Jackal*. By the time this book drops, the project should have been announced. If not, consider this the soft launch.

To James M. Scott for charging away on *Targeted: Lockerbie* while I have been immersed in these pages.

To Barbara Peters of the Poisoned Pen Bookstore, for your support from day one, but more than that, for your friendship, and for asking me to be your plus-one for your Thrillerfest Legacy Award. Congratulations! You are a true force of nature.

To Ryan Steck, a.k.a. the Real Book Spy, for championing my first book before it hit the shelves.

To the team at *Best Thriller Books* and the *No Limits Podcast* for all you do for readers, listeners, and authors.

To Katie Pavlich, best wishes on your new endeavor! So excited for all that's ahead!

To Larry Ellison for showing me and untold millions what one person can do to change the world.

To Rick and Esther Rosenfield and Jimmy and Pam Linn—Paris was magical! Let's pick our next spot on the map and make plans!

To Danny Wolfe, for providing the cigars.

To Mike Stoner, for my author photo and our weekend motorcycle adventures.

To the Cylvick family, for always being there and getting it done!

To Mitch Langberg, Brock Bosson, Karl Austin, and Marissa Linden on the legal side, and Will Price and Buwa Ijirigho on the business front, thank you for keeping things organized and on track!

To Taylor Matkins and Katie Holyfield for all you do through Lucky Ones Coffee for the Park City community, and to Bailey Nissen and Alexia Curley for all you do for our family.

To my team at Jack Carr Enterprises: Garrett Bray, Andrew Bork, Melissa Lee, Chris Warcup, and Nick Carusi, your hard work is appreciated more than I can possibly express. And thank you to Ashley Ellefsen for two great years! Best wishes on the road ahead!

To the readers and listeners who have been with me from the beginning, those who joined along the way, and those finding my work for the first time through Chris Walker and *The Fourth Option*, thank you.

To my mom and dad, who continue to be my first readers, red pens in hand just like they were when I was growing up.

And, as always, to my beautiful wife, Faith, and our three wonderful children, all of whom are markedly aware of the pressure placed on our family as deadlines near, when I am struggling to be present while my subconscious all too often remains in the pages.

THE TERMINAL LIST

On his last combat deployment, Lieutenant Commander James Reece's entire team was killed in a catastrophic ambush.

But when those dearest to him are murdered on the day of his homecoming, Reece discovers that this was not an act of war by a foreign enemy but a conspiracy that runs to the highest levels of government.

Now, with no family and free from the military's command structure, Reece applies the lessons that he's learned in over a decade of constant warfare toward avenging the deaths of his family and teammates.

With breathless pacing and relentless suspense, Reece ruthlessly targets his enemies in the upper echelons of power without regard for the laws of combat or the rule of law.

AVAILABLE IN PAPERBACK, EBOOK AND AUDIO

SIMON &
SCHUSTER

TRUE BELIEVER

A high-intensity roller-coaster ride, *True Believer* explodes with action and authenticity that cements Jack Carr as the new leader in political thrillers.

Following his brutal quest for revenge, former Navy SEAL James Reece has fled the United States, emerging deep in the wilds of Mozambique. But he can't stay hidden for long – when a string of horrific terrorist attacks plagues the Western world, the CIA tracks him down and recruits him.

Now a reluctant tool of the United States government, Reece must travel the globe, targeting terrorist leaders and unravelling a geopolitical conspiracy that will have worldwide repercussions . .

AVAILABLE IN PAPERBACK, EBOOK AND AUDIO

SIMON &
SCHUSTER

SAVAGE SON

Deep in the wilds of Siberia, a woman is on the run, pursued
by a man harboring secrets – a man intent on killing her.

Half a world away, James Reece is recovering from brain surgery
in the Montana wilderness, slowly putting his life back together
with the help of investigative journalist Katie Buranek and his
longtime friend and SEAL teammate Raife Hastings.

Unbeknown to them, the Russian mafia has set their sights
on Reece in a deadly game of cat and mouse.

**In his most visceral and heart-pounding thriller yet,
Jack Carr explores the darkest instincts of humanity
through the eyes of a man who has seen both the
best and the worst of it.**

AVAILABLE IN PAPERBACK, EBOOK AND AUDIO

**SIMON &
SCHUSTER**

CRY HAVOC

1968. A time of division. A time of civil unrest. A time of war.

Tom Reece, a SEAL operator attached to the highly classified and shadowy MACV-SOG, is about to be thrust into a bloody battle.

A spy ship, the USS *Pueblo*, is captured by communist forces off the coast of North Korea. The crew thought they had destroyed everything of intelligence value. They were wrong.

As teams of special operators infiltrating into Laos, Cambodia, and North Vietnam disappear without a trace, an ambitious Soviet advisor launches an ingenious plan with consequences that reach far beyond the battlefields of Southeast Asia, one that will forever alter the world balance of power.

From the Kremlin to the White House, from the streets of Saigon to the rugged A Shau Valley, along the paths of Ho Chi Minh Trail and into the secret war in Laos, Tom Reece has an official mission assigned by Military Assistance Command, Vietnam-Studies and Observations Group, but it's his unofficial mission that might get him killed.

AVAILABLE IN PAPERBACK, EBOOK AND AUDIO

SIMON &
SCHUSTER